To Anne as

Best Wishes

THE
BLUE HOUSE

A Tale of Two Writers

Two writers, two books, two crimes

OLIVIA RYTWINSKI

ISBN: 978-1-916981-60-7

Also by Olivia Rytwinski:

A Family by Design
I Never Knew You
Shadowlake
The Actor

For Mike, Aleks and Lily

List of Characters

Jodie Rivera - 32, Lawyer and aspiring novelist

Lucy Rivera - 62, Radiologist - Mum to Jodie and David

David Rivera - 35, brother to Jodie, living in France

Brett Anderson - 66, Lawyer and father to Jodie and David

Maxine Croyett - 63, Best-selling Novelist

Winston Croyett - Book editor and husband to Maxine, deceased

Hadrian Croyett - 34, Dry stone wall builder - son of Maxine

Evelyn Hall - 63, Sculptor and twin to Maxine Croyett

Marcus Hall - 33, Educator at Hadrian's Wall, son of Evelyn

Philip Forest - 60, Journalist

Simon Trimble - 56, Maxine Croyett's publisher and editor

John O'Mara - 38, Lawyer - O'Mara-Reeves Associates

Sheila Morgan - 21, Law graduate, deceased

Prologue - 1999

My name is Jodie Rivera, and until last year I worked as a lawyer in Newcastle, primed to search for logic and reason as the root cause for actions, crimes and their consequences. But one year on, I no longer believe that logic and reason alone can offer the explanations I need.

Until my thirty-second year, I didn't believe in fate and destiny. I'd scoff at the idea of it as something people latched onto when searching for purpose and meaning in our chaotic and confused world. Rather, I believed we chose and defined our own paths, albeit stepping through a game of chance we had less control over. But, following the unfolding of recent events I felt convinced fate had been lurking in the shadows and leading me through childhood, my teenage years and up to the present day.

Can remote coincidences really be considered coincidences? Or had fate lent her hand to the inevitable meeting of people and events through time?

One thing was certain, I still needed to digest and come to terms with all that had happened, and writing, I'd discovered, was the most effective way to achieve this.

Chapter 1

One Year Earlier - 1998

Medieval Marvel

I felt like I was in the school playground waiting to be picked by the captain of the netball team, only this was for O'Mara-Reeves Associates, team building weekend - *Medieval Marvel*.

In the minibus driving over I'd joked with my colleagues it would more likely be a case of *Medieval Mayhem*.

Our two team captains for the day were one, my boss and lawyer boyfriend, John, and his brother, Dylan, the other partner in the law firm I worked for. Seniority was already at play. I shivered with adrenaline as John stood up front and looked out at me and our nine work colleagues, with his legs apart and perfectly at ease in his medieval get up. When he glanced my way I gave a cheesy grin. But I knew he couldn't pick me first - that would show favouritism. This was about team building, not a romantic getaway.

Usually clean shaven, John had grown a thick, ginger stubble over the past fortnight. 'Are you growing it to look more warrior-like and intimidating for the weekend?' I asked him. But his denial was emphatic, and he replied that beards were back in fashion. I didn't believe him though.

As I watched him he seemed a different man to the one I'd been in love with for the past two years, and had thought I knew so well. And I suddenly got the weirdest sensation that he was a stranger to me. He stood only a few feet away with unruly blonde hair and mismatching beard, and looked like he really could have been from medieval times. The outfit suited him - he looked more rugged and attractive than in his loose-fitting Calvin Klein suits, and his curls tamed and slicked back.

We'd been given the option of female or male warrior dress and I loved my Boudicca look with long blue tunic belted at the

3

waist, leggings, faux leather boots and shining cloth body armour. I'd plaited my long black hair and a plait hung over each shoulder. It felt more exciting than my usual dress for work which consisted of a blouse, suit and sensible court shoes.

Our coach for the weekend stood between the captains and their minions and tossed a coin into the air. He directed his words at John. 'Heads or tails?'

'Heads,' John replied with an air of confidence that suggested he already knew the result.

'Heads it is!'

John turned and pointed straight at Henry who stood next to me. 'You're in, mate.'

Henry, who hit the gym five mornings a week before work, probably the weekends too, and was built like a brick shithouse, went and stood at John's side.

Dylan pointed to Mark at the other end of the line. 'Mark.'

Mark strode across to Dylan, which left eight of us.

Each captain picked more recruits leaving only Emma and myself. I already felt like a loser - the weakest and least sporty colleague that no one wanted on their team. Also, Emma was my best work buddy and I'd hoped we'd be on the same team to have a few laughs and offer one another moral support and encouragement.

When John opened his mouth to speak, I took a step forward, but when Emma also stepped forwards I realised my mistake and hesitated.

John had picked Emma, not me.

I stepped back, feeling flustered and embarrassed by my assumption.

'Guess you've got me, Dylan,' I said, and glanced at John who was already gathering his team together and chatting to them in an animated and conspiratorial fashion.

I joined my team with feigned enthusiasm and a smile. Why hadn't John picked me? If I'd been team captain I'd have picked him early on. I tried to catch John's eye but when he saw me looking he turned his back to me.

His deliberate snub irritated me and made me more determined that our team would win.

Our first challenge for the day was to perform a haka or battle cry. I couldn't recall seeing a reenactment of medieval warriors doing this or anything similar, but I'd seen how the Maori's performed one, and it looked and sounded thrilling.

The battle cry was the first of three challenges for day one, presumably designed to rouse our competitive spirit, with two further challenges for tomorrow, during which each team would earn ammunition as points and prizes. Our stash of ammunition would be used in the final challenge tomorrow afternoon when each team would build a catapult or trebuchet. Whichever team managed to fire their ammunition the furthest would be the triumphant winners of the weekend.

Chapter 2

Twisted Firestarter

'Oh my God! That's brilliant, Jodie,' said Dylan.

'What a song. Definitely has that killer vibe,' chimed Paula.

I took a bow, then leaned forward and whispered. 'Shh!' I glanced over my shoulder. 'We don't want the enemy stealing our strategies. Let's practise well out of sight and earshot.'

Myself and my team tramped away from the huts and into the woods, where the trees were already adorned with buds and leaves, and grasses and wildflowers rose up from the woodland floor. Thank goodness I'd remembered my hayfever tablets - the pollen was getting right up my nose.

We found a pretty clearing which concealed us amongst trees in all directions.

'The song isn't exactly medieval, but Coach did say we should be as creative as possible,' I said.

'Knew you'd be great to have on my team,' said Dylan.

I felt tempted to say, *'Is that why you picked me last - in fact didn't even pick me?'* But I resisted.

What mattered now was beating John, the bastard, for not picking me and instead picking my best friend Emma - three inches taller than my five foot five, with her long, shiny blonde locks, and probably physically stronger than I was.

'Pretty sure I remember the moves to it,' I said.

'Give us a demo,' said Paula, with a grin.

Dancing on a disco floor surrounded by other bad dancers was one thing, but to dance on my own in a woodland clearing, didn't fill me with confidence.

'Okay, but you have to join in or I'll feel a right pillock. We'll use a few choice lyrics as it's a battle cry not a pop production. We should include all the swear words to sound more threatening,' I added.

'Ooh, get you! Have you done this sort of thing before?' asked Mark.

'Never, but I was into punk. I loved The Prodigy. Dad hated them, which made me love them all the more.'

'Wouldn't have had you down as a rebel teenager,' said Dylan.

'No, which goes to show how deceptive appearances can be,' I said. 'You should know that as a lawyer.' I grinned.

Dylan laughed. 'True.'

'No sniggering,' I said. 'Or I'll chicken out.'

They all nodded but I could already see one or two mouths curling up at the sides.

I struck a wide stance, took some breaths and began to grunt the lyrics and stamp my boots.

'I'm the trouble starter, fucking instigator,

I'm the fear addicted, fear illustrated.

I'm a firestarter, twisted firestarter

You're a firestarter, twisted firestarter.

I'm the pain you tasted, well intoxicated.

I'm the self-inflicted, mind detonator, yeah.'

With more than a few sniggers and giggles, my team members began to stamp, pogo and chant beside me as we repeated the lyrics over and over.

'That was amazing,' said Dylan, pink faced and breathless from exertion. 'We'll adapt the lyrics and choreograph our moves, then we can go down and scare the shit out of the enemy!'

'Yeah - let's do it!' We chorused with excitement, and applauded our efforts, which I imagined to any onlookers might have looked more ridiculous and disturbing than menacing.

When both teams lined up and faced one another on either side of the decking platform, John gave me a wink and I gave a sweet smile in reply.

I was intrigued to see what John's team had created.

They went first and I'm sorry to say that I was on the verge of stuffing my fist in my mouth to stop myself from laughing aloud. At one point they were each chanting different words out of sync and when three of them turned around, the others looked confused. Thankfully, the performance only lasted a couple of minutes and when they'd finished the rest of us cheered and clapped in support.

Paula elbowed me and whispered. 'That was rubbish.'

I'll never forget the looks on our opponents' faces, and John's especially, as we performed our well choreographed haka routine. And as I had boldly predicted and hoped, we were the triumphant winners.

'The hairs on the back of my neck are never going to lie down again,' said Chris, our coach. 'Absolutely inspired, even if it was stretching the limits of medieval artistic licence.'

Our team jumped up and down and hugged one another, and when I turned and caught John's eye, I grinned, but he didn't smile in return. In fact, he scowled. That was when I noticed how close Emma stood to him - and did I imagine that their hands touched and then quickly parted?

By late afternoon, my throat was dry and my legs ached, but I was glad we'd completed our three challenges for the day. Two of which our team had won - the Haka Cry, and Blades of Glory - axe throwing, whilst John's team had won the Da Vinci Bridge Build, across a ten foot wide stream with slippery banks on either side.

Our team had struggled miserably at the bridge challenge, and we'd all ended up falling in the stream and getting soaked and smeared in mud. The other team had fallen about laughing, which in all fairness, we deserved.

The evenings' challenge was to be a Medi-Evil Cerebral - history quiz. That would include a much needed beer or two.

'Come on guys! Work hard, and play hard!'

Yes, John really did give that cliched rallying cry to his team as they headed into the hotel.

Not that I felt bitter, after all, we were the leading team.

Chapter 3

Exposed

Wivenhold House was our team building residence for the weekend - a 15th Century manor house, set amidst the Kielder forest and tastefully modernised with a dozen comfortable bedrooms. Our bedroom felt more like a five star hotel but with extra beds. I was sharing with Emma and Paula as we were the only women.

I lay in a hot bubble bath whilst listening to some meditative forest sounds on my portable stereo, then washed my hair and got ready for the history quiz. I was no history buff and the majority of my history knowledge had been gleaned from historical genre novels by the likes of Philippa Gregory and Hilary Mantel. I hoped the others in my team might be more gemmed up on the subject.

As I dressed in jeans, a red T-shirt with *L'amour - Paris* printed on the front, I looked across at Emma who was lying on her bed and stared up at the ceiling.

'I feel just the same, Em,' I called over to her.

She rolled onto her side and propped her head on her shoulder. 'What do you mean?'

'Tired, like you,' I replied.

'Yeah, right,' she said.

I sat on my bed and opened my make-up bag. 'Did you enjoy the challenges?'

'Course. It's cool spending time with you guys.'

'What about John?' I asked her.

Her brow furrowed. 'John?

'You were on his team and he seemed a bit disgruntled on the way back.'

He hadn't even sat with me on the mini-bus coming back to the hotel, and instead sat with his teammates. I got the distinct feeling he was avoiding me.

'Oh, I didn't notice,' she said, and rolled onto her back again. 'I imagine he's annoyed we're winning. He's hyper competitive,' I said.

'Not the impression I got. I don't really care who wins.'

'That's cool,' I said, applying mascara. 'I'm not bothered either. I'll talk to John after the quiz.'

'Sure,' she said, vaguely.

My team were onto our third jug of ale by the final quiz round and our voices and laughter grew more raucous. The scores were close, but annoyingly, John's team were three points ahead. I hadn't contributed successfully to many of the questions, in fact, I'd given a few wrong answers, but we were getting quite rowdy and some of the team members had quibbled over the answers and scoring. Chris, our coach was keen witted and quick to quieten those with big egos.

'Okay, guys, food is ready so we'll eat before the deciding round,' said Chris.

Three waiters carried in plates of fish and chips and I stood up to nip to the loos.

'Don't be long or I'll nick a chip,' said Dylan. 'I could eat a scabby donkey.'

'Go ahead - I'm more thirsty than hungry,' I replied.

I felt tipsy and unsteady on my feet as I headed out of the bar and along the corridor. It was dark outside and a cool draft of air wafted my hair across my face. My arms prickled with goosebumps and as I passed the door that led outside I noticed it was ajar. When I reached out to pull it shut I heard voices from outside. Instantly I recognised John's voice speaking in undertones. And then I heard a woman's voice - too softly spoken to recognise who. I tilted my ear to the gap in the door and heard the sound of feet moving on the gravel. I pulled the door a few inches wider and poked my head through. John's back was to me and he had his arms around someone, and when I caught a glimpse of white sweater and blonde hair, I knew it had to be Emma. They were smooching quietly and I saw her hand move to his head and finger his hair. She moaned softly as they kissed and my stomach lurched.

I stepped back inside and fell back against the wall. My heart thundered through the cavernous void in my chest as I sucked in the air.

How long had it been going on?

I hadn't suspected a thing.

I felt an urge to fling open the door and confront them.

My breaths shuddered, and I stepped away from the door, eyes already stinging, blurring with tears, and ran down the corridor to the toilets. I bolted the cubicle door, slumped onto the toilet seat and grabbed a wad of loo roll.

My thoughts raced around my head like flies buzzing round a corpse. Only last week John and I discussed moving in together. He'd initiated the conversation and I'd been enthusiastic. In fact, I'd been thrilled and seen it as the next step to making our relationship permanent. I'd even allowed myself to check out engagement rings in shop windows.

For a fleeting moment I wondered if he'd been comforting Emma?

No! Who was I kidding? He was either into her or a womanising opportunist.

Fucking bastard!

But what should I do?

My team was waiting for me, and dinner, although my appetite had well and truly flown. I finished peeing and rearranged my clothes, but I heard someone come into the toilets and I waited for them to lock their cubicle door. Then I wiped my eyes furiously and blew my nose again, flushed the loo and opened the door. I looked in the mirror at my mascara streaked eyes then splashed my face with cold water, pulled a paper towel and dried my face. I ran my fingers through my hair and forced a smile, which even to my eyes, looked ridiculous.

I heard the toilet flush and the door opened.

'All right, Jodie?' asked Paula. 'I wondered where you'd got to.'

'I needed some air.'

Paula stepped closer, her face concerned. 'Are you sure you're all right?'

I forced another smile. 'Tired, that's all.'

'Come on.' She took my hand. 'Let's try and whup the other team's asses.'

'Sure,' I said, and my smile faded.

When I entered the bar I glanced over and saw John and Emma sitting next to one another as they tucked into their dinners - at least, John was eating, and Emma looked his way, smiling and talking animatedly.

They weren't even being discreet.

I sat down and reached for the jug of beer and filled my glass to the brim. The sight and smell of the fish and chips made my stomach churn and I turned to Dylan beside me. 'Feel free to nick some chips. You'll be doing me a favour.'

He gave me a quizzical look, 'You okay?'

A vein pulsed in my head. 'I'm fine,' I said, feeling determined not to crumble, and picked up a chip and popped it in my mouth. I chewed and swallowed, but it tasted like mush, then picked up my fork and ate another. The food stuck to the roof of my mouth and when I swallowed it lodged in my throat making my gag reflex kick in. I tried so hard not to look over at John. Clearly he wasn't interested in talking to me, so why should I be bothered with him?

But who was I kidding, and how could I fake it for the rest of the night, or the weekend, without giving myself away? My emotions were running riot and I felt on the edge of either screaming or fainting. Fainting might be the safer option. As a child and teenager I'd grown adept at hiding my feelings, from Dad, anyway, but once he and Mum had split, I became more myself with Mum, who accepted me just as I was.

I took a long swig of beer and glanced across the room. This time John was talking back to Emma, her long hair brushing his shoulder, and even from here I could see they were flirting quietly, intimately. The fucking shitbag! And how humiliating. I opened my mouth to scream something, but quickly pressed my lips tightly together. And then before I could stop myself I pushed back my chair and with glass in hand strode across to their table.

I stopped opposite them and glared at Emma and then at John.

They broke from their conversation and straightened up, instantly widening the gap between them.

'Okay, Jodie? Enjoying the quiz?' John asked, faking a smile.

'You've barely spoken to me today,' I replied through gritted teeth.

He grimaced and picked up his glass of beer. 'Because I have to be with my team, as you have been too.'

'Why didn't you pick me?' I sounded like a spoiled child, but I couldn't control my words.

He took an awkward sip of beer. 'It would have looked like favouritism,' he kept his voice low and shifted uncomfortably in his seat.

Emma looked down at her dinner plate.

I swallowed and lifted my chin. 'I know why you didn't pick me.' I paused. 'And chose Emma instead.'

I sensed the room quieten around me and felt everyone's eyes upon me and the scene that was unfolding. My hands trembled but I didn't care. Everyone here deserved to know what sort of a man, employer and business leader John was.

'I only chose Emma because she's the youngest and newest member of the team and I didn't want her to feel that she'd been picked last,' he said, jutting his chin forwards.

'That's ridiculous, but you were okay for me, the second youngest member of the team, and your girlfriend - supposedly, to be picked last instead?'

He leaned over and spat with anger. 'Listen to yourself, Jodie, and calm the hell down.'

And instead of his words calming me, or realising how angry and crazy I sounded, I felt as if my head might explode.

He continued. 'I had no idea you were so sensitive about these things.'

'I'm not sensitive,' I said, with a calmness that betrayed my inner turmoil. 'But I am hurt when my boyfriend, who only days ago expressed a desire that we move in together, then goes and snogs my colleague and friend.' I gave Emma an accusing glare. 'A team building weekend doesn't mean getting to know your colleagues in an intimate sense, you do realise that don't you?'

And at that I raised my quaking arm and launched the contents of my glass in John's face. I resisted the urge to hurl the glass, too.

'You're a pig, John, and I'm only glad I found out now before I moved in with you. Which I would have and probably got engaged too.' I turned to Emma. 'If I were you, I'd dump the ratbag, before he spots another pretty colleague to seduce and snog.'

John's face turned pallid with rage and he stood up, still wiping the beer from his face.

His fists clenched at his sides. 'You're sacked, Jodie. In fact, you've done me a favour. All of us.' He looked around at everyone in the room and continued. 'Did you know that Jodie has been writing a chick lit novel, and a week or so ago she asked me if I'd read it - share my thoughts. With reluctance I agreed, but I'm glad I did. She kindly cast me as the main character - a right nasty bastard.'

'You didn't read far if you think it's chick lit,' I replied. 'And no, I did not cast you as the main character. Although if the label fits…'

'You called him Johnny, so it seemed an obvious conclusion to draw.' He laughed maniacally, and looked down at Emma. 'I read on thinking I must be her romantic hero yet to be introduced, but no, turns out she's cast me as Johnny, the fucking psycho of the story.'

'He's not a psycho, he's damaged and complex. And anyway, most people like to be cast as a character in a novel, don't they? Not that you were. I just liked the name, Johnny.'

'You mean as in, "Here's Johnny!" in *The Shining*? That's the trouble with your book, Jodie. It's all been done before - full of fucking cliches. Not exactly original.'

'But it's based on real events, so it is original. How much did you read?'

'Three chapters. Your book belongs in the recycling. You'll never find a publisher with that tripe.'

'I told you I still need to work on it,' I said, fighting back tears. 'It needs editing and an editor.'

'Nah, it needs deleting - burning, or whatever they do with shit books these days.'

Dylan came and stood beside me and put his arm around my shoulder. 'Listen guys. I don't know what's going on, but you can't argue here. It's not fair on everyone else and it's not respectful to one another either. Sort it out in private.'

My eyes welled and I nodded. Dylan squeezed my shoulder.

John's eyes blazed at Dylan and he leaned across and slammed his palms on the table. 'Leave it, Dylan. Don't fucking well interfere.'

'So you weren't kissing Emma?' Dylan asked.

John shook his head vehemently. 'Of course I wasn't. Jodie is paranoid.'

'So why were you standing outside embracing and faces pressed together?' I said.

'Emma was upset so I gave her a hug.'

'Is that right, Emma?' I looked at her, daring her to deny it.

For some moments Emma didn't speak and her face turned pink and her eyes shifted awkwardly. Eventually she said, 'I'm sorry, Jodie. You didn't deserve this. We have been seeing one another and I wanted to tell you.'

John clasped his head with both hands. 'For God's sake, Emma!'

'Then why didn't you?' I asked her.

She blinked rapidly then said quietly, 'Because John insisted he would. I'm so sorry.'

And I felt the full weight of their betrayal and knew I'd been defeated. To argue with them further was pointless and degrading.

'I'm leaving and don't try to stop me.' I turned away and added over my shoulder. 'And don't think about inviting me to any more team building weekends.'

John snarled. 'There won't be a next time. Like I said, you're fired!'

Chapter 4

Missing Girl

Fighting back my tears I stuffed my belongings into my bag and Dylan and Paula accompanied me outside when my taxi arrived. They tried to persuade me to stay, but I think they realised the impossibility of this.

'I'm so sorry. My brother has never been faithful to one woman for long.'

'I wish you'd told me that two years ago,' I said, and blew my nose for the umpteenth time.

'He was crazy about you. I thought he'd found the one,' said Dylan.

'Men like that never change,' said Paula and she put an arm around me and gave me a squeeze. 'I should know. I've met my fair share.'

They waved me goodbye after I assured them I'd be okay. But I wasn't okay. I'd never been cheated on. And I'd never cheated on anyone. I felt sick, frightened and alone.

On the journey back I couldn't stop shaking and sobbing and the moment I got home I threw up, then could barely get off the toilet seat for the next hour.

The following day I churned over our relationship - ex-relationship, relentlessly in my mind. Why had I not seen how close he and Emma had become? Upon reflection, I realised the telltale signs had been there. I recalled how late one night Emma had rung to speak to John and he'd left the bedroom to continue the conversation. When he came back, after twenty minutes, he said she'd been concerned about an upcoming court case.

I felt betrayed by two people I'd loved and trusted - my boyfriend and one of my best friends.

I wondered if John or Emma might have an attack of conscience and at least ring me to see if I was okay, but I heard nothing from either of them. Deep down I wasn't surprised at their lack of caring.

I rang Mum late the next night, and sobbed down the phone.

'Slow down, take some breaths,' she said.

And when she suggested I come home for a few days, I asked if she wouldn't mind if I moved back in for a while until I got a new job.

'I can't go back there, Mum.'

'Take him to a tribunal.' Mum was insistent. 'Hit him where it'll really hurt.'

'What's the point?' I cried. 'It would take forever to claim unfair dismissal. How can I move on with a tribunal hanging over me?'

'Well, he's a bloody lawyer, a senior manager, and shouldn't get away with it. Think about it?' Mum insisted.

Truthfully, although I was incensed, humiliated and gutted about John and Emma, I had to admit that I hadn't been satisfied working as a lawyer in his firm, especially during the past year. At first I'd been blissfully happy with John, more passionately in love than in any previous relationship. He'd been the first man I'd fallen completely and deeply in love with, and I'd have done anything for him, which was why I'd thrown myself into my work at the firm, working in the evenings and weekends to keep up with all that was demanded of me. But when I wasn't working, I'd been following my real passion - writing, and I knew that my law work had begun to feel less important and more of a duty that failed to ignite my enthusiasm.

I ruminated over his cruel words about my novel - and how he'd rubbished my writing and cast my book into the slush pile. But was that his genuine opinion or angry retaliation for being found out to be a cheating love rat? Either way, it only made me more determined to improve my book and prove him wrong.

I'd majored in English Literature at Newcastle University, but afterwards, with no desire to go into teaching, and at a loss as to what I could do with my degree, I'd done a law conversion course. The idea to train as a lawyer had come from Dad who had his own law firm, although he'd been estranged from me and Mum for the past decade. Dad had earned a lot of money and we lived in a beautiful home with a sea view, although none of the wealth compensated for the misery Dad had put me, my older brother David, and Mum through.

After nine years working as a lawyer I'd come to resent the excessively long hours and the niggling realisation that I'd only ever really wanted to be a writer began to dominate my thoughts. Despite continuing to write stories, blogs and poems after University, I'd struggled to start a full-length novel, or even to know what to write one about. That was, until the big idea for one had quite literally fallen into my lap eighteen months previously.

A year and a half prior to the team building weekend, I'd gone home to Bamburgh for the weekend to attend the wedding of my best friend from school, Connie. John was to travel down the next morning to join me. Growing up, Connie had been my rock, whenever Dad had upset me and before he'd eventually left. We'd known one another since primary school and had remained close ever since. And now she was getting married - the first amongst my group of friends, although two friends were living with their boyfriends, and another unmarried friend already had two children. At thirty-two, I'd felt like I was the one being left behind, but my old school pals saw me as the career girl, the successful go-getting lawyer in the city.

'Dinner in ten,' Mum called up the stairs.

Her call for dinner reminded me of my years here growing up when I'd sit in my bedroom, playing, reading, listening to music or studying. I'd spent a lot of my youth either in my room or outdoors with my friends and David.

The cooking aromas drifted up the stairs and made my tummy rumble in anticipation. 'Down soon,' I shouted back.

I'd wanted to find some old photos of me and Connie from our time at school and thought it would be fun to put a mini friendship album together to take along to the wedding reception so we could reminisce about the good old days as well as celebrating her future with her husband.

I pulled down the ladder to the loft and switched on the light.

For years I'd avoided coming up here and always asked Mum or David to help when I needed one of the suitcases we stored up here. But today I was determined to challenge my claustrophobia. As I stepped onto the ladder I felt my hands tremble and my tummy bubbled with apprehension. I gripped the metal sides with damp palms and began to climb. I only hoped Mum was right and this was where I'd find the photo albums. She said she'd hidden them up here before Dad had moved out - or what I should really say, been thrown out, and along with him, all the locks changed.

With heart pounding, I stepped onto the boarding, lowered my head to avoid the beams and moved carefully away from the loft hatch. There was more stuff and boxes than I could recall seeing the last time I'd climbed the ladder. That previous time was one memory that would never leave me, mostly because of the repercussions from what I'd discovered up here.

Mum said she thought the photo albums with me and Connie were stacked on the shelf along the far wall, and I stepped cautiously across the boarding to where two boxes sat on the top shelf, clearly labelled with marker pen, 'Photos'. I knew this was the sort of place where spiders lurked and one of my biggest fears was spiders. I took a deep breath, stood on tiptoes and reached for the nearest box. I struggled to get my hands around the edges of the box and pulled it forwards. But it was heavier than I'd anticipated and it slipped through my hands and dropped onto my feet. Dust billowed up and the cardboard box collapsed, spilling the contents - three large photo albums, and dozens of loose photographs, papers and newspaper cuttings.

I'd planned on going through them in my bedroom, but instead, I crouched down and picked out the albums from the jumbled pile. I placed them aside and leafed through the loose papers. There were photos of me and David - two years older, who currently lived in Marseilles, in the South of France. As soon as he'd finished University, he'd packed up and taken a job abroad. He told me he couldn't wait to see the back of home, and more essentially, Dad. I didn't blame him, but my loyalty to Mum never allowed me to be the second child to all but abandon her to a life alone.

She often insisted she was happy though and never asked for me to come home more often than I did. She said she wanted me and David to have complete freedom, and she meant every word, too. And although I knew she missed David more than she would ever admit to, she never complained that he didn't come home to visit. David said it upset him too much whenever he did. I told him he should get over himself and think about Mum.

For the last six years he had come home every other Christmas for a few nights with his boyfriend, Terry, but it was clear the entire time he was itching to get back to his life in France. Terry was lovely though, and he got on brilliantly with me and Mum. David was lucky to have found such a loving and loyal partner, and especially after all the trauma he'd experienced growing up with Dad.

I put some of the photos aside to take downstairs, and leafed through another pile. Here were the ones I'd hoped to find. Me and Connie in our drainpipe jeans and black T-shirts - The Ramones and The Cure. Connie had been the goth with her cropped hair dyed black, and me more into punk with the ends of my hair dyed purple and my hair backcombed and hairsprayed and sticking out like an unruly topiary bush. I found more photos of us in school uniform - skirts rolled so high you could almost see our knickers, and a few of us at a family barbecue in the back garden. Think it was the only barbecue where Dad had allowed me to bring a friend. Standing behind me and Connie in the photo was Dad taking charge of the barbecue. With utensils in hand, he glared at the camera, and even from a distance I could see the characteristic scowl he so often wore.

I couldn't ever recall seeing Dad smile, the thought of which made a lump form in my throat.

I had a good dozen photos that would make a lovely friendship album for Connie's wedding day. As I tidied up the mound of photos I spotted a folded sheet of newspaper - stained brown from age. I unfolded and straightened it out. A full sheet from the Tyne and Wear Echo, dated 7 June 1955. The main headline stood out - *Missing Girl - Law student, Sheila Morgan, 21, feared drowned.* Beneath the headline were two black and white photographs. One of Sheila Morgan and the other of divers in wetsuits and snorkels searching a lake.

I began to read.

Law student, Sheila Morgan, remains missing after divers search a lake - Crag Lough, at a Hadrian's Wall beauty spot. A red blouse was found at the lake and identified by her parents as belonging to Sheila. Trainee lawyer boyfriend Brett Anderson is still being questioned, but denies seeing Sheila on the day she was reported missing.'

I felt my scalp prickle and contract - 'lawyer boyfriend, Brett Anderson'. My father. This was the first I'd heard about any missing girlfriend. No one in my family, including David, and my Granny on Mum's side, had ever mentioned this. And by my calculations, the date was five years before Dad and Mum married.

A skeleton in the cupboard - and a bloody big one, too.

Goosebumps broke out on my skin. Dad had kept this a secret from me, but Mum must have known as she'd placed the article amongst the photographs, although possibly by mistake. What a strange thing to keep hold of. And I doubt she'd have wanted or expected me to find this. I can only imagine she didn't anticipate me coming up here again.

I rummaged around for other newspaper cuttings that might reveal how the story turned out, but found nothing.

Had Sheila been found alive, or her body discovered?

I'd find a way to ask Mum. Or maybe I should search the news archives in the library first. I loathed and despised Dad, but could he really have been the type of man to be involved in a young woman's disappearance? Dad was a partner in a law firm and had dedicated his life to Criminal Law. He'd never have been able to if he'd been convicted of committing a serious crime.

Without warning, the loft lights went out and the space plunged into darkness. I stood up and looked towards the hatch and top of the ladder.

My heart began to pick up speed again and I felt disorientated. 'Mum?' I yelled. 'MUM!'

I crouched down, too scared to move. I couldn't even see the hatch through to the landing. Disturbing memories flooded my mind. I felt my balance go and I toppled forwards onto my hands and knees.

I heard Mum's voice. 'Jodie?'

'Up here,' I called out, panting for air.

'Power cut,' came Mum's reply. 'We've had a few recently.'

I looked up and saw a flash of light from the landing below. I crawled towards the gap on my hands and knees. Mum's head appeared in the torchlight.

She beamed the torch my way. 'Unfortunate timing, my darling.'

I took some breaths to calm my heart which felt as if it was about to leap through my chest.

She held out the torch to me. 'You're all right, love, come down.'

I took the torch from her and Mum disappeared back down the ladder.

I stood with shaking legs on the landing and Mum wrapped her arms around me.

'Let's make a brew. Gas will still be working and I've got some tealights.'

I sat at the kitchen table, struck a match and lit the candle. Flames flickered up and I placed the tealight at the centre of the table. My heart had settled to a regular rhythm and I watched Mum drop tea bags into the teapot then lift two mugs off the hooks beneath the cupboard.

I looked at the candle, reached out my hand and brushed the tip of my finger through the flame, as if I was a child again. I remembered how my brother showed me this trick when I was little. I'd found it dangerous and exciting at the time and we dared one another to swipe our fingers slowly and then to tip candle wax onto our skin to find our most sensitive areas. And it hadn't stopped there.

When Dad was out at work I'd light several candles and play with the wax, always thinking I'd be able to make something from this strange pliable substance, but inevitably only making piles of finger tip shapes or adding drips down the side of the candles. Those childish explorations explained the many scented candles throughout my flat in Newcastle.

Mum carried over two cups of tea and placed one in front of me.

'You've even got scented tealights,' I said to Mum.

She inhaled slowly and sat down. 'IKEA - strawberry apparently.'

Chapter 5

I lifted my cup and took a sip of tea.

'Hopefully the electricity will be back on soon,' said Mum.

'It was quite a shock up there.'

Mum reached over and put her hand over mine. 'I know, my darling.'

'I felt like I was locked in that cupboard again,' I said, gnawing nervously at my under lip.

She nodded slowly and her eyes glistened in the candlelight. Mum always understood. She cupped her hands around her mug. 'Did you find what you were looking for?'

'Yes - some fab photos of me and Connie.' I wavered, unsure how to proceed. Then opted for the direct route. 'Has Dad ever been in trouble with the police - before you met him?'

She thought for a moment. 'You mean speeding fines, or relating to his lawyer work?'

'Neither.' I paused. 'I found an old newspaper with a story about a young woman, a law student who went missing. Sheila Morgan. The article mentioned her boyfriend, Brett Anderson.'

Mum put her cup down and propped her chin in her hands. She gave a long sigh. 'Oh, you found that, did you?'

'It fell out with the photo albums. I wasn't being nosey.'

Mum rubbed her finger under her nose. 'Well, it wasn't supposed to be there, so I can only blame myself for being careless.'

'Why the big secret?' I tensed. 'Was Dad found guilty?'

Mum shook her head. 'Of course he wasn't.'

I let out a breath. 'Phew! Was Sheila found?'

'I didn't know Dad at the time, but I remembered the story being in the news. Dad kept the articles.'

'Was Sheila found alive?' I persisted.

'Sadly, no. Her body was discovered three months after her disappearance, in Crag Lough water.'

'Where the divers were searching.' And then a memory came to me. 'Hey, didn't we go there when we were little?'

'Yes, Dad's idea, and I can't say I thought it a good idea at the time.'

'Did it upset him?'

'He said not, and insisted he wanted to go to get over the past and what had happened to Sheila. But he was quiet, and for some days afterwards.'

'Did you ask him how he felt?'

'Of course I tried, but he didn't want to talk.'

'Strange, but when I saw the photo of Sheila, I couldn't help thinking she looked like you.'

'Mmm, I know. Dark curly hair. At least mine was back then.'

'Did Dad know anything about her disappearance?'

'Your Dad had a solid alibi at the time she went missing. They were both recent graduates. They worked at the same Law firm and Dad had only been seeing Sheila a few months.'

'Did they discover how she died?'

'The autopsy and enquiry concluded accidental death by drowning.'

'What? She went out walking and swimming on her own?'

'It was such a long time ago, love. Sheila was a keen walker, and a bus driver swore he remembered her getting off the bus alone at the wall.'

'So she walked along the wall and went for a swim by herself and drowned?'

'That was what they concluded. It had been a hot spell.'

'So they found her in her swimsuit?'

Mum grimaced. 'Actually, she was naked. But according to Dad, she had been a daring kind of girl.'

'Oh God! And was she a strong swimmer?'

'I don't know the details, my love.'

'Did Dad talk about her death much?'

Mum shook her head. 'You know what Dad is like. Not the most in touch with his feelings.'

'Didn't you press for details? I would have.'

'I know, and that's the lawyer in you. But I wanted to help him forget it. We were in love, and as time went on, it didn't seem kind to bring it up again.'

'I wish you'd mentioned this to me and David. Does David know?' I asked.

'Oh no. Dad was adamant he never wanted either of you to know. He thought it would upset you both.'

How ironic, I thought to myself.

'You mean the subject became taboo in the family - a dark skeleton?'

Mum sighed and her features looked tired in the candlelight.

'Not so much taboo. More a sad event from his past. And not even my past. Way before we met.'

'Did Dad tell you about it when you started seeing each other?'

'Yes, open from the start. On our second date, in fact. I was his first serious girlfriend after Sheila.'

'You do have an exceptional memory, Mum.'

'I know it was our second date because we'd been to see a film at the cinema - Cat on a Hot Tin Roof, which if you haven't seen, you must. And afterwards in the bar next door, we bumped into an old acquaintance of your Dad's. She was tipsy, and she made a crack about hoping I wouldn't go the same way as Sheila. Your Dad was so upset by her tasteless joke that we left and he opened up about it all.'

'Had you recognised Dad from the newspaper when you first met?'

'Not until he'd told me about Sheila's disappearance, and then I did recognise him. He had, still has, very distinctive looks. Tall, dark, handsome, well-built and of course, the family nose.'

I sighed. 'Yep, at least I can thank Dad for that.'

Mum smiled. 'You have a beautiful nose.'

I laughed. 'Oh, don't worry, I quite like it now.'

The light overhead flickered on.

I looked up. 'Ooh, that's better!'

But moments later the lights went out again.

'So annoying, must be everyone cooking dinner,' said Mum.

Mum didn't seem to know much about Sheila's death, and I could hardly ask Dad about it, given I hadn't spoken a word to him in over ten years and had no intention of reaching out for a cosy catch up. But I was intrigued to know more about the case,

25

and not because I suspected Dad would have been responsible, but because Sheila's death sounded fascinating, mysterious and unsolved.

What a coincidence that Dad, a lawyer, had been so close to a young woman who had gone missing and died. That sort of thing rarely happened up our way. And to drown at a popular beauty spot along Hadrian's wall.

From as young as I could remember, Dad and I had had a strained and difficult relationship. And it wasn't just me. I never thought I was badly behaved but I seemed to bring out the worst in him. Dad had been the same with David, too. Mum and Dad rarely argued, and Mum rarely bit back at Dad when he was in a bad mood, moaning about the mess, or something me or David had done to annoy him. He rarely stopped complaining - the house, the neighbours, the weather, and our sweet dog, Suki, a golden retriever, was often shouted at for simply getting under his feet. But despite his temperament, even I could see Dad was a good looking man, and Mum was stunning with her Spanish ancestry, shapely legs and hourglass figure.

With Dad's earnings, Mum hadn't needed to work after having us, but she'd trained as a radiologist and wanted to earn and progress in her career. Dad encouraged her to give it up and stay at home, but Mum stood her ground and worked her way up to become Senior Radiologist and manager of the X-Ray department at Alnwick Infirmary. I admired Mum for that. She'd come home from a long shift and then do the washing, tidying, cooking, sit and talk to me and David about our days, and then she'd be so worn out she'd go to bed before the rest of the household. Even now at sixty-two she worked full time and spoke passionately about her work.

The first time Dad locked me in the bedroom cupboard, I was twelve years old. All I'd done was dare to answer him back. I'd been invited to Connie's birthday party but it had fallen on Dad's birthday and Mum always cooked a special dinner to celebrate. When Dad said I couldn't go and I said I refused to miss my best friend's party, he'd flown into one of his rages. Mum had been at work at the time, and David was out, so it had only been me and Dad in the house.

Dad had ranted on and on about how I had no respect for family values, or for him, and when I started crying and ran up to my room, he charged after me, slammed the door behind him and told me he was going to teach me how to behave. He grabbed me by the shirt collar and pulled me across the bedroom to the corner cupboard beneath the staircase that led to the second floor. He yanked open the door, and despite my struggles, kicks and screams, he shoved me inside, and in the process, I cracked my head against the door frame.

When the enclosed space fell to darkness and I heard the external bolt click I screamed and pounded on the door with my fists and feet. I couldn't recall much else but that I shouted - probably that I hated him, because I did. I don't know how long I remained locked in, unable to break out, but it must have been a while because in my panicked state I'd vomited and peed myself. From memory it felt like I'd been locked in forever, such was the resulting trauma. Eventually, David had come home, heard the commotion and yelled at Dad to let me out. I heard the slap and thuds of a struggle between them both and then David crying.

'I'm calling Mum,' David yelled through his tears.

And that was when I heard the bolt click and daylight entered the tiny space.

By the time I'd crawled out, soaked in sweat, feeling dizzy and faint, Dad had already left the bedroom.

After that incident I never asked Dad for anything again, at least nothing that could be construed as disobedient or challenging to him. I was always stepping on eggshells when around him and avoiding him at every opportunity. I dreaded and hated every moment of family holidays when there was no escaping from his incessant grumbling and angry tones, especially the long car journeys when he drove like a maniac and gesticulated and shouted at any driver who made an error or got in his way. I felt lucky to have even survived to adulthood when every journey made me grip the door handle and shut my eyes.

Since that day, every challenge or worry had mostly been internalised and handled by myself, or if I'd felt a need, I talked to Connie, Mum or David.

Some evenings growing up, David and I would sit together in one of our bedrooms and talk about Dad and how much we detested him. We'd fantasise about him having a massive heart attack or dying in a car accident, and even one of us pushing him down the stairs. We grew close through our shared trauma and the helplessness and inescapability of our reality.

I never told Mum about the first time Dad locked me in the cupboard, and David promised not to either. I wanted to spare her the upset. Later, in hindsight I realised we should have told her and she had a right to know. It would have saved us all several more years of his cruel words and manchild temper tantrums.

Chapter 6

Banned Books

The second and final time Dad locked me in my bedroom cupboard was when I was twenty-one, but the repeat had proven even more traumatic than the first. Again, Mum had conveniently been out of the house when the argument began. When I'd searched in the loft for the photographs and the powercut had plunged me into darkness, it had retrieved from my memory that dark and enclosed bedroom cupboard, and flooded me with the same terrifying sensations. I hated thinking about it but I could hardly ignore something that had impacted upon me so heavily since.

From childhood our home had a room dedicated to books - mostly Mum's, but I borrowed and read them freely. Mum had always been an avid book collector and reader of all genres, but especially crime and thriller novels. Maxine Croyett was a best-selling novelist but I'd first discovered her when a friend had urged me to read one of her novels at Uni. I hadn't seen any of her books in our home library, but as a postgraduate law student, I viewed reading crime fiction as supplementary reading and a welcome break from the laborious task of wading through legal documents and textbooks.

I was back from University and in my bedroom listening to music. No doubt I'd been playing my stereo loudly and certainly not the sort of music that Dad appreciated. When Dad had returned unexpectedly from work and opened my bedroom door without knocking first, to order me to lower the volume, it hadn't been my music that had launched him into a rage.

He stood squarely in the doorway. 'Turn that damned racket down!'

I jumped up, placed the book I was reading on the bedside table and reached for the knob on the stereo.

'That volume will give you tinnitus later in life,' he said, with a scowl.

I turned to face him, 'Sorry, I didn't know you were back.'

'Clearly!' He walked over and looked down at the book I'd been reading. Then he reached down, picked it up and slapped it shut. 'Where did you get this?' He demanded.

'Have you read Maxine Croyett? My friend lent me another of hers last term, and I found this in the attic...'

Dad held up his hand. 'What? You found this book in our attic?'

'Yeah, I was searching for an old textbook.'

'Were there any more of this woman's books?'

'Actually, yes, three of her novels. Mum must have stored them up there. Don't know why though.'

'Three of her books? In our attic?'

I tried to ignore his barking tone and bulging eyes.

'It's brilliant, you should read it yourself, as a criminal lawyer. You'll appreciate her insights.'

I watched him clench the book in his hands whilst his features grew taut. 'I'm not reading anything by this mad witch - and neither are you.'

'You know Maxine Croyett?'

His entire body tensed and began to jitter before he strode across to the window, flung it open and hurled my book into the garden.'

I ran to the window and looked down at it lying in the flowerbed. 'What the fuck, Dad!'

That was the moment I felt a thwack on the back of my head. I screamed and fell forwards onto the windowsill and bashed my nose and cheek. The pain stunned me; I reached up and felt blood ooze from my nose. I slumped to the floor and sobbed.

'Where are the other books?' Dad demanded. 'I've told your mum I won't have that woman's poison in my house.'

'I left the others up there,' I said. But I hadn't - I'd placed them in my bedside cabinet with the intention of reading them all.

'Get up!' Dad bellowed, and gripped my arm. 'Bring them down here, now!'

'I won't!' I screamed and wiped the blood, warm and wet on my lips and chin. 'You hurt me and I hate you. I'm telling Mum.'

'Shut up! I never wanted to have to do this again, but you need to learn some manners and obedience.' He grabbed a handful of my hair and pulled me to standing. I screamed and kicked out at him, then reached up and scraped my nails down his neck as he dragged me across the floor to the cupboard.

I kicked him in the shin. 'I fucking hate you!' I screamed.

His face turned red with rage and his eyes blazed down at me as he pulled open the cupboard door. Still gripping my hair he yanked my head and pushed me to my knees then with both hands shoved me inside the cupboard before kicking my leg which was sticking out.

'You will learn to obey and respect me,' he bellowed. Then the cupboard door banged shut and the bolt clicked.

'No! Please, Dad! I won't read her stupid books. I'm sorry. Let me out!' I wailed, and panic rose up like a tidal wave inside of me.

And when I heard Dad leave the bedroom and close the door behind him, I sat back and booted the cupboard door with my bare feet. I rammed it again and again and again, but it wouldn't budge.

If only I'd removed that bolt the first time he locked me in.

I screamed as loud as I could. 'Let me out! I'll phone the police.' I paused. 'Do you hear me?' My heart raced so fast that each beat rolled into the next, and my in and out breaths came faster and closer together. In the darkness I could no longer see where the cupboard door was until the darkness was replaced by white spots that fizzed and grew bigger into a blinding white light that filled my vision.

After that I recalled nothing. No more screams, no more pounding heartbeats, no sensation of blood racing through my veins, or panting breaths. Nothing at all.

Until I heard Mum saying my name. 'Jodie, please wake up.'

I felt a softness against my cheek.

'It's all right, I'm here.'

The moment I opened my eyes, I began to weep. 'Dad locked me in.' A sob caught in my throat. 'He did it again.'

Mum gasped and her sobs echoed mine.

With her tears falling, she said, 'I will never allow him to touch you again, ever.' Gently, she took my hand. 'I promise you.'

My clothes were soaked in cold sweat, and still holding my hand, Mum helped me to stand.

She led me to my bed, sat me down and walked to the bedroom door. She looked out and listened for some moments before she closed it.

She came and sat beside me, pulled a tissue from the box on the bedside table and dabbed the blood under my nose. 'How bad does it hurt?'

'Bad, but I don't think it's broken.'

'I'll break his bloody nose.' She blinked back tears and her eyes held mine. 'Tell me what happened.'

I stood up, walked to the window and pointed down at the book still lying amongst the flowers. 'That's what happened.'

Mum came and stood beside me and looked out. 'Did you throw it?'

'Nope. Dad did.'

'He was angry you were reading?'

'Fuming.' I paused. 'It's by Maxine Croyett - The Thief.' I watched Mum's face. 'He called her a witch.'

A flicker of uncertainty crossed Mum's features before she let out a long breath and pinched the bridge of her nose. 'Let's sit down and I'll explain.'

'You'll explain why Dad locked me in the cupboard?'

'No, I won't try to explain that.' Her eyes welled with tears and at the same time, her features flared with anger. 'Leave your dad to me.'

'I'm not staying, Mum. In the morning, I'm catching the train to Granny's, and I'm never coming back.'

I'd already made up my mind. I wouldn't stay in the house with Dad another night. Apart from the loathing I felt for him, I was terrified. Terrified of what else he might do to me.

Mum placed her hand on the side of my head. 'He struck you - is that why your nose bled?'

'He hit me and I fell on the windowsill. I did nothing wrong.' I touched my head and sucked in my breath. 'It hurts so bad.'

'I'll get savlon for the bruising. But you mustn't leave. It's Dad who must leave.'

'What? You're throwing him out?'

'My darling, I'm fuming with him. If your Dad was a dog, I'd have him castrated then euthanised.'

'No you wouldn't,' I said. 'You love him. Why else would you have stayed with him all these years?'

'I *did* love him. But each day I despise him more and more. I've tolerated his moods and anger for too long. David won't come home and I'm not having you do the same. No, Dad's got to go.'

I nodded. 'Thank you.' Tears trickled down my cheeks and washed away the rivulets of blood from my nose, mouth and chin.

Mum's tears fell too and she wrapped her arms around me. 'You're going to be okay. We're both going to be okay.'

Eventually we released one another.

'I don't understand why Dad got so angry. What's he got against Maxine Croyett? And why did you hide her books in the attic?'

Mum took a breath. 'Your dad was Maxine's lawyer. A long time ago when you were little. Maxine needed a lawyer and Dad took control of all legal issues for her books and publishing.'

'And he fell out with her?'

'Oh yes. She refused to pay his fees and there were other disagreements, too. And when he discovered I'd bought her books, he flew into a rage.'

'Has he hurt you, too?'

'Never physically, only emotionally, which I've endured for too long. But that he's abused you and bullied David, is more than I can take, more than any of us should take.'

We embraced once more and after she'd brought me a cup of hot chocolate, a piece of honey on toast, and savlon to rub into my bruises, Mum asked me to remain in my room so that she could talk to Dad.

Chapter 7

The Train Journey - Present Day

It was a Saturday afternoon in May and one month after I'd left O'Mara-Reeves Associates. I'd expected the Trans Pennine train to be busier as I made my way down the aisle of carriage number two. I found a free table, took the window seat facing forwards and placed my bags on the seat beside me. It was a forty-five minute journey to Hexham, with a few stops, which would give me time to reread the final chapter to my favourite of Maxine Croyett's novels - *In the Blood*, and to think of a question to ask if she took some after her talk. Most authors did, at least the few whose talks I'd been to. From what I understood, her talk would be a small event, after I'd originally bought my ticket for a larger venue in Manchester.

Maybe they hadn't sold enough tickets. Maxine hadn't published a novel in five years, which after her previous publication history, seemed a long gap for such a prolific and successful author. Maybe in her sixties she was slowing down for retirement. Anyway, for me attending her talk was a dream come true - quite literally. Maxine Croyett was hands down my all time favourite writer. She might not be the most literary, or poetic of writers, but her stories were exciting, original and psychologically challenging page turners. I found everything about them utterly captivating and convincing.

Her novels were one of the reasons I'd chosen to base my own crime novel on real events. I'd pondered if that was cheating? But I didn't think so. Following my discovery of the newspaper article about law graduate, Sheila Morgan amongst the photographs in our attic, I'd asked Mum what she knew, then gone to the public archives to find out all I could about Sheila's drowning and story. Not that I'd discovered a whole lot more, but the story had intrigued and fuelled my imagination and I'd come away with loads of ideas for the alternative story I could write for twenty-one year old Sheila, renamed in my novel, Sarah.

I hadn't yet told Mum I'd based my novel on the death of Dad's ex-girlfriend, Sheila, and decided I'd only tell her if and when it was ever published. I knew this was unlikely, given it was my first attempt and how fiercely competitive the publishing industry was.

In retrospect, I realised I'd all but abandoned John in my quest to get my novel written. I'd made excuses to cancel nights out, even sitting and writing in the evenings, instead of watching a movie together with a bottle of wine, and I'd stayed home at weekends when John suggested we go away or do something. Such had been my compulsion to write. Instead of grumbling about my spending less time with him, he'd chosen to chase after my friend and colleague, Emma, who obviously hadn't tried to resist his charms. I was still devastated at losing them both, but after the initial shock, I felt relieved that I hadn't gone so far as moving in with John, and at least he'd had the courtesy of showing me his true colours, even if it had been in front of all my work colleagues, to humiliate me to the max and cause me to lose my job.

Two weeks after the disastrous team building weekend, he'd phoned and tried to convince me that his 'dalliance' had been a terrible mistake and how sorry he was and how desperately he wanted me back. But I was no longer playing the fool, and had more self pride than to allow myself to give a love rat a second chance. He'd hurt and wounded me and I decided that being single would be far easier than going through the pain of rejection again. I hadn't exactly had the best male role model in Dad. In fact, Dad couldn't have been any worse, other than he wasn't afraid of hard work - his one and only redeeming feature.

My only issue now was how to support myself. My savings from the law firm wouldn't last long and I doubted my earnings as a would-be author were going to feed me, let alone pay my rent. No, I'd have to find a real job, and fast.

The train rumbled along the tracks and the carriage shuddered forwards.

A shadow fell over my book.

'Mind if I…?'

I looked up and before I could reply, a dark haired man of a similar age to me placed his rucksack onto the luggage rack overhead.

I smiled and tucked my feet into my own space. 'Of course.'

He slipped in and shuffled over to the window seat opposite mine.

I peered over my book, immediately noting his striking looks, wavy hair and hazel eyes. I wondered if his face seemed vaguely familiar and I looked down at my book again.

'Not too busy for a Saturday afternoon,' he said.

I lowered my book and glanced up the aisle - still plenty of free seats, but he'd chosen to sit opposite me.

'I thought that, although I can't remember the last time I travelled this route.'

He smiled with an easy, assured confidence. 'I'm a regular - a second home, almost.'

I placed my book on the table. 'I no longer have a car, so trains and buses will be my future friends. My legs too, I guess.'

'Ah! Well, as long as you don't need to get anywhere on time, you'll be fine.'

I glanced at my watch. 'This one's prompt, so touch wood.' I looked around and then tapped my head.

'Don't get used to punctuality,' he said with a wry smile and peered across the table. 'What are you reading?'

I lifted the book up and showed him the cover. 'I've read it before.'

He tilted his head and nodded as if with approval. 'Must be good if it's a reread.'

'Actually, brilliant, and my third reading. In fact I'm going to see this author talk today. It's a home gig at Hexham - apparently she lives there.'

'Nice. I'm going to Hexham too.'

'Oh! Do you know Hexham well?'

'I do. I grew up around there. Recently voted the happiest place to live in Britain.'

'Do you agree?'

'Certainly not, but I do visit often.'

'Well, I've never been, so now I'm more intrigued to visit.' I placed my bookmark on the page and closed the book. 'Do you know the Queen's Hall Arts Centre? That's where her talk is.'

'Yep, a five minute skip from the station, so you'll have loads of spare time.'

'Should do.' I paused. 'So you know when the talk is?'

'Why, when is it?' he replied and his lips curled at the edges.

'Six. So yes, time for me to have a wander round, which is why I came early.' I didn't add that I had nothing better to do and no one to spend my days with.

I heard raised voices further up the carriage and I peered between the seats.

Moments later a little boy dressed as Spiderman, came hurtling up the carriage. He stopped at our table, crouched down and crawled beneath. I pulled my feet in further and looked down. His cherubic face peered up at me and he giggled and pressed a finger to his lips.

I grimaced at the man opposite, and tried to ignore Spiderman fiddling with my bootlaces.

I reached my hand across the table. 'I'm Jodie.'

He took my hand. 'And I'm Hadrian. Good to meet you, Jodie.'

My brows flicked up. 'Guess your parents were inspired by Roman Emperor Hadrian's great wall!'

'Their first real date was at Housesteads Fort, just up from Hexham - walking hand in hand along a scenic section of the wall.'

'What a fabulous first date idea. Beats the cinema or a cocktail bar.'

A young woman walked down the carriage and as she passed called, 'Where's my wee superhero gone? Anyone seen a boy dressed as Spiderman? Joe?'

I raised my hand and she turned my way.

I mouthed and pointed. 'Down here.'

She gave me the thumbs up and crouched down.

Joe squealed with delight. 'I'm staying here.'

'These people don't want you at their feet.' She glanced up at us. 'So sorry.' She reached beneath the table. 'Come on. You can have that ice cream when we get off.'

The little boy crawled out with little resistance.

The boy turned and looked at Hadrian and then at me. 'Is Hadrian going to be your boyfriend?'

'Joe!' Then she directed at us. 'I'm so sorry.'

'No worries,' I said, and Hadrian and I both laughed.

'Come on, cheeky Joe.' She took the boy's hand and with the other, gave us a little wave.

As she led him back up the carriage, I caught her words. 'They would make a lovely couple - similar in looks.'

I looked across at Hadrian, whose eyes were directed towards the window. He didn't appear to have heard the woman. We had similar colouring, that was true. Deep brunette hair with hazel eyes framed by black brows and lashes. The difference was in our skin where I was distinctively olive skinned, and he was fairer skinned. Did likeness attract like, I wondered, or were we naturally attracted to opposites to mix up the gene pool? And I thought back to John and my previous boyfriends. John was the only blonde man I'd dated and fallen in love with. My other boyfriends had been dark. I was more inclined to believe that opposites attract.

Hadrian turned my way and caught me watching him.

'Kids are funny, aren't they?' I said, to cover my embarrassment.

'They are refreshingly honest. Something the majority of adults seem incapable of, from my experience.'

The image of John and Emma kissing outside the hotel came to mind. 'Sadly true, although I do try to be honest, always. I loathe dishonesty.'

Hadrian scrunched his nose. 'People rarely want to hear the whole truth. That's why so many adults perfect the art of lying, or only saying half-truths.'

I thought for a moment. 'And some adults don't care who they hurt, and lying suits them so they can get away with whatever sneaky and underhanded tricks they want.'

Hadrian nodded and his brows creased. 'Could be right.'

'I know I'm right. When you talk to someone, watch the subtle clues, the body language, the eyes especially, to work out what they're really saying, or hiding. A rare few don't try to hide their deceptions and I'm not sure which sort I prefer.'

His brow furrowed again, but a smile parted his lips. 'Have you studied this kind of thing.'

'I suppose I have. I'm a lawyer. Well, ex-lawyer to be precise.'

'You didn't like it or redundancy?'

I grimaced. 'Kinda both of those.'

'So maybe not a bad place to be. And you can decide what you want to do instead?'

'Yep, I can, although I'm not sure what yet.' I didn't particularly want to talk about me, I already felt confused about the direction I was heading, or more precisely, not heading. 'How about you? What do you do, and do you enjoy it?' I asked.

'I love what I do. It's hard physical work, but I'm outdoors and my own boss.'

I tilted my head. 'Okay. Let me guess.' I thought for a moment. 'A farmer?' He didn't look like a construction worker, although did farmers ever use public transport?

He grinned. 'Nope. Guess again.'

'You paint the exterior of houses.'

'Well, I have done that. And one in particular, but no, that's not my profession.'

'I'm hopeless at guessing.'

'Okay. I build and repair dry stone walls. My latest project is a section of Hadrian's wall.'

I laughed. 'That's ace. Hadrian is rebuilding Hadrian's Wall.'

'I know, everyone takes the piss when I tell them, but for me it's a dream job. A six month contract, too.'

'Do you think being called Hadrian tipped you in their favour?'

He guffawed. 'Might have. But I like to think my portfolio and skills helped.'

'I'm sure.'

The man on the tannoy announced we were approaching Hexham. The journey had flown by and I hadn't read any of my book. Not that it mattered, I knew it well. I stood up and gathered up my bag. 'Nice to meet you.'

Hadrian stood up too, and reached for his rucksack.

As he stretched his top rose up over his toned abdomen and I couldn't help but notice how well-built his arms were and the thick tufts of underarm hair beneath his short sleeved T-shirt.

He gestured for me to go first, and then followed me down the aisle to the doors. When we arrived at the station, I stepped down onto the platform.

As we walked up the steps off the platform Hadrian turned to me and said, 'Enjoy your talk. Who was it again?'

'I'm sure I will. It's Maxine Croyett. I'd have thought she'd be well known around here - a local celebrity.'

He nodded. 'Yeah, yeah, I know of her.' At the top of the steps Hadrian turned to me. 'So the Queen's Hall is down there.' He pointed right to cross over the road bridge. 'Head down the hill, right past the Co-op and you can't miss it. Enjoy.'

'Thanks, nice talking to you, Hadrian,' I replied.

And he turned abruptly and set off walking in the opposite direction. I watched his back for a few moments. He'd been so interesting and easy to talk to, and I'd half expected him to invite me for a coffee or something. Presumptuous of me - if I'd wanted to talk for longer, I should have asked him myself. Anyway, he no doubt had better things to do, and probably a girlfriend.

I'd always had a vivid imagination. Or what I called an optimistic imagination. I often imagined scenarios that I'd like to be real - wishful thinking. And still I expected them to become a reality but without much intervention from myself. Imagining Hadrian asking me for a coffee was a prime example. And then I suddenly thought, you're in a new town, you don't know anyone, what do you have to lose?

I watched Hadrian disappear around the corner twenty yards ahead and I set off jogging after him down the slope. I slowed and walked around the corner to see Hadrian had paused on the pavement and was reaching into his rucksack.

'Hadrian,' I called, and walked towards him.

He looked up and his eyes flickered in surprise.

'Sorry to come after you, and I'm sure you have somewhere you need to be.' I took a breath. 'But I have an hour to kill and I wondered if you fancied going for a coffee? I'd love to hear more about Hadrian's wall.'

He hesitated in thought for a moment. 'I would have loved to, really Jodie, but I'm afraid I have to meet a relative -' he glanced down at his watch. 'In ten minutes.'

I felt my cheeks burn. 'Oh, that's cool, no worries,' I said, hurriedly. 'I'll let you get on. Nice to meet you.' And I turned to leave.

'See you later, Jodie,' he said.

I turned back and threw him a wave, then jogged back up the slope as if I too had somewhere to be and someone to meet shortly. He hadn't even asked for my number, I mused. How embarrassing to chase after a handsome man - literally run down the street after him. How uncool - desperate even.

I read somewhere in a magazine, *Cosmopolitan* or similar, that if a man wanted to see you, he'd ask, and that men were genetically programmed to make the first move like the hunter primed to mate in ancient times. Not exactly a modern way of thinking and surely the human race had evolved? I'd never made the first move before, well, not so directly, and now that I had, super unsubtly, I'd think twice before doing so again. Besides, Hadrian would have been a rebound date which was never a good idea.

I headed down the other end of the railway bridge towards town. I located the Queen's Hall Arts Centre which was half-way down the High Street situated between an art gallery and a trendy looking bar. There were large frames on the wall outside the entrance to the Arts Centre, with colourful posters advertising upcoming events - theatre productions, pop artists, classical music performances, even a Parisian mime workshop. I couldn't spot one advertising Maxine Croyett's talk.

I crossed the road and headed into the public gardens. Hexham was a surprisingly pretty town, and the gardens especially, with flourishing, brightly coloured flowerbeds full of peonies, tulips, amaryllis and cornflowers. The lawns had been freshly cut and a sweet smelling scent reminiscent of midsummer, rose up and tickled my nostrils. From somewhere in the gardens I heard the rumble of a lawnmower continuing its work. A glorious variety of trees full with leaves draped their branches over the path that ran down the hill, and the lawns stretched both sides. There was a grand old building on the far edge of the park which I imagined was a stately home of some kind, and in front of it was an ornamental fountain and an ice-cream kiosk.

A gang of teenage boys, laughing and kicking a ball between them, walked up the path towards me, then split either side when I didn't step out of their way.

'Woof! Woof!' one of them called once they'd passed.

Idiot! I was almost old enough to be their mother, and I stopped and sat down on a park bench beneath a monkey puzzle tree. I looked around at the sloping lawns and at the people walking dogs, couples strolling and holding hands and parents pushing babies in prams along the paths. Two girls were throwing a ball back and forth to one another over a flowerbed, until the ball landed in the middle of it and neither of the girls could locate it despite rummaging beneath every bush and flower.

I was intrigued to see what Maxine Croyett would be like in person. After Dad's deranged reaction when he'd found me reading one of her books a decade ago, I wondered how she might come across during her talk. From what Mum told me, Dad had completely overreacted because he'd fallen out with Maxine over payments. To not even allow her books in the house had seemed extreme, but now that Dad was no longer in my life, or Mum's, I preferred not to dwell on his rages, and more than anything, the two times he'd locked me in that cupboard.

My resulting claustrophobia was an obvious trauma induced reaction, and it was something I'd always have to live with despite trying to overcome it. I couldn't bear going in lifts, and on the rare occasions when I had no choice, I'd sweat and my heart would race until I could step out again. Even small changing rooms could induce a feeling of rising panic, when I'd have to abandon a trying on session and make a quick exit from the shop. The toilets on a flight were the worst, and I'd refuse to drink anything but the tiniest sips of water to prevent my bladder from filling to bursting, even on a long haul flight. On the one occasion I had needed to use the aeroplane's loo, I'd made John come in with me, which had then taken some explaining to the flight attendant when we'd stepped out together. But, despite these terrifying reactions I refused to allow the trauma to keep me from doing normal things, within reason.

One thing was certain, I'd never try potholing. That would be a step too far.

Chapter 8

Author Talk

In size, architecture and decor, the Queen's Hall reminded me of another venue I'd been to in Newcastle, with a wooden sprung floor designed for ballroom dances, cream painted walls and lofty ceiling with chandeliers, and ornamental mouldings that criss-crossed the ceiling.

I was keen and first to enter the auditorium as I wanted to sit near the front, to be able to see Maxine's face, but not be in her face, and so I took a seat in the middle of the second row. Soft piano music which I recognised as Chopin's Nocturne in E Flat Major, filled the hall, as people began to take seats around me. I noticed the majority of the audience were middle aged or elderly women and a few men, who looked typically bookish with a fair share of corduroy jackets paired with smart trousers for the men, and dresses and scarves for the ladies.

One young man, around my age but it was hard to tell without looking too obviously, sat to my left leaving a spare seat between us. He turned my way and smiled and I said hello and smiled back. I felt young compared to the majority of the audience, and I pulled a couple of Maxine's books, dog-eared and much loved, from my bag and placed them on my knee.

I'd stuck a couple of post-it notes in the pages where I'd noted specific questions and hoped I'd have an opportunity to ask one, maybe two. Bang on time, the lights dimmed, the music faded and the stage lit up over a high-backed leather armchair and a coffee table with a glass and a carafe of water. The audience fell silent and I turned in my seat and saw plenty of seats remained empty. I was surprised given that this was Maxine's home town and assumed the locals admired her and her novels even more than the rest of the country.

A man walked onto the stage and stopping beneath the central spotlight he turned to face the audience. And it wasn't a man I'd expected to see again.

Hadrian stood at the front of the stage.

He smiled. 'Good evening ladies and gentleman. I'm Hadrian Croyett, and I've been given the honour tonight of introducing my mother, and esteemed crime writer, Maxine Croyett.'

A minor familial detail he'd failed to mention when I'd told him who I was coming to see. And no doubt Maxine had been the relative he'd had to dash off to meet. I wasn't sure if I felt impressed by his lack of openness, or annoyed.

'As some of you may already know,' he continued. 'This is the first talk Maxine has given for three years, and she is both excited and delighted to meet with her closest and most ardent of fans here in her hometown. She will be talking about her writing career to date, and of course, some of her best-selling novels many of you will have read. Afterwards, tea and coffee will be served and you'll have the opportunity to purchase signed copies of her novels and to meet the author in person.'

He glanced down to the front, caught my eye and smiled. 'Please welcome, Maxine Croyett.' He turned to the side of the stage and clapped his hands.

We all joined in and Maxine walked onto the stage as Hadrian exited the other side.

Maxine didn't look quite how I'd expected. In her author photos she had shoulder length blonde hair and looked glamorous and even youthful still. Here in front of us she looked taller and austere with her hair cropped and grey, and with hooded eyes beneath black framed glasses. Her clothes went some way to lifting her appearance and she wore a tailored red pencil skirt with matching jacket which enhanced her curvaceous figure, along with doc martin boots. Stylish, literary looking, but older and larger than I'd pictured her - probably similar to or older than my mum, which made perfect sense now I knew Hadrian was her son.

Maxine placed a folder on the coffee table and seated herself on the armchair. She sat up straight with her hands in her lap and her knees slightly apart. The stage lights drew in until only a soft white spotlight remained over Maxine, leaving the rest of the stage in shadow. I imagined Hadrian was watching from somewhere in the auditorium.

Maxine sat forwards and raised her chin. 'Good evening, dear friends, booklovers and readers. I'm delighted to see so many of you here tonight. It's been a while since I did anything like this so please bear with me if I lose track or forget what I'm talking about. My mind isn't quite as sharp as it once was.'

One or two members of the audience laughed. I didn't because I wasn't sure if she'd meant it as a joke or not. Either way, Maxine wasn't laughing but she did break into a slim smile.

'Before I talk about my writing career and my books, which is the reason you came today, I wanted first to pay tribute to my late husband, Winston. Today, by a strange coincidence, is the twenty-ninth anniversary of his death. As some of you may know, he died under tragic circumstances, and from that day on, the precise cause of his death remains a mystery. Or should I say, his murderer remains free - assuming the monster is still alive.'

Someone sitting behind me gasped.

One minute into the talk and Maxine was already sharing personal details. I was mentally rubbing my hands together and I listened on intently.

'There isn't a day goes by when I don't think about the magical few years we shared, and especially with our only child, Hadrian.' She gestured to the back of the hall. 'Whom kindly came today to introduce and support me. Every year I hope that my dear husband's passing will grow easier, but if any of you have suffered a loss you will understand that grief barely fades.'

She fell silent and for some moments cast her eyes downwards, after which she seemed to compose herself and straightened her back to continue.

Such was Maxine's genuine emotion that my throat constricted, and I swallowed at the gravity of her words. I'd read details about the loss of her husband in a Sunday supplement magazine article and had kept the magazine. It had been an emotional firsthand account she'd written several years ago, and it was clear how much his death had affected her at the time and in the years since. Death and grief had also been a recurring theme in her novels, the most successful of which had been written after her husband's death. No doubt the pain she'd experienced had fuelled the emotional depth that was so clearly evident in her storytelling. I had never lost anyone to death, not even a grandparent - Mum's parents were both alive in their mid nineties, and I'd never known my father's parents who he'd long been estranged from. I had lost my dad, despite him still being alive, but felt no grief in that sense.

Maxine continued. 'As many of you will know, death and loss is a theme I explore in my writing, and the miracle of birth, too. These are universal experiences that many of us can relate to, whether they occur naturally, or as can be harder to come to terms with, when they occur out of the blue and under violent circumstances. I view every life, including my own, as a mystery. We may think we know where we are heading, but the reality is that we never stop discovering or being surprised by what we see and experience. Trust is another theme I explore, and some of my characters learn the painful way that trusting others should never come easily. If we trust blindly we will eventually be let down by those we thought we could rely on the most. Think about your own lives, your most meaningful relationships, and tell me that you have never been let down so badly that it came as a terrible shock, was painful and that you may never fully recover from.'

Her words remained serious throughout. There were no moments of lightness, laughter or humour, which I realised was reflected in her novels. But as she drew her talk to a close and I looked at my watch, I saw she'd been speaking for over an hour and I'd been absorbed throughout by what she had to say.

Maxine took a long drink of water before she asked if we had any questions. When I raised my hand I looked around and saw that at least twenty other people had their hands up.

Most of the questions related to her plots and characters - almost as if those asking viewed her characters as people they had known personally and intimately for years.

Maxine answered each question patiently and spoke of her characters as though she knew the minutest of details about them and the emotions they experienced.

'One final question, and then I will be around afterwards to sign my books should you wish to buy one, or several.'

I sat up and raised my hand again.

Maxine directed her gaze my way. 'Yes, dear?'

As the others had I stood up to speak. 'I wondered, what are you working on at the moment, and do you have a novel coming up for publication?'

Her eyes flickered and from the silence that followed, it seemed my question had taken her by surprise. 'I'm always working and writing. So yes, I'm working on a new novel.' She tilted her chin and appeared to collect her thoughts. 'In fact, I've all but completed novel number...' She raised a finger in the air, 'eighteen.'

'Fantastic,' I said. 'Do you have a publication date?'

'Not yet, but I do have a title that might whet your appetite.'

I nodded, urging her to share.

Her eyes flickered and she gazed towards the back of the hall. 'The Tale Spinner.'

'Will you give us a clue what it's about?' I asked.

She looked at me directly. 'It's hidden treasures shall remain a mystery until publication. But you'll enjoy it in due course with a little patience.'

I felt satisfied with her reply, and thrilled to learn there'd be another of her books to devour in the near future.

Maxine stood up and stepped forwards. 'It's been a pleasure talking with you and thank you too for your rapt attention and stimulating questions. Refreshments are being served should you wish to partake.' She gestured to the back of the hall, took a bow and we all applauded, with several whoops and enthusiastic cries from the audience.

I gathered up my stuff and headed to the rear of the hall where a table had been set up with tall piles of Maxine's novels. A queue began to form but I went to the serving hatch for a much needed tea.

I handed over fifty pence to the elderly woman serving refreshments then stood aside and wondered whether to join the queue for a signed copy or wait for it to reduce.

The young man who had been sitting close by in the audience, approached me.

'You asked a great question. I was surprised no one else asked it first.' He held out his hand. 'Marcus Hall.'

I looked closely at his face, and just as with Hadrian on the train, I got the feeling we'd met somewhere before. His dark chestnut hair with rebellious curls above fine features seemed familiar, but again I couldn't think where I might have seen him. I noted his athletic build and perfect posture, which instinctively made me straighten my spine.

I placed my cup of tea down on a nearby table and held out my hand. 'Jodie, Jodie Rivera. Yes, it seemed an obvious question, and having read all of Maxine's novels, more than once, I'm keen to read more.'

His brow furrowed. 'Mmmm, me too.'

'She's an interesting speaker. I've found some authors are dry or introverted in front of their audience, but Maxine seemed confident. It makes more sense why I love her books so much.'

'She has a track record of best-selling novels which I'm sure boosts her confidence,' he said.

'True. But nothing for five years.'

He nodded slowly. 'Also true.'

I turned and watched Maxine take her seat at the table stacked with novels, pick up her pen and smile at the man at the front of the queue.

'I'd better not let her overhear us talking about her,' I said, quietly.

'Actually, I should tell you, I'm Maxine's nephew. Her twin sister's son.'

'Oh really?' I said. 'Nice for her family to support her tonight.'

'Mmm. Mum suggested I come along. I quite enjoyed it.'

'I'd hyped this evening up in my head, but even I was pleasantly surprised.'

'Maxine does have the ability to surprise, that is true.'

I looked around. 'Is your mum here too? Are they identical twins?'

'Mum couldn't come. They were born identical, but look quite different now.'

'How interesting,' I said.

'Different tastes in clothing, how they style their hair, and I'd say Mum's aged better,' he added quietly.

I looked over at Maxine, and the sparse cropped hair around her face, the double chin and the deep lines across her forehead and around her mouth that made her look like she'd lived a stressful life.

I spoke quietly in reply. 'Funny, how that can happen, especially with siblings.'

'Mum doesn't smoke for starters, plus she's active, walks and loves gardening. Guess an active and healthy lifestyle is worth pursuing.'

I nodded. 'Being an author can be a sedentary occupation.'

'It's more what you do when you're not working. Mum's a figurative sculptor so not massively more active than a writer.'

I looked at Marcus in his Levi jeans and slim fitting T-shirt. He had a broad and muscular chest, was trim with a slim waist and arms and angular cheekbones.

'What do you do, when you're not attending your aunt's author talks?' I asked.

'Have you been to Hadrian's Wall?' he replied.

'Only as a child and I don't recall much.'

'I'm an educator for The Wall Trust so I lead educational visits and residentials, and archeological digs too.'

'Sounds amazing!'

'I've been doing it for three years, and before that I taught history and archeology at Newcastle Uni.'

'I studied English at Newcastle and worked in the city centre…' I paused. 'Until recently.'

He tilted his head. 'I'm sure I'd remember if we'd crossed paths at Uni.'

'I left Uni ten years ago,' I said.

'Before I worked there,' he said. 'Have you moved locally?'

'I've moved back in with Mum in Bamburgh. Only temporarily until I get another job,' I added.

'What's your profession? Sorry, I hope you don't mind my asking all these questions.'

'Not at all. I'm a lawyer, but I'm not sure I'll go back to it.'

'You didn't like it?'

'In ten years I experienced enough to last me a lifetime. Not sure I'm argumentative enough.'

'There's maybe something you'd rather do instead?'

'I like writing, but I'm not sure yet. I need to earn a real wage and I've not even had anything published.'

'Plenty of writers write and do other jobs to pay the bills. Maybe that's an option?'

I nodded. 'Yeah, that's my thinking.'

A voice interrupted. 'Nice to be supporting your aunt, cousin.'

We both turned to see Hadrian who wore a look of amusement.

'I see you've met my new friend,' Hadrian said to Marcus, then he turned to me with a sparkle in his eye. 'We meet again.'

'You know one another?' asked Marcus, surprised, and looked from Hadrian to me.

'Not exactly,' I said.

'Jodie sat with me on the train this afternoon. We got talking, didn't we?'

I wanted to add that he'd been the one to sit with me.

'We did. And when I mentioned the reason for my journey - to see Maxine's talk, you didn't mention you were her son or that you'd be here.'

'If I'd had time for that coffee you suggested, I'd have told you.' His eyes did that creasing thing and he watched to see my reaction.

I felt my cheeks redden. 'No worries, I've had a lovely time. Hexham is charming and the public gardens especially.'

Hadrian stepped nearer and positioned himself between me and Marcus. 'Would you like me to introduce you to our esteemed author?' he asked, and leaned in so that I felt his breath waft my hair.

I looked over at the queue with a dozen or so people, although Maxine did seem to be getting through them rapidly. 'I wouldn't want to skip the queue so I'll wait my turn. Really nice to meet you both.' I drank back the rest of my tea and walked across to the back of the queue.

The two ladies in front of me were discussing which signed novel they each wanted to buy.

Hadrian appeared at my side. 'I wasn't going to push in. If Mum knows you're a friend, she'll give you more of her time. Looks like she's swift at signing and taking the money.' He laughed. 'You'd like more time wouldn't you - ask another question?'

'Then that would be nice, thank you,' I replied, not wishing to sound ungracious, and wondered what I might ask her.

We stepped forwards in the queue and I glanced across at Marcus who was collecting empty tea cups and carrying them back to the kitchen.

Maxine was rattling through the queue and as we stepped nearer my tummy nerves jangled. I felt daunted to be standing in front of the author I most aspired to write like.

When the two women in front stepped aside, Hadrian said, 'This is Jodie, Mum. She's a new friend and a huge fan of yours.'

Maxine looked up at Hadrian and raised a brow, then she turned to me and held out her hand. 'Nice to meet you, Jodie. Did you enjoy my talk?'

I shook her hand. 'I did. And thanks for taking my question.' I noted her firm hand grip.

Hadrian moved away and left us to talk.

She considered me closely and sucked in a breath. 'Ahh, the question of my next book.' She paused. 'Watch this space.'

'I love the title, so simple and yet, intriguing.'

Her tone grew business-like. 'It's all under wraps until the big reveal.' She swept her hand over the piles of books. 'Which book or books would you like?'

'I'd like them all, but as I've recently lost my job I'll have your most recent, which I have read.'

She took a book from the smallest pile and opened up the cover.

I noticed her hands were gnarled with swollen finger joints. Rheumatoid arthritis, perhaps.

'Could you sign it to Jodie, please? J.o.d.i.e.' I spelled it out.

She gripped the pen somewhat awkwardly, and held it poised on the opening page. 'Yes, Jodie, I am able to spell,' she said, and scribbled my name above hers.

'And what job were you doing before you lost it?'

'I was a lawyer for ten years.'

She handed over the signed book. 'Clever girl. And what will you do now - be a lawyer elsewhere?'

I looked down at her small zigzagged signature. 'Thank you! I'm not sure what I'll do. I've been writing a novel myself and want a job that will leave time to perfect it. I'd really like to find a publisher.'

'A competitive market, as I'm sure you know. What genre is your novel?'

'It's crime.'

Her eyes flickered and narrowed. 'Ahh, my much beloved genre.'

I reached into my purse and drew out a £10 note. 'I admire your style, not that I try to emulate it. But re-reading your novels has been hugely inspiring for my own writing.'

'Have you asked any readers for their feedback? I found that essential early on in my career.'

'Only my boyfriend. Well, ex-boyfriend.'

'And what did he think of it?'

I thought back to the team building weekend a few weeks ago and that devastating confrontation over his affair. It was an evening I was still reliving every day and imagining what I could have said or done better. I sighed. 'He hated it. At least, the little that he read of it.'

She waved her hand. 'One ex-boyfriend's opinion isn't important. And I imagine he had a grudge or two against you?'

'Yeah, he did. And he didn't like me writing when I should have been doing stuff with him.'

'Indeed. Accusations of neglect and being selfish are things any writer serious about their craft must expect, and, might I add, ignore.'

'He took his affections elsewhere, so guess I was the one who made the sacrifice.'

Her voice softened. 'No loss. A good man would have supported you, or at least understood the commitment and time it takes to write a readable novel.'

'Thank you, Maxine. Do you know, I don't think anyone else has said anything that showed they understood.'

She leaned forwards - confidingly. 'That's because they are not writers. Being a writer, or of any art that requires commitment and time, is often deemed a selfish profession. I'm not a selfish person but I will guard my writing time and woe betide anyone who tries to interfere.' With her thumb and forefinger she pinched her upper lip and looked over my shoulder at the queue behind me. 'Listen, dear, why don't you stay around while I finish signing and we can continue talking? Do you need to be elsewhere?'

I looked at my watch. The last train home would leave in twenty minutes and it took ten minutes to walk here.

'I'm in no rush, that would be fantastic, thank you.'

'Excellent!' she said. 'See you shortly.' She gestured for me to stand aside and she looked round at the man behind.

I clasped my new book and headed across to the serving hatch to see if they were still making tea. Maxine must have seen me talking to Marcus. Had she taken pity on me after my sob story about my relationship breakup and my book?

Marcus stood behind the counter and laughed. 'I'm tea lady now.'

'Want a hand? Maxine's offered to chat with me when she's finished signing.'

He gestured to the side door. 'Sure, come round.'

I walked around to the door and into the kitchen.

'Not exactly busy, but have a free brew on the house. A chocolate digestive too. How's that for a perk of the job?'

I smiled. Marcus had a friendly and easy manner. 'Sounds good to me.'

A gentleman approached the counter. He wore wire rimmed tinted glasses and a tweed peaked hat.

Marcus and I both said in unison. 'What can I get you?' We laughed in unison too.

He smiled at Marcus then said to me. 'A coffee please.'

I turned to Marcus. 'Allow me. I'm great at instant coffee.'

'Black please,' added the man.

'Coming right up,' I said, and spooned coffee into a cup.

'Do you work for the Arts Centre or Maxine?' the man asked as I placed his coffee cup on the counter.

'I'm only here for the talk and a signed copy.' I turned to Marcus. 'Marcus is her nephew though, and you saw her son, Hadrian at the start.'

He nodded. 'A family affair,' he said. 'Very nice. And good of you to help her out.'

I leaned across and confided. 'Maxine's offered me a few minutes of her time.'

'Ahh, ulterior motives,' he said, and picked up his cup. 'Good luck with that.' He turned and walked away.

I turned to Marcus. 'Am I imagining it or did he seem a bit nosey, and almost in disguise? I didn't see him here for the talk.'

'Could be right, Miss Marple. I'll keep my eye on him.'

'I do have a naturally suspicious eye.'

I heard raised voices and swivelled around to see Maxine on her feet and the spectacled man I'd served coffee standing close to her.

Marcus headed straight through the side door and I watched over the counter as Hadrian marched up to the man, back braced and poised for a confrontation. Hadrian stood nose to nose with the man and from what I overheard was ordering him to leave. Hadrian even gripped the man's shoulder and forced him to step back.

Curious, I hurried from the kitchen and watched from a few feet back as the scene unfolded. The man stood his ground and protested that he meant no harm and only wanted to talk.

Hadrian snarled back at him with blazing eyes. 'Leave! Now!' He grabbed the man's arm and led him forcibly towards the exit. The man didn't resist and Marcus followed, presumably to lend a hand if need be.

'But where's the harm in a few questions?' The man continued to protest. 'Does Maxine have something to hide?'

Hadrian didn't reply and the three of them disappeared through the double doors.

Maxine sat back down. Her eyes darted about and she looked visibly shaken.

I approached her. 'Are you all right?'

She clasped her forehead with her palm and sounded breathless. 'This is why I'm reluctant to give talks. One simply cannot avoid the nutjobs out to cause trouble.'

She waved her hand to the man and two women still waiting to buy books. 'No more.'

I leaned in and said, 'Find somewhere quiet to sit and I'll take care of any remaining sales.'

Maxine stood up. 'Would you mind? The books are already signed.'

'Not a problem,' I reassured.

She rummaged vigorously in her handbag, pulled out a packet of cigarettes and headed for the kitchen.

I took Maxine's chair at the table and Marcus returned briefly. 'Thanks, Jodie. I'll check Maxine's okay.'

Only a handful of people remained to buy signed copies and I placed the leftover books in the containers beneath the table. The smell of cigarette smoke drifted from the kitchen. Maxine must have needed a smoke to calm her, although I noticed several prominently hung NO SMOKING signs around the hall.

Hadrian approached me. 'Where's Mum?'

I looked to the kitchen where smoke billowed across the counter. 'Marcus is with her.' I turned the key in the safe box and held it out to him. 'Sales looked good, anyway.'

He nodded. 'I had to rearrange my day for this. I'm glad I did.'

'Does Maxine normally need bodyguards?'

'Hard to believe in somewhere like Hexham, but when you're a famous crime writer, you'd be amazed at the crazies who come out of the woodwork.'

'I've met plenty in my work but I'm surprised to see trouble here today. Who was he?'

'Unsurprisingly, he didn't want to share his name and number, but I know his stinking journalist face - snooping for dirt.'

'Dirt? Maxine's a crime novelist, not a criminal!'

'Some people don't understand the difference between fact and fiction. Any crime writer will deal with these sorts of issues.'

'Really? I hadn't considered that.'

'Do you write crime?'

'Well, I have written one. Still in rough draft.'

'I'm impressed. What's the title and when's it set?'

'I've not finalised the title but it's set in England, 1950's.'

'Interesting and challenging, given you weren't alive then.'

'No, but my parents were, and I've read a lot about the period.' I hesitated to mention that it was based on a true story.

55

'Come on.' He tipped his head towards the kitchen. 'As you seem trustworthy, you can come with me and we'll check on our esteemed speaker.'

A handful of people milled around holding their signed books as they drank tea and chatted, while some headed for the exit, now that Maxine had made her own escape.

In the kitchen Maxine sat in the corner and sucked on a cigarette whilst Marcus loaded the dishwasher.

'Still more cups out there,' Hadrian said to Marcus. 'If you don't mind collecting them.'

Marcus looked up briefly and I detected a lift of his eyebrows.

Maxine exhaled a plume of smoke. 'Did you get rid of the journo rat?'

'Easy. A proper weed,' replied Hadrian. 'We'll add rat poison to his coffee if he shows his ratty face again, eh?'

Maxine's mouth twisted as if she was considering his idea, then she tapped her cigarette ash into a cup. 'I've seen him before. I've no idea what these sewer rats think they'll find out. It's not like I've anything to hide.'

'Is there anything specific they ask about?' I asked.

'Just one period in my life and career. Nothing I did wrong, but the few who are interested are like a dog searching for a non-existent buried bone.'

'Well, everyone's gone now.' I reassured her. 'You sold loads of books and I loved your talk.'

'I suppose that's all that matters,' she replied, as her eyes flicked towards the hall.

'He ain't coming back, Mum,' said Hadrian, and placed a protective hand on her shoulder.

Maxine nodded and drew on her cigarette. 'I'm glad you were here.' She patted his hand.

'I'll collect the cups,' I said to Marcus.

'I'll help,' Marcus said and he narrowed his eyes briefly at Hadrian.

'I'm supporting Mum. You can see she needs me. Oh, and the remaining books need loading into the car.'

'Let me do that,' I said. 'I might not look strong, but I'm used to carrying boxes of files and my arms are like Popeye's.'

'Before or after the can of spinach?' said Marcus with a laugh.

I laughed too. 'A minor detail - maybe somewhere in between as I don't actually like spinach.'

'Here's the car keys,' said Hadrian, and he threw them my way.

I reached out and caught them.

'Gold Audi through the side door, thanks.'

Marcus and I headed for the exit, each carrying a box of books.

He whispered, 'Hadrian gets all protective with his Mum. They've been through a lot.'

It piqued my curiosity. Other than the article she'd written about the death of her husband I'd only read articles about her books and promotional editorial. Of course, I knew a little about Dad's past financial disputes with her, so maybe money issues had been another problem.

Perhaps being a best-selling author didn't even guarantee a decent income.

My future employment and financial independence was still very much up in the air.

Between us, Marcus and I tidied the hall and finished loading the books into the car.

I closed the boot and turned to see Maxine and Hadrian coming through the side door.

Maxine had another cigarette in hand and Hadrian hooked her other arm.

'I'm going to drive Mum home. She's exhausted,' said Hadrian.

I handed him the keys.

'Sorry you've not had more time to talk about books and writing,' he said.

'Not at all. It's been a pleasure to meet you and glad I could help out a bit, too,' I said to Maxine.

'Are you staying in Hexham tonight, dear? Maybe you'd like to drop by my house tomorrow?' Her eyelids flickered and her voice dropped. 'I'd like to hear more about this novel of yours.'

'I haven't arranged to stay over. But yes, I'd love that!'

'The youth hostel at the far end of the park is reasonable. I'm sure they'll have a bed,' suggested Marcus. 'I can show you where it is, if you like?'

'That'd be great,' I replied. 'Are you sure you don't need to be anywhere?'

'Oh, I'm sure Marcus can put his plans on hold for a damsel in need of a bed,' said Hadrian with a smirk.

I glanced at Marcus who appeared unphased by his cousin's jibe.

Maxine reached into her handbag and pulled out a business card. 'Here's my address and telephone number,' said Maxine. 'I'll be in all day - writing, as always.'

I took it and said, 'That's really kind, thank you. Shall I come about eleven?' I turned the card over to see the handwritten address on the back.

'I'm six miles out of town but if you catch the no.7 bus to Corbridge and ask the driver to drop you at the stop for The Blue House, that's where you'll find me. But don't share my address or leave my card lying around in case any scavenging journalists are lurking.'

'I'll guard it safely,' I said, and slipped the card into my jacket pocket.

Maxine had an unusual manner - different to when she gave her talk. Superficially friendly, but far from warm. She spoke with an edge that made me question the meaning of her words. I'd met hundreds of people through my work and some were closed books, and at the other extreme, some were happy to freely share their innermost thoughts. I got the strongest sense that Maxine was selective with what she shared. But, I reflected, I was probably the same in that respect. I needed to trust someone before I was prepared to share personal details, and trust didn't come naturally to me. No doubt a result of my childhood, when I'd been frightened and let down time and again by Dad. And recently, John, who had only reinforced my reluctance to put my trust in others.

When Hadrian drove away with Maxine I returned to the hall to fetch my bag. 'I love this venue,' I said to Marcus. 'Have you seen other events here?'

'They have a lot of bands and touring theatre groups, so yes. Not many author talks,' he added.

'A decent turnout though,' I said.

He nodded and hooked a thumb into his trouser pocket. 'Not bad. Maxine still has a loyal following, despite not having published in a while.'

'Sounds like she's going to soon though, so her revival looks set. Must be an incredible feeling to be an established author, and know that whatever you write will be successful.'

'Yeah, I'm sure,' Marcus said, but he sounded unconvinced. He took a step closer. 'Between you and me, Maxine has been talking about this so-called new book for three years. No one's seen evidence of it.'

'Is that unusual to take so long?'

'She was one book every year or so, prior to that. I don't think she's being entirely honest, but don't share that with her when you visit tomorrow.'

'I wouldn't dream of it.'

Chapter 9

An Eventful Night

The youth hostel looked more like a newly converted barn than any hostel I'd stayed in before.

'How lovely,' I said as we walked through the double doors and gazed around the entrance hall at the exposed beams and colourful weaved wall hangings.

'Thought you'd like it,' said Marcus.

We crossed to the front desk and a young man looked up from the computer screen and smiled. 'Can I help?'

'It's rather late, but do you have a single room or bed for one night?' I asked.

'We're unusually busy but I'll check.' He shuffled the mouse and clicked on the computer.

'Happy to share a room,' I said, after a minute or two.

'Ah ha! You're in luck. One of the ladies' dorms has a spare.'

I turned around to Marcus. 'I'm in. Thanks for bringing me here.'

He smiled warmly. 'Been great to meet you, Jodie. And best of luck with Maxine tomorrow, and your book.'

As we said goodbye and he walked away through the doors, a strange and unfamiliar feeling came over me. I wondered if I'd ever see him again.

I turned back to the young man at the desk, who placed a key attached to a wooden fob with an engraved number 4, on the desk.

'Do any of the shops stay open late?' I glanced at my watch. 'I need one or two provisions.'

'Try the Co-op on the High Street. You'll be fine walking through the park, but don't stray from the path,' he added with a grin.

'Can't imagine you get much trouble in such a quiet town. It couldn't feel more different to Newcastle where I've been living.'

'Only rarely.' He peered outside. 'Could rain though.'

'I'll run if I have to.'

As I turned to the stairs to check out my room, Marcus walked back in.

'Hello again,' I said, surprised.

His face creased with a smile as he stepped closer. 'I wondered if you'd like to swap numbers? I realise you're probably not hanging around after seeing Maxine, but if you're ever over this way again, or me your way, we could meet up, or call, if you like?' He smiled and his eyebrows lifted expectantly.

'Yes, sure.' I pulled my phone from my handbag. 'Not sure what I'll do after seeing Maxine.'

We said our goodbyes once more and as I headed up the stairway to my room I couldn't help but smile as I reflected on my day. Nothing like I'd envisaged. A chance meeting with Hadrian on the train, who I'd found attractive, interesting and confident. Then spontaneously running to catch up with him, and him rejecting my invitation for coffee. Maybe with genuine reason but without giving an honest explanation. Followed by a journalist causing trouble after Maxine's talk but then a surprise invitation to visit Maxine's home. What a fortuitous opportunity that could be if I gave it some thought. And finally, exchanging numbers with Maxine's nephew, Marcus - a surprise that I had to admit to being the highlight of my day.

What might tomorrow hold?

I knocked on the door to Room 4, and turned the handle. It was unlocked and I walked into a large room with six beds against opposite walls. On one bed sat two young women - cross legged and facing one another.

They looked up and smiled.

I closed the door behind me. 'Hi, I'm Jodie.' I gazed around and spotted the only unmade bed in the corner by the window with a pile of folded sheets and duvet.

I crossed the room. 'I guess this one's mine.'

'Yep,' said one of the girls with curly brown hair piled up in a ponytail. 'Our friends are in the pub. Couldn't possibly wait for us.' She laughed.

'Keen to start drinking,' said the other girl, freckled faced with a messy, blonde bob. 'I'm Pippa.'

'I'm Simone,' said the other girl. 'Are you here with anyone?'

'On my own. Didn't think I'd be staying over so I have nothing with me. I'm nipping to the Co-op for a toothbrush.'

'You're welcome to join us at The Angel in town. We're eating, having a few drinks. We've been digging up at the wall all day so in need of food.'

'Archeology students?' I asked.

'Yep, our last night, too, so we're celebrating.'

'I don't want to intrude,' I said.

'You won't be, and you don't want to sit up here all night. You'll be bored rigid,' said Pippa.

I looked around at the magnolia walls, beige blinds and blue floor lino. It was only half-eight and I wasn't tired. 'Then I'd like that, thank you.'

'Fab,' Simone said. 'We're heading up now. Far side of the park, across the road.'

I nodded. 'Yeah, think I saw it. Up from the Queen's Hall. I've been to an author talk.'

'Ooh! Anyone famous?' asked Simone.

'Big in the literary arena. Maxine Croyett. She's a crime novelist.'

Pippa grimaced. 'I thought she was dead.'

'No, very much alive. You heard she'd died?'

'I thought so. She's old isn't she?'

'Only in her sixties.'

'I'm not much of a fiction reader,' said Pippa. 'My gran has some of her books.'

'My mum's a devoted fan,' I said. 'She's working today so couldn't come.'

'That's a shame,' said Pippa.

'Are you dressing up? I haven't got a change of clothes,' I asked.

'Nah, what we're wearing, and maybe some lip gloss. I love your jacket,' Pippa added.

'Thanks,' I said, smoothing down my leggings and denim jacket. 'I'll nip out and see you at The Angel. Are they still serving food?'

'Yeah, orders 'til ten,' said Simone.

I looked down at my bed - I'd make it up later.

What remained of daylight was fading fast, and as I headed through the iron gates and into the gardens a grey mist hung over the grass, and rose in wisps through the trees. Victorian lamps and strings of white lights lit the pathway that curved its way between the lawns up towards town. The swirling mist gave the impression of the trees dancing a slow, unpartnered waltz. I felt as if I'd landed in a magical fairy-glen as I followed the path, crossed the footbridge over the stream, and up the other side to where street lamps and bars beckoned.

I heard a rustle in the undergrowth closeby, as if a creature, a dog or someone walked through leaves. I turned around and paused for a few moments to listen. But the only sounds I heard came from the distant cars in town, and I continued walking, cautiously with my senses heightened. I heard a sneeze, muffled but nearby, and I stopped again, spun around and scanned the trees and bushes.

Someone was near. Despite being short-sighted, I didn't wear my glasses unless driving, and I rifled in my bag for my glasses case. I put them on and the lights, trees and bridge sharpened into focus. A flash of movement. At the bottom of the slope a man crossed the path and walked quickly over the grass. In the half-light his outline looked vague until he disappeared behind a cluster of trees. Had he been following me or was I jittery because I was alone in a park at dusk?

I turned towards town and sprinted up the path.

At least I wouldn't be alone when I returned to the hostel later.

What a strange and unnerving encounter - well, close encounter.

The woman serving in the Co-op placed my toothbrush and paste, shampoo, hand towel, soap and flannel in a carrier bag. At least I'd brought my makeup essentials along with me, as I usually did. As a lawyer, well, unemployed lawyer, we'd often go straight from work to the bars, and I'd take a change of shoes for a night out. The hours I'd worked, all of us in the law firm, left little time for much else other than more work and some drinking, which had become a regular evening routine since starting at O'Mara-Reeves Associates. But in the four weeks since leaving, I couldn't say I'd missed any of it, even the socialising. I missed John, but I suspected this was only because I'd got used to his company, going out with him, and of course, the sex. I knew I'd soon miss my salary, too.

I couldn't deny I was missing that physical closeness of being with a man. No doubt that was why I'd gone chasing after Hadrian earlier - fit, charming and handsome, and not interested in me. But men faced rejection, unless they were extremely lucky or gifted in the ways of charming women. I realised that had been John, although he hadn't pursued me for long before I'd fallen for his looks, smooth talk and intelligence.

I left the Co-op, crossed the road, and smiled to myself. Life was full of surprises when you did something different, stepped out of your comfort zone and dared to take a risk or two.

John had done me a favour, and good riddance to him.

Music, laughter and the low buzz of voices travelled onto the street as I approached The Angel Inn. I glanced through the windows as I passed - the bar was already full of people talking in clusters, and I hoped I'd be able to spot the students. When I opened the door the rising hum of conversation grew louder and a warm fug of air and food aromas hit me.

I scanned the faces at the bar and to both ends of the room. It was then that I spotted a familiar figure, but not the girls' faces I'd expected to see. To the left of the fireplace, sat a man in profile, and beside him a woman with long, sleek blonde hair. I noticed the unmistakable dark auburn curls and slightly hooked nose of Marcus - who had so kindly asked me for my mobile number only an hour ago.

Was any man, however kind and sensitive he might strike you upon meeting, capable of pursuing only one woman at a time? I couldn't see the woman's face and luckily Marcus hadn't seen me, such was the intensity of his focus on her. I made my way to the far end of the bar which led to another room.

I heard someone call my name and a hand waved from the table in the corner, round which sat five young women.

'Hello,' I said, and headed across.

The girls paused in their talk and looked up.

'This is Jodie,' said Pippa. 'Our roomy for the night.'

They all smiled and Pippa pulled out a stool beside her.

I sat down and she placed a glass in front of me. 'Here we go.'

'Thanks! Exactly what I need.'

'Been a long day, has it?' Pippa asked, and she raised her glass to her lips.

'Could say that. Some interesting encounters and surprises. Some, like yourselves, better than others.'

She nodded knowingly. 'Ahh, one of those days.'

'But, I'm in a new town with some new friends,' I said, and looked around the table. 'So let's waste no time.' I raised my glass and took a long drink of my iced gin.

My new friends, I discovered, were Masters students who'd been on a dig at Hadrian's wall for the week and were heading back to Manchester University early the next morning.

I thought about Marcus, who'd told me he was an educator at Hadrian's Wall, and sat at the other end of the bar with his girlfriend.

'I don't suppose you met a teacher called Marcus?'

'Yes, we did.' Pippa quickly replied. 'Marcus Hall. Super smart, handsome, and eyes that hypnotise when he talks?'

I nodded. 'Oh yes, that's the one.'

Had he hypnotised me when he talked? After seeing him with a girl in the bar, I doubted I'd ever find out.

I sipped steadily on my gin. The effects were immediate and I enjoyed the sensation of the alcohol slipping like silk through my blood, and found the lightness of my thoughts intensely pleasing. I was glad not to be sitting alone in that dorm and felt grateful to the girls for inviting me along.

We ordered meals and I headed over to the bar for a round of drinks. I peered between the people at the far end of the bar to see if I could spot Marcus again, but he'd gone and another couple sat in their seats. At least I was unlikely to bump into him again.

As I stood and waited to be served a man came and stood beside me.

He turned to me. 'Excuse me, you were at Maxine Croyett's talk. I bought a coffee from you.'

I recognised him instantly as the interfering journalist Hadrian had escorted from the building.

'Can I get you a drink?' he asked.

He was well spoken with traces of an accent I couldn't place - Northern, anyway. And handsome in a craggy, strong-jawed kind of way.

As a rule, accepting drinks from strangers wasn't something I did, but I was in a safe place, and I was also curious to hear what he might have to say.

'I'm buying the round for my friends too - three gin and tonics and three pints of lager.'

He raised his eyebrows. 'No worries. I'm feeling generous.'

He looked different from earlier in the hall - hatless, minus the long coat, and a clear pair of glasses, unlike the tinted pair he'd worn in a weak attempt at a disguise earlier. His tone was altogether more relaxed, too.

I imagined he wanted to sound me out about Maxine, so he could pay for whatever I might be able to tell him, which given I barely knew Maxine, would be minimal. I wondered if he'd spotted Marcus in the bar. Marcus could tell him far more than I could.

As the barman filled the tray with our drinks he introduced himself as Philip Forest and explained that he was a freelance journalist. He produced his photo ID which showed him as a member of the British Association of Journalists, and it looked legitimate.

I picked up the tray. 'Thank you. I'll take these. Back in a mo.'

'Who's the man at the bar?' asked Simone as I placed the tray in the middle of the table.

'A journalist who wants to talk about Maxine Croyett, the author I saw. Free drinks for us, so I'll give him a few minutes. Not that I know anything about her.'

'Are you sure he only wants to talk?' asked Simone, with a doubtful tone.

'Well that's all I'll be doing and not so much of that either,' I said and returned to the bar.

'Shall we sit down?' He gestured to a free table. 'I won't keep you long.'

I guessed he was sixtyish, and he looked a little rough around the edges in his gold-rimmed spectacles, well-worn shirt and slacks. When he handed me my drink I spotted a chunky gold ring on his wedding finger which I found reassuring. I'd known married men who removed their rings when out in bars. As he spoke his eyes had a curious and unblinking intensity which made it impossible to let my eyes drift elsewhere.

The chatter around me seemed to fade.

'You know Maxine, personally?' he asked.

'Not really, but I met her son earlier today and offered to help out after her talk.'

'I'll be open with you. I'm working on a story about Maxine early on in her career. It might end up being a revealing and groundbreaking article if I can link some missing pieces from the jigsaw.'

'Why don't you ask her for a proper interview? She might be more forthcoming.'

He shook his head. 'Unlikely. You see, Maxine knows I wrote a story about her when her husband died, and she and her family objected. In fact, they demanded a written apology in the same paper my article was published.'

'What did you write to upset them?'

'Nothing that wasn't factually true, although I did intimate that the death of her husband may not have been an accident and his murderer was known to him, that was all.'

'Maxine herself suggested he was murdered in her talk - still unsolved. And I don't know anything about her husband or his death.'

'Before your time - 1960's.' He sat up and drank back the last inch of his pint. 'If you don't know her then I doubt you can help me.'

'I'm a fan of her books. I write too.' I hesitated. 'Actually, Maxine has invited me to her house. I told her about the book I'm writing and she seemed interested.'

He nodded slowly. 'How generous of her.'

'I thought so, too.'

He removed his spectacles and polished them with his handkerchief. 'What do you hope to gain from meeting with her?'

'Hopefully some writing advice and some tips on getting published.'

He replaced his glasses on his nose. 'Not what you know, but who you know, eh?' He remarked, casually.

'Not at all. I want my book to be good enough for publication, not to try and win favours.'

'Of course.' He nodded again, and I could see his mind ticking over.

'What's the mystery surrounding her husband's death?' If he could ask me questions, so could I.

'You should read the articles I wrote for The Daily Echo.'

'I might do.'

'There was an inquest issued by the coroner and a few people were taken in for questioning, but it never went to trial or court.' He inclined his head. 'Something else you might be interested in.'

He spoke as if he knew my profession. 'Who was taken in for questioning?' I asked.

'Maxine and her sister, but the inquest ruled death by accident so that was final and no one was charged. But there was evidence to suggest his death was suspicious and there was a lengthy investigation and inquest.'

'I can only imagine that Maxine is completely innocent if she's still searching for answers to his death, too.'

'Ahh. Double bluff, maybe.' He clicked his tongue. 'Not unheard of in these cases, and she's never done a lot of searching from what I've seen.'

'If all were found innocent why so interested?'

'I can't name my sources, but I'm only interested in the truth of the story. And I know others would be too.'

'If there is more to know...' I trailed off.

'Maxine is satisfied to let her husband's death remain a mystery, which is why she refuses to talk to me.'

'She didn't sound satisfied today,' I said.

He nodded thoughtfully. 'What Maxine intimates publicly contrasts with how she treats any questions from interested parties.'

'Hence you were escorted from the room,' I said.

'I didn't expect a warm reception, but any journalist with half a brain knows that when someone refuses to talk or is overly defensive it's a strong sign there's more going on than we're aware of.'

'But as it's long in the past I'm sure she'd far rather forget and move on than keep being reminded of his death, or worse, feeling as if she's being investigated. She must have been devastated to lose him, and Hadrian, too. How old was he when it happened?'

'Young - four or five.'

'So even more traumatic for Maxine. You should leave them be.'

'Jodie?'

I turned around and noticed Pippa calling me over as a waiter laid our plates of food on the table.

'I have to go,' I said, and stood up. 'Sorry, I really don't know the family well enough.'

'Not yet, anyway,' he said, and reached into his jacket pocket. 'Here's my card.'

I took it from him and slipped it into my jacket pocket alongside Maxine's. 'I'm only seeing her tomorrow and I've no intention of poking my nose into their family history.'

'I wouldn't mention to Maxine that you've spoken to me, it may not make her warm to you.'

'Wouldn't dream of it. Thanks for the drinks, and sorry I can't help.'

'No, you've been a great help.' He touched my arm briefly. 'May I offer you a bit of advice?'

Whenever anyone uttered the words *bit of advice*, I felt a tremendous urge to run in the opposite direction.

I smiled. 'You may.'

'Be wary of what you share with Maxine. Fine, take her writing advice, but leave it at that.'

How naive did he think I was? I was a lawyer, for goodness sake.

'Writing advice is all I'm going for,' I replied, tersely.

And irritated by his advice that was about as welcome as a snake joining me in the bath, I turned away and rejoined the girls.

I'd ordered fisherman's pie and when I sat down and the aromas filled my airways, my taste buds tingled. I hadn't eaten since breakfast and I picked up my knife and fork.

'Looked like you couldn't get away,' said Pippa.

'He's investigating something from decades ago. Anyway, he bought us drinks so it was worth my time.'

I glanced over at the bar. It looked like my journalist friend had already gone.

'This is tasty,' I remarked, looking round the table at the girls tucking in too.

'The guy in the hostel recommended the food. He was spot on,' replied Pippa.

'Last round's on me,' I called across the table.

Pippa tapped my arm. 'How about we save our money and head back to the hostel?'

'We're just getting going, aren't we?'

She threw her head back and laughed. 'I can see that. But Mae has baked some of her special recipe chocolate cookies and we thought we'd nibble on those.' She paused. 'For dessert.'

'I am quite stuffed but I never refuse a cookie.' I looked across at Mae who gave the tiniest wink.

'Ahh, I see.' I winked back. 'Then it would be rude to refuse.'

When we left the pub and headed across the road and into the park I felt giddy and veered across the path. Pippa grabbed my arm and hauled me straight. 'Coffee for you when we get in.'

'Can we help ourselves?'

'Yeah, if you sweet talk the cute receptionist,' she said.

I giggled. 'Why can't you?'

She nudged me. 'You stand a better chance.'

'How about we drink water instead?' I suggested.

We tumbled chattering and laughing through the doors of the hostel and a tall woman with a head of curly white hair stood in place of the young man who'd checked me in earlier.

'Evening, girls,' she called with stern disapproval at our rowdiness. 'Having an early night?'

'Yes,' Pippa replied, with a chortle. 'So tired after all our digging.'

'Very wise,' the woman said. 'Bright and early for breakfast at seven?'

'Oh, yes, we'll be down by then,' I said. 'I have a meeting with a *V-I-P*!'

'Who's that?' the woman asked.

'Maxine Croyett - the famous crime writer.'

The woman's eyes widened and she inhaled a breath. 'She's a lesser spotted celebrity in Hexham.'

'I've been invited to her place.' I hiccupped. 'Is she a recluse?'

'Thankfully,' the woman replied, and I saw her lips tighten.

'You know her?' I asked.

She folded her arms across her chest. 'I've had a few dealings.'

'You've read her books?'

Her top lip curled. 'Tried one years ago. Not my thing.'

She sounded unkind and bitter, and anyone who didn't appreciate Maxine's brilliant creative mind and books, had poor taste in fiction, as far as I was concerned.

'Fine. I won't pass on your regards.' I peered closer at her name badge. 'Lisa.'

'I was Detective Holland when I knew her.'

My new friends headed up the stairs and I called after them. 'Be there soon.'

I turned back to the woman, alert. 'Were you around here when her husband died?'

'Yes, and if I may speak frankly, Maxine couldn't have been more obstructive during the investigation and inquest.'

'She was probably traumatised - grief does strange things to people.'

'She never appeared grief-stricken.' The woman gave a half-shrug. 'Still, it's history and we've all moved on.'

I got the impression that Lisa, aka Detective Holland, was reluctant to reveal more. 'You thought her husband's death might be suspicious?' I suddenly felt quite sober.

'The inquest concluded no, but I was the lead officer on the case and I found Maxine difficult, and unconvincing.'

'Interesting. Our esteemed author seems quite the dark horse,' I said.

She inhaled sharply. 'I'd say a dark personality is needed to write crime novels.'

I thought for a moment about my own motives for writing my book. 'It's more likely Maxine has a vivid imagination and her own experiences have fuelled her writing.'

'No smoke without fire. I've seen that time and time again through my work.'

'Or innocent until proven guilty,' I replied, and felt annoyed by all the negative talk I'd heard about Maxine tonight. 'I'm going up. Early start.' I turned and walked away.

On the bottom step I tripped and stumbled onto my hands and knees.

I heard a snigger from the desk. 'You okay?'

I stood up hastily and glanced around. 'Fine thanks.' And I continued on up the stairs.

In the dorm, I found the girls sitting on their pillows in the aisle between the beds, with an open tupperware box full of chocolate cookies.

'You keep getting accosted by weirdos,' said Simone, one of the students.

'I shouldn't have mentioned Maxine Croyett. Seems her name stirs everyone up around here.' I grabbed the pillow off my bed and the girls shifted round to make space for me in their circle.

'Small town politics and gossip,' said Pippa. 'It's why I love Manchester.'

I sat down cross-legged on my pillow. 'You're right about small town talk. Plus, have you noticed how successful women are so often demonised? Look at Jemima Hawkins. What's she ever done, other than to write brilliant stories that capture children's imagination and encourage them to read? Same for Maxine Croyett. Any scent of controversy and people cling onto it like poison to drag them down. Wouldn't happen if it was a male author of course. Makes me sick.'

Mae lifted the tupperware box. 'Have a cookie then. Promise it won't make you sick.'

I reached over and took one. 'How potent are they?'

'Not overly. I have a tried and tested recipe.'

'I can vouch for their safety, and effectiveness,' said Pippa, as she took another bite. 'The trick is to eat them as a delicacy, not to bolt them down because they're chocolatey.'

'There's enough for one more each, but we'll give them a good hour to take effect first,' advised Mae.

'I confess I've never eaten space cakes.' I took a tentative nibble. 'I smoked weed at Uni once or twice.' I chewed and the chocolate flavours burst across my tongue. 'Oh my God!' I savoured the sweetness and swallowed. 'Good job you advised me to eat slowly.'

Pippa reached into her rucksack and pulled out a tape player. 'How about some music to get us in the mood. The Doors anyone?' she asked.

'Perfectly psychedelic,' I replied.

'Fun to dance to,' Trish said, and stood up, ready.

'Here she goes,' said Mae. 'We all look like bumbling baboons next to Trish.'

I watched as Trish took a few steps back into a clear space. When Pippa turned up the volume, Trish gyrated her hips and twisted and curved her hands and fingers.

I loved dancing too, well, after a few drinks, so with my space cake in hand I got up and joined her. I felt giddy as I raised my arms and wriggled my hips.

'Oh, you've been practising too,' someone said.

'I always thought I should become a dancer rather than a lawyer,' I joked.

Pippa jumped up and joined us. 'There's still time, my friend, as you're between professions.'

'True. I can do anything I want now I've been betrayed, dumped and sacked,' I said, feeling bold and carefree. But even as I spoke, I knew all I really wanted to do was to write.

For now, and tonight, nothing mattered.

By the next song, "Light My Fire", the others had joined in and we pranced around the room. I pulled off my boots, jumped onto my unmade bed and bounced up and down, then leapt off and tumbled into a heap on the floor.

Someone rapped on the dormitory door and we all stopped in our tracks and looked at one another. Pippa reached for the tape player and lowered the volume. I ran over to the door and opened it a few inches.

Lisa from reception stood there, her pointy features fixed and stern. 'There's an 11 p.m. curfew when we expect music and voices to be silenced so that other visitors can sleep. Is that clear, ladies?'

I stifled a snigger and set my features straight. 'I'm really sorry. We'll turn it to barely audible and speak in whispers.'

She frowned. 'Good, thank you dear.'

When she'd walked away I closed the door.

I turned back to the room and we waited a few moments before collapsing into giggles.

'We could sit on the bandstand in the park?' I suggested.

The girls agreed and we put on our jackets and shoes. Mae grabbed the box of cookies and Pippa brought the tape player. We all trooped downstairs in silence.

'We have a midnight curfew so please don't be late. I'd like to sleep, too,' Lisa said firmly.

I looked at my watch. That gave us almost an hour.

'We'll be back, don't worry,' I said.

As we headed into the park, I gazed up at the strings of lights between the trees and they shimmered, bright and vibrant. A gratifyingly cool breeze swept in, brushing my cheeks and I opened my arms and inhaled the fresh night air. The tips of my fingers tingled and I felt the darkness wrap itself around my exposed skin.

The lights overhead sparkled and rocked in the nightly shadows and I raised my arms and felt as though I could almost touch them. My limbs felt weightless and when I turned around and looked at the girls' faces, the whites of their eyes appeared bright in the curious half-light.

The bandstand was part-way up the slope, and we trooped up the steps to the wooden platform.

'I'd love to see a band play here,' I said.

'I'll play Portishead, and we'll pretend they're performing,' one of the girls said.

I walked around the platform trailing my hand along the iron rail.

Mae peeled the lid off the cookie tub. 'Seconds, anyone?'

We all stepped forward eagerly, bar Pippa, and picked another cookie.

'Don't think the other has affected me yet.' I took a bite and resisted the urge to stuff it in whole.

I stood at the top of the steps and looked out at the trees beyond the benches to where the lights winked, and where strange silhouettes swayed in the breeze and danced upon the grass.

'I went to a house party in Bristol last year and some of the members of Portishead were there. Beth, the lead singer, was so cool,' said one of the girls, somewhere behind me.

The music played; my new friends chatting, laughing, but I felt invisible, a ghost looking on at a group of cheerful revellers. My thoughts drifted back to the afternoon - some pleasurable moments, a few mystifying, and others troubling. Firstly, talking to Hadrian on the train, then meeting his cousin Marcus and their barbed and rivalrous exchanges. Maxine had been composed and eloquent on stage, but turned on a sixpence to becoming frantic and enraged about the journalist. And the same journalist, Philip, who later approached me in the pub. Coincidence - possible but unlikely? Had he been the figure lurking in the park? What about Marcus, welcoming and kind? And later on that barstool, talking with a blonde.

How many hours until I saw Maxine again, and in her own home? Did she live alone? I tried to imagine what her house might look like. She'd have quality furniture, bookshelves stacked with books, an antique writing desk, a standing Tiffany lamp to light the plush curtained rooms where framed family photographs and original paintings hung on the walls. A cat or two, and perhaps a golden retriever she walked along Hadrian's wall. Maybe a small orchard at the back of the house with apple, pear and plum trees amongst grasses spotted with butterflies and colourful wildflowers. There'd be bees buzzing lazily amongst the flowerbeds, birds chittering in the trees, and a summerhouse with Scandi style decor, and a rustic table with wicker seats around. She'd write there in the summer with the doors and windows wide open, using notebooks and ink pens to jot down thoughts as they came to her. A few loose papers lying around, an empty tea cup, and an oil lamp so she could continue working into the warmer evenings, when moths would be drawn to the flame and flitter in the glow. From her window she'd admire the sunset radiating pomegranate pink above the hills and Hadrian's wall as it had done through the centuries. When darkness fell she'd lean in closer to the page as she wrote.

The image of Maxine at her writing desk faded. And in her place there was I at her desk in the summerhouse, not writing, but holding a book and reading. Someone else was in the summerhouse, too, and I lifted my eyes from the page. There was Dad, who I hadn't seen in years. He stepped squarely up to the desk, his full height towering over me. His features had aged almost beyond recognition - his nose bulbous tipped and his lips thin, cracked and pinched, with grey brows hanging heavy over dark eyes. He opened his mouth and began to hurl abuse at me, but I only saw his lips curling and changing shape, whilst his teeth bared in an angry growl. I cowered in my seat, my body shrinking further back each second. The rage in his features paralysed my instincts to stand up and run, rendering me dumb and fixed to the chair. I glanced past him to the open door. I wanted to slip past and run into the evening, to hide amongst the trees so that he couldn't hurt me. But instead he turned away and walked through the door, leaving me pinned to the seat by the fear that gripped my belly. He slammed the door behind him, just as the ceiling and four walls began to move inwards. I stretched out my arms to hold them back but their shadows kept pressing in, inching closer until I felt their weight bear down on me from all sides.

I cradled my arms over my head and screamed. 'Stop!'

'Jodie! Jodie, it's okay.'

I felt someone beside me and a hand on my arm.

My eyes shuttered, and in that moment I was back on the bandstand with Pippa beside me, her expression full of concern.

My eyes darted behind to see who else might be near. 'My dad. He shut me in.'

'No, Jodie. It's us, your friends from the hostel. We're in the park.'

I looked into her eyes. 'But…' I hesitated. 'Dad was here.'

'No,' she reassured. 'It's the marijuana. You're having a bad reaction. Here.' She placed a plastic bottle in my hands. 'Drink some water.'

I took the bottle from her. The liquid cooled and soothed my throat. But my mind felt confused. I tried to separate all that had happened today, with events from my past which had returned to the present. Like a parasite that refused to leave its host, they'd sent my thoughts and memories into a spin.

I felt I was teetering on the edge - that something unavoidable and dangerous was happening to me. It was wrong being here in the dark with people I barely knew. When I looked up I saw the girls dancing and carefree, the railings around the bandstand and beyond that the darkness which swelled with shadows, lurking like the memories from my past.

The plastic bottle fell from my hand and I turned to Pippa. 'I'm tired. I'm going to bed.' I turned towards the pathway illuminated by the lights through the trees. 'I'll see you soon.'

'Okay, I'll watch you. Go straight in and up to bed.'

When I reached the footbridge over the stream, I turned and waved to Pippa, still watching from the bandstand. She lifted her arm and waved. When I turned back my step faltered and my vision swayed. The path ahead shimmered like black water flowing towards me and I made a concentrated effort to place one foot in front of the other up the hill.

That second cookie had been a big mistake - probably the first, too.

I heard strange noises - footsteps and rustles in the undergrowth closeby, followed by the haunting cry of a bird. Or was it a fox? As I walked I twisted round to check if anyone was behind me.

The lamps at the gate to the hostel came into view, but beyond that everything became a blur.

Chapter 10

Lost Memories

'My God, Jodie, where the fuck have you been?' cried Pippa as I walked into the dormitory.

I stumbled across the floor to my bed, flopped onto my back and stared up at the ceiling.

A voice closeby said, 'We were about to send out a bloody search party.'

But I closed my eyes and within seconds I fell into a deep slumber filled with vivid and disturbing dreams.

I pushed my legs over the side of the bed and looked around the empty dormitory. The curtains were open and daylight streamed in but there was no bedding on the other bunks, no bags and shoes, and none of the girls.

At least I could remember who I'd shared the room with.

I spotted a handwritten note on my bedside table.

We didn't want to wake you. We were worried about you last night. I hope you're feeling all right this morning. Thanks for coming out with us and good luck with the author, Pippa and friends xx

She'd written her mobile number at the bottom. I wondered with embarrassment what I might have said or done when I'd been high on hash.

I looked down at my watch. Nine o'clock already!

Downstairs in the canteen, I placed my mug under the hot water boiler and pulled down the lever.

'In need of caffeine?'

I turned around and Lisa from reception stood behind me with her cup.

'My second cup, so yes, dire need.' I pulled the lever back up.

I stood aside and stirred the teabag.

She frowned darkly. 'Not surprised, given the state you were in last night.'

I couldn't remember seeing Lisa when I came in. But then, I barely remembered anything beyond the bandstand.

I felt my cheeks burn. 'I hope I didn't say anything to upset you.'

'Not at all. You didn't even notice I was at the door when you came through.'

'I was very tired.'

'Mmm. A thank you would be nice.'

My mind turned over. 'Thank you?'

'I didn't want to lock you out. Your friends came in before the midnight curfew. I saw you weren't amongst them.'

'I thought I came in before them - my memory is a bit muddled.'

She tutted. 'Nope, you were late.'

I poured a splash of milk into my cup and turned to face her. 'Well, that was kind of you to wait, I appreciate it.'

'At least you weren't wandering around alone in the dark.'

'I wasn't?' I tried to piece together my patchy memory. 'One of the students?'

'Don't know if he was a student. From where I stood, he looked older than that.'

'He?'

She raised her eyebrows. 'As you seemed to be talking intimately at the end of the drive before coming in, alone, I assumed you knew his name.'

My heart thudded. 'Of course. I was tired...' I grappled for memories and stumbled over my words.

Her eyes narrowed and she nodded. 'Enjoy your breakfast.' Then she squeezed her teabag with a spoon and dropped it in the bin before heading out of the canteen.

I returned to my table and looked around at the now empty tables. Last down to breakfast and last to leave. And it was the last time I'd ever eat marijuana.

I finished my tea, set the cup down and looked up again. The corners of the room blurred and shimmered as though a wind pressed against the walls. My arms felt light as if I might at any moment lift off my seat and float up to the ceiling, and from there look down upon myself sitting here, alone at this table. Recent memories appeared before me, a flickering mirage with disordered images moving into the frame and out again.

I heard my breaths loud in my ears, and I rubbed my eyes to try and clear my vision and my mind - to regain some clarity on last night's events. When I opened my eyes again I was back in the hostel canteen with sunlight illuminating the walls and tables.

I glanced at the clock above the breakfast counter. Almost 10 a.m. and I still needed to shower, catch the number 7 bus and find Maxine's house.

Who was the man I'd been talking to intimately outside the hostel last night?

Had it been Philip the journalist I'd spoken with in the pub? I must have been high as a kite. The only other time I'd experienced memory loss was when I'd been staggeringly drunk as a student. The sensation of feeling out of control, loss of memory, plus the horrendous hangover, had been enough to deter me from repeating it. I took another bite of toast and hoped as the day progressed, my memory of last night would return, and that I hadn't done anything foolish or embarrassing.

Chapter 11

A Strange Encounter

I took a seat near the front of the bus and gazed out of the window as we headed out of Hexham, and over the bridge to where fields, farm buildings and woodland took the place of houses. The driver assured me she'd give me a call at the correct stop, so I sat back and enjoyed the views of the hillside on top of which I could see the line of Hadrian's Wall.

I tried to picture Maxine's house, what any best-selling author's country house might look like. And then an unsettling memory from last night came to me. Or had I been dreaming? I got the feeling I'd visited Maxine's home before. But that must have been the marijuana spiking my imagination, even bringing Dad into the mix.

Still, as a writer Maxine was sure to have shelves of books. You could tell plenty about a person by the books on their shelves. I always sneaked a peek when visiting friend's houses, to check out reading preferences. Maxine would have her fair share of crime novels. Not that she'd need to steal ideas. Her novels were rich with originality in every respect. Maybe she had a partner - it had been years since her husband passed away. Although most likely a partner would have come to her talk. She'd probably have a cleaner and gardener. I know I would with her success.

The bus slowed and we pulled into a layby.

'Stop for The Blue House,' the driver called back.

I stood up and slung my bag over my shoulder.

'Is it far?' I asked.

She pointed over the road. 'Narrow lane, so keep in. About a mile up the hill. I've walked there and it's a lovely spot.'

I thanked her and stepped onto the verge.

'Good luck!' she called and pulled onto the road again.

I waited for two screaming motorbikes to whizz past and I crossed the road.

Open country spread all around me, and as far as I could see, field after field lay like a patchwork quilt across the land, stitched in olive, jade and emerald greens. The sounds of traffic faded and overhead puffed up clouds, crisp white in the sunlight drifted across the sky, with a few hanging over the pale violet hilltops in the distance. The air felt cooler than yesterday and I buttoned up my jacket and walked along the verge to the lane that led up the hill. As the bus driver warned, it was narrow, a few feet side to side, and after walking only a hundred yards or so a silence filled the empty lane.

At the first brow I turned and looked back. Acres of sloping fields fell away to create a captivating view. In the valley, Hexham was visible, but tucked in and cosied away from the elements and softened by distance from up here. A Victorian brick tower stood out amongst a factory on the edge of the town, with ribbon lanes winding along either side of the river which meandered through the valley. Sunlight between the clouds created shifting shadows over the land - and sparkled on the surface of the river. Fertile pastures and clusters of trees lay below, full with leaves, where nesting birds sang. Somewhere in the distance I heard the faint chuffing of a train as it travelled the Tyne Valley. Moments later the engine and carriages appeared between woodland and moved into what could be a John Constable painting, where farm buildings, cows and sheep dotted the fields and tree lined lanes.

How I'd love to wake to this view each morning, to pull back the curtains and greet the new day. I'd sit at my window with a novel and a cup of tea in hand, and gaze out every so often to be reminded of nature's artistry beyond the walls of my home and garden.

Such a view must inspire Maxine's writing.

I turned around to continue up the lane and heard the rush of wheels on gravel, but even before I could register the direction they came from, three cyclists raced around the corner only yards away. From where I stood in the middle of the lane I was unsure for a second which direction to jump aside. But there was no time for calculation and the cyclists picked up speed as if they hadn't registered my presence. As I dived for the verge one of the cyclists swerved into my path, ran over my foot and knocked me sideways. I pitched headfirst into the wall, banging my head and scraping my hand. As I scrambled to sit up I watched the cyclist, as if in slow motion, do a somersault over his handlebars and roll over the gravel. He came to rest in the middle of the lane. The other two cyclists braked hard, skidded and pulled up twenty yards in front.

The side of my head felt painful to touch and my left ankle throbbed. I pulled up the hem of my jeans, then wiggled my foot and rubbed the skin. It felt sore, but thankfully, nothing seemed broken. When I raised my hand to my head it felt tender and already swollen, but I looked at my fingers and felt relieved to see no blood. By the time I registered that all seemed to be intact, the offending cyclist had clambered to his feet.

His eyes blazed as he stormed towards me. 'What the fuck were you doing in the middle of the road, you idiot? You almost killed me.'

I rose to my feet slowly and straightened my clothes.

The cyclist stepped closer - his stance confrontational.

'Hey Rob, you all right?' Called one of his friends, approaching.

'Think so,' he called back.

'Yeah, I'm okay too, thanks,' I said with sarcasm. 'You came at me like lunatics - it's a public road.'

'Exactly, *a road,* not a spot to stand and admire the view. The footpath is on the other side of the wall, clearly marked, if you'd opened your eyes.'

'I didn't know. Besides, if I'd been a stopped car you'd have come off far worse. So consider that next time you're hurtling three abreast around corners down a single track lane.'

My tears threatened and as I turned away I felt a shooting pain above my eyes. The pain intensified and for a few seconds I clutched my head and closed my eyes until the pain subsided. I blinked tears from my eyes, and the road ahead sharpened beneath a burst of sunlight. I was in no mood for an argument and I set off up the hill to escape his anger.

'Wait up,' one of the cyclists called out from behind.

I heard footsteps and turned around.

One of the other young men jogged up. 'Are you hurt?'

'I'm fine, no thanks to your mate.' I gestured to his friend.

'I saw you fall. Sure you're okay?'

'I'm shocked, that's all.'

'Have you far to walk?'

'No.' I glanced over his shoulder. 'Is your friend all right?'

He leaned closer. 'He wouldn't be making such a noise if he wasn't.'

I smiled. 'True, but better keep an eye on him all the same.'

'He's my little brother, so that's in my job description.'

I nodded. 'Thanks for checking I'm okay, and don't worry, I won't sue him. Although I'm a lawyer so you can inform your little brother of that in case he thinks he might want to yell at me again.'

'Ahh right, that I appreciate. We'll be more careful in future.' He turned and walked back to join the others.

My head throbbed and feeling lightheaded and unbalanced, I crouched down on my haunches. The dizziness slowly eased and I straightened up and watched the cyclists mount their bikes and set off down the lane in single file.

Despite my ankle twinging with each step, I wasn't limping and I felt relieved I hadn't sprained it, or worse. Around the bend a signpost over a stile read, Hadrian's Wall, half a mile. Peering up at the signpost and squinting against the sun, the strongest and strangest sensation came over me - a certainty of having been here in this spot before. I turned around and looked at the ancient oak tree on the opposite verge. It had a gnarled trunk and branches that twisted and reached across the lane towards me. Like the wooden signpost it appeared strikingly familiar and I sensed with certainty that The Blue House was only yards away up the lane.

With each footstep and as my perspective altered, I felt I was retracing steps I'd walked before. Each rock by the side of the road, each tree and view over the wall was no surprise to me. When I rounded another bend and spotted three tall chimneys that emerged above a thicket of trees, I knew it to be The Blue House. I approached the driveway with a five bar timber gate and once more, the slate nameplate nailed to the gate aroused a familiarity in me.

The house was partly hidden behind tall elm trees, but I saw it vividly in my mind. Had I dreamed of visiting before, or seen photographs in a magazine? My hands trembled as I unlatched the gate, pushed it open and stepped through, before securing the latch behind me.

The lawns on either side of the potholed drive grew lush and long, and a neat stone wall surrounded the garden as far as I could see. I continued up the drive, between the trees, until I stopped in front of the three-story stone Manor house with creeper-covered walls, and a pitched slate roof with high dormer windows. The flagged path to the front door was well trodden, and the stone pillars on either side of the door had crumbled in places, and the paintwork on the door and window frames had weathered and cracked. There was a brass wall plaque next to the door engraved with *The Blue House*, and above it a bell with dangling rope to sound your arrival. The only thing obviously blue about this house, grand but frayed at the edges, was the front door painted teal blue, but in much need of a recoat. Nevertheless, the house, which to all outward appearance could have belonged to a different time, stood sure of itself - strong and solid in a way that houses built a century ago still were today.

It seemed a curious name for a house almost entirely devoid of blue, I mused.

I sensed movement in an upstairs window, and when I glanced up saw the curtains twitch and a figure step back from the window. I hoped Maxine hadn't changed her mind about my visit. I stepped up to the door and even before I reached up and pulled the bell rope I sensed I would return, stand on this same doorstep and ring the bell once more.

A breeze swept through the trees behind me and crows cawed overhead. Something brushed against my leg, and I startled and looked down to see a ginger Tom curl his tail around my leg. When I reached down to stroke him, he hissed, splayed his claws and arched his back.

I'd always been wary of cats, or perhaps they were wary of me, and I was allergic to them, too. No doubt this one sensed my unease.

'It's okay puss. I'm friendly.' But he hissed again and continued to eye me with suspicion. I reached for the bell again, but heard the scrape of a bolt drawn back and the door creaked open. The cat darted forwards and slipped through the gap.

Maxine pulled the door wide and looked out at me. Her brow furrowed.

I smiled. 'Hello, Maxine.'

She gave the briefest of smiles in return. 'Ahh, so you came.'

'Is it convenient?'

She shifted sideways, holding one foot loosely, and looked over my head towards the lane. 'Of course. I'm distracted because I was in the middle of a chapter and my mind was elsewhere. My housekeeper would normally answer the door.'

I stepped inside. 'Sorry to interrupt your flow. I know how engrossing writing can be.'

I wondered why Maxine had been at the window if she was in the middle of writing. Perhaps that had been someone else.

We stood together in the entrance hall.

'Yes, I write all morning without a break and I don't tolerate interruptions, as a rule. Jonie, isn't it?'

'Jodie,' I corrected.

'Of course.' She tilted her head. 'We've met before?'

'Before yesterday, you mean?'

'Yes, you're familiar. I thought so at the hall, too.'

I recalled the feeling of deja vu as I approached the house.

'I have walked in the area once or twice. Not for many years.'

'You know Hadrian, though? He'll be here soon.'

'Actually, I only met Hadrian and Marcus for the first time yesterday. I met Hadrian on the train.'

'I thought you two must be friends.'

'Well, he is easy to talk to.'

'That he is. He gets his agreeable genes from me,' she said with a snort of laughter. 'Although most of the time I'm happy in the company of my characters, I do make exceptions.'

'I feel honoured,' I said.

'Indeed, you are.' Her eyelids flickered, and I detected the faintest smile through closed lips. 'Come through and we'll talk over a cuppa. You can tell me about yourself and I can maybe share some writing insights.'

As we walked through the entrance hall, high-ceilinged, but windowless and unlit, Maxine continued. 'I'm afraid the house is in a state. My housekeeper left me in the lurch a fortnight ago.' She tutted. 'I can't even get hold of the damned woman.'

'Did she say why she was leaving?' I asked.

'No real reason, other than I didn't do something she asked. But I paid her to do the doing, not me.'

I followed her into a living room, long and narrow with tall windows at either end and a high ceiling with floral mouldings. The curtains were part-drawn and in the dim light we passed two maroon sofas on either side of a coffee table overladen with newspapers, magazines, pens and sheets of paper. A selection of tea cups with dregs of tea rested on the coasters. In the middle of the table was a domed glass case through which a stuffed crow peered out at me with green eyes. The ginger Tom I'd encountered at the front door lounged on the back of a sofa and followed me with his eyes whilst his tail swung back and forth. As I'd imagined, there were mahogany framed paintings and photographs on the walls, and a grand piano at the far end of the room. The old stone fireplace was full of embers and discarded crumpled paper - some trailing over the hearth and onto the rug.

Maxine paused and looked around, then seemed to decide against sitting in here, and gestured for me to follow her out. We walked through to a gorgeous conservatory, no, orangery, at the rear of the house. It must have been built as an extension and it stretched well over twenty feet along the back of the house. It was light filled and deliciously warm with sunlight shining through the roof lantern. There were several orange trees spotted with fruits, and French doors that opened onto a patio. I inhaled a refreshing scent of greenery mingled with spicy citrus.

I looked out through the windows onto a sprawling garden, vibrant with flowers amongst grass that swept gently downhill. Beyond the lawn and flowerbeds was a mini woodland with a variety of broadleaf trees, and beyond, fields and a hillside that rose up the other side.

'What an amazing room and garden,' I said, with genuine admiration.

'I'm fortunate, and I often write here to take advantage of the natural light and view.' She gestured to two high-backed chairs. 'Have a seat and I'll make us tea. Out of milk, so is black okay?'

'That would be lovely, thank you.'

Maxine left to make tea and I went and stood at the window. Looking out at the garden, deja vu began to flood my senses once more. Perhaps the collision with the cyclist and the bang to my head were causing these strange sensations. I spotted a swing hanging from a tree part-way down the slope and for some moments I imagined myself on the seat with legs dangling down as I swung back and forth. I began to sway on my feet and felt as though I were falling forwards, until I grasped the window frame to regain my balance.

I walked to the French doors and turned the handle. Locked, but there was a key. I turned the key and pushed open the door, then feeling compelled, stepped out onto the patio.

A warm breeze blew my hair across my face and I swept it away and tucked my hair behind my ears.

So silent out here - no birdsong, sounds of tractors in the fields or traffic on the lane. But then I heard a voice close by - a child talking and giggling, softly but distinct enough to hear the words.

'Higher,' said the child. 'Push me higher.'

I peered closer at the swing which swung forwards and back, forwards and back. Was it the wind? A chill travelled down my back, and my arms prickled with goosebumps. Did Maxine have grandchildren here? Or was it an echo from a garden further up the lane?

I heard the creak of a floorboard behind me and I turned around.

Maxine stood watching me from the doorway with a tray in hand. 'You like my garden?'

'I do! It's how I imagine the Garden of Eden.'

Why did I say that? I was feeling awkward - daunted to be in my literary heroine's home.

Maxine tilted her head, but if she noticed my discomfort she didn't draw attention to it. 'It's grown wild and needs attention.'

'Better for the bees, birds and wildlife.' I wondered whether to ask about grandchildren until I realised the child's voice I'd heard had silenced.

Maxine stepped back inside. 'Not quite warm enough for me out here.'

'Sorry, I hope you don't mind,' I walked back in and closed the door behind me. My hand felt clammy on the door handle and my breath steamed the glass.

'On warmer days I sit out and write. Further down though,' she said.

I peered to where she pointed. Perhaps there was outdoor seating further down.

The tray wobbled in her hands as she set it on the low wicker table and we sat on the chairs facing one another.

Some of the tea had spilled onto the tray, but I lifted my cup and took a sip. 'Mmm. Earl Grey, thank you.'

'You found me okay, then?'

'Yes, and I'd have been earlier if a lunatic hadn't run me over.'

She sucked in her breath and her face shot through with alarm. 'A car?'

'Thankfully, no - a cyclist. Three hurtling abreast round a bend. I didn't stand a chance.'

'I've seen plenty of mad men in lycra. Shouted at dozens speeding past my house. They either don't care about other traffic or pedestrians, or they have a death wish. A young man, I assume?'

I nodded. 'Sent me flying. Then ranted and blamed me!'

'I trust you got his name? You must sue him.'

'I'm fine and I wouldn't want the hassle right now.'

'He'll do it again and the next person won't be so lucky.'

'I hope he'll be more careful. He came a cropper, too.'

'I'm a firm believer in people paying for their mistakes. I'd sue and make him pay for it.'

'I'll bear it in mind,' I said, wanting to move on.

She sat back and rested her cup on its saucer. 'So, now you're no longer a lawyer, you want to write, and you've written a book?'

'I've always wanted to write, but I can't rely on that for income.'

She inclined her head and tutted. 'There's no easy money in writing.'

'But it does happen for some,' I said. 'And it did for you.'

'Takes a lot of talent, persistence and rejections.'

'You were rejected?' I said, surprised.

'A dozen times or so until I found a publisher. But I knew I had a good book and I persisted until someone took a chance on me.'

'And the publisher never looked back, I'm sure.'

'Indeed. A win win on both sides.' She placed her teacup on the table and leaned forward. 'But enough of me. You're an unpublished writer which is why I invited you here. Tell me about it? Do you have your manuscript with you?' She glanced down at my bag.

I took a breath, feeling determined to sound confident and competent. 'I've wanted to write forever. From childhood - illustrating my stories, too.' I paused for a moment. 'I read a news story a while ago. It was about a young woman that went missing in the 1950's - Sheila Morgan. Not far from here, as it happens. It was a mystery how she died and I used her story as the basis for mine, but changed and fictional for the most part.'

'How intriguing,' she said slowly. 'Sheila Morgan?'

I nodded. 'Yes, she'd graduated in Law. So, I was intrigued from a personal perspective too.'

Maxine tilted her head thoughtfully. 'That is interesting. I possibly do recall such a news story. I was an Oxford undergraduate at that time and immersed in college life.'

'Were your family living round here then?'

Maxine hesitated before replying, 'No, we lived in Maidstone.'

'Nicer up here, though,' I said.

'Indeed, I wouldn't move back down south. And did you conduct thorough research for your book?'

I nodded. 'Newspaper articles at the library mostly. But, as I said, I've used it as a framework and springboard.'

'How old are you, dear?'

'Thirty-two.'

'I could have done with a mentor early on.' She paused. 'Perhaps you'd like me to read your manuscript and offer feedback?'

I sat forward. 'Really? The full manuscript?'

'If it seemed worth my time. I'd know after a chapter or two.'

'You might change your mind.'

'I might, but I'm prepared to start it. If you think my opinion would help?'

I gasped and my eyes lit up. 'I'd be immensely grateful.' My insides bubbled with adrenaline.

'I shall be honest with you, too. It's what writers need if they want to improve and find a publisher.'

'Of course.'

'Have you printed it off or I could print it here?'

'Only for my ex-boyfriend. But I've edited since. Mum has a printer.'

I sometimes carried my book on a memory disc if I travelled, but as I'd only planned an afternoon away for the talk, I'd left it safely at home.

Some moments elapsed as Maxine paused, thoughtful, 'How about you come again with your disc and a print out?'

'Really? That would be incredible!'

'You drive?'

'Yes, but I don't have a car.'

'I rarely drive mine, but my housekeeper did. We could arrange insurance for a day or two. How does that sound?'

'That's so generous of you. How can I thank you?'

She waved away my thanks. 'It's timely for me as I was going to take a day or two off from my current novel. I like to reflect on what I've written. You'll find this, too. A writer must step back and allow their story to be digested, rather like a good meal.'

'I can see that makes sense.'

'Would you like to look around my home? It's untidy because I don't do domestic work and it's why I employ a housekeeper. Writers and artists rarely have the time, head space or organisational mentality for such menial work.'

'I'd love to look round!'

I thought about my own domestic habits. I considered myself a tidy person, but equally, I'd block out the mess when busy.

John on the other hand was fastidious and fussy and had often complained about my untidiness. But in my work, I was thorough, could prioritise and didn't miss appointments or actions.

Maxine stood up, and I drank the remainder of my tea.

'I've never been in an author's home. Oh, wait, I did visit Beatrix Potter's cottage in Ambleside. So pretty and charming.'

'Couldn't get two more diverse genres - illustrated children's stories and hard-hitting crime. Only thing me and Beatrix have in common is our gender and country living in the north.'

I heard a door slam and a voice call. 'It's the delivery man!'

Maxine clapped her hands together. 'My groceries. I'm down to my last crust and over ripe banana.'

'And they walk into your house? Do you know them well?'

'It's Hadrian, my dear.'

Maxine called back in a flamboyant French accent, 'We're in the orangery.'

Hadrian walked in and huffed. 'Grocery shopping is more exhausting than building stone walls.' He flopped onto an armchair before looking at me. 'You made it then?'

'Of course.' Did he think I wouldn't bother? 'I stayed at the hostel in town.'

'I know.' He nodded and his mouth turned up at the sides.

'Marcus kindly showed me,' I said.

'Yes, I know that too. And what have you ladies been talking about? Your novel?'

'Mostly, yes. I haven't been here long,' I replied.

'I was going to show Jodie around and I've offered her my car for a day or two.'

Hadrian nodded his approval. 'When Mum decides she likes someone she rarely hangs around. You're privileged.'

'And even more generously she's offered to read my manuscript, which I'm immensely grateful for.'

'You can at least expect an honest assessment, eh, Mum?'

'Life is too short to waste people's time,' Maxine confirmed. 'Actually Hadrian darling, would you mind showing Jodie round after putting the groceries away? I have some urgent admin.'

'I can help with the groceries,' I offered and picked up the empty teacups.

Without waiting for Hadrian's agreement Maxine was already heading out.

'Are you sure about the car? I could always get the train,' I asked.

Without turning round she said, 'Hadrian will organise the insurance for you.'

When Maxine had disappeared, Hadrian said, 'Don't mind Mum. She has high expectations of all people and is quick to delegate. A pity about the housekeeper absconding and me being her only child.'

'I have one brother but he's moved to France, so I feel like an only child most of the time.'

'Your parents are still around?'

'Only Mum. I've moved back home for a few weeks.'

'Your dad passed away?'

'Some years ago.'

Hadrian nodded. 'Sorry to hear that.'

'Thanks. We weren't close.' It always felt wrong lying about my dad's death, but I hated people asking about him, if they thought he was alive.

'My father's death was sudden, too. But I was only little,' he said.

'So you never really knew him?'

'Some vague memories. Photos help.' He crossed to the wall adjoining the house and pointed to a framed photograph. 'Mum and Dad on their wedding day.'

I stepped nearer for a closer look.

It was a family group with Maxine and Hadrian's dad holding hands. I couldn't believe how different Maxine looked. Tall and slim, with a cream body hugging knee-length dress. Her hair was left long and loose - blonde curls shaped around her heart-shaped face. Unrecognisably pretty and naturally so. 'That's your dad?' I couldn't hide the surprise in my voice.

Hadrian was tall, broad shouldered, dark eyes, hair and features, whereas his father was also tall but finely built, and clear to see in the photograph, green eyes that sparkled, beneath light brown hair.

Hadrian sensed my surprise and said, 'I know, we look quite different. But Grandad was built like a weightlifter, and dark like me, so his genes skipped a generation.'

'I imagine that happens more than you'd think.'

'I've got Dad's nose though,' he added and tapped the side of his nose.

'Oh yes, I can see that,' I turned and glanced at Hadrian's profile. In truth, I couldn't see the resemblance with his father, but it was a front facing photograph.

'I look like Mum and Dad,' I said. 'Mum's parents are Spanish, living in England now, and Dad is, I mean, was from Northumberland, but could have been Spanish, at least until he opened his mouth.'

'You don't have a Spanish accent either.'

'I speak fluent Spanish, though. Me and Mum sometimes chat that way.'

'Cool - two sultry senoritas with geordie accents,' he said with a light laugh.

'The Spanish think we're natives when we visit relatives, even with the geordie accents.' I pointed to a pretty woman with long fair hair and a pink hat that almost obscured her face. 'Who's that?'

'Aunt Evelyn. Mum's identical twin, and Marcus' mum.'

'Marcus mentioned she's an artist?'

'A sculptor and a successful one. Evelyn Hall. You've maybe heard of her?'

I thought for a moment. 'I'm not sure. What a talented family heritage you have.'

'Dad was a publisher. Well, a book editor,' he said.

'Your mum's editor?'

'Originally, yes, then she joined Albatross Publishing, where she's been since.'

'How interesting.'

He turned to me and with eyes that smiled, said, 'At least I could never accuse my family of being dull.' And he gave a cynical and dry laugh which suggested he had some reservations. 'Better get these things in the fridge.'

We walked through to the living room, down a narrow corridor and into the kitchen at the back of the house. There were three bulging shopping bags on the kitchen table, along with dirty plates with various scraps of food, used cups, and empty cans and bottles. The cat stood on the table nibbling at what looked like days old tomato pasta.

Hadrian marched up and swiped at the cat. 'Down you dirty minger.'

The cat growled, twisted round and snapped at Hadrian's hand before springing off the table and scuttling past my legs. He cast an evil eye back at Hadrian before he slipped through the cat flap to the garden.

Flies buzzed around and there was an unpleasant and cloying stench of stale food and fish. Scattered vegetable peelings and crumbs lay on the floor and the bin in the corner was full to the brim with packets hanging over the sides.

'Christ on a scooter! Natalie's only been gone a few days.'

'Your mum said she's too busy to keep on top of it,' I said.

'Nah, she just doesn't give a toss. Must have a stomach of iron.'

'Let me clean up while you sort out the shopping.'

'That's cool, thanks.'

We located a roll of bin liners, dishwasher tablets and some kitchen cleaner, and I set to work. When I saw the plug hole clogged with bits of food I rummaged under the sink and found a pair of rubber gloves still in their packet. It didn't take long for me to get the kitchen looking a whole lot tidier and the table and kitchen surfaces wiped clean. The varnished pine units were dated and some of the quarry tiles on the floor were cracked, and there were a few burnt pan marks on the wooden tops, but I could see it must have been a stylish kitchen many moons ago. An unpleasant scent drifted from the cat's tattered bed in the corner.

'Had Natalie been working here long?'

'Eleven years, so it's a blow she's left. Imagine she couldn't take Mum's moods any longer.'

'Your mum seems even tempered.'

Hadrian huffed. 'Only when she makes considerable effort, which she will with you today.'

I looked out of the kitchen window onto the garden. 'Did you grow up here?'

'Aye, which is why I couldn't wait to get my own place.'

I turned back to him. 'It is quite remote. Where do you live now?'

'Hexham, a two up, two down terrace.'

'How about Evelyn and Marcus?'

'Evelyn's in Corbridge. A few miles east. Marcus has his own pad in Hexham.'

'It's such a pretty area,' I said.

'Would you like to see the garden? It's much prettier than the house.'

'I'd love to,' I replied. My visit was proving to be more interesting and lengthy than I could have anticipated.

I followed Hadrian through the kitchen door onto the patio.

He pointed and arched his eyebrows. 'It's magical down there. Just wait til you see it.'

We set off down the pathway at the edge of the lawn which narrowed and curved beneath the trees, and past the swing which hung still now. The sun overhead felt hot on my shoulders and I felt as if I'd entered a secret garden - wild, luscious green and abundant. I gazed around at the sun-gilded grass and leaves and thought I'd never seen a more beautiful and inviting garden. The flowerbeds were overgrown and last year's blooms stood tall and dried amongst this year's growth, which in contrast was captivating and colourful. Underfoot, twigs and branches fallen in the winds of winter lay strewn in our way and I stepped over and between them.

Hadrian stopped, turned to me and asked casually, 'How are you feeling today?'

His question took me aback. 'Fine. Why?'

'You don't remember then?'

I hesitated. 'Remember... what?'

His eyes creased into a smile. 'We met in the park last night.'

'With some girls - students?'

He pressed his lips together for a moment. 'Not exactly.'

Oh, God, I thought, and realised he must have seen me when I'd been spaced out. Was it Hadrian who Lisa, the woman at the hostel, had seen me with late last night?

I felt my cheeks warm. 'Where was I?'

His brows lifted and his eyes sparkled. 'You really don't remember?'

I shook my head. 'I really don't.'

'It was late and you were heading towards the hostel - I guess. I was walking home after meeting friends and when I saw you in the park we talked. Sat on a bench for a while.'

'The students offered me space cakes and my mind's a blur. Was I talking nonsense?'

A half smile parted his lips. 'Not so much talking, more, how can I put it?'

I felt my face burn. 'What?'

'You were friendly.'

'In what way?' But I knew where this was leading.

He masked a smile that suggested more. 'I really didn't mind.'

'I don't even remember seeing you.' And it was true.

'I assure you we met and talked. I insisted on walking you back safely.'

I felt confused. Hash didn't make you forget what you were doing, unless I'd passed out. But my memory of the latter part of the evening was patchy, to say the least.

'My friends were worried and the hostel manager was annoyed.'

'Good job I turned up or God knows where you might have ended up. You were spaced out and giggly.'

'But I was headed in the direction of the hostel?'

He grimaced. 'More wandering across the grass towards town - talking away to yourself.'

'Then I must thank you. I'm embarrassed.' And I was, my cheeks were burning.

He put his hands up. 'Please. I didn't mind.'

'I remember seeing Marcus in the pub earlier.'

He tilted his head and we continued walking. 'Did you speak?'

'No, he was with a woman.'

'He generally is. A different one each time from what I've seen.'

'Really? He doesn't seem the womanising type.'

'Dark horse, is Marcus. Quietly seduces and reels 'em in.'

'Okay.' I'd exchanged telephone numbers with Marcus, I reflected, and in a way that made me think he wasn't presumptuous.

I gazed up into the trees, and inhaled the scents of wildflowers amongst the grasses that spread before us like a finely woven blanket. 'This is breathtaking. Must have been fun when you were little.'

'I spent more time having adventures on the hills and along the wall. Did what I wanted as soon as I was of school age.'

I turned to him, surprised. 'You were allowed to go off on your own?'

'Yeah. Mum liked me being out of the way and we had no TV. It gave her peace for her writing.'

'Did you have friends round?' I thought back to my own childhood when I'd play with my friends amongst the dunes and on the beach.

'Not so often. Mum didn't like other kids around making noise.'

The sun burst between the clouds again, casting diamonds of light through the trees.

With each step I felt the long grass brush against my legs. 'You could be in the middle of nowhere here.'

'We almost are,' Hadrian replied.

The sound of the wind rushed past, wafting the branches and leaves, and it seemed as if nature's orchestra played her tune for us.

'It's paradisiacal.'

'I didn't appreciate it as a child. But you're about to see the real surprise.' He raised his arm and pointed. 'Behind that rock.'

I looked through the trees. A rock, at least as tall and broad as a house, came into view. That in itself took me by surprise.

'That's pretty cool. Do you climb it?'

'Yep, this side is too sheer but round the back there are plenty of footholds and it slopes gradually.'

'This place reminds me of the book, *The Secret Garden*. This garden is…' I searched for the words. 'Breathtaking, captivating, labyrinthine!'

I tried to imagine what might be beyond. 'It can't be Hadrian's wall round the back?'

'That's way up on the ridge.'

'A Roman fort - a fish pond?'

'No but there is a stream that borders our land.'

And then I felt my skin prickle and my heart began to beat faster as we walked beneath the shadow of the rock which towered over us.

Chapter 12

Hadrian continued speaking, but his voice grew distant. 'I wasn't supposed to climb it, but I did. Fell a few times...'

My limbs grew heavy and I felt disoriented as we continued on past the rock, and emerged into a clearing dappled with sunlight. My step faltered as I gazed upon a summerhouse surrounded by trees and nestled amongst wildflowers and shrubs. So here was the properly named Blue House.

Its walls were made of bricks laid at angles to form alternating diamonds, with supporting wooden beams painted teal blue - the same shade as the front door to the main house. The slate tiled roof rose sharply to a central joint topped with a cockerel weathervane. Wooden steps led up to timber decking and a porch where vines climbed the pillars and trailed across the roof and handrails.

I stopped and tried to frame my vision in the light that played upon the windows and dazzled my eyes.

When I blinked the white light remained imprinted on my retina - fading as I turned to Hadrian. 'So, here is the real Blue House.'

His eyes smiled. 'Yep, until people see it, and you're privileged to be able to, first time visitors always expect the main house to be blue.'

As had I. But, now that I was here it confirmed what I already knew, somehow. But how? My prior knowledge must have been through seeing it in a publicity feature.

Hadrian continued talking. 'Mum often writes down here. It's the silence. There's electricity and water, so it's a mini home, but more of a study. As a child I discovered where Mum kept the key so I'd come down and sneak in, or occasionally she'd bring me with her.'

I gazed upon the summerhouse - enchanting in this wooded glade. The blue paint had peeled in places, and moss, tufts of grass and weeds sprouted between the roof tiles. Its shabbiness and neglected appearance, only enhanced its appeal and mystery.

'It captures the best of the sun, and from the back the views up the hillside...' Hadrian continued.

I stepped closer to the summerhouse and his words faded into a hum. My skin buzzed with pins and needles and my mind wrestled between stopping and retreating. The breeze hushed, but still the crows chattered amongst the tree canopies, and again I sensed I had prior knowledge of this place - the pathway down, the wildflowers and lawn that led us to the rock, but most of all this strange garden idyll - the blue house.

I sucked in a breath to push aside the hesitation in my steps and the heavy weight of foreboding that came from within.

Hadrian noticed my reluctance. 'Come on. It's pretty inside,' he said beside me.

'Are you sure?' I muttered and I forced myself to follow him up the steps. My legs felt unsteady and I gripped the bannister with damp palms as each thunderous heartbeat rolled into one. Fear spiralled inside of me, my vision sprinkled with white spots and I felt on the brink of passing out.

Hadrian bent over and lifted a plant pot. He placed it back down and lifted another pot. Then he stood up and reached onto the wooden rim above the door.

'That's annoying,' he said.

'What?' I said, sounding breathless.

'The key. It's usually under the pots or on the ledge.'

'It's locked?'

'You've no idea how protective Mum is of this place. But I thought you'd like to see it.'

'Then we shouldn't go in,' I said, and relief already flooded through me as I stepped back down the steps. 'I don't want to intrude where I'm not welcome.'

Hadrian walked along the decking lifting more flowerpots. 'She's always changing her hiding place.'

He cupped his hands against the glass and peered through. 'Come closer.'

As I stepped up to the glass I saw my reflection, and my eyes stared back at me - a startled appearance that mirrored my trepidation. I refocused on the interior and gazed straight through to the windows at the back and the garden beyond.

Hadrian continued talking, but his words washed over me, as the windowpane shimmered before me. I spotted a movement beyond the summerhouse. A figure with a face in shadow and I couldn't tell if I was seeing my own reflection or that of another woman. I peered closer. No, there was a girl, with long hair and wide, fearful eyes. I couldn't tear my gaze away until her lips parted and her mouth opened wide in a terrifying, soundless scream.

A cold hand gripped my shoulder and I stumbled forwards and cried out.

'You okay?' Hadrian said.

I turned around. 'Oh God, I forgot where I was.'

He looked into my eyes. 'Could be the marijuana in your blood, still. Your eyes look bloodshot.' He reached forwards and brushed a curl from my forehead.

I stepped back, surprised at his physical closeness. 'Last time I'm eating hash.'

'Wise. I'm not anti-recreational substances, entirely. That would be hypocritical, but safer if you know where the supply came from, and the potency. I imagine whoever made those space cakes sprinkled way too much.'

'I ate two, so it was my fault. I never do drugs.'

'Course not,' he said with smiling eyes.

'No, I don't.' I insisted. 'I'm anti-drugs.'

'Look, forget it. We can't go in anyway.'

With a slowing pulse and much relief, I walked back along the deck to the steps.

'Come on, I'll sort that car insurance,' Hadrian said, and we set off walking beneath the shadow of the rock and up the pathway through the trees.

Chapter 13

The Family Home - Bamburgh

Back in Bamburgh the following day, I looked down at my suitcase spread across my bed, and wondered what else to pack. The weather had warmed up but was still unpredictable, plus I might want to walk along the wall so I'd need some jeans and T-shirts.

How long would Maxine take to read my manuscript - two or three days at least, if she read it all?

There came a knock on my bedroom door.

'Come in,' I called.

Mum walked in and peered down at my suitcase.

'How was work?' I asked.

She flopped onto the end of my bed and sighed. 'Crazy. They're wanting us to reduce time with each patient so we can squeeze in more appointments.'

'Surely you have some say in that?'

'I do, but my persuasive powers don't result in better funding for the hospital or more staff to cover the waiting lists.'

'You could retire, you know?'

She sighed again. 'I know. But I feel too fit and young and wouldn't know what to do with myself all day.'

'At least you've got a job you enjoy with a decent salary,' I said with an edge of regret.

'You'll find another job,' she said.

'I'll probably continue with law. A different town, maybe.'

'Did you mention to Maxine that she knew your dad?'

'Christ, no! If they fell out I doubt she'd be keen to read my manuscript, least of all lend me her car and a room.'

'What will you do with yourself?'

'I mentioned her housekeeper has left?'

Mum grinned. 'You mean you'll do her washing, cleaning and cooking?'

'Hey! I can be domesticated.' I folded a sweatshirt and dropped it in the suitcase.

'Course you can,' she said, with a lift of her brows.

'The only reason my flat was untidy was because I worked seventy plus hours a week as well as writing my book. It's not exactly difficult to turn on a washing machine and load a dishwasher.'

'I know it isn't. But you're not the housekeeper sort.'

'Maybe I won't want to be a lawyer again, so I need to rethink my options. This is an incredible opportunity to improve my book and my writing.'

'So, what's Maxine like as a person? You've not said a great deal.'

'I'm not sure yet. Seems friendly and honest. Not as easy to talk to as her son, Hadrian. But I'll find out more soon. She's generous enough to read the book of a rookie writer and trust me with her car.'

'Ahh, so her son's called Hadrian. An apt name for a boy born near the wall. I wonder if there are lots of Hadrian's over that way.'

'Maybe I'll find out. The name suits him anyway.'

'Is he handsome?'

I nodded and sighed. 'Ridiculously. Sure to have a girlfriend and get tons of women chasing him, too.' I pictured myself running down the hill to catch up with him.

'How old is he?'

'Early thirties, I think. Oh, and Maxine has a twin sister with a son, too.'

'She's a sculptor, I believe, and a successful one. Has Maxine mentioned her husband, or has Hadrian?'

'Yes, early in her talk. A mysterious death, and she believes he was murdered and the culprit is unpunished.'

Mum nodded slowly. 'Mmm, I recall his death in the news.'

'I wonder if he really was murdered. Anyway, it'll be interesting staying with her. I shan't pry though.'

'No, best not and it is all in the past.'

'If she wants to talk about him I'll be supportive, obviously.' I paused. 'From a selfish perspective having her name linked to critiquing my crime novel could win me some interest from a publisher.'

'Absolutely.'

'She might hate it and tell me so.'

'She won't. If it's anywhere near as well written as your short stories and poems, I'm sure she'll be impressed.'

'I love you, Mum. You're always so encouraging and sometimes that's exactly what I need.' I hugged and kissed her on the cheek.

I loaded my suitcase into the back of Maxine's Audi.

'You could always ask me to read your book? I'll give you honest feedback.'

I turned to Mum. 'Aww, thanks. But I'd really like you to read the finished thing, should it ever get that far.'

'Fine, but if you do need another pair of eyes.'

'I'll bear it in mind.' We hugged one another. 'Thank you.'

Mum waved me off and I set off on my hour and a half journey from Bamburgh to Hexham. I'd printed off my manuscript and brought a fresh notebook in case Maxine made some suggestions I could work on.

I had genuine reasons for not asking Mum to read my manuscript, not least because through the fictional characters I'd explored some painful memories from my childhood, and particularly my relationship with Dad and his physical and emotional abuse. I'd also seen the way he'd spoken to and bullied Mum and David. Mum would recognise a lot of what I'd written was personal to me and to our family.

Even though Dad was completely out of my life, and never likely to return, in some respects he still had a hold over me and had left me with issues I'd never fully resolved and probably never would. My journals had given me another outlet for exploring the trauma and emotional fallout, but I hadn't been tempted to write a memoir. Exposing myself so openly in public would be abhorrent to me. Fiction was my realm, or at least I hoped it might be.

I drove out of Bamburgh beneath low, black clouds, and when I joined the A1 a fleeting but torrential cloudburst gave way to blue skies studded with white wisps that drifted towards the

North Sea. I ramped up the volume on the radio and when a Stone Roses track started I sang along and tapped the steering wheel.

I reflected on my relationship with John, and as I felt myself emerge from the shock of our break up, I realised I'd been in a rut both with him and my professional life. Deep down I think I'd known all along he wasn't right for me, although I hadn't wanted to admit it to myself. John had obviously known this too and hadn't bothered to talk to me first. Anyway, I'd never forgive a man for cheating on me, and so despite the hurt and sadness that I hadn't been enough for him, I made it clear there would never be any going back. All the cruel and hurtful things he'd said that night, too, which had upset me even more than catching him kissing Emma. I hoped Emma would see John for what he was and dump him before he treated her the same way.

And of course, I was the one to lose my job. Why was it always women who ended up having to leave a job because of a relationship that went wrong? Probably because men held the most senior positions. That was changing, but nowhere near fast enough.

Acutely aware I was driving my literary heroine's car, I drove steadier than I would normally. I didn't overtake the slower cars and stayed in the slow lane. On the outskirts of Newcastle I pulled into a garage to use the loo and buy a coffee. I placed the cup on the dashboard and when I checked my phone I saw I had a missed call and a text. The call was from an unknown number, but when I read the text I knew who the call had been from - Marcus.

"Hi Jodie, great to meet you on Saturday. You're likely back in Bamburgh, but I wondered if you'd like to meet up sometime? Maybe we could go for a walk along the beach or visit Bamburgh castle. Marcus."

I read it again. What a nicely worded message. But, I mused, he'd been in the pub with one woman, and not at all shy in asking for my number, and then texting two days later. Was he confident or keen?

I wasn't sure if or how to reply and so I put my phone back in my pocket and set off. As I drove and wondered whether I would or wouldn't like to meet up with him, I realised I'd have to reply anyway. Once I'd decided that I felt my phone burning a hole in my pocket. It was only early afternoon so no rush to get to Maxine's, and when I saw a lay-by ahead I pulled in.

I was glad of my new Blackberry which made texting a lot easier.

"Hi Marcus, I'm staying at Maxine's for a few days whilst she reads my manuscript. Driving back to Hexham now. Maybe we could go for a walk from there? Jodie."

I could subtly sound Marcus out about other relationships he might be in, and either way, it would be nice to see more of the area, and as an educator he'd know plenty about the history.

I was an expert at justifying my motives.

I doubted Maxine would be interested in walking for leisure, but I could be wrong.

It was just past three when I pulled into Maxine's drive. I lugged my suitcase to the front door and as I reached for the bell, the latch clicked and the door swung open.

Maxine peered over my shoulder. 'Car still in one piece? No scrapes, I trust?'

I smiled. 'I was super careful. And I filled her up, too.'

'Good girl.' She stepped aside. 'Have you printed your manuscript?'

'Yes,' I replied and hauled my suitcase into the entrance hall.

'I've set aside my own work so I can read a few chapters of yours. You won't mind if I scribble notes and ideas?'

'No, scribble away. I'll be grateful for any thoughts.'

'Splendid. Your bedroom is ready.'

Wow, I thought, no chit chat and straight down to business.

From the hallway I followed Maxine up a gorgeous, wide wooden staircase that turned twice before we stepped onto the first landing. It was dimly lit with windows at both ends of the long corridor. The ceilings were high and the walls decorated in Laura Ashley wallpaper, blue with small white flowers beneath a white corniced ceiling. A second flight of stairs led to the upper floor.

Maxine turned left along the corridor, stopped at a door and turned to me.

'You're in the guestroom, although I can't recall the last time I had a guest stay over.' She paused. 'I don't generally encourage visitors.'

'I feel privileged.'

She nodded and her lips twitched as though she might say more.

I was usually good at reading faces, but Maxine was proving trickier than most.

'I hope I won't get in your way,' I added.

Her brows drew together. 'I'm making an exception because I know how much I'd have valued some expert advice early on.'

When she turned the door handle and opened it wide, sunlight spilled from the bedroom window into the corridor.

'The back of the house gets all the sun. My bedroom's at the back too, at the other end of the corridor.'

I set my suitcase at the foot of the iron-framed double bed and looked around. The room was large but the air smelled musty and it had a neglected feel. The floral curtains and the walls papered with a green trellis pattern had faded over the years, but I judged them to be of good taste and quality. There was a visible layer of dust on the dressing table which had a vintage ewer and basin on top, and I spotted several dead flies across the windowsill and on the carpet below. I'd sweep those up.

'The bathroom is along the corridor, and next to it is the airing cupboard where you'll find fresh bedding.'

Maxine stood at the window. She glanced down at the windowsill and swept the flies onto the floor with her hand. She exhaled and straightened up. 'Your room has the best view of the garden and the hillside. You can see Hadrian's wall and if your eyesight is sharp you'll even spot walkers along the path.'

I went and stood beside her avoiding stepping on the flies. I slipped my glasses onto my nose and my eyes followed the sloping lawn with the trees and the pathway down to the rock and the summerhouse beyond. Only a few roof tiles and the weathervane were visible through the trees.

Crows circled the treetops, some swooping from one tree to another, and the sounds of their squawks and caws travelled.

'You have a lot of crows,' I commented, as I watched them disappear into the treetops.

'Disturbing my peace all year round, but especially now the eggs are hatching. Constant feeding and activity, as you'll see and hear.'

'We have gulls in Bamburgh, but I barely notice them now.'

'Oh, well I'm afraid crows are quite different. Vermin, really, but short of chopping the trees down they won't be going anywhere.'

'The trees are beautiful and add privacy down at your summerhouse, too.'

Maxine huffed and I sensed her disapproval. 'I saw Hadrian showing you down there.'

I stepped away from the window and sat down on the bed. 'Must be a quiet place to work,' I said. 'Will you read my manuscript there?'

'Maybe, but I tend to read in the orangery.'

'We didn't go into the summerhouse,' I said.

'I keep it locked. My private space, although Hadrian has always been curious to go in. Not sure why.'

'Perhaps he's curious by nature.'

'That is true. It's a pity this quality didn't boost his learning at school.' Her brows furrowed and she looked down at me for some moments. 'Hadrian was born in this room. In this bed actually.'

'Oh, wow! So you had a home birth?'

'Yes, intentionally. Winston was opposed, but once I decide on something, there's no changing my mind. It's my body, after all.'

She moved closer and I began to feel unsettled under her gaze. I shuffled back on the mattress.

'Mum's a hospital worker and she gave birth to me at home, too. She had an easy birth with my big brother.'

But Maxine continued without acknowledging my words. 'Took me a while to conceive and I had no intention of being drugged up to the eyeballs which could put my baby at risk. I wanted to experience a natural birth, and that was what I got.'

'It went smoothly, then?' This was the first time Maxine had been so open and forthcoming and given that she'd written about childbirth a few times in her novels, I was intrigued to hear if her experiences echoed anything I'd read.'

'My dear, girl. You may or may not give birth one day, but let me tell you, there is nothing smooth or normal about a woman birthing a child. Birthing is an otherworldly experience.'

'And you took no pain relief?'

'Nothing. I wanted to remember the experience. I wanted to feel my child make his entry into this world and that included the pain and the moments of relief in between.'

'Was it a long labour?'

'Two days, and for the majority I laboured alone.'

'Where was your husband or midwife?'

'I couldn't get hold of Winston who was working away, and I only wanted the midwife when I knew I was close.'

'You're brave. I'd want to be in a hospital surrounded by doctors and nurses who know exactly what they're doing.'

'Well, I never have been one to follow expected norms which for a writer I'd suggest is essential.' She tutted as if she'd already assessed my low risk approach to life, and possibly my ability as a writer.

'I suppose boldness and taking a few risks are important when creating original stories.'

'Essential if you don't want to churn out the same mind appeasing bilge one so often finds in stories. Some novels are more effective than swallowing a sedative. A writer should have a rebellious streak or they might as well not bother lifting a pen,' she said through narrowed eyes.

I hoped she wouldn't find my story mind appeasing bilge. If she did I'd have to scrap the whole manuscript.

She placed her palm over her belly. 'Men will never understand the excruciating agony and transformation a woman goes through when she gives birth.'

'They're lucky,' I said, without hesitation.

'No, Jodie. They're extremely unlucky. I may have only experienced it once, but I recall every moment in profound and vivid detail. I lay on this bed, alone, with only the low moan of the wind and the crows to mask my cries. When each contraction came, I embraced the pain, knowing that each stab through my belly and each banshee howl brought my baby closer to being in my arms. If you can try to imagine lying on your back with three knives thrusting and twisting through your abdomen whilst a vice ensnares your belly and back, and with each breath and contraction the pain penetrates and burrows deeper - consuming your whole being, then you may begin to comprehend the power that we have when we bring new life into this world.

Close your eyes and take a breath, Jodie. Imagine it for yourself. My boy, your own child who has been a part of you, growing and feeding from inside of you for nine long months, doesn't want to leave the safety, warmth and sustenance of your blood and womb. But he has no choice - his time has finally arrived to make his entry into your real world.'

As instructed, I closed my eyes and after taking some long breaths I felt the muscles in my stomach twinge into a strange and uncomfortable spasm. Something akin to a period pain, but more intense. A pressure began to press down on me and with my eyes still closed, I placed both hands upon my abdomen. The tiniest limb slipped and moved beneath my fingers, and as I slid my hand upwards, I felt the length of a spine. I exhaled then sucked in my breath as a stronger wave of pain and pressure rose up inside of me. Instinctively I lay back against the pillow.

I heard a voice, distant. 'Do you understand how it feels?'

'Yes, yes, I do,' I replied, and my voice juddered.

Maxine continued in the full throes of a storyteller. She could have been reading from one of her books, but her words were new to me. 'The pain brings about new life, and a transition from a foetus to a living and breathing child, allowing them to begin their journey to becoming a separate and independent human. We are the privileged gender and by embracing and immersing ourselves in that life giving pain, we allow our child's life to commence normally, without drugs and intervention or interference from the outset. That is how every child should begin their life, and when the time comes, that is how we should meet our death. Pain is a natural part of who and what we are, and to deny this is to live without depth of experience.'

Pressure inside my abdomen built again and as the pain and spasm intensified a flood of nausea made my mouth fill with saliva and sweat seeped from my pores. I sat bolt upright, pressed a hand to my mouth and leapt off the bed, then I lurched towards the door, opened it wide and raced down the corridor.

After frantically trying three doors I located the bathroom, and leaned over the toilet seat just in time. I knelt there for what seemed an age with saliva and bile spooling from my mouth until my eyes streamed and my throat burned.

Still sweating and breathing hard, I yanked some loo roll and wiped my chin and mouth before spitting again. I sat back on my knees for some moments as my face cooled and my breaths and pulse slowed.

At the mirror over the sink my ghostly complexion and watery eyes looked back at me. I splashed my face with water and rinsed my mouth before returning to the bedroom, keen to apologise to Maxine for my dramatic exit. What had made me vomit so violently? But Maxine was no longer in my bedroom.

I studied myself in the full-length mirror and saw in my reflection the same woman I'd seen at home in Bamburgh before I left - loose hair, minimal make-up and dressed in denim jeans and red T-shirt, but in my eyes I noticed something else - a difference I hadn't perceived before. The Jodie staring back at me appeared changed. Her eyes looked blacker and sharper, narrower than the almond shaped, kind eyes I knew so well. My reflection had a curious gaze - a questioning gaze that suggested a vulnerability, but at the same time an eagerness to explore her new environment and the people within.

I turned away from my reflection.

Where was Maxine? If our positions were switched I'd have been concerned and gone after her to check she was all right. Perhaps my sudden reaction had disturbed her. And yet she'd been the one describing her birthing experience, in lurid and graphic detail. I hadn't expected it, clearly, and my mind and body had reacted in a way that had taken me by surprise.

I walked from my bedroom and down the corridor to the stairs. Maxine was coming up and carrying two glasses.

'My dear girl,' she said as she stepped onto the landing. 'Are you okay?'

I nodded. 'I've no idea what made me so ill.'

'Ahh, you see, that's the trouble with my storytelling. I forget how deeply affecting real life stories can be when I describe them.' She handed me a glass. 'It is I who should apologise.'

I held up the glass - a shot of brandy - and when I took a sip and swallowed, its pungent heat slid over the back of my tongue and down my throat.

'It's odd, because I can read and hear about the worst crimes, watch horror movies and hospital surgeries, so I don't know what came over me.'

'I think I do,' she said, and nodded.

'You do?'

'You're an empath, Jodie. If I may be open, I saw this when I met you at the Queen's Hall. And because of all the female energy I experienced in that bedroom, and as you listened so intently, you began to feel what I had felt. I was sick as a dog throughout my labour.'

'But I felt physical pain. That is surely more than empathy.'

'Did you indeed?'

I nodded and took another sip of brandy, unsure whether alcohol was a good idea after vomiting.

'Yes, intense pain, and pressure whilst it lasted.'

'Perhaps you'd prefer to sleep in another bedroom?'

'Please don't go to any trouble. I'll be fine now.'

She nodded. 'If you say so, dear. Now, why don't you give me your manuscript and I'll begin reading while you settle yourself in.'

'Wonderful! I'll fetch it.' And still holding my glass, I hurried down the corridor to my room and grabbed the manuscript from my suitcase.

I handed over the file. 'I feel quite nervous.'

'The brandy will help, and like I promised, I'll be honest, and constructive.'

'Do you read a lot of books?' I asked, realising I hadn't yet seen any filled bookcases or stacks of books lying around.

'I have one or two shelves. But I prefer newspapers and quality magazine articles. I read the occasional novel when it appeals.' She tapped the top of the file. 'As does yours.'

'I always thought writers loved to read novels and it helped to improve their craft and language.'

'Of course I read all the time when I was younger, but when one gets to my level of literary success one can read as much or as little as one likes.'

112

'Don't you miss getting hooked and lost in a story? I love that feeling of escapism and total immersion.'

'My dear, that is why I write my own books,' she said. 'They are the stories I want to lose myself in.'

'I'd love to know what your latest book is about,' I said. 'Without giving away any spoilers, of course.'

She looked up and her hooded eyes met mine. 'But if I told you, I'd have to kill you.' And then she chortled.

There was something in her eyes that made me feel vulnerable and exposed, and I gave a nervous giggle. 'Like we're living in a crime novel.'

'Exactly. We live, we make mistakes, we pay for them and we learn from them.' Her brows drew slowly together. 'And then we write about them.'

'I need to do a lot more living then,' I said, and laughed again. 'Thanks for the brandy. It's soothing and not something my mother ever recommended.'

'I'm a firm believer in its medicinal benefits. Far too many are taking prescribed medications when a shot of brandy works far more effectively and without the toxic ingredients and nasty side effects.'

I nodded. 'I hadn't thought of it that way.' I decided against mentioning the medication I'd taken on and off for anxiety during my teens and twenties. 'I'll sort out my stuff then I'll make us a cuppa, if you'd like one?'

I was gasping for one.

'Excellent. And I shall be in the orangery - reading a novel!' And with my manuscript clutched beneath one arm, and her glass of brandy in the other, she turned and headed back down the stairs.

Chapter 14

Hidden Story

When I opened my eyes it took me some moments to register where I was. My eyes were bleary and my body felt heavy with sleep as I pulled myself upright against the pillows. I looked around the dimly lit room - at the tall chest of drawers, mirrored wardrobe door and the framed paintings and photographs with their shadowy faces and figures.

I saw through the window that daylight had already descended into a muted charcoal-blue sky.

How long had I been asleep?

I recalled talking to Maxine on the landing, sipping brandy and returning to my room to unpack. When I glanced at my watch it was too dark to see the hands so I got up and switched on the bedroom light. My suitcase lay open on the floor still full of clothes. One of the chest drawers had been pulled open and the wardrobe door too, with empty coathangers on the rail. Either that shot of brandy had gone to my head, or the sickness I'd experienced prior to that had left me in need of a rest. It was seven o'clock, so I'd slept for two hours, at least.

I placed my spongebag on the vanity chest in the bathroom, then ran the tap and splashed my face with cold water before gulping down a few mouthfuls. My tongue felt thick and there was an acidic taste on the roof of my mouth so I grabbed my toothbrush and paste and brushed them well.

When I looked into the mirror over the sink I looked washed out and my eyelids drooped from sleep. I pinched my cheeks to revive some colour and washed and dried my hands before heading downstairs.

The entrance hall and corridors were in near darkness other than the traces of light cast by the windows. In darkness the house appeared altered and I felt disoriented as I made my way to the living room to where Chopin's melancholy nocturnes played. A soft light glowed from the orangery, and as I approached the doorway I saw Maxine sitting with knees wide and leaning over, intently immersed in what she was reading.

She glanced up as I walked in. My manuscript lay open on her lap and I immediately noticed by the thickness of the pages on the left that she must have read a few chapters. With a pen in hand she peered at me over the rim of her glasses.

'I'm afraid I fell asleep.'

'No harm in that. Brandy is a fine relaxant.'

I was keen to ask what she thought of my story, but no, I'd wait for her to volunteer her thoughts.

'Did you mention you'd make tea?' she asked.

'If you've not eaten, perhaps you'd like some dinner too?'

'I don't eat late in the evenings, but help yourself to something,' she said and cast her eyes back down to my manuscript.

'Thanks, I might. Black tea?'

She looked up again briefly. 'Yes, my preferred cup is on the draining board.'

As I went to the kitchen I turned on the lights. Maxine might not mind the dark, but a large unlit house in the middle of nowhere with numerous rooms and corridors felt creepy at night.

There were three cups on the draining board so I turned them over and tried to work out which one might be Maxine's preferred cup. Sure to be the china tea cup with a pretty floral design. The inside was thick with stains and I picked up the scourer and scrubbed until it gleamed white again. Dad had been anally fastidious and clean, and had expected us to be too, and although I was more relaxed these days, I always spotted dust and dirt, even though I didn't jump to clean it. Maxine, it seemed, was typically creatively messy, although rather too extreme for my liking.

Maxine took her tea, thanked me then set it aside on the coffee table. I'd obviously selected the correct cup. She didn't offer any writing feedback so I left her alone and returned to the kitchen. When I opened the fridge door a fly buzzed lazily past my ear. An uncovered chicken carcass sat on a plate on the bottom shelf and I detected a cloying, unpleasant odour.

I reached for the plate and lifted it to my nose. When I sniffed the rancid chicken my stomach heaved. 'Gross!' I said aloud. I held the plate at arm's length and carried it to the bin. Maxine really did need a housekeeper. Still, my time and help was a small price to pay for a once in a lifetime mentoring opportunity.

I found a tin of minestrone soup in the cupboard, a fresh brown sliced loaf and a tub of butter in the fridge. The moment I sat down to eat at the kitchen table and lifted my spoon, a telephone pierced the silence. I rose and went into the corridor where an old fashioned, black phone fixed to the wall rang loudly.

I lifted the receiver. 'Hello, Maxine Croyett's residence.' I realised how ridiculously formal I sounded. When no one answered I said, 'This is Jodie, can I help?'

I detected voices in the background, but no one replied.

'Hello,' I said again, and waited. But there was only silence from the other end, until just audible over the silence, a soft breath. I replaced the receiver and looked at it. I picked it up again and dialled 1471 to see if I could hear the number that had called.

'You were called at eight twenty-four p.m. The caller withheld their number,' came the automated reply.

I replaced the receiver and goosebumps pricked my skin. Back in the kitchen, the window rattled in its frame and I heard gusts of wind that blew through the trees and skirled around the outside of the house. My soup was lukewarm and too salty, but I spooned it up and dipped my buttered bread until I'd emptied the bowl, then I loaded the pan and crockery into the dishwasher.

When I passed the living room and adjoining orangery the haunting piano music played on and I assumed Maxine was still reading. Not wishing to interrupt her flow I headed upstairs to unpack.

Amazing how much more human I felt with a little food inside me.

I hung my clothes in the wardrobe and folded a few T-shirts and underwear into the chest of drawers then went to close the curtains. The night was black against the bedroom light but in my peripheral vision I detected a bright light blinking below. I pressed my forehead to the glass, cupped my hands around my eyes and peered into the dark. A wild animal - a fox or a badger maybe. And then there came a long and pained screech and my back went rigid. I reached for the curtains and pulled them together. The strange sounds unnerved me and my heart thudded, but I knew from hearing the same from my bedroom in Bamburgh, that it had to be a fox on the prowl. It could probably smell that stinking chicken carcass.

Mum had asked me to ring her once I got settled and I reached for my mobile on the bedside table.

Marcus had replied to my message. "Hi Jodie, that is generous of Maxine. Great! How about a walk tomorrow? I'm working until three at Housesteads fort. If you like, we can walk from the fort, or I can drive over to Maxine's?"

I doubted Maxine would have finished reading my book by tomorrow, and I texted back.

"Hi Marcus, I'll drive to Housesteads. Been years since I walked there. See you tomorrow." Maxine had said I could use her car during my stay and hopefully she wouldn't be needing it.

When Mum answered I reassured her all was well and I described the glorious garden and the views of the hillside and wall. But I didn't mention my sickness episode or Maxine going into ghastly detail about her labour. That would only unsettle Mum, and I sensed she already felt uncomfortable about my staying here.

I headed back downstairs to see Maxine but the orangery was in darkness. The kitchen light was off too, and when I popped my head into the other downstairs rooms they were similarly unlit and with no sign of her. It was only 9 p.m. and I didn't feel sleepy, although I could go up and read. I went back to the kitchen, made a cup of tea and plucked an apple from the fruit bowl, gave it a rinse and headed back to my room. I crept along the landing and saw Maxine's bedroom door was ajar and a shaft of lamplight cast onto the floorboards.

I detected voices and paused to listen. The radio? No, it was Maxine speaking. Perhaps she was on the phone to whoever had rung earlier, but had remained silent to me. I hadn't heard the phone ring again, but she might have a landline in her room or be talking on her mobile.

Curious, I stepped closer to the doorway. But I couldn't decipher any words and it seemed she either whispered down the phone or was possibly talking to herself. And that was when the apple slipped from my hand and with a thud it hit the floorboards and rolled past her bedroom door.

For a moment there was silence as Maxine stopped talking.

'Only me, Maxine,' I called out and reached for the apple. 'I dropped an apple.'

Her bedroom door opened wide and I saw by the straight line of her mouth and her frown that she wasn't happy to have been disturbed.

'I'm going to sleep, dear.'

'Sorry to have disturbed you,' I said. 'I was coming to say goodnight.'

'If you want to stay up I don't have a TV but there's a radio in the living room and a stereo in the orangery. But please keep the volume down!'

'Of course, and thanks. Would it be okay if I borrowed your car tomorrow afternoon? I thought I'd drive over to Housesteads for a walk.'

'That's fine. A scenic spot.'

'Yes, I love it up there from what I remember.'

'You might see Hadrian. He's rebuilding a section of the wall.'

'Yes, he said. And Marcus works there too.'

She nodded and her brow creased again. 'I believe so.'

I smiled. 'Well, see you in the morning.'

'Sleep well, dear.' She turned and pushed the door closed, leaving the corridor and me in darkness.

Maxine still hadn't mentioned anything about my book, I mused as I returned to my bedroom. I couldn't help thinking that if she had been me, I'd have at least said where I'd got to chapter wise. But she wasn't me. I was getting the impression she either didn't like my story or regretted asking me to stay over.

Maybe she was annoyed because she suspected I'd been eavesdropping on her talking, which of course, I had.

I found the airing cupboard and made up my bed before washing and changing into my nighty. I read a couple of pages of my latest read - Birdsong, but realised the words were barely going in. My mind was all over the place, hopping from one encounter to the next - Hadrian, Marcus, Maxine, the speeding cyclists, Philip the journalist, even Mum with her curious well-meaning questions, and all the resulting conversations and exchanges that whirled through my head. I felt wound up and on edge. No doubt staying in an unfamiliar house and bed, down the corridor from my writer hero, with my beloved manuscript under her sharp scrutiny, only compounded my agitation.

I was neither tired nor relaxed enough to sleep and I sat up, finished my lukewarm tea, and walked onto the landing.

The floorboards felt cold beneath my feet and when I tiptoed down the corridor to Maxine's room I saw no slither of light escape beneath her door.

I thought about going down and listening to the radio, but instead I switched on the light and crept up the staircase to the upper floor. The top landing was smaller and the corridors left and right, narrower. With each step the floorboards creaked, and I stood still for a moment. I tiptoed stealthily, aware how sneaky I must appear. Why did every floorboard in this damn house conspire to reveal my every step and movement?

The panelled door opposite the top of the stairs was shut and when I reached for the handle it turned and the door clicked open. I stepped inside and pressed the light switch which didn't work. But as my eyes adjusted to the darkness I could see the room was bare other than a few picture frames piled against the wall beneath the window. I closed the door softly and crept down to the next room, with the door similarly closed. Again it opened and I saw this room was also bare, save for an unmade bed against one wall and what looked like a full-length mirror hanging on the far wall beside the window.

I came out and found a light that lit up the end of the corridor. Maxine obviously had no use for these rooms - maybe never did. It was an enormous house for one woman who used to have a husband, and their only son who had flown the family home.

Each attic room had an abandoned and neglected feel. There didn't appear to be a bathroom or even a toilet, which would put most people off today from using them as bedrooms. The views must be stunning though, especially the back with her own personal atrium and rocky outcrop, and the hillside that rose to the historic Roman wall.

I tried the only door I hadn't opened, which I estimated to be directly above Maxine's bedroom. The door creaked slowly open like in a horror movie and I grimaced and held my breath. I slipped through the half-open doorway. Must tread carefully. As with the other rooms I tried the light switch and this time a bulb in the middle of the ceiling filled the room with light.

This room was furnished with a blue Chaise Longue on a threadbare Persian rug, a tartan chequered armchair with matching footstool and an antique writing bureau set directly in front of the window to take advantage of the view. It had to be Maxine's alternative writing space - successful authors could have as many as they wanted. There were shelves with a dozen or so books, but which were mostly filled with dusty old files and folders. I crossed the room to the writing bureau and trailed my fingers along the wood. It was elegant and French in style, made of mahogany with small drawers and shelves, and delicately inlaid with fleur-de-lys. The desktop was messy and piled high with loose papers, but with a red leather inlay at the centre, and a newish computer and keyboard. I pulled the handles on some of the drawers, but they were all locked. I searched the top of the bureau - shuffled under the papers and peered inside the china stationery pot, but found no keys.

I was perfectly aware I shouldn't be up here prying into Maxine's papers and drawers, but I was curious to see what she might be writing. She was reading mine, after all. Admittedly, me reading her unpublished work wasn't entirely the same. No doubt her latest creation was saved on this computer.

I leafed through the loose papers which looked to be mostly bills and utility paperwork. Not terribly organised, but a lot of it looked dated. I went to the bookshelf and reached for a loaded lever arch file. When I pulled it out I'd expected the papers to be punched and filed, but they slipped from the file and onto the floor.

'Shit!' I muttered as the papers drifted and scattered across the floorboards, and I stepped away only to stand on something sharp. I yelped and clapped a hand to my mouth.

I held my breath and didn't dare move - listening out for any movement on the floor below. Unless Maxine was a deep sleeper I must have woken her. I lifted my foot and saw a drawing pin sticking out of my heel. I pulled it out and placed it on the floor beneath the shelf, then crouched down and began gathering up the fallen pages. It was a typewritten manuscript with each page numbered.

A door closed somewhere below and I quickly gathered up the remaining pages, then clutched the file and hurried to turn off the light. I slipped through the doorway and closed the door behind me.

Had I closed my own bedroom door? Would Maxine see the light on the stairway up here - she'd be sure to unless she thought I'd left it on purposefully when I'd come to bed? Chances were my yelp had startled her, and now I had to think of a plausible reason for being up here with her folder in my hands - and fast.

Or I could leave the folder in one of the other rooms and sort the pages into order and replace it on the shelf in the morning. Yes!

I pushed open the door to the room beyond the study, tucked the file behind an old board propped against the wall, then swiftly and silently closed the door behind me and walked calmly down the stairs to the landing. I caught sight of Maxine's back as she went into the bathroom and the door clicked shut behind her.

I flicked off the stairs light and dashed on tiptoes down the corridor to my bedroom. I dived into bed and pulled the duvet up to my chin, trying to slow my breathing and the sound of my heart thundering in my ears. The toilet flushed, the bathroom door opened and moments later there came the unmistakable creak of a floorboard outside my bedroom. Through slitted eyes I watched as my bedroom door opened a crack and the outline of Maxine's head and shoulders appeared through the gap. She remained still and watched me for some moments before withdrawing and closing the door with a click.

I let out a breath of relief. If she suspected I'd been snooping around in the attic rooms when she was asleep, she'd be rightly annoyed. But would she confront me about it? And if she did what would I say to appease her? Christ, the number of times my curiosity had got me into deep water. And did I ever learn?

No, I simply kept on repeating myself.

Chapter 15

When Lightning Strikes

I slept badly that first night, not helped by my overactive mind, and the wind that wandered around the house, sighing against my bedroom window. Before sunrise, the crows stirred and began their chatter and calls. At some point one of them landed on my window ledge and wouldn't cease cawing, until eventually, tired of its incessant noise, I threw back the duvet, padded across the room and swept the curtains aside. Unphased, it tilted its head and peered through the glass then opened its beak and cawed. How bold! I tapped on the glass expecting it to take flight, but its eyes seemed to widen and it pecked the glass.

'I've got nothing for you. Bugger off!'

But still it didn't move, and in defiance turned its head to the trees and continued cawing.

I released the catch and slid the sash window up. 'Get lost!' I hissed through gritted teeth.

I didn't anticipate what happened next.

The crow spread and flapped its wings then flew in through the gap in the window. Up close its wingspan was huge as it flapped in front of my face. I staggered back but the crow flew right at me. It squawked and screamed in my ears, its wings beating furiously, and I felt its claws and wings catch in my hair. I ducked down but my hair must have caught in its feet. The bird scratched and clawed at my head to try and free itself. Instinctively, I raised my hands and swiped and batted at the bird until I caught it full force, launching it across the room. It crashed into the wall with a thud and horrible squawk.

The crow fell to the floor and began frantically flapping one wing whilst the other wing hung twisted at an unnatural angle. The bird's head lolled awkwardly and as it writhed it opened its beak emitting pitiful cries.

What to do? I knew I should put it out of its misery, but I stood there, paralysed and unable to act decisively.

I took a deep breath and crouched down as the crow twitched and flapped its wings feebly and looked at me with terrified eyes. Its writhing and shuddering movements went on and on, and I watched helplessly. I clutched my head - desperate to act, but too hesitant and unsure. Warm liquid dripped down my cheek and I moved my fingers to touch. When I looked at my hand my fingers were smeared with blood.

I reached for the towel on the radiator. If only it would stop flapping I'd wrap it in the towel, and try to soothe its pain. Gradually the bird's movements slowed and I watched it rest its head on the floor as its wing and legs twitched and juddered. It was near to death, and there was nothing I could do to relieve its agony.

What made it fly in through the window when it could have flown away to its nest in the trees? What if she had eggs to keep warm or hatchlings that needed feeding, and now they were going to starve and perish too? I covered my mouth and stifled a sob.

When the crow's movements stopped altogether I knelt before it. Its eyes remained open with the lifeless stare only evident when a heartbeat has ceased and blood no longer flows. I leaned over and trailed my finger along the crow's black downy back and drops of my blood dripped onto the back of my hand. Gently, I scooped the bird into the towel, folded its wings against its sides and cradled it in my hands. The bird felt warm and heavy.

'I'm so, so sorry, little bird.'

I stared down at it and a shiver rippled through me. There was something unusual about its plumage which I hadn't spotted before. The crow had a white marking on its otherwise downy black head - the size and shape of a perfect fingerprint. I carried the bird to the open window, reached my arms through, and placed it carefully on the ledge.

In the morning I'd take it to the garden, dig a grave, and lay a stone cross and some flowers. It might not have been the friendliest crow, and the cuts on my head were evidence, but it had panicked when it flew in instead of flying away.

I drew down the sash, closed the curtains and headed to the bathroom.

With a warm flannel I pulled my hair aside and wiped away the streaks of blood. They were only scratches and nothing deep enough to need stitches, thankfully. My head had taken a beating since I'd arrived - first the cyclist and now the crow.

At least I'd survived to tell the tale, unlike the poor crow.

I climbed back into bed and pulled the duvet up to my chin, and as I lay there, wide awake with my heart still thumping, I wondered if Maxine had heard the commotion. Hopefully not. I didn't fancy explaining that I'd opened the window for a crow to fly into my room, then accidentally killed the poor creature.

What a nightmare!

When I closed my eyes, I realised I could no longer hear the crows, or any birdsong for that matter.

My pulse slowed and eventually my thoughts drifted from the crow on the window ledge to where in my story Maxine might have read to. But I shouldn't expect her to rush. She could take as long as she needed, and no doubt she'd be keen to get back to her own writing, too.

Exhausted by the upset and drama, I fell into a deep and troubled sleep where I dreamt that a ring of crows circled overhead, watching and waiting for me to fall asleep so they could fly down and peck and feed from my body to take revenge for what I'd done to a member of their rookery.

When I awoke, with that feeling of relief I'd only been dreaming, the wind had dropped and a beam of light shone between the gap in the curtains. I drew the curtains aside and sunlight nuzzled my bare skin. It took me several moments to register that the dead crow no longer lay on the window ledge. I lifted the sash right up, leaned out and peered down to the path below. But the bird hadn't fallen - the path was empty.

Could a larger bird have flown down and carried it away to feed on, or a fox sniffed it out? Those were the only explanations I could imagine. The bird wasn't stunned - it had died.

But as I dressed, I felt baffled. For certain I hadn't dreamt the whole episode, and I touched the scratches on my scalp, still raw and tender.

From my window it looked like summer had finally arrived and I dressed in a short skirt, vest and sandals. I'd brought some trainers with me - I'd need those today over at Housesteads Fort.

I went outside and checked the path beneath my window and the few shrubs nearby, but there was no evidence of any crow - not even a black feather.

At lunchtime I sat out on the patio alone and ate a cheese and tomato sandwich, after which I set off on the seven mile drive to Housesteads fort.

As I drove, I reflected on my conversation with Maxine that morning. She'd been in the kitchen when I went down, and she showed me where the cereals were kept and poured me a cup of tea from the freshly brewed pot.

'You slept well?' she'd asked.

'So so. I'm never great the first night in a new bed.'

She gave me a pointed glance as she poured my tea. 'I'm convinced I heard footsteps on the upper floor last night. Was that you creeping around trying not to wake me? I'm assuming a family of rats hasn't taken residence up there.'

There was no point in my denying I'd been up there, and at least she hadn't heard me fighting off a crow in the early hours.

'Yes. I hope you don't mind. I felt restless after my earlier nap and thought I'd take a wander up there.'

'I don't use the top floor. I used to write up there - you may have seen my old study?'

'I looked in, briefly.'

Her eyes narrowed with obvious disapproval, but she didn't comment further.

'Where do you usually write? Do you have a laptop?' I asked, changing the subject.

'Yes, and I find it so much easier to carry around. I mostly write in my summerhouse and light the stove when it's chilly.'

'Peace and quiet, and pretty views.'

'Exactly. Do you have a writing space at home?'

'I had my flat, where I lived alone, and now my old bedroom at home.'

'Brave to move home again,' Maxine said. 'Once I was free of Mother's clasp, I never looked back.'

'I'm lucky Mum's always been supportive, but relaxed.'

Maxine turned to face me. 'And your father?'

I hesitated to frame my words. 'He and Mum divorced a decade ago.'

'You still see him?'

'No. We didn't have the easiest relationship. And he's passed away now.' I lied, hoping to move on from the subject.

'Perhaps you and your mum are better off without him?'

'She tolerated his moods for too long.'

'Didn't he want to keep in touch with you?'

'Not especially. I rejected his efforts and never wanted to see him again.' My eyes stung and I swallowed. But I wasn't sure if I was emotional because I was lying about Dad, again, or how his memory made me feel.

She nodded. 'Painful memories will give your writing an edge. No experience, especially bad, is wasted when you're a writer.'

I nodded. 'I hope this edge comes through in my book, too?' I said, and awaited her response.

But she avoided my gaze and busied herself at the sink, making a big deal of rinsing a teaspoon, drying it with the tea towel and placing it on the wet draining board. 'I'm going to work in the summerhouse, so if you wouldn't mind clearing up the breakfast things?' She picked up her teacup and slice of toast.

'Of course. Is it still okay if I borrow your car to drive over to Housesteads Fort?'

'That's fine. Would you also put a clothes wash on and hang it out?'

'Anything to help.'

'And cook a meal for later?'

'Sure. Any menu preference?'

'Look in the freezer - plenty of meat in there. Vegetables in the fridge. I'm not fussy as long as my meat isn't cremated.'

'I'm sure I can manage that,' I replied. As someone who preferred meat to be well cooked, I'd have to take extra care.

I pulled into Housesteads visitor car park at the foot of the hill that led up to the wall. Maxine still hadn't commented on my book and my thoughts were preoccupied about her thoughts on it. I had to admit to feeling slightly annoyed as well as anxious.

Hopefully, her feedback would be well worth the wait and nervous anticipation.

I laced up my trainers and asked the elderly man serving in the cafe if he'd mind filling my water bottle.

'We do sell water.' He gave a disapproving frown but took my bottle.

'I'm short of cash. And I will be paying to enter the fort,' I added.

Unsmiling, he pushed the filled bottle briskly across the counter. After thanking him with a smile, I set off.

As I walked I remembered the stony path and view even though it had been years since I'd come here. The path dropped down into a dip to where a stream flowed beneath a bridge, before meandering up a steep incline to the magnificent ruins of the sprawling Roman fort and Hadrian's wall. I was breathing hard by the time I'd marched up to the visitor centre.

I glanced at my watch. Ten past three so Marcus should have finished work for the day. We'd arranged to meet at the entrance to the museum and visitor centre and I found an empty bench, sat down and looked around. The views were breathtaking and for some moments I imagined what it must have been like to be a Roman settler living up here two thousand years ago. How many soldiers and their wives had tramped up and down this hill and along the wall, or slept together and given birth to new generations at the fort?

Today, the sun felt warm on my face and there was only the lightest breeze despite the altitude, but the winter months must have been tough to endure. Of course, the Romans had been far more advanced than other civilisations with their inventions and modernisation of homes and buildings, with water supplies, toilets and sanitation, fireplaces and cooking, but even so, miles apart from the home comforts we took for granted today.

I stood up and walked to the corner of the terrace and back. Almost twenty past and still no sign of Marcus.

And then I recognised a familiar face walking down the slope, with his shirt sleeves rolled up and dark curls tumbling around his face.

'Hey, Jodie,' Hadrian said, scraping a hand through his hair.

I stood up. 'Hi.'

127

He shielded his eyes against the sunlight. 'How's it going with Mum?'

'Yeah, your mum's great and I'm so grateful to her.'

He nodded slowly with a sharp and curious expression. 'Long may that last.'

'What do you mean?'

'Oh, I'm only teasing.'

'Okay, but if there is anything I should know…'

He interrupted. 'I heard you arranged to meet my cousin here?'

'Marcus told you?'

Hadrian looked back up the slope and replied, 'He might have mentioned it.'

I suppose they did both work here and were cousins.

'Any idea where I might find him?'

Hadrian pointed to another stone building fifty yards down the hill outside of which a group of students stood chatting.

'That's where he works but he's had to dash to his mum's.' He cleared his throat. 'Some urgent matter.'

'Oh no! Hope everything's okay.'

'He asked me to pass on his apologies.'

'With any explanation?' A curious mixture of emotions came over me.

Hadrian sat on the bench and with a grimace said, 'Guess it must be a private matter.'

'So, I've made a wasted journey, and fuel, too.'

He gestured for me to sit down and I slipped onto the bench opposite him.

His eyes came back to me with fixed and searching attention. 'So, how's it really going with Mum?' And he spoke softly as if he didn't want our conversation to be overheard.

His close attention made me turn away for a few moments to the grassy slope that led up to the ridge.

'Really, it's fine. She's reading my book and spending time with it so what more could I ask?'

His gaze seemed unremitting. 'And what are her thoughts so far?'

'She's keeping them close to her chest.'

He nodded, unsurprised, and his tone was smooth and intimate. 'You're lucky though. Don't think Mum's ever read the efforts of any other fans - or many writers, for that matter.'

'I do feel lucky. And I'll be patient, despite not being the most patient person.'

'I'd have thought training to be a lawyer and communicating with criminals and fraudsters, you'd have to exert tremendous patience and restraint.'

'True. But I'm not dealing with a criminal, rather a crime writer, which is a different thing entirely.'

'Possibly quite similar. I shouldn't say this, but mother is a law unto herself. Love her madly, of course.'

'She seems quite reserved in some respects.'

'Aren't most writers, unless pushed to be otherwise?'

'I don't really fit that mould,' I said.

He cocked his head to one side as though to enquire. 'No, you don't seem your typical literary introvert. Hey, why don't I show you round a bit seeing as Marcus has stood you up? The section of wall I'm rebuilding is up there.' He pointed and paused. 'Unless you'd rather get back?'

'No, I'd like that, if you can spare the time.' I wasn't desperate to return to Maxine's to spend another evening most likely alone, and given that my novel was based on a crime that happened round here, it would be helpful setting research.

He beamed and clapped his palms together.

At least someone was pleased to show me around, I thought, and my disappointment faded as we headed up the incline beside the fort walls.

Three young women approached down the slope. One of the girls, petite and wearing the shortest shorts I think I'd ever seen, stopped in front of us. The other two girls whispered something to one another and continued on.

'Hadrian,' she said, but turned her eyes my way.

'Hey Melissa,' Hadrian replied with an enquiring lift of his brows.

She pulled her sunglasses onto her head and scraped her wavy auburn hair off her face. 'Are you going to introduce me to your friend?' She cocked her head to one side, like a bird.

'This is Jodie - she's a writer and lawyer. Staying with Mum.'

'Okay.' She stepped closer to Hadrian and spoke quietly but loud enough for me to hear. 'I thought we were doing something.'

'I'm sorry. Marcus has let Jodie down and she's only here a day or two.' Hadrian didn't try to moderate his tone.

Melissa bit her lip and gave a small, disappointed shrug. 'Sure. Maybe tomorrow?'

'Yeah, yeah. I'll catch you later,' Hadrian replied, with a dismissive tone.

She jutted her chin, then turned swiftly and headed off in the direction of her friends who were waiting and watching from the picnic benches.

'I feel bad,' I said. 'If you've got plans, I can walk up on my own. I'm not nervous about that.'

'I wouldn't dream of it, plus...' he said with a grimace. 'Melissa is behaving a little oddly.'

'Is she your girlfriend?'

'God, no, nothing like that. But we all went out for a drink last week and she latched onto me.'

'She only looks school age,' I said.

'A uni student, so she's mature enough.' He paused, and his eyes searched mine. 'But I really prefer women my own age.'

'You're not her teacher though?'

'No.' He stepped closer and lowered his voice, 'That never stops Marcus from dating his students here on field trips.'

'What? Is that even legal?'

'Like I said, Marcus has a different girl every week - well almost. The majority of those are students on residentials. All eighteen plus, I must add, so technically, it's legit and legal.'

'Possibly legal yes, but hardly appropriate for an educator, and if the authorities found out what he was up to...'

Hadrian interrupted. 'Well, I try not to be his judge, but I must admit I agree.'

'Does anyone at the training centre know about this?' I asked.

'I doubt it. Marcus keeps his private life away from work.'

I huffed. 'I'm not surprised.' I didn't hide the irritation in my voice and began to feel relieved that Marcus had stood me up. And given that he hadn't even bothered to ring or message me made me realise he wasn't the sort of man I'd want to meet up with.

On top of the ridge, and where a cliff fell away in front, we stopped and gazed out at the plateau and moorland below.

I gasped. 'I remember this view so vividly.'

'Once seen never forgotten,' said Hadrian. 'One of the reasons I love working up here.'

'But I imagine you work all over the place?'

'Of course, so these past couple of months have been perfect. Close to home and now the weather's hotting up, even better.'

'Heavy work though. You must feel exhausted each night?'

Hadrian ran his hand slowly over his forearm, already tanned and speckled with freckles.

'Sometimes, but I usually have energy for doing a few jobs at home or heading out with friends. I recently saw Chekhov's *The Three Sisters* at the Queen's Hall. Hexham might be a small town but there's a rich cultural scene for those who enjoy that sort of thing, as I do.'

'Fantastic. I'd love to have seen that.'

'If you're around for a few days there's a band playing on Friday. The lead guitarist is a mate.'

'Who are they?'

'Blameless, Indie rock, had a track in the top forty a while back.'

'Wow! I know them, and I love Indie rock.'

'I could get you in for free?'

'Yeah, if I'm still here, that would be fun.'

He nodded and smiled. 'Excellent! I look forward to it.'

We turned left along a track that followed the ridge of the cliff. Ferns grew in abundance amongst the mossy rocks beneath the trees - ancient, gnarled and wind bent. The air felt thick with heat, and bugs darted hither and thither in front of me. One landed on my top lip and I picked it off.

'Where did all these thunderbugs come from?' I said, swatting away another.

'It means a thunderstorm's coming,' Hadrian replied, in an ominous voice.

I glanced up at the sky. 'Is that even a thing - bugs before a storm?'

When I turned to him he shrugged and grinned.

I paused at a gap in the trees where an enormous rock jutted out over the cliff edge. Stepping closer, I pressed my hands against the cold stone and the trees hissed and juddered around me in a sudden gust of wind. I leaned over the precipice, and swept away the hair that fell over my eyes. With the wide expanse of sky above us, and moorland stretching endlessly below, there was a frightening and wild openness about it that made me gasp.

'Oh my God! Nature's ultimate creation. I should have brought my camera.'

Hadrian came and stood beside me. 'Please, be careful.' He reached his arm out in front of me just as another gust of wind rushed past.

But I was in no danger of falling and I turned and saw the alarm in his eyes and how his cheeks paled.

I stepped away from the rock. 'I'm not afraid of heights and I'm not daft enough to fall.'

He stood away and gave me more space. 'I'm sorry. I know you're sensible, but there are some who don't respect these heights and drops. I know youngsters who did exactly what you did.'

'Why? Have people fallen?'

He nodded and stepped back onto the path. 'Let me explain.'

When we set off walking, Hadrian didn't immediately speak and I got the strongest feeling he was about to reveal something that troubled him.

'This isn't easy to talk about, but it's why I have massive respect for this wall and the drops and heights which have taken too many walkers by surprise, and even those who know the paths and terrain well.'

He turned to face me, and a sadness came over his features. 'Mum talked about the death of my father at her talk.'

I nodded. 'She was brave. And because his death is a mystery your loss must be doubly painful.'

He nodded and a furrow formed between his brows. 'Dad's body was discovered at the foot of this rock face - that precise spot.'

I gasped. 'Oh God! I'm so sorry. And there I was leaning over and going on about how lovely the view is.'

'And it is a lovely view. But I can't help imagining Dad in that spot leaning over admiring the view before he fell... or was pushed. And I see it every time I come this way, without fail.'

'Can't be the easiest place for you to work then.'

'In some respects it isn't, but it's my living. I've avoided this stretch previously, but working here now has forced me to confront these demons head on. I usually walk straight past.'

'Do you or anyone else have any suspicions who pushed him - if someone did?' I asked.

'I do have a couple of suspects in mind. And each time I pass I picture one of them standing beside him, or behind him, and taking him by surprise.'

'Someone he knew?'

'Has to be. Most murders are.'

'People were arrested?' I already knew this but perhaps Hadrian had others in mind.

'Three people, all with alibis - apparently. Mum was questioned, and Aunt Evelyn, as of course any close relative was.'

'If you want to talk about it with someone completely neutral, I'm a sympathetic listener.'

'I sense that about you.' His eyes held mine. 'I don't know you well, yet, but you seem smart and kind. I suspect Mum knows this too.'

'Thank you. I hope I get to know her better.'

'She's not overly forthcoming, but if you're patient, she'll open up.'

'She already has in some respects,' I said, then decided it wouldn't be wise to mention how Maxine described giving birth to him in painful detail.

And after my dramatic reaction, not something I particularly wanted to go over again either. Perhaps her description was a warning for me to avoid childbirth in the future, I mused. Not that having children had been on my radar up to now.

We continued walking and neither of us mentioned his father's death again. If that had been my dad I wondered how disturbing it might feel to be here. The memories could be overwhelming, and I was concerned I'd upset Hadrian, even if he had been so young when it happened.

How strange a coincidence that I'd leaned out at the exact spot his dad fell to his death? I felt a sense of unease rise within me as we continued along the path.

'Why is the wall a different height in places?' I asked.

'There's only around ten percent of the wall remaining. Most of it crumbled away centuries ago.'

'How high was it originally?'

'Five metres in places, but it varied. Three metres wide. I'm restoring a section that's lower and narrower than the original, but it requires so many stones that restoring it all to the original dimensions is unfeasible.'

'Fascinating work.'

'It is. It's physical, outdoors and takes thought, precision and skill. How many jobs can you say that about?'

'And who wouldn't want to spend their days up here?' I said, and gazed over the wall at the expanse of open skies, wild moorland and distant hills.

We walked side by side along the path, which narrowed down a gentle incline.

'Sorry for getting all weird back there,' he said, without looking my way.

'Please don't. It's me who should apologise.'

Up ahead I saw a mound of stones piled in front of the wall, with a sign and cones diverting walkers around.

'This is me,' Hadrian said, and I heard the pride in his tone.

I looked in admiration at the neatness of the stonework with freshly laid stones fitted perfectly together like a thousand piece jigsaw puzzle. 'Beautiful work.' I trailed my hand along the stonework. 'How do you carry all the stones up here?'

'We use a lorry and then a smaller truck to bring them closer.'

A man's voice called from behind. 'How's it going, mate?'

We turned and an elderly man approached along the path we'd walked down moments ago.

'Hi Pete. This is Jodie, my new friend, and a talented writer and lawyer.'

Hadrian turned to me. 'Jodie, Pete works for English Heritage and I'm lucky to have him as my boss for the project.'

I thought Hadrian had such a warm and generous confidence. Entirely different to Maxine who I couldn't imagine giving any compliments or praise.

'Aye, good to meet you, Jodie.'

I shook his outstretched hand, thin fingered and weatherworn.

'Hadrian's been showing me his fine work.'

The man nodded. 'Aye, the lad's doing a grand job.' He turned to Hadrian. 'Could I have a brief word?'

'Course.' Hadrian turned to me and his brows flicked up. 'Won't be long.'

They wandered away and I watched them for a few moments as they talked closely.

My phone rang and I reached into my pocket. I was surprised there was any mobile reception up here. It was Marcus. I toyed with the thought of letting him go to answerphone, but I was curious.

'Jodie?'

'Hi Marcus.'

'Are you still at Housesteads?'

'Yes, it seemed a shame to leave after I'd driven over.'

'I am so sorry for messing you about.'

He sounded genuine enough, but he hadn't tried to ring or message me earlier.

'It's fine. Hadrian explained you had something to deal with so he's kindly showing me around.'

There was silence on the other end.

'Marcus?'

'Everything's fine with Mum,' he continued, finally. 'Seems there wasn't the urgency I was led to believe.'

'Oh, you must be relieved.'

'Of course, yes. A shame I couldn't be there. I can drive back now.'

'Please don't worry,' I said. I felt a drop of rain on my arm and looked up. The sky had darkened and rain clouds formed overhead.

'It's no trouble,' he said, insistent.

'Sorry, no,' I replied. 'I'll head back to Maxine's soon. I've offered to prepare dinner.'

'Maybe if you're still around tomorrow we could meet up?'

I felt several more drops of rain and looked back up towards Hadrian and his boss who appeared deep in conversation. 'Yes, maybe. I'll let you know if I'm still around.'

Marcus seemed keen, and persistent, at least in words. His actions revealed otherwise.

Rain spattered onto my hands and phone. 'I have to go. It's raining and I'm up the hill.'

'Sure, I'm really sorry again for the mix up,' he said.

We hung up. The only mix up was that he hadn't bothered to let me know. But I was glad that nothing serious had happened.

Hadrian jogged down the slope. 'It didn't forecast rain.'

I looked down at my bare arms and legs and laughed. 'At least you checked the forecast.'

The rain fell harder and I blinked the drops from my eyes.

'Come on. There's a spot to shelter at the bottom.'

We set off running down the path. Well, jogging as fast as the rocky terrain allowed.

I slipped but recovered, laughing, and jogged behind Hadrian.

We stopped at a stile at the bottom of the slope, and I clambered over, taking care not to display my knickers beneath my skirt on the way down the other side.

Rain droplets ran down my chest and I wiped away the wet hair that clung to my cheeks as the storm intensified.

We hurried down a sheep track that curved around the foot of the cliff we'd walked on top of only minutes ago. I ran behind Hadrian until we reached a small cave, just high enough for us to shelter beneath and miss the torrents of rain.

We stood breathless and looked out at the rain that poured in sheets only feet away.

'Jeez! Does this happen often when you're working?'

'Yeah,' he replied. 'But it won't last long. A cloudburst - they come and go.'

'It was so warm and sunny when I set off.'

Hadrian's head brushed the roof of the cave and he hunched his shoulders and looked down at me. I watched his eyes lower and linger on my chest.

'I hope you're not cold,' he said.

'I am a bit, actually,' I said, and rubbed my arms.

'Thought you might be.' He gave a cheeky smile and raised his gaze.

I knew he referred to my breasts beneath my camisole and vest.

'Next time I'll bring a cagoule.'

'Not quite as pretty, but a good idea when walking,' he said.

He turned to a rock behind us. 'Let's sit it out. There's room for two.'

A thunder clap sounded, making me jump, and lightning flashed and lit up the sky as rain pelted the ground. Rivulets of water dripped from the roof at the front of the cave.

I tucked my skirt beneath me and sat on the lichen covered rock, then shuffled along to make room for Hadrian.

Two sheep walked up to the entrance of the cave, and watched us watching them, before thinking better of trying to squeeze in and instead continued on past. 'Sorry, mates,' said Hadrian.

'I think we've stolen their shelter,' I said and laughed.

'First come first served,' he said, and laughed with me.

I sensed his nearness and when his leg touched mine I didn't move mine away.

'Jodie?'

I turned to him. 'Yes?'

'I wanted to say how bad I felt the other day, after the train, when I had to turn down your invite.'

'No worries,' I said. 'I felt silly for asking. I don't normally do that kind of thing.'

'I'm flattered. I only wish I'd insisted we meet up another time instead.'

'Well, we have, by chance, and again today.'

'I'm glad. And I'm glad that it rained too,' he said, as he lifted his hand and pushed a wet curl from my eyes.

'Hadrian?'

'Yes?' His black lashes flicked up and down

'Have we met before? You look familiar.'

He tilted his face and thought for a moment. 'I must look like someone you know. And if I'd seen you before I doubt I'd forget.'

I smiled. 'Then if you can't remember, and I can't remember, then I'm having another deja vu moment.'

He reached for my hand and I felt his fingers trail over my damp skin. 'I'm almost glad it rained - so we could shelter in here.'

When I looked into his eyes, the darkest brown, and his pupils intensely black, I saw my reflection looking back. I blinked and watched myself lean closer, until my reflection faded and my mouth met his lips - soft and cool. For a moment our lips remained slightly parted and still, until I felt his hand move to the back of my head bringing us closer. We kissed slowly and I felt the tip of his tongue against mine. As we did so I had the strongest sensation I'd been here in this cave before, with Hadrian, and yet stranger still, I couldn't remember how I got here. Confusion washed over me, holding me back from responding to his kisses.

Was it the rain that grew cold against my skin and seeped into my clothes and creases, or the thunderous clouds that sank lower over the land? A chill crept through me and I began to tremble. But Hadrian didn't appear to notice as his lips pressed mine with greater urgency and his hands curved around my waist and slipped beneath my vest and up my back.

Instinctively I jerked away, but he pulled me nearer.

I pushed him away and jumped up. 'I can't do this.'

He stood up and reached for my hand. 'What is it?'

I shook his hand away.

'It's only a kiss,' he said.

A feeling of nausea came over me, almost knocking me off balance. 'I'm going back.' I turned and hurried from the cave as thunder rumbled overhead and rain pelted my skin once more.

'Sorry,' I called, and raced back along the sheep path.

Hadrian shouted something, but I didn't stop running.

The rain fell harder and each drop pricked like a needle, cold and sharp against my skin and scalp. My shoulder bag and water bottle thumped against my hip as I clambered over the stile and jogged up the slope, and my breaths rasped whilst my lungs screamed for reprieve. But I kept on, even as I slipped and scrambled up the rocky slope. At the mound of stones I glanced behind me and saw Hadrian pacing up the slope only a hundred yards away.

He called out. 'Wait! Jodie!'

But I had no intention of waiting. I only wanted to get away from the feeling that I'd done something I shouldn't, and I'd regret. No, that I already regretted.

Up here the air felt cold and gusts of wind lashed my hair over my eyes and slammed into me, almost throwing me off the path. Rainfall streamed down the pathway and with every flash of lightning the water lit up - splintering like glass fragments beneath my feet. At the top of the incline where the ground evened out, I picked up my pace, sprinting once more. The trees all around me tossed and twirled in the wind, their branches reaching down, turning and lifting back up to the sky like they danced the flamenco. A fork of lightning split the sky and landed amongst trees near the edge of the cliff, whilst simultaneously a crack of thunder made me duck down as the air rumbled and shuddered all around me.

Beneath the trees the deluge eased and as I neared the rock that jutted over the ledge, a lightning bolt lit up the sky amidst an awful growling sound, booming and at half speed. When it came down and struck a tree twenty yards in front of me, I stopped and staggered backwards - every hair on my body stood on end and my skin prickled intensely. As the lightning bolt flared and crackled like a sheet of paper tearing slowly I was momentarily blinded. My vision readjusted and I watched the tree almost in silhouette, split apart. Half of the tree toppled and crashed onto the pathway - its branches reaching over the cliff edge. Heat rose and pressed against my skin and smoke billowed, but as quickly it receded and swirled phantom-like from the smouldering wood and bark. A pungent smell of burning and chlorine filled my nostrils and throat, and I stopped still - unable to move.

I'd been a fraction of a second away from that lightning bolt and the fallen tree, which, had I been running faster, would have wiped me out in an instant. Thunder rumbled on, guttural and unearthly. I recovered myself, turned and leapt over a ditch to a different path that ran parallel to the main path.

Without looking back I ran onwards until I reached the fort remains at the top of the hill. I bent over to catch my breath, resting my hands on my knees, before straightening up and raising my eyes to black clouds and drizzle. The rolls of thunder grew more distant as the storm passed over.

My clothes were soaked through and I shivered uncontrollably, but I didn't stop at the visitor centre to dry off. If Hadrian caught up with me, I wouldn't know what to say. How could I explain running away from a harmless kiss, that I was equally a party to as he was - possibly more so? My reaction had been visceral and extreme and I couldn't even explain it to myself.

I avoided the curious glances of other walkers, and I jogged across the car park, scrabbled for the car keys in my bag and unlocked the car. I didn't turn back to see if Hadrian had followed me down and I turned onto the main road.

A mile down the road, my thoughts whirled and raced and I pulled into a layby. What if Hadrian rang Maxine and told her what happened or he asked her to look out for me because I was behaving irrationally? I reached into my bag for a pack of tissues and dried myself as well as I could, including my mascara that had smeared around my eyes.

Thankfully I'd brought a hairbrush and I made myself look presentable again despite my wet clothes and tresses which could easily be explained. Maybe I'd be better volunteering to Maxine that I'd seen Hadrian?

When I arrived back at Maxine's, I wiped down the car seat and headed indoors. There was no immediate sign of Maxine or the sounds of Chopin's nocturnes I'd already grown accustomed to hearing in the shadows, so I jogged up the stairs and to my bedroom to change.

The moment I stepped through the bedroom door I knew someone had been in. I also knew that someone could only have been Maxine. I'd left the door closed and the window open a few inches, but the window was closed and the bedroom door had been ajar. Nothing immediately struck me as being out of place, not that I had much stuff. I wondered what she'd been looking for. She obviously hadn't crept in and left it the same, so clearly didn't care if I knew she'd been in.

I closed the door, stripped everything off, and hung my clothes over the chair by the window. Sunlight glowed through the open curtains and I lifted the sash window to allow the air to circulate.

Chapter 16

A Proposal

I blow-dried my hair, scrunched it into a bun and dressed in jeans, a blouse and some pumps. My toes felt cold still and I did some star jumps to warm up. Downstairs, I went into the orangery to see if Maxine was sitting quietly, but when I found it empty and with no sign of my manuscript, I headed down the hallway to the kitchen. Maxine wasn't in there either. I poked my head through the living and dining room doors which were similarly empty. As I passed through the hall again, the telephone on the wall rang. I waited a few moments to see if Maxine came to answer it and when she didn't I picked it up.

'Hello,' I said, and waited. 'Hello?' I repeated.

'Hello. Is that Jodie?' The woman had a friendly tone.

'Yes, I'm staying with Maxine for a day or two.'

'I'm Evelyn, Maxine's sister.'

'Oh, I met Marcus at Maxine's talk.'

'Marcus is right here. He mentioned he was supposed to meet you but was sent on a wild goose chase to mine.'

'A wild goose chase?'

'Indeed, but nothing to worry about.'

'Did you want to speak to Maxine?' I asked.

'Not particularly. It was you I hoped to talk to.'

'Oh, really?'

'Yes, I wondered if you'd like to come over for dinner tomorrow evening? Marcus will be here too.'

I was taken aback. 'That's kind, but I might not be here if Maxine's finished with my manuscript.'

'You can always cancel if you have to return home. I thought it would be nice to meet, and especially as Marcus was disappointed he missed your walk today.'

She sounded so warm and genuine, and that Marcus had been disappointed made me feel more forgiving towards him. 'Then that would be lovely, thank you.'

'Let me reassure you, I'm no interfering mother, but I love to cook and to meet new people, especially young people. I have many friends - mostly middle-aged, naturally, given my age.' She laughed. 'I'd be delighted if you'd come.'

She gave me her address and we arranged a time and hung up.

I reflected on our conversation. Evelyn couldn't have sounded more different to Maxine, not so much in voice but in her tone, open expression and more than anything, her warmth. She'd been honest in her reasons for inviting me, and truth be told, I felt quite alone in this big old house, with the lights always off and the windows closed. Maxine seemed very much the recluse - in her sixties and already an old lady who had turned inward and eccentric, and more essentially, barely present in any conversational sense during the time I'd been here. And even when she was visible, wasn't good company unless it suited her. Still, her magic was in her writing, and, I conceded, in her willingness to critique my amateurish attempts.

Maxine wasn't in her bedroom or the attic study so I assumed she must be working in the summerhouse. I hadn't yet reordered the file of papers I'd dropped last night so I headed to the attic room where I'd left it and carried it down to my bedroom. I hid the file in the bottom of my wardrobe to sort out when I came to bed, then I went downstairs and out through the kitchen into the garden.

The late afternoon sky was still bright and almost clear of clouds and it was hard to imagine the ferocity of the storm Hadrian and I had been caught in earlier. I inhaled and the scent of the lightning bolt still lingered in my nostrils. As a girl I once tried to photograph fork lightning from my bedroom window, and when the film came back all I got for my efforts were black skies and streetlamps. I'd never before experienced such a dramatic storm as today, and I knew I'd been lucky, not only to witness it, but not to have been struck myself or to have had the tree crash down on me. And for it to have happened at the exact spot that Hadrian's father had fallen to his death struck me as frighteningly coincidental.

I shuddered at the strangeness of my afternoon. It seemed a shame I couldn't talk to Maxine about the lightning tree. She might be interested, but it could also upset her. And I doubted I'd see Hadrian again - it would be far easier if I didn't have to explain myself to him, especially as I couldn't rationalise my reaction myself.

The summerhouse came into view through the trees and the sinking sun reflected on the windows, which meant I couldn't see if Maxine was sitting at her desk. But as I neared I heard the telltale piano nocturnes and the door was open. Approaching, I saw Maxine at her desk looking out my way. I raised my hand in a wave but she didn't smile or wave in reply and instead looked down again, presumably reading my manuscript. When I reached for the handrail and walked up the steps, I felt my heart begin to thud and pick up speed just as it had the previous day when I'd walked down with Hadrian.

Maxine must have sensed me standing there and when she glanced up she waved for me to enter. I hesitated - trying to summon an excuse for why I should retreat and return to the house. I felt a compulsion to turn around and run, but I forced myself to step forwards, and with my heart still pounding, I pulled the door wide and walked in.

I forced a smile, but my knees shook and I clenched my hands in an attempt to steady them. The interior space wasn't small, there were plenty of windows, and I was inches from an open doorway, so it couldn't be my old claustrophobia returning. Or could it?

'Come forwards, dear.' And with a probing expression she said, 'I don't bite.' She snapped her teeth together and followed with a chortle.

I laughed feebly and crossed to her desk, where the pages of my manuscript lay open. I saw she neared the end of the one hundred and eighty typed pages.

She gestured for me to take the chair opposite her desk.

The seat was low and I sat down, placed my hands in my lap, and felt as nervous as if I was attending a job interview. My knees trembled and I felt a chill sweep through the room.

'Are you shivering, dear?'

'I got caught up in that storm.'

'Storm? It's been lovely here.'

'No rain? Or thunder and lightning?'

She ran one finger slowly along the bevelled edge of her desk as though clearing away the dust. 'I vaguely recall some distant thunder.'

'It was biblical at Housesteads. Sheeting it down with the loudest claps of thunder I've heard.'

'How unpleasant. But I've been distracted.'

I turned and looked out of the window at the trees. Everything looked dry and untouched by rain. I hoped she meant she'd been distracted by my manuscript.

'Must have been an isolated storm. How odd,' I said.

'The weather here is patchy and changes in minutes.' She gestured dramatically with a sweep of her hand. 'One must be prepared.'

'I'll know for next time.' I cleared my throat. 'Dare I ask how you're finding my book?'

'Ahh!' She patted the pages in front of her and her brows knitted together. 'Firstly, I have a question.'

The hardness in her tone and her expression made my stomach lurch.

'Okay,' I said, but with hesitation.

'You said your story is based on true events?'

I nodded. 'Loosely, yes.' I lied.

'But the events didn't take place in the setting you chose - Yorkshire Moors?'

It was beginning to feel like a grilling - more of an interrogation, and I felt the tension between us building in waves. 'No, as I explained I set it elsewhere - dramatic licence, and my interpretation is explorational - fictional, given the conclusions drawn at the time.'

Maxine would find out for herself that it was a story about the evil some humans are capable of, the tragedy of a young woman's death without living the full life her family expected her to live, but most of all, the terror she experienced before she'd drowned. The sort of crimes Maxine wrote about too.

Her focus on me intensified. 'And will you credit that it's based on a true story?'

'I should, but with the caveat and emphasis that it's largely fictional.'

She nodded slowly. 'Mmm. The drowning of the young woman was an accident, I seem to recall.'

'That was the official verdict, yes,' I replied.

'But not the conclusion you come to in your story.'

I'd witnessed questioning in the courtroom where a prosecuting lawyer would ramp up the questions like a dynamo building in power and pace, ready to catch the guilty party's admission of guilt.

I nodded and held her eye. 'As a lawyer I'm primed to search for other possible scenarios, and when I read the articles, other lines of enquiry emerged. Of course, they are my interpretations to build suspense, and it is a crime novel, so I wanted my novel to be about a crime that wasn't easily solved.' I thought fast to voice a plausible explanation but without giving too much away.

She nodded, thoughtfully. 'That makes sense. And I can almost read it as believable,' she added.

'But not convincingly?'

Her voice was clear and her words harsh. 'No. In my honest assessment, not convincing.'

'Will readers be convinced?'

She clicked her tongue. 'Readers are far more astute and critical than us writers, my dear.'

'What would you suggest to improve it?'

'I recommend you think about an alternative ending - a more believable scenario.'

'But wouldn't that mean rewriting entire chapters? I'm not sure I want to do that.'

'And...' Maxine said, then paused.

'Yes?'

'Let me speak frankly. It could be better written. A lot of flimflam could be removed to make the language tighter. In short, you need a damn good editor.'

'But I have already cut it down to keep the language tight.' I felt my eyes watering. It was clear she hated it.

Maxine continued and her words grew more blunt. 'It's a rookie writer's mistake - try to include too many ideas and repeat details which assume the reader has little intelligence and a memory like a goldfish. This dilutes the central message and ultimately, the readability and impact of the story.'

I sighed. 'Then my boyfriend - ex-boyfriend was right.'

She rubbed her chin, slowly. 'I don't know about your ex, but all is not lost.'

'It isn't?'

'Indeed. If I might speak plainly, I have a proposal for you.'

'A proposal?'

She placed both hands on top of the manuscript. 'I need a housekeeper, and you my dear, need an editor. I propose that you take on one role whilst I take on the other?'

I gasped. 'You'd do that?'

'Yes. Because I like you. You're interesting, your writing has emotion and you're obviously smart.'

'But can I craft a novel?'

'You may have it in you. But you also need a job.'

'That is true. How long would it take for you to edit it?'

'I'd say two, maybe three weeks. Would you be prepared to take on this house and me?'

'Yes!' I said, decisively. 'I'd love the opportunity. Thank you!'

I felt elated. If Maxine edited it, an international best-selling novelist, I felt confident that with her skills and ability, my book would become publishable.

'And would you mind if I altered the ending?' she said.

My heart juddered. 'Really? Perhaps if you suggest how I should alter it first?'

She nodded. 'Leave it with me and I will decide on an exciting and convincing conclusion.'

'And discuss with me first?'

'Of course. I'll draft those parts once we've decided on the ending?'

'Maybe, if that's your preference.' But what I really wanted to say was, I would prefer to rewrite any parts myself.

I felt sick and anxious that someone else could decide how my story ended. This was my book - my baby. But I didn't want to say no outright and risk her rejecting the project. I should be grateful she felt it worthy of her time and talent. Plus, I still had the final pages I'd written that I could use if I chose to once I got it back from her.

'Thank you. I'm immensely grateful, and I know I'll learn so much from your guidance.'

She pursed her lips in an odd way. 'Now, if you'll leave me to work, could you prepare dinner? I haven't eaten a morsel all day.'

I got up and pushed my chair back. 'I'll see what's in the freezer and rustle up something tasty.'

'As you leave your book in my hands, I leave the menu to you. The raw ingredients are all there,' she said.

'Righto! Leave it with me.' And I turned and walked out of the summerhouse, relieved to be out of there so that I could reflect on our exchange.

Maxine said some contradictory things - for instance, saying she hadn't eaten anything all day, when I'd seen her eat three slices of toast for breakfast.

My pulse and thoughts raced and I wrung my damp palms together as I returned up the path. I turned around and looked back down the slope. How picturesque and inviting her summerhouse looked from a distance, nestled in the evening light. But the discomfort and apprehension it evoked in me belied any of its outward loveliness.

If it was my garden, I could never relax or work in there. In fact, if I owned the land, I'd have the summerhouse dismantled, burned, and in its place sow wildflowers and cherry trees.

Despite Maxine's surprise offer to edit my manuscript, the stress and anxiety were getting to me. Maxine's home felt weirdly familiar and yet I knew I hadn't been here before. It wasn't so much that I felt intimidated by Maxine, but I couldn't separate the brilliance of her writing and her books from her real self. Certainly not the warmest of women, and yet her offer was beyond anything I could have hoped of her. No, I needed to get a grip of myself, calm the hell down, and be grateful for this once in a lifetime opportunity to improve my novel.

Back in the kitchen I lifted the lid of the six foot long chest freezer and surveyed the contents. Cold air billowed out in an icy cloud. There were six baskets, each part-filled. Four contained plastic bags of meat and two held what looked to be frozen fruits and vegetables. I reached in and pulled out a couple of bags of meat. They weren't labelled and as I'd rarely cooked or eaten meat since childhood, I couldn't decipher what animal they might be from.

One bag was squashed up but I could see it was some type of mincemeat. I'd defrost it and make a bolognese - a simple dish. I placed the meat in a bowl in the microwave and located a tin of tomatoes, an onion, cloves of garlic and a packet of spaghetti. Hard to go wrong with a bolognese and I'd add plenty of veggies to make the meat more palatable.

We sat on opposite sides of the kitchen table and Maxine filled our wine glasses.

'Rioja - Italian, 1990,' she said. 'A fine vintage.'

I took a sip. 'Delicious. Cheers!' I raised my glass.

Maxine swilled the wine around her glass then gave a cursory toast and raised the glass to her lips. 'I might be no chef but I know my wines and I only drink the finest.'

'Where do you buy from?'

'A wine merchant in town.'

'My ex was a wine connoisseur. I'm not,' I said, and raised my glass again. 'But I can appreciate a decent vintage.'

'And this is a decent dinner to accompany it. Not just a pretty face,' said Maxine, twirling spaghetti round her fork.

'Mum worked shifts when I was young so I'd often cook dinner.'

'For your father, too?'

'Sometimes, if he was in.'

'A shame your mother and father were always out working.'

'Mum still works in healthcare and she loves it, plus she's helping others.'

'Splendid, and worthy.'

'Yes, she's wonderfully caring.'

'And you weren't tempted to follow her into that line of work?'

'No, I followed in my father's.'

'He was a lawyer?'

I hesitated - I didn't want to let too much slip. 'Yes.'

'I've had a few dealings with lawyers. Almost none of it favorable. To put it mildly,' she said.

I figured she referred to her fall out with Dad when he was her lawyer. 'Lawyers are a bit like teachers in that they tend to have strong opinions on most things. I'm probably no exception.'

She swirled the wine around her glass once more and nodded her agreement. 'Even when they are misinformed or know almost nothing about a subject. From what I've observed.'

'Apart from me,' I said with a laugh.

'I'm sure,' she said, and narrowed her eyes.

I raised a fork of spaghetti to my mouth. 'Not cooked a bolognese in ages. Is it minced pork?'

'No, I believe this is rabbit.'

'Oh!' I failed to mask my alarm. 'I've never eaten rabbit.' I thought about Bobbins, the sweet Dutch bunny I had as a child.

'I have a mincing machine in the larder. A most useful instrument for using up scraps and cuts of meat.'

'Mmm, I can imagine,' I said, and pushed the meat to the side of my plate. 'I've only ever eaten meat packaged and labelled from a shop.'

'I only buy from the butchers. Or freshly caught and skinned by farmers. Better for flavour and supporting the local economy.'

'True, though I'm not much of a meat eater.'

She peered at me closely over her bolognese. 'That'll explain the translucent tint to your complexion,'

'Mum is Spanish born, and Dad was dark.' Shit, I must stop mentioning my dad, I reminded myself.

'Yes, but you appear anaemic. A woman's curse if she isn't careful.'

'I eat plenty of pulses, greens and beans.'

Maxine huffed, clearly unconvinced. 'I'm blighted by fair and sensitive skin which is why I avoid the sun.'

'But you must enjoy your magical, sunny garden?'

'Yes, but I prefer the shade and my summerhouse - less glaring to my sensitive eyes.'

I looked at her tinted reading glasses propped on her head. They were a permanent fixture.

'I like wearing sunglasses and they protect our eyes,' I said.

'I'm a firm believer in protecting one's space and wellbeing. Coming into contact with too many people with germs and god knows what can threaten one's physical and mental health.'

She didn't seem to be overly fussy about germs, I mused. The state of her bathroom had made me want to clean it before I risked cleaning myself.

'I have to admit I love being with people and socialising,' I said. 'I get a bit bored with my own company after a while.'

'Whereas I quickly tire of other people's company.'

I repressed a grimace. 'Then I shall respect your privacy whilst I'm here.'

'Good. One favour returned by another. Now eat up.' She peered across at my still full plate.

Eating rabbit didn't sit well with me - in my head or stomach.

'Any suggestions for dinner tomorrow? A vegetarian dish perhaps?'

She sighed, and I sensed she'd already grown tired with my conversation. 'The freezer and fridge will inspire you.'

'Righto,' I said.

'But there is one food item you must avoid.'

'Yep?' She hadn't mentioned that earlier.

'It's in a blue bag.' She paused as though to give weight to her words. 'My placenta from Hadrian's birth. Well, what's left of it.'

I felt my dinner rise in my throat and I swallowed hard. I'd spotted that blue bag earlier, lifted it out and wondered what the reddish-brown granular substance had been.

'When I'm unwell I defrost a spoonful or two, cook it and I'm inevitably right as rain after a day or two.'

'But that must be over thirty years out of date!' My words came out too strong.

'Not at all. The freezer has never broken - only short-lived power cuts. My placenta is as fresh as when I gave birth to it. My continued good health is testament to that.'

My face grew hot as my stomach turned, and vomit threatened to make its presence all over my dinner plate.

I took some breaths. 'Have you ever served it to anyone else?'

'Yes, of course.' Again she paused. 'Hadrian benefited when unwell as a child. No one else though. I'm not wasting it on those I care nothing for.'

I felt like saying I doubted anyone would want to touch it with a pitchfork, but again I held back.

After Maxine had eaten and left, and as I cleared up the dinner things, I reflected on our conversation. I wondered if there was anyone other than herself or her son who she did care for. Possibly her twin sister Evelyn who I would meet tomorrow, and Marcus.

By contrast, in her books Maxine's characters often cared passionately about their family and friends. They may be crime novels, but they always involved a love affair portrayed in ways that convinced me Maxine had experienced for herself those powerful and intense feelings. Maxine must have loved her husband profoundly, and his death affected her deeply.

Curious, I lifted the freezer lid and peered inside. Visible in the fruit basket amidst the steaming ice lay the blue bag, and I reached inside, lifted it out and held it at arm's length. A shiver ran through me and I returned it to the same spot. I knew other people boiled up their placenta in the belief there were health benefits, but thirty plus years later, she was still eating it. Gross! And there could be nothing healthy or nutritious about it - more likely to cause a lethal dose of food poisoning.

Before leaving the kitchen, I took a strawberry yoghurt from the fridge and a pear from the fruit bowl.

Like yesterday, Maxine disappeared to do whatever it was she did in the evenings. Maybe she'd start editing my manuscript. The light was on in the orangery and the nocturnes echoed through the rooms.

Didn't she enjoy any other composers?

I popped my head in. 'If there's nothing else you need I'll head up to read - *Birdsong* by Sebastian Faulks. Have you read it?'

Maxine tapped her cigarette into the ashtray. She peered over her glasses. 'What?'

'*Birdsong?*'

She shook her head, confused. 'You mean early in the morning birdsong?'

'No, a novel by Sebastian Faulks. I wondered if you'd read it. It's beautiful - heartrending…,' my voice trailed away as she looked down again, uninterested.

With her pen poised in one hand and cigarette in the other, she replied, 'Goodnight, dear.'

Like a servant dismissed, I left her alone.

As I passed the telephone in the hallway, it rang out, shattering the silence.

'Jesus!' I said, and stumbled and fell into the opposite wall. I quickly straightened up, reached for the receiver and held it to my ear. There was a click followed by the dial tone.

My arms prickled with goosebumps and I replaced the receiver.

Back in my bedroom I felt chilled and grabbed a woolly jumper from the wardrobe. I lifted up Maxine's lever arch file that I'd dropped in the attic, then I closed my bedroom door, sat on the bed and placed the file on my lap.

I opened it up and turned all of the pages over so they were typeface up. Now to sort them into order which is how I assumed they'd been filed on the attic shelf. I couldn't have got them more mixed up if I'd thrown them out of the window to scatter in the wind, and I began the tedious task of sorting them into numerical order.

I finally located the first and title page, *THE LIE by Maxine Croyett*, typed in big and bold letters. The novel was obviously in draft form with Maxine's jagged scrawls in the margins and line edits. I noted it wasn't the same title as the upcoming book she'd mentioned at her talk. The yellowed edges of the paper made me think she'd worked on it a while ago. Although I wondered if it might have been published under a different title. All of Maxine's novel titles were short and punchy - the sort of easy to remember and uncomplicated title to catch a reader's attention on the shelves. I'd followed the same principle with my own.

My eyes settled on the opening paragraph and I began to read.

I immediately recognised it as an unpublished novel. The scene opened in a courtroom where a woman in the dock was being questioned by the prosecuting lawyer. The unnamed woman was angry and bitter in her responses but she answered the questions succinctly. On the outside the woman came across as eloquent and sharp minded, but her inner dialogue and thoughts revealed a different picture as she ricocheted between resentment at being questioned at all, to conflicting confusion as to how she should reply to each question. She fought against an impulse to object to certain questions, but she answered them - some evasively and measured. As I turned the page and continued to read I sensed a familiarity with the setting, not least because I'd been in court many times, but because the crime the character was being questioned about was for her lover's murder.

And when the prosecuting lawyer mentioned the character's profession, her young son and her sculptor's studio, it clicked in my mind precisely who Maxine had put in the dock - none other than her twin sister, Evelyn.

My God! Her writing had me gripped though. Where would the story lead? And would it reveal who had murdered Maxine's husband, Winston - fictionally or factually? Had Maxine been concealing evidence from the police all this time or was it speculation and storytelling on her part?

I had to read it all, but I couldn't afford for Maxine to suspect I held it in my posession.

Before I could read further I heard Maxine call my name - high-pitched and insistent, followed by hurried footsteps along the landing that grew louder with each step.

I leapt off the bed, clutched the pages and the file, quickly lifted the duvet and slipped them beneath, just before Maxine pushed open my bedroom door without bothering to knock.

I hauled the duvet back into place.

Her eyes had a wild look and there was fear in her tone. 'There's a man in the garden!'

'What? Do you know who?'

She wrung her hands together and her eyes darted to the window. 'I couldn't see his face. I was sitting in the orangery, and sensing movement in the garden, bolted up and looked out. He knew I'd spotted him and darted behind trees.'

I switched off my bedroom light, crossed to the window and peered out. Darkness had fallen and only the black outlines of the trees were visible. I gazed down to the patio, dimly lit by the light cast from the orangery. I stepped aside to hide from view, but continued watching for any sign or movement.

When I turned to Maxine she was perched on the edge of my bed and I noted her one hand resting precisely where I'd hidden the lever arch file beneath the duvet.

'Do you have a house alarm? Any security?' I asked.

'Yes, but I haven't used it for years. When Winston died I got two Alsatians and they went ballistic if anyone came to the home. Later on I had the alarm installed.'

'Do you know the code to set it? And we should alert the police.'

But she shook her head. 'I don't want the police anywhere near me or my house.'

'But he's still out there.'

I closed the curtains and turned on the bedside light.

The fingers of Maxine's right hand moved over the duvet and I saw her features register that there was something hard beneath. No doubt she thought it odd that I'd put a book or a file under the duvet and I hoped to god that she wouldn't ask, or worse, pull back the duvet.

My pulse raced and my forehead felt damp with perspiration. I puffed air through the side of my mouth, sending a draft up my face.

Hopefully the garden intruder held her thoughts.

'Has this happened before?' I asked.

She shook her head. 'Never!'

'Are you sure you didn't get a glimpse of his face? What about his height or body shape?'

I bombarded her with questions to distract her from the file hidden beneath the duvet.

'No! It's too dark.'

'What about that journalist at your talk? And there have been a couple of silent phone calls on your hall phone,' I continued. 'Is that something new?'

I switched the main light back on. The moment I did I spotted a single page from Maxine's manuscript file lying on the floor by the wardrobe - typeface up.

Fuck!

I looked at Maxine and she lifted her eyes from the paper to me, narrowing them slightly.

Christ, she'd seen it, but maybe assumed it was one of mine. I reached down, picked it up casually and placed it face down on top of my empty suitcase. There were a couple of handwritten words on the back and I folded up a vest that had fallen off the chair and placed it neatly on top. My cheeks simmered. Would Maxine think me capable of swiping one of her manuscript pages - or indeed the whole bloody file?

Time would tell, but I had no intention of admitting to taking anything unless her suspicion forced my confession.

Maxine's mouth twisted from one side to the other as her eyes continued to hold mine. 'It could be that journalist. But why would he be creeping around my garden at night?'

I turned to the window to break her gaze and made a show of peering through a slit in the curtains. 'What about your study in the summerhouse? Might there be anything of interest to him down there?'

'You think I'm stupid enough to keep anything of value down there?'

I swivelled around. 'Not at all. I only meant because you write down there.'

The colour in her face rose. 'My garden retreat is my sanctuary. To imagine it being violated or damaged by an intruder - that disgusting, fucking journalist. I keep my address private and for good reason.'

'Do you want me to go down and check if it's okay? If he realised you saw him, I'm sure he'd imagine you'd call the police.'

She inclined her head. 'You're not afraid to go down at night?'

'Not if I have a torch.' Of course I hadn't mentioned to Maxine I'd spoken with the journalist, Philip, from her talk, if it was him she'd seen.

Maxine nodded. 'I only want to know it's not been broken into. Check the door is locked and no broken windows or damage.'

'If you stand at the orangery window you can watch me.'

'I'll not see you or the torch beyond the trees and rock.'

'I'll shout if I need help. Stand at the open window.'

I gripped the torch in my hand and left Maxine watching me from the orangery. With my rational mind protesting, I set off down the garden path. The full moon, lilac rimmed and dusted, had risen in the night sky, and its luminosity shone through the tree canopies to guide my way along the path. With each step the grass felt cold and damp against my sandaled feet. The dew laden air clung to my skin and crept into the gaps and seams in my clothes, and in front of me my breath fogged and furled in the torchlight. My footsteps broke the silence and the wind whistled softly through the leaves and undergrowth carrying with it a scent of the mysterious and unknown. Even the crows had retreated to their nests - silent and sleeping.

When the outline of the summerhouse came into view, fear crept through me like a physical ache, and slunk through my innards, making them twist and protest. My inner child wanted to turn and flee back to the house, but I forced myself onwards, placing one foot in front of the other. As I neared I watched the branches beneath the moonlight wavering above the roof tiles breaking the stillness and making the summerhouse shift and shudder in the half-light.

With one foot on the bottom step I directed the torchlight at the door, then I beamed the light slowly to one end of the deck and back to the other end. With hesitation I climbed the steps, crossed the decking and placed my hand on the door handle. When the call of an owl pierced the silence I startled and spun around, but saw nothing other than grey shadows stealing a pinch of light from the house.

The hairs on my arms quivered, and I got an eerie sensation that I was being watched by someone lurking in the shadows. I took a determined breath and twisted the handle, expecting the resistance of a lock. But it turned and I pushed the door open.

Maxine had forgotten to lock her precious summerhouse. Standing on the threshold I shone the torch over the floorboards to her desk and chairs and then over to the dresser with its papers, ornaments, magazines and books, and across to the sagging sofa in the far corner. The earlier heat had given the room a stuffy feel and when I inhaled, the stench of damp and mould filled my airways.

Something unexpected, a movement, caught my eye through the far window - somebody was down there. Instinctually, I stumbled back a few steps, fearful I'd been seen.

My heart pummelled my ribcage and I clicked off the torch and trod softly past the desk to the far window. Hidden by the curtain I peered round into the muted greyness watching silently and still, and waiting for the figure to move and reveal their identity. The clouds parted and they stood clearer in the swollen moonlight - facing away and down to the stream at the bottom of the slope. But it wasn't a man, as Maxine thought, but the unmistakable curved hips and narrow shoulders of a woman. A chill snaked down my spine and I pressed my palms and forehead to the glass.

Who was she and what was she waiting for or looking at? My breaths condensed, clouding the glass and I wiped away the moisture with my fingers. When my view cleared I saw no sign of the woman, not a trace of a human shape or shadow, or any movement at all.

Footsteps sounded outside on the deck and as I spun around the door swung and clicked shut. I stumbled to the door and when I turned the handle it didn't move. Someone had locked me in. I twisted the handle and rattled the door. No one was out on the deck. I flicked the switch on the torch, but it didn't light up. I flicked it back and forth again. 'Shit!'

Sweat sprung from my every pore, and heat rose through my chest and neck. The torch slipped from my hand and with trembling fingers I felt along the window ledge to locate the catch, but there was no catch. There had to be one on the vertical frame and I moved my hand up until I could reach no further.

'Let me out!' I called. Panic rose within me as I banged the glass with my fists. 'Let me out you mad bitch!'

Who was she?

I had to get out. With arms outstretched I crossed to the dresser. I felt around and touched and gripped what felt like an antique iron - heavy, hard and cold in my hand. I stumbled back to the door, raised my arm and thrust the iron at the glass panel. It shattered, and fragments sprayed and clattered to the floor.

Using the iron I scuffed off the shards that clung to the edges of the frame, then I felt my way to the desk, grabbed the chair and dragged it over to the door. I had to get out and away from whoever had locked me in here, man or woman. I climbed onto the chair, gripped the door frame and stepped onto the ledge. I heard more glass fragments crunch and clink to the floor and I jumped onto the decking, stumbled and threw out my hands to break my fall. I scrambled up, leaped down the steps and fled back up the grass, between the trees. Whoever locked me in might be close behind, but I didn't pause to look around and I raced on until I saw the light from the orangery only yards ahead.

The orangery door was wide open but I saw no sign of Maxine.

I hurtled through and slammed the door behind me, then twisted the key in the lock.

Breathless and with panic in my voice I shouted, 'Maxine? There is someone outside.' I raced into the passageway and down to the entrance hall. 'Maxine?' I called again. 'Where are you?'

'I'm here.'

I spun around and Maxine walked calmly along the passageway I'd raced down only seconds ago.

'Is the summerhouse all right?' She sounded breathless, too.

I leaned over, panting hard to catch my breath. 'Yes.'

She stepped closer. 'Your hands are bloody.'

'Where did you go? You said you'd watch out for me.'

'I thought I heard the front door.'

'And was anyone there?'

'No - I looked from the window. Did you fall?'

I looked down at my hands and saw blood streaked across both palms and felt the sting of glass fragments caught in my skin.

'The door to the summerhouse wasn't locked so I checked inside.' My breaths heaved. 'I saw someone, a woman. She locked me in and I panicked and smashed the window to get out.'

Maxine looked startled. 'But I'm the only one with a key, and I was here.'

'You don't understand,' I insisted. 'I saw someone.'

'You panicked and tried to open it the wrong way,' she said.

'But I left the door wide open,' I said.

'That door swings shut. Only takes the slightest breeze.'

I shook my head. 'Someone locked me inside.'

Maxine gave an accusing glare. 'So, you've smashed the glass and left it unsecured, and there could still be a stalker, thief or murderer on my land.'

'I told you - it wasn't locked.'

Her eyelids flickered and she tilted her head to one side. 'Until someone locked you in?'

She didn't believe me. I was wasting my breath.

'Yes,' I said, insistent. 'I should clean my hands.' I paused, angry that she doubted my word. 'You must alert the police.' I turned away and headed for the stairs.

In the bathroom I placed my hands beneath the flow of cold water, then inspected to see if any fragments of glass remained. Without the blood the scratches looked superficial and I dabbed them dry on my flannel. Sore but nothing that a few plasters wouldn't fix.

Maxine thought I was imagining I'd been locked in. But she'd been the one to see the intruder and come running to me. I'd done her a favour by going out alone in the dark to check on her property. I'd been a fool to offer.

When I returned downstairs I found Maxine sitting at the kitchen table with a cup of tea in hand.

She hadn't made me one and I refilled the kettle.

When I turned around Maxine was watching me.

'Sorry I didn't make you one.'

'It's fine,' I said, staggered at her thoughtlessness. I could have done with something stronger but tea would do. 'You're probably in shock,' I added.

'I rang the police as you suggested. They're coming over,' she said.

'Good. They can take a proper look.'

Maxine sniffed. 'They won't find anything. The law round here are bigger bumblers than Inspector Clouseau.'

The kettle bubbled and clicked off and I poured steaming water into my cup. I turned to her. 'You've had dealings with the police?'

Her gaze drifted to the window. 'Not for years. Had no need to.'

'Maybe you need another dog. A guard dog.'

She looked at me straight. 'You've had experience with dogs?' Her tone was sarcastic.

'No, but they sound the alarm.'

'I might consider it,' she replied. 'A pet is another burden.'

The doorbell echoed through the hall, and she got up.

'I'll come too - just in case.'

'No stay here. Sure to be the police,' she instructed and left the kitchen.

Feeling physically drained and shaken, I leaned against the worktop and sipped my tea. Voices sounded from the hallway and Maxine returned, followed by two male officers, one elderly and the other looked in his early twenties.

'This is Jodie. She's here for a few days,' Maxine said, introducing me.

'I'm a lawyer, between jobs. Maxine's reading my manuscript so I'm helping her out with the housekeeping.' I didn't want Maxine speaking for me, which I suspected she'd be only too willing to.

The elder officer introduced himself. 'I'm Officer Lloyd and this is PC Donaldson. When did you arrive, Jodie?' he asked.

'Only Monday - yesterday.' I mused how it seemed an eternity ago.

Officer Lloyd walked around the table. 'I hear you had to break the door in the summerhouse?'

'Yes, someone locked me in.'

His brows lifted, surprised. 'You were locked in?'

'But,' Maxine spoke up. 'I have the only key and I was up here.'

'And where is the key now?' he asked.

'I never reveal the whereabouts of my key, but it's safe,' Maxine assured.

'You could check where you think it is,' I said. 'Keys can go missing, are stolen or copied.'

Officer Lloyd spoke. 'Firstly, if you can both stay here, we'll head down and check things out.'

'Maxine saw a man, an intruder outside. You've told them, Maxine?' I asked her.

'An intruder?' Officer Lloyd turned to Maxine.

'Yes,' she replied. 'Which is why I called you.'

'But you reported a break in?'

'Not exactly,' Maxine corrected them. 'I spotted an intruder outside and then found out about the broken window.'

'Please,' I said. 'Let me come down too and I'll explain what happened as we go.'

'No, Jodie,' Maxine interrupted. 'Stay with me.' She sounded fearful, suddenly.

'Okay,' I agreed. 'But when the officers return, I'll explain what I saw and what happened.'

It seemed Maxine and I were approaching this from different angles and I was beginning to sense I was the one under suspicion - not the mysterious intruder Maxine had reportedly seen.

Armed with torches, the officers headed through the back door from the kitchen. I glanced at my watch - ten to eleven.

'I told them there was an intruder.' Maxine turned to me, with an accusing glare. 'Our police are damned useless.'

'At least they came promptly.'

'Only because I'm well known. If you were alone calling in distress, they'd tell you to calm down and come to the station in the morning to make your statement.'

I didn't contradict her. Her cynicism could be related to previous dealings and didn't reflect my experiences with the police in my professional role. Granted, some officers were less diligent than others, but I'd always found the police helpful in prosecution cases.

I stood at the back door, looked out into the darkness and saw torchlights moving amongst the trees down the slope. There was a cold and eerie stillness that made me step back in and close the door. I was mad to go down alone in the dark.

I turned to Maxine. 'Your sister rang earlier, Evelyn. She invited me over tomorrow evening.'

Her brow furrowed. 'What on earth for? Do you know Evelyn?'

I pulled out a chair at the table. 'I've met Marcus, obviously, and he mentioned I was staying here. That's all.'

'Evelyn and I are virtually estranged,' said Maxine.

'Oh, I didn't realise. You don't mind me going?'

Maxine twitched her shoulders. 'You're a free agent so do as you please. I'd only ask that should my sister start prying about me, which I have no doubt she will, and highly likely to be the reason she asked you over, that you keep my affairs strictly private. Could you do that?'

'I wouldn't dream of talking about you. And I don't know you well enough to do so either.'

She huffed and her eyes narrowed. 'It is when people don't know someone well, that they get things wrong - fabricate stories. So yes, keep myself, Hadrian, my work and my home out of the conversation.' She sniffed. 'And why Evelyn thinks she has the right to invite a perfect stranger beggars belief.'

All I wanted to do was to explain what I needed to to the police, ensure all the doors and windows were locked, then head up to my room. Maxine's manuscript that I'd stashed away awaited, but I wasn't even sure I had the energy to read.

Maxine's eyes flitted from me to the back door. 'Where on earth have they got to?'

'Maybe they've found something or they're being thorough.' I swallowed the remainder of my lukewarm tea.

Voices approached outside and the door swung open and the officers stepped back into the kitchen.

I watched their expressions, but they gave nothing away.

'Would you like some tea?' I asked.

PC Donaldson nodded. 'Thank you.'

He had an altogether friendlier demeanour than Officer Lloyd.

'You'll be reassured to hear we saw no one down there,' said PC Donaldson.

'I'm not surprised,' I said. 'They'll have seen your blue lights as you arrived.'

A frown formed across Officer Lloyd's brow. 'You said you were locked in the summerhouse which is why you broke the glass to get out?'

'If it hadn't been locked I'd have opened the door,' I replied.

He nodded. 'The door was and still is unlocked.'

'But I couldn't open it!' I protested.

'And you panicked?' PC Donaldson asked.

'Yes, I was terrified.'

'Then the door must have been stuck. It is a damp night,' he said.

I stood up. 'That isn't what happened. I saw a woman further down from the summerhouse. It was she who locked me in.'

The three of them looked at me, each with dubious expressions, implying I'd imagined her or lied about what happened.

'Could the woman you *thought* you saw have been your own reflection in the window?' asked Officer Lloyd with a probing expression.

'Not at all,' I said, insistent. 'She was full height with wide hips and standing on the grass.'

'And yet, it was a man that I saw from the orangery.' Again Maxine pronounced orangery with her exaggerated French accent. 'And I was right here the whole time you were checking the summerhouse.' Her tone was dry. 'Unmistakably a male intruder.' She repeated, turning to Officer Lloyd.

'If you'll give us the key, we'll lock the door, but you'll need to contact our response security services to fix the window panel,' the young officer directed at Maxine.

'Thank you. And we'll take care of the window,' replied Maxine with an uncharacteristically compliant smile, and she promptly headed out of the kitchen to retrieve the key from wherever she'd hidden it.

As soon as Maxine was out of earshot I said. 'Did Maxine phone and report her summerhouse had been broken into?'

'That is what we were led to believe,' replied Officer Lloyd.

'Thank you,' I replied. 'I hope you now realise that wasn't actually what occurred.'

They looked at one another.

'Indeed it would appear so,' Officer Lloyd replied.

I let out a breath. 'Maybe I overreacted, in the dark alone, and obviously I'll clear up tomorrow and pay to have the glass replaced.'

'That would be wise. There didn't appear to be other damage, a few papers on the floor, but no structural damage, and more essentially, no intruders,' said PC Donaldson.

Chapter 17

A Strange Scent

I awoke late the next morning, feeling cool beneath the duvet, but refreshed. I'd intended to read more of Maxine's manuscript but fell asleep within moments of getting into bed and slept deeply.

After the officers had secured the summerhouse and left, Maxine and I had gone round and checked all the doors and windows, and before heading up to bed, she'd set the house alarm. I felt reassured we were safe and the house was secure, but remained confused about the evening's events. Had I imagined seeing that woman, and why couldn't I open the door when the police assured me it had been unlocked? Either I'd panicked, or there really had been an intruder - and not only an intruder, but a malicious weirdo.

I drew back the curtains to daylight and with a sigh, gazed upon the garden. The view from here was breathtaking - the rich variety of plants and trees and the rock beyond, and further still, a copse of trees and the hillside that rose up like a tidal wave to Hadrian's wall along the ridge. I lifted the sash window and a breeze blew in making the curtains billow. I raised my face to the sky and inhaled the sweet summer air. How I wished I lived somewhere like this - a gorgeous manor house with its own orangery, acres of land with a stream and rocks. I'd renovate and decorate the house, make it light, pretty and homely, and write all day long, then when I wanted a break, I'd walk my dog, maybe two dogs, up the hillside to the wall and enjoy the vistas and glorious landscapes.

The views alone would fire my imagination to create endless stories.

I wondered if Maxine realised how lucky she was. Of course, she'd worked incredibly hard to get here and there was no doubting the immensity of her talent, but I couldn't help thinking she wasn't making the most of her fortunes, her reputation or her situation living here in the heart of stunning countryside and an ancient historical wonder. She seemed more of the disgruntled recluse jaded by people and life, and not outwardly kind or warm.

But I was determined to make the most of the opportunity, even if there were going to be issues to get my head around. I opened the wardrobe door, and closed my suitcase with Maxine's manuscript hidden beneath. Then I picked out my denim shorts, a blue cropped vest and sandals. After I'd showered and blow-dried my hair I headed downstairs.

Again, I wandered into the various rooms to locate Maxine, and eventually, after following the fumes of cigarette smoke, I found her in the living room, ensconced on the sofa with a newspaper. I noticed an opened bottle of sherry on the coffee table and a glass with a dreg or two left in it.

She'd opened the velvet drapes and windows. Scents of summer, grasses and new leaves drifted in, helping to waft away the smoke that plumed from her cigarette, and the colourful walls and fabrics transformed in the natural daylight. I noticed for the first time the delicate leaf patterns on the wallpaper with exotic butterflies and birds. They might be faded but with the furnishings, antique furniture, dado rail and framed prints I could see this had once been a sumptuous living room. Even now, it had a charm that invited one to sit and relax.

Maxine looked up from her paper and peered over her glasses. 'Ah, Jodie. You're up.'

I didn't miss the sarcasm in her tone.

'Yes, I was exhausted.'

'No doubt all the excitement,' she said with a lift of her brows.

'Indeed, a day I won't forget in a hurry.'

She inhaled sharply through her nose. 'We must diligently lock doors and keep a vigilant eye out for unwanted visitors.'

'Of course. I feel reassured by the security alarm.' I paused. 'Is there anything you'd like doing - washing, hoovering, dusting perhaps?'

She pulled out a piece of paper from her trouser pocket and cast her eyes over it. 'Firstly, can you sweep up the broken glass?'

'Of course. I'll pay for the glazier, too.'

'Yes, if you would,' she said through tight lips. 'As you're dining out tonight will you prepare something I can heat up later?'

'Maybe a beef risotto? I'm good at paellas and risotto.'

'Yes, there's beef in the freezer and parmesan in the fridge. Thank you, dear,' she said, and lowered her eyes to the newspaper.

And that was that. Conversation over.

As I removed the wet clothes from the washing machine and heaped them into the wash basket, I mused what an easy job it was to be a housekeeper to only one adult with no children. If Maxine were elderly, that might make the work more challenging, but other than that she was rather stern in her manner and could never be accused of being overly familiar, the housework itself was a breeze. Judging by the dust and cobwebs in every room she didn't have exacting standards either. I'd learned that was often the way with talented people focused on their work - houseproud wasn't amongst their sphere of everyday concerns. I couldn't decide which category of people I belonged to, yet.

I stepped outside with the basket of washing in my arms. Maxine had said the clothes line was at the front and I found it strung between three poles, and the clothes pegs huddled in a basket amongst twigs and leaves. Some of the pegs had snapped whilst others were intact but covered in mildew. They'd have to do, and I hung each clothes item by joining two pieces together with one peg. It felt odd hanging someone else's underwear, and I couldn't help but think Maxine could really do with some new bras and knickers that weren't grey or holey with raggy elastic. Maybe when you were single and sixty plus, fresh and pretty underwear wasn't a priority.

'Now that's a beautiful sight,' came a voice from behind.

I spun around holding a pair of Maxine's knickers. Hadrian leaned casually against the side of the house.

'I didn't hear you arrive,' I said.

He walked forwards, his eyes bright and keen. 'Sorry, I wasn't creeping up on you. But I couldn't help but admire the view, and I'm not talking about my mother's underwear.' He chuckled.

I dropped the damp knickers back into the basket.

He really did have an attractive face, I thought. Fresh, sunkissed skin that glistened, curls in need of a trim, but which gave him that unkempt, rugged edge. He was the sort of man you could imagine playing Heathcliffe or Mr Rochester.

'Well, it is a nice day and I'm all for taking advantage of the rays,' I said.

I noticed his gaze lower unashamedly to my midriff and down to my legs. 'I imagine you tan easily with your exotic looks.'

'Guess so,' I replied. 'But I'm careful with sunscreen.' I paused and tried to frame my words. 'I want to apologise for running away during the storm. You probably think I'm quite mad.'

'I can't say I'm used to that reaction. Was it the thunder and lightning freaking you out or my kissing technique?'

'Yes, I mean no.' I forged a lie. 'I knew a man who got struck by lightning on a golf course - he died outright.'

'That is unfortunate,' said Hadrian.

I picked a blouse out of the basket and pegged it to the line. 'Yes, a close friend of my father's,' I elaborated. 'Left behind three young children.'

'Christ! You could maybe write your next novel about that? Perhaps don't mention the part about sheltering from a storm in a cave with a man you barely knew. Or then again…'

I turned back to face him.

He laughed and gave a lazy shrug, and I realised he hadn't believed a word of my lie.

'Hey, did you see the lightning tree up on the ridge?' I said, promptly moving on.

'I did. Right next to where…' his words trailed off.

I nodded. 'I was right there when the lightning struck. Scared the bejeebers out of me.'

'I heard the crack and was concerned you might be close.'

'Thank God not too close. Anyway, I really wanted to say sorry. I'm not long out of a relationship and I freaked out.'

'You mean, I might be in with a chance?'

I thought for a minute. 'I'd only be on the rebound.'

'Sure.' He looked down and twisted the heel of his boot in the grass. 'How's it going with Mum? She rang me about the trouble last night.'

'Yeah, apart from that, all right, I think.'

'You'll get used to her.'

'I'm sure.' I spotted the toolbox further back. 'You're replacing the glass?'

'Yeah, I'm handy with stuff like that. I'm Mum's unpaid handyman.'

'I feel bad for breaking it. Your mum told you about the intruder?'

'Yeah, she should have rung me last night. But at least you have the alarm. I wondered if it might have been that sneaky journalist.'

I didn't want to explain what I saw, or thought I saw, so I nodded. 'Yeah, I wondered too.'

'Mum mentioned Aunt Evelyn's invited you round.'

I nodded. 'I hear she and your mum aren't close.'

'Aunt Eve's all right. But you'll discover that for yourself. I expect Marcus will be hanging around for a free dinner and a chat with pretty Jodie.'

'Maybe.'

'Listen, if there's more trouble, don't call the pigs, ring me. They're bloody hopeless.'

'Hopefully we won't need to.'

'It'll be no bother. Mum doesn't have a man around to protect her so I help out.'

'You must let me know how much the glass is.'

He made a flipping gesture with his hand. 'Nah, don't worry - I get it cheap.'

'That's kind, thanks.'

'Anything to help out, milady,' he said, and bowed. 'Better check out the damage.' And he picked up his tool box.

'Can I get you a cuppa or anything?' I offered.

'No, but I'll drink a beer with you once I'm done.'

'Maxine has beers?'

'Yep, I buy a stash for when I visit - check in the pantry.'

He set off down the pathway with toolbox and a sheet of glass in hand, and I hung out the rest of the washing before heading back inside to put on another load. I rummaged in the freezer for a bag of beef to defrost. Frozen meat was far harder to identify than unfrozen meat labelled in the shop, but I found what appeared to be diced beef and left it on the worktop to defrost.

The cat wandered across the kitchen floor, sniffed the air and rubbed against my legs before he leaped gracefully onto the worktop.

He slunk up to the frozen bag of meat and prodded it with his nose.

'Oh no you don't, young man.' I reached under his belly and when I lifted him up, he hissed, twisted his head around and snapped at my wrist with needle-sharp teeth

I dropped him lightly to the floor and held up my arm. A minor scratch which I ran under the tap. I couldn't stop the cat from jumping up so I found a plastic bowl, put the bag of meat inside and placed a plate on top.

Hadrian had been down the garden for well over an hour and I found two bottles of beer, unchilled, removed the caps and set off down to the summerhouse.

When I arrived Hadrian was polishing the new window pane with a cloth.

'Good timing,' I said, as I walked up the steps. 'Thought you might be in need.' I held out a beer. 'Looks neatly done.'

'Not bad eh?' He wiped his hands on the cloth and reached for the bottle. 'Cheers!'

We chinked bottles and took a swig. I wasn't much of a beer drinker but it tasted delicious.

'A brewery from over your way - Kielder IPA,' he said.

'Surprisingly tasty,' I said, and took another swig. 'Nice fruity flavour.'

Hadrian sat on the top step, stretching out his legs, and I leaned against the porch rail.

'Don't you have to be at the wall today?' I asked.

He placed his beer bottle on the decking, leaned back and folded his arms behind his head. 'I'm my own boss, so I can be flexible. I do have an apprentice but he's in college some days.'

'Must be great being your own boss. I'd like that.'

'Has many benefits. A lot of responsibility, too. Maybe you'll be a best-selling author one day, like Mum.'

'Well, I can't say I don't dream of that.'

'Keep writing, less dreaming and you might get there.'

'Maybe.'

The sun felt pleasurably warm on my arms and legs and as the alcohol took effect my all too frightening experience in this precise spot last night, faded from my thoughts.

I placed my bottle on the deck and feeling emboldened said, 'I'm going to check inside.'

Hadrian twisted round. 'Did you see the intruder?'

'Yes, but down towards the trees at the bottom. I was scared witless.' But I didn't want to explain that I'd seen a woman not the man his mum had seen.

I could only assume Maxine had mistakenly presumed the intruder to be a man. It had been dark, after all.

The door to the summerhouse opened smoothly, without sticking, and I stepped inside. In daylight the place didn't feel half so creepy and I didn't experience any jitters or racing heartbeat as I crossed to the rear windows. I inhaled a woody scent I hadn't noticed yesterday, and then as I gazed out and searched the view down to the trees and stream, I smelt a different aroma. I breathed in deeply through my nose. What was it? Not unpleasant exactly, but a familiar odour, cool and musky. The air in the room grew colder suddenly and goosebumps broke out on my arms and legs. The strange scent grew stronger and I walked around sniffing and cast my eyes around the floor and over the desk and shelves.

I walked back to the doorway. 'Hadrian?'

He swivelled round.

'Would you come in here for a minute?'

He stood up. 'Sure.'

I stepped aside and he walked in.

I sniffed. 'Do you smell something odd?' The pungent scent clawed at the back of my throat and I coughed.

He breathed in. 'What, you mean a musty old smell because no one's cleaned in here for donkey's years?'

I shook my head. 'Not that kind of smell, but I can't figure out where it's coming from.'

Hadrian walked around. 'Think you're imagining it. I don't smell anything unusual.'

'Wait.' I wafted the air to my nose. 'It's sulphurous. Maybe clay.' I turned to Hadrian. 'Is the soil here clay based?'

'There is clay in the soil. Sand, too. But in here?'

'Well, I definitely smell something unusual, and I couldn't yesterday.'

He laughed quickly and wrinkled his nose. 'I think that beer's gone to your head.'

I laughed too, as if to shake off that anxious feeling that had begun to creep back in. 'It definitely has.'

'I like you, Jodie. Even if you don't like me. You're different.'

I grimaced. 'Different is one of those words people use when they are really thinking, she's weird.' I smiled. 'Anyway, I never said I didn't like you.'

He gave a lopsided smile. 'True, you didn't.'

I inhaled through my nose again, but the scent had faded. How odd.

'I should get back,' I said, and headed for the door. 'I need to earn my keep if I'm to stay in your mum's good books. And thanks for fixing the window.'

'Good luck tonight with Aunt Evelyn,' he called.

'Thanks. I'm sure I won't need it.'

Chapter 18

The Sculptor

The twenty minute drive to Corbridge was easy, but finding Evelyn's house wasn't so straightforward. After crossing the bridge over the river I consulted my road map. Quarter of a mile straight on, past The Pack Horse Inn, and left onto Willow Lane. Except the lane didn't have a sign and I continued past only to realise I'd missed my turn. After a few uncharted twists and turns, I found a terraced row of four Edwardian cottages along a quiet lane out of town. They looked rather more grand double-fronted houses than cottages, I thought, switching off the engine and securing the handbrake.

Evelyn lived at Sweetbriar Cottage, the last house on the right and as I lifted the catch on the iron gate I admired the trimmed hedges, and the colourful and scented shrubs - azaleas, lilac, lavender, and Lily of the Valley. Marcus had mentioned his mum liked gardening and the flowers were coming into bloom. The topiary bushes were immaculate and more like sculptures - a peacock, a pyramid, spiral and spherical bushes. Rose bushes of cream, yellow and red added colour, along with coneflowers, sweet peas, snapdragons and pink clematis that climbed around the front porch.

I spotted movement in the window and continued down the cobbled pathway. As I reached out to rap the knocker the door clicked and swung open.

A slim and attractive woman beamed out at me.

'Hello Jodie. Glad you found us okay.'

'Hello.' I smiled and held out my hand.

She took my hand in hers which felt warm and welcoming.

She stepped aside. 'Please, come in.'

'Your garden's lovely,' I said.

'One of my interests - more of a passion. Marcus is already here. Did I mention he would be?' She smiled and fine lines radiated from her pale blue eyes.

I smiled in reply. 'Yes, you did.'

'I count myself lucky. He usually comes round once a week to see his old mum, despite being busy with his own life.'

Busy dating various women, from what I'd seen and heard, I thought, as I followed her down the hallway and into the living room. Marcus was sitting in the armchair by the window, with a glass of wine in hand.

He placed his drink on the windowsill and stood up. 'Nice to see you again, Jodie. I'll get you a drink - wine, beer, gin and tonic?'

'Thanks. I'll have the same as you.'

'Righto.' He gave me a warm smile and headed out of the room.

I looked around, and to the bay window where the evening sunlight streamed in bringing out all the gold and terracotta in the furnishings. There were vases of flowers, too, pink roses at the centre of the coffee table, and another vase on the windowsill with lilies and stems of myrtle. I already knew Evelyn was a sculptor but I hadn't known what sort of art she created. All the various art pieces and figurines had to be hers.

I turned to her. 'These are your artworks?'

'Mostly. I own a few pieces from other artists, and most of the paintings aren't mine.'

Several figures stood on the dresser and mantlepiece. They looked to be made from clay or bronze.

'If you're interested after dinner I'll show you my studio and some of my works in progress.'

'I'd love that, thanks,' I replied.

What immediately struck me was how alike facially, and yet equally, how unlike she was from Maxine. Where Maxine was plump with cropped grey hair and wore baggy, dowdy clothes, mostly slacks, slip-on shoes and shapeless tunic tops, Evelyn was a woman who cared about her appearance. She wore no makeup apart from a splash of pink lipstick, but her long, tousled hair shone like copper and was pinned up on her head with strands that fell over her shoulders. She wore a blue jacket over a lilac dress covered in delicate white flowers and cinched in at the waist with a wide suede belt to enhance the curve of her hips and ample bust. Pinned to the lapel of her jacket was a bright pink rose made from felt. Beaded bangles jangled on her wrists and her heeled shoes were green suede with a large silver buckle. Her ankles and calves were slim too. The only thing that revealed her profession were her hands, slim ringless fingers, and short unpolished nails tinged with stains. An exquisite musky perfume wafted in the air as she moved. Like Maxine, her voice and accent was Queen's English and eloquent, but when Evelyn spoke she had a softer and warmer tone.

Marcus returned carrying two glasses and handed one to me and the other to Evelyn.

I took a sip and the chilled wine tingled on my tongue and teased my tastebuds. 'Pinot Grigio by any chance?'

'Well done,' said Marcus. 'Bit of a connoisseur?'

'Definitely not, but Pinot is my favourite tipple and I'd recognise it anywhere.'

'How serendipitous,' said Marcus, and his grey eyes sparkled.

'I wasn't sure what you'd like to eat, but I've cooked a vegetarian lasagna,' said Evelyn.

'Mostly because she knows it's my favourite. I hope there's garlic bread?' Marcus said, putting an arm around his mum's shoulders.

Their closeness seemed so natural.

Evelyn squeezed up against Marcus. 'Most certainly. Prepped and ready to pop in the oven.'

'Sounds lovely,' I said. 'I eat meat, but not often.'

'Unlike my sister, which I'm sure you've realised. She eats meat for breakfast, lunch and dinner. She believes it keeps the neurons firing at full throttle.'

'I made her a beef risotto for dinner. At least I think it was beef.'

'We haven't been invited round for years, but I recall that freezer crammed with various cuts.'

'It still is.' I grimaced as I remembered the bag of minced placenta.

'Our parents were excellent cooks and when Maxine was young she liked to experiment with her cooking, although with

174

rather less success than her storytelling. Our parents passed away ten years ago within a year of each other, but sadly, Maxine was estranged from them and didn't attend either of their funerals - she said she couldn't cope with the upset.'

'I'm beginning to see Maxine as quite the recluse,' I said. 'Writers can be a strange breed, I believe - often introverted.'

'Trouble is, Maxine pushes people away. She's happier in her own company with her writing and her fictional characters.'

'I'd say Hadrian and her are close, though,' I said.

And here we were already talking about Maxine and Hadrian, as I'd been instructed not to do. But Evelyn seemed so easy to talk to, and truthfully, I preferred to talk about real things and not only make small talk.

'Oh yes, an unbreakable bond there.'

'Maybe more so because of losing Hadrian's father so young,' I said.

A shadow fell across Evelyn's features. 'A terrible thing to happen. And all the mystery and controversy over Winston's death made it harder for Maxine to accept.'

'You knew Winston, too, I imagine?' I asked.

'Of course, he was my brother-in-law. A kind, intelligent and lovely man.'

As Evelyn lifted her glass I noticed she wore no wedding ring. Maybe she was divorced or widowed, or perhaps she'd never married. Maxine still wore her wedding ring. At least I assumed the diamond ring she wore was one. I wondered if Marcus had been born out of wedlock - that wasn't so unusual.

'I shall leave you with Marcus whilst I finish dinner preparations.' She glanced at her watch. 'I have a friend joining us soon.'

We both sat on armchairs in the bay window.

Marcus leaned forwards. 'I'd like to explain about yesterday.'

'There's really no need.'

'I received an urgent message that Mum needed help, but it wasn't genuine.'

I frowned and shook my head. 'But who passed on that message and why would they?'

He pressed his lips together and seemed reluctant to say more.

'Sorry, you don't need to explain.'

175

He paused before he spoke. 'As you may have gathered, or possibly not, Hadrian and I don't always see eye to eye. We were close as youngsters and often stayed over at one another's houses.'

'It was Hadrian who passed on the message?'

'Afraid so, and entirely fabricated. And then conveniently saw you upon your arrival to meet me.'

'That's strange. I thought it odd that you hadn't tried to ring or message me earlier.'

'Exactly. I dashed here. I was concerned, until Mum reassured me she was fine and all was well.'

'Did something happen between you and Hadrian?'

Marcus took a slow drink of his wine. 'When I was thirteen and Hadrian fourteen, he discovered my mum had been arrested and questioned in relation to his father's death, back when it all happened. But, every family member was questioned, and it goes without saying that Mum had nothing to do with Uncle Winston's fall and was cleared. But since Hadrian found this out our relationship changed - possibly as a result of how accurately or inaccurately this news was divulged to him by Maxine.'

'But you came to Maxine's talk to support her and help out.'

'Truth is I want to build bridges. Other than Mum, Hadrian and Maxine are my only other living family, and I know Maxine can be baffling and perverse, and Hadrian's complicated, but Mum doesn't deserve the coldness and detachment they show her.'

I nodded. 'Your mum seems lovely. I admire you're doing what you can to improve relations, but rifts sometimes become too wide.' My experiences with Dad clouded my thoughts.

'I was hacked off with Hadrian for his meddling yesterday. I nearly went round to have it out with him.'

'I'm glad you didn't. But I'm also glad you've told me. Hadrian does seem quite complex,' I added.

'We all are, I guess, but I always try to be upfront and honest. I'm not into playing games. Well, not mind games, anyway.' He smiled.

'Me neither,' I said decisively. 'And I'll drink a toast to that.' I raised my glass.

Marcus leaned across and we chinked glasses.'

'So, anything either Maxine or Hadrian say about you or Evelyn I shouldn't take too seriously?'

'Might depend on what they say, but if it's negative I'd take it with a pinch of salt.'

'That's sad, but the nature of some families.' I knew how I sometimes talked about Dad with Mum, but my experiences justified my negativity. 'Should we offer to help your mum?'

'Probably, yes.'

With glasses in hand we went through to the kitchen at the rear of the house.

Evelyn drizzled olive oil over a bowl of salad. 'More wine?'

'I'll put it on the table,' said Marcus. 'How about cutlery?'

'Yes, thanks darling,' she said, flicking some fallen strands of hair from her face.

The doorbell sounded.

'That'll be Philip,' said Evelyn.

Marcus smiled at me and headed out.

'Philip is a good friend,' said Evelyn. 'I'm sure you'll like him.'

I heard voices and laughter in the hallway and Marcus returned followed by a spectacled man with dark olive skin - and more essentially, a man I'd met before.

'Philip, this is Jodie, Jodie, Philip.'

Philip held out his hand and smiled.

'Of course, we've already met,' I said, without returning his smile.

Chapter 19

A Married Man

When Evelyn had rung to invite me over, she'd conveniently forgotten to mention that her journalist friend, Philip, would be coming too. Would I have accepted her invitation anyway? Yes, most likely. And what about Marcus with his, *I don't play games?* Did he know Philip would be here? And why was Philip here - to meet me or purely for the social occasion?

By the time we sat down to eat I'd already drunk two glasses of wine and given that I'd barely eaten, my head swam with questions and thoughts. But I didn't want to appear rude amidst Evelyn's hospitality and so I made polite conversation up until we'd eaten our main course.

I'd hoped Evelyn or Marcus may be forthcoming about Philip's presence, or even Philip himself, given how forthright he'd been with me at the pub only a couple of nights ago.

'That was delicious. Thank you.' I placed my knife and fork on the side of my plate.

'You've a good appetite,' Evelyn said, with approval. 'Or perhaps you've not been eating well at my sister's,' she added.

'I can be a fussy eater,' I said.

'Probably why you're slim,' said Marcus, sitting beside me.

'Thanks, but my curves have never been easy to control. Thankfully I love to exercise.'

'What's your sport - or do you hit the gym?' asked Marcus.

'I swim and run. Neither very well.'

'Ahh, then you and Marcus have something in common,' said Evelyn with a satisfied smile.

I turned to Marcus. 'Running or swimming?'

'Swimming. More wild swimming than lengths in the pool.'

'I've never done that, other than the sea. Any wild swimming spots around here?'

'Yeah, a few lakes, or loughs - nice and quiet.'

'Isn't it freezing?'

He laughed, his eyes shining. 'Yeah, that's part of the fun! Sometimes I wear a wetsuit.'

'Wise. The cold can be treacherous to an unsuspecting swimmer wanting to cool down.'

'Is that so?' said Philip, who'd been quietly listening and taking it all in.

'Yes, umm...' I hesitated. I didn't want to share how I knew that - through writing my book - so I didn't divulge. 'I only know that people can get caught out and paralysed by the cold water. Not a pleasant way to go. Well, no way is a good way when you're young.'

Philip nodded. 'There have been tragic cases locally, too.'

'It must happen all over, which is why there are warning signs in popular spots.' Tired of skirting around why he was here, I said, 'Philip, you didn't mention you were friends with Evelyn when you approached me in the pub and asked about Maxine.'

He nodded and gave the slimmest of smiles. 'My apologies. But in my defence I didn't know you'd be coming for dinner tonight.'

Our eyes gravitated towards Evelyn.

'It's a surprisingly small world. Don't you think?' Evelyn said, and laughed with pleasure.

'Is it?' I said, but I couldn't help laughing too. 'There's coincidence and then there's quietly avoiding sharing pertinent details.' I sipped more wine.

Marcus laughed beside me. 'You know Jodie's a lawyer, Mum?'

'Ex-lawyer right now,' I added.

'A crime writer, too. So, I don't think anyone can pull the wool over her eyes.'

'Thanks, Marcus. I'm only here for dinner and good company, but if there is something I should know then I'm all ears.' I blinked innocently.

'I should explain,' said Evelyn. 'No, *we* should explain.'

Philip took hold of Evelyn's hand and nodded.

'I mentioned that I'm writing a biographical article about Maxine which will focus on the mysterious and unsolved death of her husband, Winston,' said Philip.

'You did. And I got the feeling you thought I might be able to root out and share details about Maxine.'

'Maybe so,' he admitted.

'Which, given that Maxine is far from forthcoming about private stuff, I doubt I'll be able to enlighten you more than you already are by knowing Evelyn and Marcus, and having covered the story at the time. I'd also feel disloyal as Maxine is mentoring me. Correction, editing my book.'

Philip nodded. 'Fair points, Jodie. I'm afraid making enquiries is second nature to me. My apologies if I appeared intrusive.'

I sighed. 'Glad you understand.'

'I'd love to read your book,' said Evelyn. 'Have you had many readers?'

'Only Maxine so far. My ex read a page or two before getting bored,' I said with a laugh.

'It can't possibly be boring,' said Marcus.

'I don't think it is. It needs editing, but it isn't dull.'

'If you'd like another pair of eyes I've read all of Maxine's and average one book a week. I'd be a fair critic,' Evelyn offered.

I thought for a few moments. Would Maxine mind? Yes, probably. But would she find out?

'Then I'd appreciate it. Please don't let on to Maxine though. I need to be tactful and especially whilst she's so generously editing it.'

'I wouldn't dream of telling her,' reassured Evelyn. 'Could you send me a copy?'

'Yes, I carry it with me on a floppy disc.' I pushed my chair back. 'I'll fetch it.'

Evelyn waved her hand. 'Please, no rush.'

'I'll forget if I drink more vino.' As I walked from the dining room, I felt unsteady and tripped.

I giggled to myself, and straightened up.

In the living room I reached for my handbag.

'Mum didn't say Philip was coming tonight.'

I spun around and Marcus stood a few feet away.

'Mum only said a friend.'

'Hey. I'm not worried. I'm having a great time,' I said.

'Oh good. Mum will make an excellent reader. She'll be honest and constructive, I'm sure.'

'Yeah, I sense that. I get a good feeling about your mum. So, is Philip her boyfriend?'

'Yeah, long term. Well, as long as I can remember.'

'It's such a small world.'

'He's like the dad I never knew.'

'But they've never married?' I recalled the wedding ring Philip was still wearing tonight.

'Mum's not the marrying sort. She's loyal though.'

I was tempted to ask about Marcus's dad, but even with the alcohol loosening my inhibitions, I held back.

'If Evelyn and Philip have been friends for that long then surely Maxine and Hadrian know about their relationship?' I thought for a moment before adding. 'And you acted like you didn't know Philip at the talk?'

Marcus looked at me with a soft expression, but didn't immediately answer. 'I had no choice. Luckily Maxine lives far enough away and Hadrian rarely visits us here. Mum and Philip prefer to keep their relationship private.'

'Ahh, so Philip is married?' I asked, quietly.

'Well, kind of.'

'He's either married or not.'

'It's not always so straightforward.'

'A marriage certificate is supposed to be binding - or until divorce or death.'

'But very often it isn't,' said Marcus.

'Anyway, it's none of my business.'

He came closer and lowered his voice. 'In truth, I've had similar conversations with Mum, but she's happy with the arrangement and she's free to do as she pleases.'

'But your mum is loyal, as you say, unlike him.'

'Mum makes her own rules. And she breaks them when she wants, too.'

A voice came from behind. 'What rules are those?'

We both turned to see Evelyn in the doorway.

'I was just saying, you're a bit of a rebel.'

She laughed and walked into the room. 'I live by the philosophy - we're free to be who we want to be. If we don't like

181

something we can either try to change it, ignore it or simply let it go. Within the law and always showing kindness, of course.'

'I like that idea and I'd go along with that too,' I said, my cheeks burning at being caught talking about her.

Evelyn smiled, unoffended. 'Come on, dessert and digestif?'

'Sounds good.' I held out the disc. 'You can print it off or save it on your computer.'

She took it from me. 'Thank you. I feel privileged that you trust me with your work.'

'I do trust you, and I'll value your opinion too.'

Chapter 20

Natural Beauty

We returned to the dining room where Philip was rifling through Evelyn's CD's. 'What do you fancy - classical, jazz, indie?' He glanced over his shoulder.

'How about The Sundays?' said Marcus. 'The one I gave Mum for Christmas.'

'Nice choice,' said Philip, as he trailed his fingers along the shelf. 'Ah, here it is.' He slotted the CD into the player.

We sat back at the table and the female singer's tones filled the room.

My arms and scalp prickled and a feeling of euphoria rushed through me. 'Her voice is so melodic,' I said. 'I've got goosebumps.'

'That's when you know you've found a good singer,' said Evelyn. 'My taste is eclectic but I usually listen to instrumental when I'm sculpting. Lyrics dilute my thoughts.'

'Interesting. I write and read in silence,' I said. 'Although I don't mind background noise, as long as it isn't sport.' John watched football and rugby and I couldn't think straight.

'When I worked for *The Times* we were expected to write with a cacophony of telephones, shouting and conversations going on around us. I used to slot in ear plugs,' said Philip.

'I wonder if the newspapers still work like that,' said Marcus.

Philip nodded. 'They do indeed. I was down last week. Couldn't get out fast enough.'

'So you still work for a newspaper?' I asked.

'Only freelance. I write something and find a buyer or I'm commissioned to cover a specific story.'

Evelyn turned to Philip with an admiring gaze. 'Makes a good living, too.'

'I get by,' he said.

'Because you're damn good,' she said.

'Thanks, my love.' He took her hand and raised her fingers to his lips.

Such a loving gesture, I thought.

'Plenty of silence at Maxine's, I imagine,' said Evelyn.

'Well, she listens to Chopin's nocturnes on repeat. Doesn't go in for chit-chat though.'

'No, she never has. When Maxine speaks, you know she's not making polite conversation. Not such a bad thing,' Evelyn said.

'I'm not writing anything whilst I'm staying though. But it's refreshing to come out tonight. I'd feel isolated staying at Maxine's for long. Did her housekeeper live-in?'

'No, Patricia lives in Hexham,' said Marcus.

Evelyn stood up. 'Apple pie and ice cream for dessert.'

'Can I help?' I asked.

'Lovely, thanks, Jodie.'

In the kitchen Evelyn slipped her hands into her oven gloves and reached into the oven. 'Looks nicely browned. The tub of ice cream is in the bottom drawer of the freezer.'

I opened the freezer drawer. 'I shouldn't have drunk so much. Seeing as I have to drive back.'

Evelyn turned to me. 'You can sleep here. I should have offered on the phone.'

'Are you sure?'

'Yes, then you can indulge a little more,' said Evelyn, as she placed the steaming pie and four china bowls onto the tray. 'Could you grab another bottle of white from the fridge?'

When I walked back into the dining room carrying the tub of ice cream and a new bottle of Pinot Grigio, I saw that Marcus and Philip were talking in earnest.

They fell silent and looked my way.

'More wine anyone?'

'Please,' said Marcus. 'Aren't you driving though?'

'Evelyn's offered me a bed. I'll ring Maxine.' I uncorked the bottle and poured wine into our glasses. 'Shan't be a minute.' I took my mobile phone into the hallway. Thankfully Evelyn had decent phone reception, unlike Maxine's house which was patchy. The dial tone rang out and went to her answerphone. I hung up and redialled. Again it went to answerphone and I left a brief message. I tried Maxine's mobile instead and wasn't surprised when that too went straight to voicemail.

I typed out a text and hoped she'd get at least one of my messages.

It was only half-eight, surely too early for Maxine to head up to bed. But she might still be editing and couldn't be bothered to answer the landline.

Back in the dining room I sat down to a bowl of apple pie topped with ice cream that had melted and oozed.

'Delicious,' said Philip, spooning another mouthful.

'You're a great cook, Mum,' said Marcus.

'Do you live alone, Marcus?' I asked.

'I have a flat in town. I was living with a mate, but he's moved in with his girlfriend. They've got engaged.'

'Yeah, I've got friends settling down. One or two with babies.' My thoughts went to John and the plans we'd tentatively discussed, but that was all history now. Then I saw Evelyn looking at me intently.

'If you don't mind me saying, you have such beautiful and striking features. Are your parents from the south?'

'Mum's parents are Spanish born, and Dad had dark hair and colouring,' I replied.

'Have you ever done any modelling?' she asked.

'Gosh, no. I'm too short and curvy for conventional modelling, and it isn't something I've ever considered.'

'I create my sculptures based on real people. I've done some of Marcus, and Philip.'

'They look like me too, which can be embarrassing,' said Marcus.

'Why embarrassing?' I asked.

'If you saw them you'd realise.'

'Ahh, they're nudes?'

'Exactly.'

'But they are contemporary and beautiful and so one can hardly complain,' said Philip.

'True.' Marcus nodded and turned to his mum with an admiring gaze. 'Incredibly lifelike. Flattering in some ways.'

'No, they are truthful in every aspect, other than height and colour,' said Evelyn with a warmth to her tone revealing the pride she felt for her son.

I looked at Marcus too. I could understand - he was exquisitely handsome and even more attractive because of the combination of his unique features.

Evelyn turned to face me once more. 'I wonder if you might consider allowing me to create a sculpture of you?'

I was taken aback. 'Really? But yes, if you think I'd make a decent subject.'

'Of course you would. It isn't often I create one from such a natural beauty.'

I felt the colour rise in my cheeks. 'Would I need to sit for you?'

'Not for long. I take photos and make sketches to work from.'

'Would I need to pose naked?' I grimaced.

'Preferably, but only if you feel comfortable. I've had models who posed in underwear and I used my imagination.'

I felt emboldened and with the alcohol flowing through me, I said. 'I'm not overly body shy, so I wouldn't mind.' I glanced across at Marcus who had his chin propped on his hands, as he watched me with the faintest of smiles.

'Tomorrow morning okay?' said Evelyn.

'How about tonight? I'd hate to chicken out tomorrow.'

She clapped her hands. 'Good girl. I'll show you my studio, too. And we'll lock the boys out.'

'Please. I'm not that brave.' I laughed and felt my cheeks blush.

Chapter 21

Sculptor's Studio

Evelyn's studio was a cultural cornucopia to lose yourself in. 'So this is what a sculptor's studio looks like,' I said, and gazed around.

I inhaled an aroma of linseed oil mixed with clay, copper and wood, and I felt intrigued and welcome, all at once.

There were figurines of people, a few animals and other unusual shaped creations on the shelves. Some sculptures looked complete with a shining bronze sheen, and others were matt clay and works in progress. The worktops were laden with jars of pencils and paintbrushes, sheets of paper covered in sketches and portraits, hands and various other anatomical details.

'This is quite small as studios go, but equally as messy as others I've been in,' Evelyn commented, and laughed.

I crossed the studio to where three eye-catching bronze figures stood proudly on a shelf, each figure around a foot high. Two of them had the distinct features, including the wide-set eyes and long-limbed build of a man I instantly recognised to be Marcus. The standing male figure in the middle, was of a finer build, similar facial features and a goatee beard. The likeness and accuracy of the two to Marcus was uncanny and it was clear why Evelyn had achieved such a respected reputation and success in the art world.

I tried to imagine Marcus posing naked for his mum. That was an interesting thought. But Evelyn was a cool lady and I doubted she had any hangups about the human body and nudity. And that was probably the same for Marcus too - easy and relaxed in his own skin. Naturally masculine, but none of the alpha male posturing evident in my ex John, or Hadrian.

In both figurines, Marcus struck a different pose. One sitting and resting with his chin on his hand. Not dissimilar to Rodin's, The Thinker. His limbs were longer and finer though, and his hands, face and hair were exquisitely crafted and detailed. Evelyn was certainly pretty at sixty plus, but I could only imagine that Marcus must have had a handsome father. It can't have been Evelyn's present boyfriend, Philip, of that I felt certain. Plus, Marcus and Philip didn't seem to have a father son connection you might expect to see. A friendly and easy familiarity, yes.

I traced my finger over the shoulder of the sitting figure. 'I can't believe how lifelike these are.'

'Truthful representation and likeness are vital in my work, to the art I bring to life, and I try to bring out the personality and essence of each person I sculpt.'

'I see that in this one, particularly.'

'I know I'm biased, as every mother is, but Marcus does think deeply, too deeply, sometimes, although I cannot fault him for that.'

'Mmmm. Some men don't think deeply enough, at least from my experience.'

'You're still hurting from your previous relationship, I think?' she asked, softly.

I nodded once. 'Yes, but I'm better out of it.'

Evelyn walked closer and placed a hand on my arm. 'When a man treats us badly, there can be no going back.'

'You don't believe in second chances?'

'I do not. When a man loves you, he doesn't cheat - ever.'

But what about Philip? I wanted to ask. He was a long term adulterer, at least from where I was standing.

I pointed to the middle bronze figure. 'This one isn't Marcus?'

'No, that is someone I knew years ago…' she murmured and her words trailed away.

'Fits perfectly between those of Marcus.'

Evelyn turned away and I sensed her reluctance to disclose the identity of the middle figure.

'Is it warm enough for you? I could turn on the heater?' she asked.

'It feels fine,' I replied, and felt a flutter in the pit of my stomach.

'You can undress behind the screen. There's a robe you can wear and all you need to do is stand on this podium. I'll take photos from a few angles, but only when you feel comfortable, and closeups of your features, too.'

'I trust you, Evelyn. You're the artist and I'm honoured you want to sculpt me. I also hope to see the completed sculpture.'

'Of course you will. Plus it'll be a good reason for us to meet again.'

I stood behind the folding screen which was decorated with delicate Chinese figures, pagodas and flowers. Evelyn put on some music - an instrumental version of The Beatles, *I'm Only Sleeping*.

'I'm a big Beatles fan - my era,' said Evelyn with a laugh. She hummed along.

'Mum was a hippy chick,' I said. 'Still is.'

'How about your father? Was, or is he a free spirit?'

I hung my clothes over the chair and pulled a blue silk robe off the hook on the wall.

'No. There was nothing remotely flowery or free spirit about him. A lawyer. And an unpleasant one at that.'

'I'm sorry to hear that. I know you're a lawyer, and I already sense you're a genuinely lovely person, but truthfully, I've met one or two lawyers who were the most disagreeable people.'

'The profession does attract a mixture - or maybe it changes those who work in the profession for long. In my ex-boyfriend's firm there were caring and kind lawyers, and those who were hard-edged and driven by their humongous egos.'

'Happens in the creative arena too. I'm forever mindful not to let my success and ego make me unsympathetic to the views and needs of others.'

'My ex, brilliant in the courtroom, is an egotist and walks all over those around him to get what he wants, as I discovered to my cost.'

'He didn't deserve you.'

'No, he didn't. I'll get over him, and as they say, what doesn't kill you, makes you stronger.'

I walked out from behind the screen.

'Do you believe that?' she said, but with doubt in her tone.

I nodded and replied with conviction. 'Yes, I really do.'

'A woman needs to be strong. Far too many rogues out there take advantage of lonely or vulnerable women.'

I stepped onto the podium and sat on the stool with my bare feet resting on the foot bar. 'I've had my lifetime share of rogues.'

Evelyn hung her Nikon camera around her neck and made some adjustments to the lenses. 'I only photograph in black and white.'

'That's interesting,' I replied.

'I only want to see the fine details, shades and tones, and colour photography can confuse my eye when I come to create in a single material.'

'So different to painting, I guess,' I said.

'Principles are the same, but yes, the result being a whole different perspective to two-dimensional art. I'll need to use the flash even though the room is well-lit.' She went round and switched on three lamps suspended from the ceiling around the podium.

I slipped the robe from my shoulders and Evelyn stepped forwards to take it from me. I felt exposed beneath the lights and pressed my knees together. To try to appear relaxed and natural I resisted the urge to fold my arms over my breasts, and rested my hands on my knees. But Evelyn expressed no awkwardness in her eyes and her features remained relaxed.

'What might make an interesting pose would be to cross your legs and rest one hand on your thigh and the other arm relaxed at your side.'

I adjusted my position as she suggested.

Evelyn crossed to a worktop and reached into a woven basket. She searched inside and pulled out a small blue object.

'Would you mind wearing this hair clip?' She brought it over and held it in her palm. 'This butterfly can represent a transition to a new life - as yet unwritten by you, but with endless potential for creativity and freedom to be your truest self.'

The blue butterfly was decorated with jewels and sparkled beneath the studio lights. 'It's so pretty.' I smiled and took it from her.

I lifted some strands of hair away from my face, and clipped the blue butterfly above my ear.

Evelyn stepped away. 'That's lovely. Can you turn your face towards the window? Imagine you're gazing upon something that holds your interest.'

Immediately, and I wasn't sure what prompted the idea, Marcus came into my mind's eye.

'Wonderful. Such a natural expression, Jodie.' The camera flashed twice. 'Now can you look directly at the camera?'

I did as she asked and the light flashed again.

'How do you feel?' Evelyn asked, and stepped closer.

I considered her question. 'I guess I feel vulnerable. Not in any threatening sense,' I added.

'That's normal. You're in your natural born state, you're young and beautiful, comfortable in your own skin, but you may also realise how alluring you appear.'

I nodded. 'I never really think of myself in that way.'

'Your modesty is charming and only enhances your beauty.' She moved and steadied her camera for a new angle. 'I've also photographed and sculpted dozens of women, and men, so feel reassured.'

I felt at ease, so when she asked me to stand up it felt natural. As directed, I assumed various poses, all that I would make if I were standing and looking around. Nothing felt either provocative or forced. Evelyn spoke encouraging words and in some photos I smiled and in others my features remained neutral.

'I like how your mouth turns upwards even when you're unsmiling,' she said.

And then,

'You're effortlessly feminine.'

'Am I?' I said. 'No one has ever said that to me before.'

'It's not the sort of thing people compliment on.'

'True.'

'And you remind me of Juliet Binoche,' she added. 'The actress.'

'Thank you.' I felt my cheeks warm.

I caught a flash from the corner of my eye - and not from where Evelyn stood. I hadn't noticed before that the blinds remained half-open. It had grown dark and from the back of the house where we were, there was the garden and fields beyond.

Instinctively I folded my arms across my breasts and stared at the window. Perhaps another electrical storm was brewing, but I couldn't see or hear rain or thunder.

I turned to Evelyn. 'Could you draw the blinds fully?'

'Of course, although nobody can see. Other than sheep, potentially.'

'No, I'm sure. But I saw a flash of light.'

She crossed to the window and looked out for a few moments. She wiped her hand against the glass. 'We're a bit steamed up anyway...' she broke off and stared out of the window.

'Evelyn?'

She reached for the chain on the roman blind and the material lowered to the windowsill.

'I can't see anything.' She turned to me. 'But I've got what I need, photos wise.' She lifted up the robe from the chair and handed it to me. 'You're truly a photogenic wonder, Jodie. You looked so relaxed which is no easy feat. Thank you.' She went round and turned off the suspended lights. 'Now I'm keen to get these processed and see what I can create from them.'

'Thank you, too. I appreciate the opportunity,' I said, and wrapped the robe around me.

'I'll leave you to change.' She placed her camera on the sideboard and left the room.

After dressing, I checked my hair in the mirror before turning off the main light and returning to the kitchen.

Philip stood at the sink with his sleeves rolled up and his hands in the washing up bowl. Marcus leaned against the granite worktop with a can of beer in his hand.

'How was the modelling shoot?' asked Marcus.

'I didn't feel like Naomi Campbell, that I do know,' I said and laughed.

'Rather more sophisticated modelling, I'd say,' said Marcus.

'Albeit in the nude,' I said and giggled. 'I liked the sculptures of you. They should be in an exhibition.'

'They often are, but staying here for a bit,' said Evelyn.

'Good of you to offer to pose. I know Mum only asks those she thinks will be interesting to create from,' said Marcus. 'And her commissions, of course.'

'Well, I'm no prude, plus it was fun and your mum made me feel comfortable.'

Evelyn turned to me from the dishwasher. 'I'm glad. Do you want to see the photos before I begin?'

'If I'm still around. Do you process yourself?'

'Yes, I've a mini darkroom just off the studio. Much easier and quicker than sending film away.'

'Fantastic.'

Evelyn walked to the back door and tried the handle. She turned the key in the lock and tried the handle again. Then she crossed to the window behind the sink, reached over Philip still washing up, and pulled the blind down.

A thought struck me. Had Evelyn also seen something from the studio window when I'd seen that flash of light? Where did she go after she left the studio so abruptly?

We returned to the living room and sat up talking and listening to music. Past midnight Evelyn stood up and announced she needed her bed. Philip got up too.

'No need for you two to retire like us oldies, and the music won't bother us. Everything's locked up,' Evelyn said, as she headed out of the room.

'Good night. A lovely evening, thank you both,' said Philip. He pressed his hands together and bowed.

How polite and thoughtful Philip seemed - an entirely different impression from the one he'd made at Maxine's talk.

That left me sitting on the sofa with my feet tucked beneath me and Marcus leaned back in the armchair with his legs stretched out.

I felt pleasantly tipsy as I continued sipping from my glass.

'I love your mum's sculptures. Not often you see modern art today that looks like what it represents.'

Marcus nodded. 'Yes, so much contemporary stuff isn't that aesthetically pleasing.'

'Has your mum sculpted many of you, other than the two I saw?'

He ran his hand through his hair. 'Yes, I'm an easy target and I've got over any shyness of being her model.'

'You shouldn't be shy. I'm honoured your mum's offered to sculpt me, especially now I've seen how incredibly lifelike they are.'

'Yes, more flattering in some ways.'

'I'd say completely honest.'

'Those two in the studio have been in Tate Liverpool. She had an exhibition there, and in Edinburgh too.'

'My goodness.' I swallowed another mouthful of wine.

I looked closely at Marcus - his chiselled lips, the prominent curve of his cheekbones, and a thought occurred to me, prompting me to ask. 'Are you in touch with your father?'

'I've never even met him,' Marcus replied.

For some moments he swirled the wine around his glass before he rose to his feet and came to sit beside me on the sofa.

'Can I tell you something in confidence?' He studied the back of one hand, before raising his eyes to mine. 'I rarely talk about my father, mostly because I know nothing about him. My friends rarely ask about my father, and if they do, I say I was born from a love affair that went wrong. It's easier and safer than telling the truth - that I don't know who he is.'

'Do you know if your father deserted your mum when she fell pregnant?'

'Not sure, but I know Mum was devastated - she at least told me that.'

'I'm sorry. I shouldn't have asked.'

He reached out and touched my hand. 'Don't be. I'm grateful to talk with someone I can trust.' He took his hand away and rested it in his lap.

'I'm glad I've met you and your family. I feel like I've known you all for far more than a few days.'

'Funny how we can meet people and find an instant connection.'

I smiled. 'It's nice on the rare occasions it happens.'

'Maybe losing your job and leaving John has opened new doors for you.'

'I think it has. Not that I was given much choice. But it's been a surprising week so far.'

'Listen, I know you have to go back to help Maxine in the morning, but if the weather's fine would you like to walk down to the Lough? It's only a mile or so from Maxine's.'

I nodded. 'I'd really like that.'

The dawn chorus was already starting when we finally climbed the stairs. Marcus stopped at the first door on the landing.

'The spare room.' He opened the door, and reached round the doorway to turn on the light. 'The mattress is old and squishy but I can guarantee a good night's sleep, well, the few hours left of it'

I poked my head in. 'I'm sure I will.'

He gestured along the corridor. 'The bathroom, and then my room is next down if you need anything.'

'Thanks. I'm sure I won't need to disturb you,' I said, as my mind ran through scenarios where I might feel the need to.

'Night then.' And with a final smile, he turned and walked away to his room.

'See you in the morning,' I called quietly after him.

I saw that dawn approached as I gazed out of the bedroom window and down at the shadowy shapes of the topiary bushes in the garden. Across the lane and hedgerow there was a field with sheep huddled beneath a tree, and above the hillside beyond, the sky glowed gold as the sun crept towards a new day.

Chapter 22

A Moment Shared

I awoke with a start.

'Jodie,' a voice murmured.

I opened my eyes and sat bolt upright.

Marcus stood beside the bed. 'Sorry to startle you.'

'Is it late?'

He whispered. 'Still early. I wanted to show you something in the garden. Come to my room.' He hurried out.

I pushed the sheet away, swung my legs out of bed and reached for my skirt on the chair. I couldn't imagine what he wanted to show me.

With bare feet I padded softly down the corridor to where his door hung open. He stood at the far window, turned, and in silence gestured for me to join him.

My eyes followed where he looked to the back garden below. Twenty yards away down the sloping lawn, three deer nibbled the dew covered grass. Two long legged and graceful females stood beside a fawn which looked only days old.

'Oh look,' I whispered. The mist, glistening luminescent in the dawning light, swirled around the three deer as they feasted, unaware they were being watched.

'I've never seen them in our garden,' said Marcus.

'A magical sight.' I turned to Marcus. 'I'm so glad you woke me.'

He blinked with a childish glint. 'I had a feeling you wouldn't want to miss them.'

We turned again to the garden. 'I wonder what time it is?' I whispered.

'Early.'

'Why were you awake?'

'Not sure. I felt awake and restless.'

I yawned and my breath misted the window.

Marcus raised his hand and wiped the glass. 'Now you can see again.'

One of the deer raised her head and turned towards our window. We remained still, hardly daring to breathe, as she watched us. After some moments, and with a flick of her tail, she turned to the fawn and nudged its neck before stepping through the grass and between the bushes. The other two followed and in seconds all three deer had disappeared.

I felt my eyes sting. 'Such graceful and beautiful creatures.' And I wiped the dampness from the corner of each eye.

I turned to his bedroom interior and looked around at the band posters on the walls - Duran Duran, Visage and Human League. 'Your childhood room by any chance?'

A record player and tape deck stood in the corner of the room with two shelves above crammed full of records and cassettes.

'Nicely preserved from your teenage years.'

'But at least I was into decent music,' he said, with a laugh.

'Some of my faves here, too.'

'If it wasn't so early, I'd play you some,' he said.

I yawned. 'Can you see the garden and fields from your bed?'

He wandered across to the bed, sat down and stretched out his legs, then propped a pillow behind his back. 'I can. And why I rarely draw the curtains.'

I went and stood beside the top of his bed and looked out.

Marcus shuffled over a few inches and patted the mattress beside him.

I sat down and leaned against the headboard. 'A perfect view. And so comfy.'

'It's old and saggy, but I always sleep well here.'

'Nice that you come and stay with your mum.'

He turned to me. 'Do you go home much?' he asked.

'I'm staying at Mum's when I leave Maxine's. But yeah, me and Mum make a great team. Especially after Dad left.'

'Did your mum never meet anyone else?'

'I reckon Dad put her off men for life. She has male friends who'd have liked to make it more, but she's happy as she is.'

'And has your dad put you off men?'

'Surprisingly, no, but I am wary about who I get involved with. And I'll never accept shoddy treatment again.'

'That's wise. Was John cheating for a while?' he asked.

'Long enough, but I was in the dark. Makes me wonder if others at work knew.'

'Trouble is, people are reluctant to get involved where affairs and secrets are concerned, so they keep quiet or pretend ignorance.'

'It's really shitty.' I gave a deep sigh. 'Have you had any long term relationships?' I remembered Hadrian's comments about Marcus having a different girlfriend every week.

He paused for some moments. 'A few months ago I split with my girlfriend, Fiona. We were together for six years.'

'Oh,' I said, surprised. 'That must have been tough.'

He nodded slowly. 'She had a few issues and we both made the decision to end it.'

'No regrets then?'

'Not for me, no. Fiona wanted to meet up to talk about 'us', so we had a drink in the pub at the weekend.'

Ah, so the blonde woman was Fiona, his ex.

'She was keen for us to try again…'

'Gosh…'

'I told her it was too late for me, and I hoped she'd meet someone else.'

'Was she disappointed?'

'Yes, and she got upset. But I don't believe in going backwards, even if that feeling of familiarity is tempting. Not that I've been in that situation often before.'

'I agree. There's no going back for me and John - not that he wants me now he has my best friend.'

'He's an idiot - even if I have never met him.'

I laughed and nudged him with my shoulder. 'I should go back to bed.'

'Lie here if you like. The deer might come back.'

When I turned to him he gave a slim smile and his grey eyes seemed to change shades in the dawning light.

'Okay.' I shuffled my bottom down the bed, pulled my skirt over my thighs and laid my head back on the pillow. Marcus lay back too and I felt the warmth of his body beside mine. Instinctually, I moved my head an inch or two along the pillow and felt him do the same until our hair touched. He took my hand in his and I closed my eyes.

Chapter 23

An Honest Conversation

Before I left Evelyn's later that morning, I thanked her for everything, and arranged with Marcus that he'd drive over to Maxine's later that afternoon so we could walk together from there down to the Lough.

I turned from the lane onto Maxine's drive and hoped that when I got in she wouldn't ask me too much about my evening at her sister's. I also hoped Maxine had received one of my messages. For certain, I wouldn't be mentioning meeting Philip the journalist there. That wouldn't go down well and would seriously jeopardise my stay here and Maxine's editing support.

I slotted the key into the front door but the lock wouldn't turn. Maxine must have left her key in when she locked up the previous night. I walked around the side of the house and peered through the kitchen window to see Maxine standing at the hob and stirring a spoon in a saucepan. I tapped on the window and her head twisted my way. I waved and smiled but she didn't smile in reply and I went to the kitchen door. When I tried the handle, that too was locked, but I soon heard the key turn and Maxine pulled the door open.

She stood squarely in the doorway and looked down at me. 'You're back, are you?'

'I hope you got my message?'

'Only this morning when I discovered your bedroom was empty.'

She scowled, turned around and stepped back into the kitchen.

I climbed the steps and closed the door behind me. 'Sorry. I hope you weren't concerned?'

'Not my concern what you do, but I'd prefer to be kept properly informed.'

'I had a couple of drinks. I didn't expect to be offered a bed.'

'How generous of Evelyn,' Maxine hissed through barely parted lips.

'Was lovely to meet her, anyway. You're quite different, not least your professions,' I said, but their professions were possibly their least glaring difference.

Maxine continued stirring the pan which bubbled and gurgled on the hob. 'The only thing I have in common with my sister is that we share genes, live in the same county and have one son each. Other than that we share no common interests, and almost no conversation for the past decade.'

An aroma of spices and cooked meat filled the room. 'That smells good. Would you like me to take over?'

'No need, it's cooked. You can clean up. This is my own recipe and it usually lasts a few days.'

'Soup?'

'Yes, we'll have it for lunch. I've defrosted some crusty bread.'

'Lovely.'

Maxine turned off the gas and looked around. 'And how was my sister - well?'

'She seems to be. Marcus was there too. And she showed me some of her sculptures.'

Maxine sniffed. 'Not my kind of art, but it seems others don't agree.'

'I liked them. Not an art form I'm that familiar with. She's going to…' I broke off. I'd been about to mention Evelyn was going to make a sculpture of me, but realised how tactless that would be.

Almost as if she'd read my mind, Maxine said, 'Evelyn tried making one of me a while ago. Obviously thought she might sell it at an extortionate price to a fan or a gallery. But I got wind of what she was doing and put a stop to it.' She turned to face me. 'I hope you didn't see any naked figures of me down there?'

I shook my head. 'Not at all,' I replied quickly. 'I'm sure she respects your preference and privacy.'

I tried to picture a statue of Maxine in Evelyn's distinctive naturalistic style. But it was hard to imagine what Maxine's figure might look like unclothed as her attire gave little away. Although Maxine may have been a lot younger when Evelyn had begun to create it, I realised Maxine would never have willingly posed for the preliminary photographs as I had.

'I'm going for a quick shower,' I said. 'What time shall we eat?'

Maxine glanced at the clock on the wall. 'Twelve-thirty. As it's a pleasant day, we'll eat in the summerhouse.'

'Oh, yes, okay,' I said, and tried to summon some enthusiasm into my tone.

Adding salt to the soup, Maxine looked over her shoulder. 'And we can talk more about your book.'

'Fantastic!' No need to feign enthusiasm on that score.

An hour to shower and with Maxine occupied I could read a few more pages of her manuscript concealed in my wardrobe.

At least the bathroom was modernised and the strong water jets of the shower sprayed exquisitely sharp and hot over my skin. As I watched the soapy bubbles pool and swirl around the plughole, I reflected on my night at Evelyn's. Particularly posing for photographs, the mysterious flash of light through the window, talking late into the night with Marcus, and only hours ago watching the deer in the morning mist before falling into the welcome arms of sleep beside Marcus. Being so close with him physically had felt intensely romantic and intimate, but at the same time only hours later, quite surreal as if I might even have imagined it all.

I'd be seeing Marcus again in a few hours, and I felt excited at the thought. He seemed such a genuinely thoughtful and gentle man, and there could be no denying his intelligence, looks and fine physique.

I hadn't anticipated swimming during my stay here, but I found a crop top and a pair of cotton shorts that would do just as well. The lake water would be freezing so I'd take along a towel and a sweatshirt to warm up afterwards.

I blow-dried my hair then pulled my suitcase from the bottom of the wardrobe. When I registered that Maxine's manuscript was no longer beneath, I wondered for some moments if I'd hidden it elsewhere. I opened up the suitcase, all the drawers, reached onto the top shelf of the wardrobe, then looked under the bed to see if I'd placed it there. But no, the folder had gone. And there was only one person who could have taken it - Maxine.

201

Knowing I'd been caught prying where I shouldn't, my face grew hot with embarrassment, and I slumped onto the bed, wondering what I could say to explain why I'd taken her file and hidden it in my wardrobe. Maxine had obviously seen the loose page when she'd walked in unexpectedly yesterday. She must have been curious to know what I'd been reading and possibly recognised it as one of her printed pages, somehow.

'Shit!' I muttered under my breath. I could hardly deny taking and hiding it. Not that I'd had a chance to read many pages. But Maxine wouldn't know how much or little of it I'd read.

I should have driven home last night, read some more and returned the manuscript to its proper place on the shelf in the attic. Damn!

No wonder Maxine had locked me out and been frosty with me.

I'd come clean over lunch - I had no choice. At least I could say in all honesty that I had only read a few pages, although I'd keep to myself that I'd found it suspiciously revealing.

When I returned downstairs I felt sick with nerves - more so than I'd ever felt walking into a courtroom to speak in a client's defence. No, this was brought on because I'd been found out. I was guilty of snooping into the private property of a best-selling novelist, and one who'd generously invited me into her home to mentor my own writerly efforts.

When I found Maxine sitting at the kitchen table, I felt my cheeks simmer even before we exchanged any words.

Who would broach the subject first?

I watched Maxine pick up the knife and cut into the loaf of bread.

'Such a lovely day - it would be criminal not to take advantage of it.' She sounded surprisingly bright.

I ladled the gloopy brown soup into the bowls Maxine had set beside the hob, giving myself a smaller portion.

'Yes, lovely out,' I replied. 'I'll carry the tray.' I couldn't help but think that the steaming bowls of soup would be lukewarm by the time we'd traipsed all the way down there.

I stepped out onto the patio. 'Shall we lock up?'

'Yes, we don't want any intruders thinking they can nip in, snoop around and take what they damn well please.'

Was that an intentional reference to the manuscript in my wardrobe? Had to be.

Maxine locked the door behind her and slipped the key into her trouser pocket.

It wasn't easy walking down the slope with the laden tray - the bowls slipped and soup sloshed over the sides. And now that my nose was directly above the bowls I didn't much like the aroma. The chunks of meat swirled amongst diced carrots and peas and a greasy film had risen to the surface. Still, I'd have to eat some or risk appearing ungrateful and rude.

On the far side of the rock and as we approached the summerhouse, the nerves in my belly bubbled up like a hot spring and my heart began to thud to a quickened rhythm. I tried to calm my breaths. How ridiculous to be feeling this way. It was only a shed, and a pretty one from a distance. And Maxine was twice my age and just because she was a successful author and it was her home, it didn't mean I couldn't hold my own and be assertive.

I was an experienced lawyer, I reminded myself. But I didn't feel like a professional walking behind Maxine in my cutoff denim shorts and sandals, with my curls flopping about my face and obscuring my vision.

What would Maxine say about my book and why did we need to come down here to eat? We were supposed to be enjoying the sun, but as we walked into the shade beneath the trees and up the steps to the door, I felt a chill in the air and my skin prickled with goosebumps.

'Let's sit on the steps?' I suggested. 'We'll feel the sun that way.'

'No, dear, we'll sit at my desk,' she said, allowing no room for manoeuvre.

A shudder ran down my back as I waited for Maxine to find her key and unlock the door. I wished I'd brought my sweatshirt.

The bowls rattled on the tray - if I wasn't careful, she'd spot my hands shaking.

Maxine cleared away some papers to make space on the table and I set the tray down. We sat opposite one another and she offered the plate of bread. I took a slice and laid it on the side of my plate.

'Do you often eat down here?' I tried to sound upbeat and normal, but felt acutely aware of the tremor in my tone.

Maxine, however, didn't appear to notice my discomfort as she dipped a hunk of bread into her soup.

She peered at me over her glasses. 'Eat up, dear, then we'll talk shop.'

'We can talk now,' I offered.

The sooner we talked the sooner I could get out of here.

My belly churned but I lowered my spoon into the soup then raised it to my lips. How hard would it be to chew and swallow whilst feeling sick with worry? I opened my mouth and closed my lips over the spoon. The meaty broth and lumps spilled across my tongue and to avoid the flavour, I quickly chewed and swallowed. I inhaled a breath as the soup hit my stomach.

I lifted my eyes and looked across at Maxine who watched me.

Her eyebrows lifted. 'Good?'

I nodded and shifted in my seat. The small of my back felt damp with sweat.

'Mmm, you must share the recipe.' Jeez, I was a shit liar.

A rush of wind blew in followed by a sudden bang as the summerhouse door swung shut.

I jumped and my knees knocked against the table.

Maxine laughed with a sneer. 'Why so skittish?'

Oh, she was enjoying my discomfort.

'It was unexpected, that's all.'

Maxine cocked her head to one side, blinking several times in succession. 'I wanted to update you on where I've got to in your manuscript. I'm about a third of the way through - made many amendments and edits.'

'Oh, right,' I said. 'I know it still needs work.'

'But what I really wanted to ask you were two things...'

The mood in the room had shifted and my body tensed. 'Yes?'

'You said you read about this news story and found it interesting as a basis for a novel. But as I read it again I'm utterly convinced that you must know the main character - Johnny. He is described in far greater depth and for a female writer portraying a man that's a positive.'

I wasn't sure how to respond and I considered my words before replying.

'I'm glad he comes across as realistic. That was always my intention.'

A flare of light fell across her features. 'Uncanny, almost.'

I felt my heart judder. 'How?'

She seemed to be baiting me, interrogating me.

'Your said your father was a lawyer?'

'Yes, he passed away some years ago.' I lied again. 'But the character isn't based on my father, just because he's a lawyer.'

She peered over her glasses. 'Can I be honest with you?'

The meaty concoction rose in my throat; I didn't want to hear what was surely coming, trapped in this room. I glanced towards the closed door. Despite the sunny day the air inside felt chilled - unnaturally so. The cold clawed at my skin and I rubbed my hands up and down my arms to regain some warmth. My legs began to tremble beneath the desk.

Maxine continued. 'I used to know a man, a lawyer, very much like this monster in your story. He fits the mould like a glove. Okay, he has a different name and a different physicality.'

I saw by the glint in her eyes how much she was enjoying her finely prepared words.

I however, was not.

She waited for my response and as I deliberately slowed my breathing, I felt my vision sway.

'And do you know if the lawyer you knew personally was involved in this real life case at all?' I said it with more confidence than I felt. 'It's purely coincidence.' The moment the words came from my mouth I knew I shouldn't have spoken them.

Maxine shot me a sharp, unblinking look, 'I think we both know the answer to that.'

I shook my head. 'Nope. I've never met the lawyer involved in the real life story, and obviously neither do I know this lawyer friend of yours.'

The corner of her mouth twitched and her eyes flicked sideways. 'Are you quite certain of that?'

'Of course.' I squirmed inside. 'What was the name of your lawyer friend who reminded you of Johnny?'

She waved a dismissive hand. 'I don't recall his name,' she said, without any pretence of conviction.

Clearly, Maxine was sounding me out, unprepared to be forthcoming or honest with her own knowledge. I must assume there were details she'd leave unsaid - a human trait I'd learnt early on in my career.

Could she really suspect or know her ex-lawyer, my father, was the boyfriend of the girl who'd drowned? Yes, of course she could, and I only had my own writing and my naivety to blame.

I held her gaze. 'Other than the newspaper articles I read for research, I don't know what the lawyer was like personality-wise - he's purely fictional. But I've met many lawyers and understand the way they behave and talk.' I hoped my voice sounded confident and convincing.

Maxine tapped her pen on the desktop with irritation. 'Then I'll ask my next question.'

And again I knew precisely where she was going with her choreographed dance of words.

Strangely, I no longer felt chilled and my scalp prickled with heat and sensations that began to creep down the back of my neck to my shoulders. I scraped my hands through my hair, opening my armpits which felt damp with perspiration.

'Why did you take my manuscript from the attic?' She watched me, cold-eyed and silent, daring me to spin a lie into her spider's web.

Saliva filled my mouth and I felt droplets of sweat dampen my skin.

She tilted her head and her eyes probed like needles, 'Well?'

I kept my voice low and level. 'I went upstairs to check out where I might have to clean and when I came across the file I thought it might be interesting to read some of your unpublished writing. Was that okay?'

She leaned forwards, pressing her palms on the desk and her neck flushed red with angry blotches. 'No! Most certainly not okay. My writings are private unless published. How would you feel if you'd offered your time to read and edit *my* manuscript with virtually a free bed and board, and I then repaid you by snooping and reading your private journals?'

I mumbled, 'Sorry…' But my head began to swim and the room rotated, until I felt in danger of toppling off the chair.

I needed air. I had to get out.

'I only read two pages. And I was going to put it back…'

She scoffed with a cunning snarl on her lips. 'Two pages?'

'Yes, and it was compelling, which is why I wished to read more.'

The muscles in her jaw clenched and stood out like pulled cables. 'There will be no further opportunities to read it. I have locked the attic rooms as I can no longer trust you not to snoop.'

'Then I must leave your home.' I pushed back my chair and as I stood it felt as if the ceiling had dropped and the walls were closing in. I turned and stumbled to the door, twisted the handle and yanked it open. Barely able to remain upright I staggered down the steps onto the grass, dropped to my knees and with my head spinning, retched. I coughed, vomited and spat until my eyes streamed and the back of my throat stung.

I wiped my eyes and mouth with the back of my hands and when I refocused I saw Maxine's beige shoes and trouser legs. My eyes, still watering and blurred, travelled up to her face.

She looked down at me and shook her head. 'Do you enjoy drama?' But her words had a sympathetic tone.

Slowly I stood up and brushed my hair from my face and straightened down my clothes.

'If you'll give me my manuscript, I'll pack my bag, call a taxi and leave you in peace.'

Maxine put her hands up. 'There's no need for a rash exit. Come up to the kitchen for some water. And I trust it wasn't my cooking that made you vomit?'

'I'm hungover from too much wine and lack of sleep,' I said.

'Mmm, Evelyn always was a dreadful lush. No doubt she kept refilling your glass.'

'She didn't force any alcohol on me.'

In truth, I hadn't felt hungover, but I could hardly accuse Maxine or her homemade soup of causing my sickness.

No, my vomiting was a result of either being in that summerhouse with the door closed, Maxine's questioning and accusations, or what was in that revolting soup.

Despite still feeling queasy, I was no longer trembling or dripping in sweat.

'I really am sorry about reading those pages. I realise I should have asked first,' I said. 'Snooping isn't a habit of mine.'

But that wasn't true. I'd got myself into trouble before by stumbling upon things I shouldn't - not least when Dad had found me reading Maxine's book I'd discovered stashed away in our attic. But I was curious by nature and one of the reasons that becoming a lawyer had appealed to me, and now to become a writer.

What greater way was there to satisfy one's curiosity than to explore and express through people, words and language?

Maxine and I walked together back up the slope to the house, but this time Maxine carried the tray.

'You remind me of someone, Jodie,' Maxine said slowly as we walked.

I waited for her to say who, but she didn't. And I felt so ill at ease that I didn't ask. As far as she was concerned my surname was Rivera, not my father's surname, Anderson. Plus I'd said I was from Newcastle, not Bamburgh where my mother still lived and where my father had lived at the time he'd been Maxine's lawyer. One thing was certain, I needed to keep a track of what I'd told her, or not as the case may be. Maxine was too switched on to be fooled.

How close had my father and Maxine been before they fell out, I wondered? Some of the details in my manuscript had been specific to Dad and I hadn't for one moment expected Maxine to recognise it was him.

But Maxine was smart and I'd been naive. I should never have given her my manuscript and I certainly couldn't risk letting her know my relationship to her ex-lawyer.

No, it would be safer to pack and leave today, I thought as I sat at the kitchen table and sipped water. No one held a gun to my head. I was free to make the right judgement and leave today. And yet, Marcus was driving over later, and I really didn't want to miss going for our walk again. If the atmosphere didn't improve dramatically with Maxine I'd leave in the morning. I could continue working on my book at Mum's whilst applying for a new law position.

John had already assured me he'd write me a good reference - it was the least he could do for someone, his girlfriend, that he'd sacked because I discovered his affair with a junior colleague. If he didn't follow through as promised I'd damn well sue him for unfair dismissal.

Maxine poured the remainder of the soup into a plastic tub, sealed the lid and placed it in the fridge.

I pushed back my chair. 'I'll wash up.'

'Hmmm, if you're feeling well again there's plenty of other jobs you can get on with, too. My sheets and duvet need changing and the toilets need a good scrub.'

'Of course,' I said. 'I like to keep busy.' I felt hesitant to say that Marcus was coming over later. Not that I'd invite him in. Not unless Maxine asked me to, and I thought that unlikely.

I ran the dishcloth under the tap. 'Give me a shout if you think of anything else you need doing.'

Chapter 24

Crag Lough

When I pulled back Maxine's duvet and saw the sheets gathered in creases and scattered with bits of dirt and cat hair, I realised neither Maxine or her housekeeper changed the bedding regularly. Maxine had said the cat didn't come upstairs, and I'd barely seen it other than the occasional glimpse of it giving me the evil eye in passing, or slinking round the kitchen at mealtimes. As I was allergic I was grateful it hadn't come to me for affection - I doubted it got much from Maxine either, even if it did clamber onto her bed.

As I shook the duvet I glanced out of the window and saw Maxine carrying my purple manuscript folder down to the summerhouse. So, she still trusted me to be alone in the house. Or was she testing me? My paranoia intensified.

Both toilets took ages to clean thoroughly after which I headed down to the kitchen. My appetite had recovered and I opened the fridge and reached inside for the cheese and a jar of pickle. When I caught a whiff of Maxine's soup on the middle shelf I felt another wave of nausea. God only knew what she'd put in it. I closed the fridge and opened the back door and hungrily inhaled some fresh air.

Maxine and I might share an interest in writing, but our tastes in cuisine were an entirely different matter.

After eating my sandwich I still had an hour to kill before Marcus arrived. I headed upstairs to freshen up, then I packed a bag with a towel and a hairbrush. On the landing I glanced up the staircase to the attic rooms and paused in my step. I rested my hands on the bannister and peered down to the hallway. All seemed quiet and I placed my bag on the bottom step and crept up the stairs. Silently, I approached her old study, stopped and listened. She couldn't have returned from the summerhouse without me hearing and I tried the door handle. As promised, she'd locked it. I continued down the corridor to the room where I'd originally hidden her manuscript, and tried the handle. The door opened and I stepped inside. The floorboards creaked as I crossed to the window and I looked out over the tree tops and garden. I sensed a movement to my right and I jumped and turned abruptly.

When I saw my shadow move against the wall I heaved a breath and chided myself for being so keyed up. The windows were grimy and insect corpses with legs sticking up speckled the window sill. Ivy vines trailed over the window, but through them I saw the sky overhead was a bright cerulean blue, with a clear view up to Hadrian's Wall on the peak of the hill. In contrast a white mist hung over the trees and rock as far as the summerhouse in the dip beyond. From here the garden looked even more abandoned, untamed and mysterious. And what a treasure trove of flowers, insects and wildlife thrived down there in this utopia, half-way between cultivated garden and wilderness. No crows circled the treetops, and I heard none of their caws I'd grown accustomed to hearing - as a low but continuous background noise.

'A murder of crows,' I spoke aloud, wondering why anyone had thought up that peculiar collective noun. Did crows murder one another? I recalled more - a mischief of magpies, a murmuration of starlings, a parliament of rooks. Oh, and my favourite, and the one that always made us laugh at school - a booby of nuthatches.

I sniggered. Maybe I should become an ornithologist with my abundance of bird phrases, and if I didn't fulfil my aspiration of becoming a writer. The latter was probable, I realised, things were going badly with Maxine, and a sense of gloom descended over me.

Unlike my mood, no clouds hung in the sky and the patch of mist over the lower end of the garden seemed isolated, which I assumed was a result of evaporating dew and water from the stream.

The garden had a dream-like, unreal quality, and a feeling - a sensation that the view from this exact window was familiar grew inside my mind. I rubbed my eyes and blinked to clear my vision then with the tip of my nose to the glass I peered at the trees - tall, pale and ghostlike. My gaze dropped to the tree swing and I tried to imagine the last time someone had swung on it. Surely not for years or since Hadrian was a boy. A sense of deja vu rushed through me so fast it felt like vertigo, arousing sensations similar to my first walk up the lane to The Blue House, and the same disorientating feelings I'd experienced stepping into the summerhouse.

I wondered if my coming here had been fated, somehow, and that my standing looking out from this window had always been an inevitable part of my future. And if that was so, then it applied to whatever might happen over the next few days, too. My future had already been decided long ago - a shadow bound to me, watchful and hovering from close behind. I pressed my palms upon the windowsill, icy cold against my skin, and I shivered.

I moved my hands away and straightened my back and shoulders.

My mind played tricks on me - confusing and toying with me until I no longer saw clearly what was real and in front of me. And yet I sensed that something from the recesses of my memory was breaking through to my present day. But what and why? There could be no such thing as a future already written. No, it was I who decided where I went, and what I did or didn't do.

I was aware that new experiences and stressful situations could do strange things to blur our perception and our rational mind. But despite the trauma of my childhood that I still struggled with, I wasn't one to shy away from new experiences. My therapist once advised that facing our demons worked wonders to challenge and overcome them, and she was right. I was still young and not prepared to allow my father's cruelty to darken my future, more than he already had my childhood.

I would not be one of his victims.

One of the reasons I felt compelled to write creatively, and most of all during the writing of my novel about the drowned girl and my father's relationship with her, was the relief and catharsis it offered. Often as I wrote it felt as if I were living another life, and with this came a lightness of being that not only distanced me from the pain of my past but enabled me to delve deep into it as though I moved through it again, but with a strength and understanding I hadn't possessed at the time.

In the garden below, a figure emerged slowly from the mist - Maxine returning so soon. Startled, I jumped back from the window, lest she spotted me here, and I dashed across the floor and onto the landing, closing the door behind me. If Maxine knew I'd been up here again, she'd be fuming and I couldn't face more run-ins with her. The atmosphere between us was awkward enough already.

I ran down the stairs, grabbed my swim bag and strode back across the landing and into my bedroom. A minute later I heard Maxine plodding up the stairs. Thankfully, she didn't move quietly around the house so I could always pinpoint where she was if she wasn't sitting quietly.

Knocks at the front door echoed through the house. It had to be Marcus. I checked my watch - a minute past four.

As I headed out with my bag over my shoulder, Maxine stepped out of the bathroom.

'I'm not expecting anyone. Are you?'

'Yes, Marcus has invited me on a walk.'

'Marcus is here?' Her tone was sharp.

'I'm assuming it's him,' I said. 'I'll be out an hour or so.'

'Why didn't you mention him coming before - this is my home after all?'

'Sorry, but I didn't think it was important you know.'

'Really, Jodie. For a lawyer and someone supposedly intelligent, you are lacking in common courtesy.'

'Like I said, I'm sorry.' I tried to keep my face composed and hide my annoyance at being spoken to like a naughty child.

The door knocker sounded again.

'I'll take a key with me.'

'Fine, but don't lose it! And if you don't mind, please return alone?'

It wasn't a question, but an instruction.

'Of course. I had no intention of inviting Marcus back.'

'Go on, or he'll be coming round the back.' She waved her hand to shoo me along.

I jogged down the stairs and across the hallway. Just as I turned the key in the door, the bell rang again.

I opened it wide.

Marcus smiled.

'I was upstairs,' I said, sounding breathless.

'I was beginning to think you'd changed your mind,' he said.

I laughed, leaned forward, and said quietly. 'Far from it. I could really do with getting out.'

The late afternoon rays picked out the sheen and colour of his curls and for a moment I saw my reflection in his sunglasses. I looked different - older. Marcus lifted his glasses onto his head and smiled again. He really had the widest and most infectious smile of any man I'd met in a long time. Not a hint of the macho moodiness I seemed to bring out in some men, or in Maxine's unsmiling coldness. Even when she did attempt a smile I don't think she'd once shown her teeth.

'I've not had the easiest of afternoons.'

He nodded his head towards the lane. 'Let's go and you can tell me all about it.'

I remembered Maxine's words - *"Don't be talking about me to Evelyn or Marcus."*

'I don't want to bore you.'

'Whatever suits you. I'm a good listener, though.'

I closed the front door and we set off down the drive. Marcus had parked his mini on the verge and he opened the boot and pulled out a picnic hamper and a red tartan blanket. He draped the blanket over his shoulder and with the hamper in hand we set off up the lane. Where the lane veered left, we crossed the road to a small turnstile gate.

Once through the turnstile Marcus turned and looked down at my feet. 'It's quite uneven up the hill. Better watch your ankles.'

'Will do. As long as we don't have any sudden storms and lightning bolts I'll be fine.'

'Ahh, the storm I fortunately, or unfortunately missed.'

'I told you about the lightning splitting that tree on the ridge? Weirdly, I feel now I might have even imagined it.'

'Yes, and you didn't imagine it. I saw the wreckage myself this morning. I wish I'd been there to witness it too.'

I hadn't mentioned that the only reason I'd been on the ridge was because I was running away from his cousin. That detail might not go down so well.

Marcus was right - the footpath was uneven and rocky up the short but steep incline, and more than once I almost lost my balance when loose stones slipped beneath my feet. Marcus was like a mountain goat, and because he knew the route he nimbly negotiated the rocks and stones ahead of me.

'Much easier from now on.' He paused and stood gazing out across the plateau, his cheeks radiant in the afternoon sun. 'Up here it's the sheep path, narrow but relatively even.' He pointed down over the ridge to a lake about a mile across the plateaued moorland. 'Can you see the boathouse on the far side?'

I shielded my eyes against the glare of the sun lowering over the land and water. 'Oh, yes.'

'There's a jetty to sit on, and if you feel like it, we can swim.'

'I've come prepared,' I said. 'And I'm feeling brave, and hot.'

Strands of his hair danced around his head. 'It'll be fun.'

We continued walking.

'Mum's started the preliminary drawings for your sculpture.'

'That's quick.' I wondered if Marcus had seen any photos.

As if he'd read my mind he said, 'Don't worry, Mum won't leave your photos or sketches lying around her studio. She keeps them all in a folder.'

'I suppose I wouldn't have posed if I wasn't happy for her to use them. But I'm glad she's discreet.'

'She is. She totally understands what she's sculpting is someone in their most natural state, but equally, their most honest and vulnerable.'

'I really like your mum. You're lucky.'

'I am. I maybe don't tell her enough.'

'Who does with their parents? We take them for granted.'

'And what about Maxine? How's it going being the new temp housekeeper?'

I grimaced. 'She's no slave driver in that respect, and I'm glad I'm doing most of the cooking after sampling her soup at lunchtime.'

He laughed. 'Grim?'

'Worse than grim. I threw up.'

'Bloody hell!' He guffawed. 'Sorry - not funny. Does Maxine know?'

215

'In hindsight it was pretty hilarious. And yes, she was right there when I puked. I blamed it on last night's booze.'

He sniggered. 'Yes, well I really enjoyed last night. I hope you did too.'

I turned to him. 'So much. I loved it.'

He smiled and his eyes became strangely bright. 'I'm pleased.'

And in that one mesmerising glance and moment it struck me precisely who Marcus reminded me of. Not Evelyn especially, but his uncle Winston on his wedding day to Maxine - the framed photograph on the wall in the orangery, in which Winston was clean shaven, and of course, the slightly disguised bearded sculpture in Evelyn's studio. How blindingly obvious, I thought, and Evelyn had even placed Winston between the two sculptures of their son, Marcus. If my suspicions were correct.

Without speaking I considered his face - the wide mouth, the curve of his jaw, the slope of his forehead, but most of all, his eyes.

'You all right? You look like you've seen a ghost,' he said with a nervous laugh.

I blinked. 'Sorry, was I staring?'

He nodded, and looked straight back at me. 'I was beginning to wonder if I had something on my nose.'

Feeling embarrassed, I looked away. 'I do stare when I'm lost in thought. Ignore me.'

We walked along the ridge in companionable silence and took in the views that stretched for miles on both sides. The distant hills rose up in shades of blue and grey beneath the afternoon sun. Nearer, the moorland was criss-crossed with farm tracks, stone walls and footpaths, and in between cows and sheep dotted the grassland. The sky above and the land surrounding us appeared soft and tranquil, despite the rugged terrain beneath our feet. Here, wild nature and farmland lived in harmony.

I thought about the sculptures in Evelyn's studio. Surely if I saw the resemblance of Marcus to Winston, then Maxine did too? Was it a dark family secret that caused the irreparable rift between the sisters? And did Marcus know or suspect who his father was? That's if it wasn't pure coincidence that Marcus had no father at home but who happened to hold an uncanny resemblance to his uncle, and especially in those wide, distinctive eyes.

And Hadrian, I thought - he looked nothing like his named father, Winston.

Most families had their skeletons, and mine was no different. I thought about Dad and what he might be doing now. He'd reached retirement age. Did he look old and grey with a middle aged spread, or was he still trim and good looking? Not that his looks made him a better person - no, he was a despicable monster and I had no wish to see him again, ever. I was glad I'd broken all ties, and in name, too.

'Marcus?' I said.

'Uh huh?' he replied.

'At the talk Maxine mentioned she'd written a new book. You don't have any idea what it's about do you? Only she's not hinted at any and I've seen no evidence of her working on a new one.'

He tutted. 'That's because I don't believe she has written one. Previously her books were written in a year and published months later. That's consistently been her pattern. How long since her last published novel - five years? Totally out of keeping with her career. Not that she needs the money or to prove anything to anyone. If she wanted to retire she'd never have to worry about income.'

'But she did say she'd written something, and most writers never want to stop, from what I understand. They only give up because they have no choice.'

'You mean dying?'

'I guess,' I replied. 'Or illness.'

'Interesting.' He paused. 'Better watch out she doesn't want to keep hold of yours, especially as it's a crime novel.' He laughed.

I laughed too. 'I doubt it would be up to her standards, so it's unlikely.'

He scrunched his nose. 'But she is editing it…'

'True.' I laughed again.

'You think it's impossible?' he said, lifting his brows.

'It would be criminal, plus she's a brilliant writer. She doesn't need my amateur efforts.'

'Unless, she's lost her mojo, her fire, her drive to create.'

'You're kidding me, right?'

'Yeah, would probably be too underhand, even for Maxine.'

'Actually, I've found a manuscript of a book she hasn't published. Appeared to be written some time ago.'

The path dipped to where some steps crossed over the wall.

Marcus turned to me. 'Is that so?'

'Yep.'

'Did you read any of it?'

'Only got chance to read a page or two. But what I read intrigued me.'

Marcus climbed the wall ladder and spoke over his shoulder. 'In what way?'

'I'm not sure, but I got the distinct feeling that where she was going was autobiographical, in a way that none of her published novels could have been. The opening chapter was a court scene building up to a crime.'

He looked down from the top of the wall. 'Why didn't you read it all?'

I gripped the handrail and climbed the steps. 'Mmmm, that's a whole other story,' I said. 'Caught in the act, so to speak.'

'Blimey, Jodie. Must have been awkward,' he said, descending the other side.

I looked down at Marcus. 'Like swallowing glass. The confrontation - that was just prior to my throwing up her soup. I offered to leave. Felt like a sneaky thief.'

'But Maxine didn't want you to go?'

I shook my head and climbed down. 'She must be quite forgiving.' I jumped down the bottom two steps and landed beside Marcus.

He looked doubtful. 'Maxine, forgiving?'

A mobile phone rang.

'Is that yours or mine?' I said, and rummaged in my shoulder bag.

'I think mine.' Marcus pulled his rucksack off his back and reached inside for his phone. 'Hi.' He walked a few yards off the path amongst the heather.

I caught some of his words, but he tried to keep his voice low.

'Look, I'll call you tomorrow...'

He turned around and grimaced. 'Oh dear. She hung up.'

'Who was it?'

'Fiona, the ex I told you about. Somehow she heard I'd spent the night at Mum's with a woman and was meeting her today for a walk.'

'Not happy?' I said.

'More like furious. She refused to say who told her. What sort of person tries to shit-stir like this? And who the hell knew other than me? Mum, Philip?'

Of course, Maxine knew, but why would she care to stir up trouble. Unless she'd mentioned it to Hadrian.

'A jealous one with a grudge against either you or me. I'm sorry. I appear to be causing trouble wherever I go recently.'

'No, you've done nothing wrong,' he reassured.

'I brought my phone too. People can ring us anytime they want. It's both a blessing and a curse.'

'I often carry mine, too, but sometimes I wonder why.'

'Maybe you should turn it off?' I suggested.

'Now that's an idea,' he said, and pressed the off button on his phone.

'I will too.' I retrieved my phone and powered it off.

'I don't like being on call twenty-four hours a day. Sometimes we need privacy, from work, friends, and angry exes.'

'Totally agree. And especially on a lovely evening.' I looked at my watch. Not even five, so hours until nightfall and the sun still felt blissfully warm on my arms and face.

It took us another twenty minutes following the sheep path to reach the nearside of the lake.

'Is this Crag Lough?' I asked.

'Yes, how did you know its name?'

I thought for a moment. 'Because this is the lake that features in my novel. It's where the missing girl's drowned body was found.'

'What? In real life?'

I nodded. 'I based my book on a true story, loosely. But I haven't set the story up here and so the fictional lake is elsewhere with a different name.'

'Have you walked here before?'

'Only with my family when I was little. I only remember because Dad took a few photos at the time and Mum labelled them up in an album.'

'I bet you were a cute kid,' he said.

I smiled. 'I was kinda chubby.'

'Hard to imagine that,' he said.

'We change when we grow up. I got into keeping fit, and I had a few unkind comments, so I guess I wanted to show them.' What I didn't mention was that it had been Dad who'd made the snide comments about my chubby thighs and cheeks.

'Well, you look amazing now.'

'Thanks, Marcus. I always accept a genuine compliment.'

'So, if scenes in your novel happened here - fictionally speaking.' He swept his hand in front of him, 'This could be extra research?'

'Yeah, I'm still refining the details.'

'Have you brought a camera along?'

'I didn't think to.'

'Me neither,' he said. 'We'll use our eyes to gather sights and memories.'

'Definitely,' I replied, and as I followed him I tried to drag my eyes away from his bottom and long muscular legs.

I turned and gazed across the lake to the boathouse. 'Who owns the boathouse?'

'No idea. A wealthy landowner, I imagine.'

'They won't mind us going on the jetty?'

'Nah, I've been down to swim before. Rarely see anyone other than a walker or two.'

I stopped and turned to look back at the crag. 'Quite an impressive sight, isn't it?'

'It is. Why so many people are drawn to the area, and it's why the Romans built their wall along a magnificent natural boundary.'

Marcus continued along the path and as I followed I spotted the silhouette of a figure up on the wall. I squinted against the sun. He appeared to be standing on top of the wall with legs slightly apart, shadowy and completely still. I got the strangest sensation he was watching me watching him. I stopped. And stranger to me still, was a familiarity in their build and stance.

How was that possible from such a distance?

'Are you coming?'

I glanced back at Marcus. 'Yes, sorry.'

'What've you seen?' Marcus asked.

I turned back and shielded my eyes from the sun's rays. 'There's a man on the wall.'

Marcus followed my gaze. 'Where?'

I scanned the ridge left and right. 'I didn't imagine him.'

'He must have jumped.'

'What?' I asked, alarmed.

'Back onto the path, obviously.'

'Christ! I thought you meant he'd jumped to his death.'

Marcus walked back to where I stood, eyes still directed at the ridge on the cliff. 'I wouldn't joke about that sort of thing. But it has happened.'

I searched his eyes. 'I'm sorry, your Uncle Winston?'

He nodded. 'It is possible he jumped deliberately.'

'I know you wouldn't joke about such things,' I spoke softly. 'But what if the man I saw did jump? He disappeared in an instant.'

Marcus straightened up and shielded his eyes. 'He won't have jumped this way.'

'But why stand on the wall? It can't be safe.'

'I didn't see him, but anyone up there will only have been after a better view. Plus, on that stretch there are a few feet on this side of the wall before the cliff drops away. He'd have had to have jumped off the wall and then jumped again.'

I let out a breath. 'Ignore me - I'm being paranoid.'

'It isn't paranoia to worry about someone and their safety.'

But in truth, it hadn't only been their safety I was concerned about.

The moment passed and we continued on.

'So you run, do you?' asked Marcus.

'Yes, only a few kilometres, sometimes ten or so. It clears my head and I always sleep well.'

'You don't fancy a marathon then?'

I laughed. 'Oddly, not at all. Never been competitive or into challenging myself that way.'

The sheep path curved to the right and passed near to the water's edge, where the water looked still and deep beyond the rocks and reeds.

'How deep is it?' I asked.

'Deep, I reckon. You can't touch the bottom once you're more than a few feet in. Rocky as well, so you can only jump in certain places.'

'I was thinking I'd do more of a gentle drop in from the jetty.'

'Conveniently, there's a ladder.'

'Even better,' I said.

The water looked inviting - a gleaming silver disc beneath the afternoon sun, and the sky overhead shimmered and glowed with a gauzy haze. As we neared the boathouse I saw it was a simple three walled structure with no doors and no boat inside either. It had a dilapidated feel with planks missing from the walls, and a rusty corrugated roof. In contrast, the jetty was in good repair, recently renovated and wood stained. We walked to the end of the jetty and Marcus laid out the blanket and hamper. Inside the hamper, all neatly in place, were two sets of cutlery, plates, and wine glasses. And nestled inside, a bottle of sparkling wine, tub of grapes, chicken drumsticks, crusty bread and hard-boiled eggs.'

'How lovely! A proper hamper,' I exclaimed.

He reached for the glasses. 'Are you hungry?'

'Absolutely ravenous.' My belly had been rumbling for the past hour or so.

I pulled out two plates and placed them on the blanket whilst Marcus untwisted the wire around the bottle top and popped the cork. I watched the cork fly in an arch over the water before plopping onto the surface and making the water ripple. The ripples spread outwards across the water - on and on, seeming to reach the far side. As I watched, mesmerised by the patterns in the water, a thought came to mind. The silhouette of the man on the wall - the reason he seemed familiar was because in shape and proportion he could have been my father. It was as if he'd followed me here - his memory, anyway. Tall and well-built, and so often as I'd seen him, standing squarely and watching me and my brother. Watching and waiting to catch one of us doing something he didn't approve of. Dad had a knack of always making me anxious and fidgety. He was too quick to pass comments and judge me, however harmless an activity - whether watching TV, reading a book, writing my homework, sucking on a straw, or eating my dinner.

"Don't eat with your mouth full...Slow down, it's not a race...Don't fold the corners of your pages over - use a bookmark...Are you deaf? Turn that volume down! You should watch something educational..."

Other than the more obvious and traumatic physical assaults, those were the things I remember about him. Not in the least like Mum who would counteract his aggression by being sympathetic, gentle and understanding, and by giving me freedom to do what I wanted when he was away or at work. I'd sometimes wonder how much Mum saw or was appalled by his treatment of me and David. Why didn't she tackle him or put a stop to it, or at least try to?

If I'd had two parents like Dad God knows what sort of an emotional wreck I'd be now.

Marcus picked up a glass. 'Vino?

'Lovely, thanks,' I replied.

I took the glass and sipped. Still nicely chilled, given the warmth of the day.

It seemed my past had come to haunt me - my father had come to haunt me. For years I'd tried my hardest to forget him and what he'd done to me, but the old wounds of memory refused to heal.

Of course whoever was on the wall can't have been Dad, but this spot, Crag Lough, was where an important event in his life had occurred. Although that mystery had never been solved, Dad, as Sheila's boyfriend, had been considered a suspect for a while. But even as I'd researched and written the story based on her death, I hadn't been able to get to the bottom of it. Hardly surprising given the police investigation had failed to. It was too long ago and I'd found no additional evidence, other than knowing the truth of what my father was really like as a man. But in my fictional story, and in my mind, I'd concluded that the young woman's boyfriend, the character based on my father, had been responsible for her drowning. I felt no guilt writing my story to exorcise my father's ghost - to feel fractured with each memory, to weep as I wrote and to repair the tears in my heart.

In truth, I'd known from the moment I began writing that casting Dad as the murderer had been a risk. If Maxine recognised the news story, so would Mum, if and when she read it. And if Dad ever read it, he'd immediately know I'd implicated him as the guilty party. Not that I cared a damn what he thought - he deserved all the bad feeling and fear of being found guilty, fictional or otherwise, that I could throw his way.

'Are you someplace else?' asked Marcus.

I blinked and turned to him. 'I was for a minute. But I shouldn't be.'

He gave a genial smile. 'I'm glad you're relaxed.'

'It's gorgeous - thanks for bringing me here.'

And as we sipped our wine and talked, I started to relax and to put aside my book and the bad memories.

Marcus stood up and I wondered if he was going to suggest a swim, but I watched as he walked back up the jetty and off the path towards a thicket of trees. He appeared to be searching for something before he crouched down.

He stood up and gestured for me to join him. 'Come and see.'

I headed across and joined him, and when I looked down I realised why he'd invited me over.

I gasped. 'Wild strawberries!'

We crouched amongst clusters of bright red berries which glistened in the evening light.

'I'm surprised the wildlife haven't nibbled them all,' I said.

'Lucky timing,' he said, and plucked two plump strawberries and placed them in his palm.

He offered his hand.

I took one and held it up. 'It's perfect.'

'Wait til you taste it.' He lifted his eyebrows, and popped the other strawberry into his mouth.

He closed his lips around the strawberry.

When I popped the strawberry into my mouth and bit into it, the sweetest and juiciest flavours burst across my tongue. My saliva buds exploded into life.

He watched me with a glint in his eye. 'Nice?'

'Unbelievable!' I swallowed and sighed. 'Why do they taste so much more strawberryish than shop bought?'

'Even more so than those you pick in strawberry fields,' he said.

'I reckon so,' I said, trying to recall the last time I'd done that.

He reached down and picked two more.

'Here we go.' He lifted one to my lips.

My insides fluttered as I opened my mouth and he placed the strawberry on my tongue. His fingers brushed my lips and a warm and sensual feeling skittered through me.

In silence we ate more, savouring the sweet berries, our eyes meeting every now and then. He really had the most beautiful eyes - wide set and the palest grey.

'I feel I should leave a few for the rabbits and squirrels to enjoy,' I said.

He picked another. 'Very generous.'

I stood up and stretched my back and shoulders. 'Shall we swim? If the sun sets, I might wimp out.'

'You mean when the sun sets,' he laughed. 'It'll be just as cold, either way.'

Back at the jetty I finished my second glass of wine. 'Dutch courage needed.'

Marcus picked up the bottle, took a long swig and handed it to me.

'That's more like it.' I gulped back some mouthfuls.

Marcus unbuttoned his shorts and let them fall to the floor. I couldn't resist taking a sneaky look to admire his trim waist and broad chest as he pulled his T-shirt over his head and stood there in his swimming trunks. The hairs on his chest were so much darker than the chestnut hair, swept back from his face. I wondered if the Roman soldiers had come down here to bathe, and thought how Marcus would have blended in perfectly.

I felt a little self-conscious and I turned around and undid the buttons on my blouse. Then I pulled down the side zip on my skirt and let it slip down onto the blanket. When I turned back Marcus averted his eyes to the water. It felt like a curious ritual - me watching him and him watching me. My eyes followed him as he walked to the end of the jetty. It came as no surprise that his physique was exactly as Evelyn had sculpted him. Long limbs, not overly muscular but well-defined. Paler skinned than me, and I noticed tan marks where the sun had caught his exposed skin. My breathing quickened as I joined him and I wondered if this was the effect Marcus was having on me or the anticipation of swimming in the freezing water.

He scraped a hand slowly through his hair then turned to me and smiled.

'I usually swim to that rock jutting up over there.' He pointed left. 'I know there are no shallow rocks if we head that way. Okay?'

I nodded and looked out across the water and at the sunlight shimmering and dancing pirouettes upon the surface. 'How deep is it here?'

'Twelve feet or so and free of rocks,' he replied.

'Here we go then!'

I took a breath and leapt off the jetty. The chill of the water engulfed me and for a few moments my eyes searched the black water, until I kicked my feet and bobbed back to the surface. I gasped a breath and swivelled round to face the jetty. The jetty was empty and moments later Marcus' head popped up a few feet away.

'You've done this before!' He laughed.

I swirled my arms and legs to tread water. 'Here is a definite first.' I drew in some breaths. 'Christ Almighty, it's icy.'

'Better get moving,' he said.

From the water, the rock looked quite a distance.

We swam breaststroke at a steady pace until we neared the rocks at the far edge.

'It feels warmer in the shallows,' I said.

'Like a hot spring,' he turned to me and we both laughed. 'Go steady - there are some sharp rocks here.'

I saw reeds below and I felt stones and gravel beneath my feet. Marcus scrambled onto the rock then turned and held out his hand. I grabbed hold and clambered up beside him.

I squeezed the water from my hair. 'So this is what wild swimming is all about?'

'Sure is, and beats an indoor pool and excited kids.'

The air felt cold upon my skin and I shivered.

Marcus turned to me, and without inhibition put his arm around me and pulled me close. 'Come here and we'll shiver together.'

I turned to face him and laughed. 'How come you feel so warm?'

'Maybe I'm used to the cold.'

I rested my head on his shoulder and it felt such an easy and natural thing to do. As I gazed out across the water, and with our closeness and his skin against mine, my teeth stopped chattering and my breathing slowed. The water rippled in the breeze and I felt mesmerised by the tiny undulations. Sheila, the young woman who drowned here, came to mind. She'd been a dark haired beauty and by all accounts a strong swimmer. But in the few photos I'd seen of her she'd looked petite and delicate. The chill of the water could easily have overcome her had she tried to swim right across the lake. But had that been her intention - and had she been fleeing from someone? Her body had eventually been found bloated and decomposed towards the far side, but her body may have drifted from any point where she'd initially drowned.

We'd swum close to the edge, but I wouldn't feel safe swimming far out and alone. Had Sheila really come here alone that day? Not in the version I'd written based upon my own theories and speculations.

I felt Marcus' hand move down my arm, warm and firm. 'Shall we swim back or would you rather walk round?'

'Let's swim. It's writing research, remember?'

'Fun too, I hope,' he said.

I felt his breath warm on my cheeks and my eyes lowered to his lips - strawberry red and wide, with a prominent cupid's bow. His face was only inches from mine and when I sensed him move closer I did the same. His lips met mine and I closed my eyes as we kissed tenderly.

When I felt his hand on the back of my head and his fingers trailed through my wet hair, the nerve endings on my scalp and neck tingled with yearning. Instinctually, I moved closer until my thigh pressed against his and the touch of my skin upon his stirred sensations that flickered like fireflies through my blood. My body cleaved to his and I heard the softest moans.

Still kissing, I pulled my top up over my arms and we drew apart and he lifted it over my head and threw it behind him. Side by side we wriggled out of our shorts.

My eyes moved from his mouth down his chest and further to between his thighs. I felt a hunger to be closer and I pressed my lips to his once more. With his hands around my waist he urged me to sit astride him and as our kisses grew more urgent he cradled my breast and brushed my nipple.

'Are you sure?' I said.

'Are you sure?' he replied, and his eyes blinked and shone in the setting sun.

I nodded.

He cupped my cheek and his eyes locked with mine. 'I was drawn to you from the moment I spotted you in the audience.' He pulled me closer still. 'And when you lay beside me in bed this morning, how I stopped myself from taking you into my arms and kissing you I'll never know.' With the softest caress his hand moved round to the back of my neck and we kissed again.

In that moment I was lost to him, and the great expanse of land and sky around us shrank to the rock upon which our hearts and minds joined.

Our breaths quickened and desire stirred me deep inside, and when I looked into his pupils - coal-black and wide, I saw my own, unrecognisable reflection - impassioned, fervid and free. I'd left behind the girl from my past and become a woman unconstrained - who knew her worth, and most of all, was finally released from her father's cruelty.

When I opened my eyes and looked over Marcus' shoulder I knew without any shred of doubt, that this was the spot where Sheila had perished. And I sensed too, the presence of another close by - a man known to her, but his image remained obscured by the passage of time.

I closed my eyes, shut out the past, and with a desperate yearning to be close, I leaned into him - to the warmth of his mouth and tongue and the heat of his limbs entwined with mine.

Intense pleasure cascaded through my every nerve and cell. I felt as if I'd been journeying towards this moment here with Marcus my entire life, while at the same time knowing this moment would pass, with no knowledge of where it would lead.

I only knew it was happening here and now. And when I threw my head back and called out his name, Marcus cried out too.

We clasped one another as our breaths came together, and our hearts slowed and beat in rhythm.

'Be mine, Jodie,' Marcus whispered close to my ear.

'I'll always be yours,' I replied, and pressed my lips to his.

The final rays of sun slipped like a cloak down my back and the crisp evening air took its place. We remained there, blissfully relaxed in one another's arms and I rested my cheek upon his chest. The sounds of water lapping gently against the bank merged with our breaths, and the breeze that rustled the reeds comforted like a blanket in our lakeside bed.

In my peripheral vision I sensed a movement beyond the heather, amongst the trees. A shadow passed between a clearing in the trees and disappeared behind bushes. A deer, I thought, like the ones we'd seen that morning.

Marcus stroked the back of my hand, turned to me and smiled. 'I didn't expect this.'

'I know you didn't.'

'But I'm glad.' He paused. 'No, far more than glad.'

I nodded and nestled close. 'Me too.'

'Are you cold?' he asked. 'We should dress.'

'We should. Someone might see us.' I giggled.

'Bit late for that.' He laughed. 'Anyway, no one comes down here.'

'Do you want to know something strange?' I asked.

'You bet, the stranger the better,' he said, and smiled.

'It's more like strange things I've been experiencing.'

His brow crinkled. 'Today?'

'Not only today, but since I arrived in Hexham, and especially at Maxine's.'

He wrapped his arm around me. 'You're shivering.'

'Well we are naked.'

'My aunt is quite strange.'

'I don't know, Marcus. I think it's more than that.'

'What sort of strange things?'

I thought for a minute. 'I imagine I'm seeing people - flashing lights, peculiar smells that come and go, the swing in Maxine's garden swinging on its own. And the crows in the trees - I'm sure they're watching me.'

'Those crows never shut up.'

'And I keep experiencing deja vu - like I've been here, seen everything here before.'

'Your book is about the area though, so your imagination is probably all stirred up and working in overdrive.'

'Possibly, yes.' I paused. 'I ate space cakes that night after Maxine's talk. I'm wondering if there was something in those. Or the chemicals have disturbed and triggered long forgotten memories.'

'Could be if there was something other than hash in them. Where did you get them?'

'Some students I shared the dorm with. They seemed trustworthy.'

'Difficult to know then,' he said.

'We were in the pub in town on Saturday night, when I saw you with your ex, Fiona. I imagined she was your current girlfriend.'

'Ahh. That could have been confusing when I'd asked if we could meet up.'

'It was.' I didn't want to mention the things Hadrian had said about Marcus.

'If you feel worried at Maxine's at any time, ring me. Night or day. I'll give you my home number too.'

'Thanks. I'm only staying until she's finished editing my book. I shan't hang around after that.'

He nodded. 'Sensible. Are you okay to swim back?'

I looked up at the crag and the line of the wall where the sky had turned burnished orange, and blood red streaks spread out like the wings of a phoenix taking flight.

I reached for my top and shorts. 'I'm up for another swim.'

We struggled into our wet swimwear. My body shook and my teeth chattered but I felt determined to swim back.

'It won't feel as cold this time,' he said as he stepped into the shallows.

I laughed. 'You're just saying that.'

He reached out and I took his hand.

'Your hand is so warm,' I said.

'Sure you want to swim?' he asked again.

'Yes.' But in truth, if he'd said he preferred to walk back around the edge, I'd have been relieved. I stepped into the shallows and gasped as the icy water rose over my hips and waist.

There was nothing for it but to dive in and race back to the jetty. That would warm us up. I stretched out my arms and plunged forwards as Marcus did the same. We set off at a steady breaststroke.

'It feels colder,' I gasped through chattering teeth.

'Kick your legs. Take lungfuls of air,' he said.

Every other stroke, Marcus dipped his head beneath the water but I swam turtle style with my eyes fixed firmly on the jetty a few hundred yards away. With every stroke the water grew colder and the distance between me and the jetty seemed to lengthen. Marcus had taken the lead but my limbs were slowing - dragging behind. I renewed my effort but my legs felt numb and heavier the harder I kicked. The gap between Marcus and me widened and I opened my mouth to call for him to wait. I felt out of my depth. I didn't want to swim alone. Something brushed against my toes. A reed or a fish? Whatever it was brushed my foot again, but this time it wrapped around my ankle and I jerked my foot to shake it off. But its grip only seemed to tighten, and so much so that it felt more like long fingers and the grip of a palm and nails clasping my skin - its weight holding me back. I opened my mouth to scream but before any sound could emerge, water filled my mouth and nostrils. I choked and spat. Whatever held my ankle began to drag and pull, until my head was fully submerged. I couldn't shake its hold on me.

All was ink-black beneath the surface and I could see little other than the dimmest light overhead. But the surface grew more distant with each second. Water consumed my nostrils, mouth and throat, and in reflex I swallowed to empty my mouth so that I might take a breath. Oh God, no, I must free myself. I twisted and wrestled against the drag of the weight and turned to see what held me fast.

What I saw filled me with terror. An image so horrifying it will never leave me. It was no river weed clasping my ankle, but a hand, long fingered and waxen white, and down in the depths, an arm, and beyond that I saw nothing other than murky black water swirling in motion to hold me hostage. I kicked again and struggled against the hand's vice-like grip, but I only sank deeper into the whirlpool until the water pressed against my chest and squeezed what little air remained in my lungs. The strength in my limbs faded fast, and my every kick and twist grew weaker than the last. I was falling, drowning - helpless against this monster, this creature of the depths, transporting me to my inevitable death.

Without breath, the oxygen in my blood had gone, and without the strength to fight, exhaustion consumed me as water flooded my airways. The light from above blackened and a strange calm came over me as my vision faded and the arms of death embraced me.

But amidst this transition between life and death, my silent voice whispered for mercy, *I don't want to die, not here, not today.*

And then something bumped into me, someone was beside me. I was sinking blindly but hands grabbed my arms and hauled me from whatever clutched my foot.

My ankle came free and I was suspended in the swirling black water - rotating slowly, neither sinking or rising. The obsidian murk of the water lightened until moments later I was carried upwards and my head rose above the surface.

I spat water and gulped mouthfuls of air - blinking water from my eyes.

'Christ! Are you all right?' Marcus clutched my shoulders.

I gasped hungrily for air. 'Get me out!'

With his arm hooked through mine, I kicked my legs and we swam. And with every breath and stroke, my need to escape from what lurked beneath drove me onwards. Overhead the sky had darkened to indigo blue but light remained to see the jetty like a lifeline as we neared.

With Marcus at my rear, I climbed the ladder then staggered to the blanket and sank to my knees. I spluttered and coughed up more water.

Marcus put his arm around me. 'My God, Jodie. What the fuck happened out there?'

I coughed some more then turned over and lay on my back.

Marcus grabbed his shorts and T-shirt and placed them under my head for a pillow.

'Was it the cold?' he asked.

I gasped. 'I got caught in weeds, or an old fishing line.' The truth of what I'd really seen made me terrified to speak of it.

Marcus looked down at my feet and moved to take a closer look. 'You have red marks and bruises forming - scratches too.

I sat up to take a look and pulled my ankle closer. 'Whatever it was, didn't want to release me. The more I struggled, the tighter it gripped.'

'And yet, when I dived down, I felt no resistance pulling you up.'

'Then I must have kicked it free.'

But Marcus frowned and I could see the doubt in his eyes.

'I've never seen anyone fishing down here, although they must do.'

'This doesn't look like fishing line,' I said, quietly.

'No...' he knelt closer and gently held my foot in his hand. 'I'd say it looks more like scratches...' he pointed to red marks that formed a ring around my ankle, 'or fingerprints, which is impossible...'

He looked up at me, and I could no longer hold my emotions in.

I reached over and clasped his arm. 'It was a hand.' My voice trembled. 'Not only did it feel like a hand when I tried to kick it free, when I looked down I fucking saw it. White, bony and long fingered, like a corpse.'

Marcus shook his head. 'No, Jodie. That's impossible.' He came forward and wrapped his arms around me. 'You're freezing. Are you able to dress?'

I nodded. 'I think I'm going mad.'

'You're not going mad, I promise you. But I think you are anxious about your book and the subject you're writing about.' He paused. 'And staying with Maxine is exacerbating these feelings.'

'You might be right.'

'How about I ask Mum if you can stay at hers until Maxine's finished editing? You got on well and she likes you.'

I thought for a moment. 'If I could I would. But I'm housekeeping as part of the exchange and it would cause huge resentment on Maxine's part.'

He looked into my eyes and rested his hand on my arm. 'You could even stay at mine?'

I bit my lip. 'I am tempted. But we've only just met.'

'A little bit more than that, I hope.'

I leaned forwards and kissed him on the lips. 'Yes, far more than that. But I don't want to rush anything. I loved it back there.' I glanced back to the rock that jutted from the water's edge.

'I loved it, too.' His eyes smiled. 'Maybe between the sheets next time.'

My tummy turned over and I felt relieved he was already thinking about a next time.

'I'd love that.'

'Okay, dress, hot bubble bath at Maxine's, then tonight think about where you'd like to stay. You can always drive in during the day to do her housekeeping.' He gripped my hand and pulled me up.

I put my weight on my ankle and took a step forward. 'Phew, at least my foot's still working.'

Chapter 25

Black Out

By the time we'd retraced our steps along the sheep tracks, the wall itself and down the hill to The Blue House, the sky had turned coal black and star sprinkled with a disc of moonlight that helped to guide our way. I'd stopped shivering, although my airways and ankle felt sore, and the taste of lake water lingered in my nostrils and mouth. It could have been a whole different story if Marcus hadn't been there and quick to see I'd disappeared. My life might have been over.

Could the same thing have happened to Sheila? Or was it her ghost - her memory floating in the depths, that had almost caused me to drown? I couldn't help but wonder if I'd imagined the whole thing, panicked and done this to myself. Maybe I'd never find out and I'd be left reliving it and questioning what really happened. I'd take a closer look at my ankle - maybe that would provide the answers I needed.

Marcus held my hand as we stood together at the end of the drive and I turned to the house. My eyes were drawn to a light in an upstairs window. A curtain fell back into place, and I knew Maxine had been looking out for me. Was it out of concern for my whereabouts or annoyance at my being out late again?

'I don't care if she's spying on us,' said Marcus.

'She could be worried I got lost.' But I doubted it.

'Hmm, maybe.' He leaned forward and held me in a hug and I felt his cool cheeks against mine, and in contrast, the warmth of his breath.

He whispered, 'Ring me, soon.'

From the front doorstep I turned back and threw Marcus a wave who I could just make out watching for me to go inside.

I was almost surprised when my key turned and the door opened.

I stepped into the hallway and called up the stairs. 'I'm back Maxine. I've locked up.'

Footsteps echoed above on the landing, but I heard no acknowledgement from Maxine that she'd heard me.

I called out again. 'Maxine?'

Suddenly I felt frustrated and annoyed by her rudeness and walked up the unlit stairwell.

Her bedroom door was ajar and lamplight shone from within.

I reached to flick on the landing light and walked across the hallway.

'Maxine, are you in there?' I stopped in her doorway.

I heard a movement behind me and that was when I felt a thwack on the back of my head, followed by intense pain and the sensation of falling until my vision went black.

One moment I was adrift, sinking deeper beneath the water, until I realised I was in a dream and waking up.

My limbs felt weighted down, my eyes so leaden and sleepy I thought I must have been drugged or sedated. When I forced my eyes open my vision pulsed in rhythm to the throbbing in my head. Feelings of disorientation overwhelmed me and I tried to lift my hand to my head to work out what could be causing the agonising pain. But my hands remained fixed to something - both hands pressed together and bound tightly behind my back. I was sitting upright and my shoulder joints burned from being pulled into an unnatural position.

'What the fuck!' I groaned, and my vision flew into a violent spin.

Could this be my final moment? Was I about to die?

Gradually the pain and spinning subsided, and taking care to make no sudden moves I turned my head to try and figure out where I was. I peered into the darkness and saw slithers of grey light filtered between curtains at both ends of the room.

Each time I moved my head too quickly the pains intensified and nausea made my head spin. I was soaked in sweat and I closed my eyes, took some breaths and the pain eased. When I tried to stand I felt the force of resistance beneath me. My hands and feet were bound so tightly to the chair that I couldn't move more than a few millimetres.

'Maxine!' I cried. 'Maxine!' Fear throbbed in the back of my throat and pins and needles travelled down my neck and spine.

I remembered the blow to my head, and before that, walking up the stairs to find Maxine.

And then I thought, had Maxine been hurt, too?

Could she be beaten unconscious here with me? Was she still alive?

Perhaps it hadn't been her looking out from the upstairs window for my return. Was it the man or woman, the intruder, we'd seen in the garden? Some weirdo stalking her? Had they returned to hurt her and then I'd turned up?

At least they hadn't killed me, yet, I thought miserably. One thing was certain, going by the deathly silence, no one was around to help me. I was on my own. When I twisted and wrestled against the bindings, the throbbing in my head only worsened. I strained to stand and threw my weight left and right but the chair barely moved beneath me. It was a dead weight.

Where were the painkillers when you needed them? Any migraines I'd suffered previously paled into insignificance.

When a chink of daylight crept through the curtain and fell like a candle flame upon the floorboards, I knew where I'd seen the chair I was bound to - the blue house at the bottom of the garden. Whoever brought me here, had to be strong to have carried me unconscious all the way down from the house. Was Maxine that strong? What about her intruder? Other than my pounding head and dizziness, I was intact, with no feelings of discomfort between my thighs that might have added another sinister layer to my capture.

Memories of being at the lake with Marcus returned. Mostly kissing and making love - beautiful and unexpected, bringing to the surface feelings for him which had blossomed so rapidly. Then there was the swim back to the jetty and the hand from the depths that almost dragged me to my death. Details from last night, like the way Marcus' lips had parted as we made love, and how his eyes remained stubbornly open so that he could watch me, as I watched him - these were forever imprinted in my mind. Nothing could steal those incredible, life-changing moments.

And then I began to experience a creeping terror. What if last night had all been a dream, a nightmare or a hallucination that had then brought me here?

No, the headache and discomfort of being tied up was all too real. I shifted one foot and gasped as the rope scraped against my bruised ankle.

Now I knew where I was, my breaths and pulse quickened. Of all the places to be confined, and not only confined but bound to a rock of a chair. This room had triggered anxiety in me from the moment I stepped up to the door. Did the person who put me here know that, or was it a coincidence? And what difference did it make other than no one from the road would hear my cries, and no one would come down here to look for me? I shivered from the cold, but at the same time, fear soaked sweat crept down my back and belly.

'What do you want?' I shouted. 'Show yourself! Let's talk!' I yelled, then coughed and gasped from the strain.

The nerves in my head fizzled and my ears buzzed with strange sounds. I teetered on the brink of losing it, big time, but I took some breaths and clung onto what remained of my sanity.

I craved water. My tongue cleaved to the roof of my mouth, and my throat felt like I'd swallowed a cup of sawdust. The wine I'd consumed last night. The miles of walking and talking with Marcus. The last time I'd touched water was the lake water I'd swallowed when I'd almost drowned, and that I'd coughed up. I was already dehydrated and the longer I remained here without water, the thirstier I'd be, the weaker I'd feel and the less rational I'd become.

No, if they hadn't killed me yet, whoever brought me here, had a plan.

I'd arrived back at Maxine's at ten last night, and judging by the daylight creeping through it was approaching dawn.

Outside the crows stirred and I heard their caa-caa's from their nests. More crows joined in the tuneless chorus and grew to a steady rumble, like a storm was brewing close by.

A new day was beginning. But would this be my last?

Above the crows' calls came a strange rattle and tip-tapping sound on the roof. The sounds started and stopped, then started again. A crow hopping across the tiles, perhaps. Then above the pounding in my head I heard another sound - this time words, but whispered and unclear.

Were they coming from outside or in my head? I tried to quieten my breathing and listened intently. It seemed to be coming from behind me, and I turned my head, but saw only vague outlines. The words were muted - more murmuring than specific. But it was a man's voice, with a dark and menacing tone.

'Who are you?' I said.

I listened again.

'What do you want with me?'

The crows' cacophony intensified, making my head pound to the jarring rhythm, then sensing movement I turned towards the door. A figure, shielded by the curtains, moved across the decking.

'Who's there?' I called. 'Show yourself!'

Whoever it was stepped up to the door so that I saw them in silhouette, his shape sharp and clear. My heart juddered and I began to pant with fear of what might follow. There was something recognisable in the outline of his head and hair. Whoever it was remained still. Certainly a man - tall, well-built. His hair thick over broad shoulders.

Surely not Hadrian? Could he have struck me and tied me up here?

A wave of nausea sent my head spinning, and at the same time a flash of light filled my vision, blinding and transporting me back to my childhood - to a memory locked away in my subconscious until now.

My memories gained clarity moment by moment - creeping with silent steps to the forefront of my mind. And they explained the impression that I already knew this place. I realised why the foreboding and deja vu had held me back from entering - striking a shattering, blood-stained blow whenever I'd stepped inside.

A shimmering vision hovered before me like a ghost from my past - my young self, right here in this room. I wore a green summer dress and my hair hung loose over my shoulders. My father had driven me here when he'd visited Maxine, as her lawyer. Dad only ever dragged me along when he had no other childcare option.

I watched myself hide and curl up beneath the enormous desk, then when I'd been found by a boy, I laughed, jumped out and he chased me around the room. That young boy must have been Hadrian. Memories and scenes emerged and played out before me - of being yelled at by a woman for running down corridors in the main house where we'd been playing hide and seek.

For punishment, the boy and I were instructed to play here - in the summerhouse. At first we thought it was a game.

More memories with the smallest of details flooded my mind. My younger self had dragged a chair to the window, climbed up, banged the window and screamed to be let out. I had no recollection of how long we'd been confined, but the terror I'd experienced back then returned to me today. The boy huddled silently in the corner of the room, until eventually after what seemed an eternity, the woman unlocked the door and released us.

Why was it only now I remembered this cruel and terrifying imprisonment?

Had the trauma from that day suppressed it in my memory until history repeated itself?

As each minute passed I recalled more with old scenes unfolding in my mind.

When we left that afternoon, Dad pushed me into the backseat of the car and smacked my legs. Such physical reprimands were nothing new. And like most occasions I wasn't told what I'd done to deserve his cold anger and violent treatment. I doubted he'd needed an excuse. I got in his way or was an easy target when he needed to vent his anger.

I looked again at the shadowy figure keeping guard at the door, now more clearly visible as daylight crept closer. Despite the disturbing memories I knew it couldn't possibly be my father.

Or could it?

I might be concussed, with paranoia setting in and imagining the impossible. Or was I merely assessing the tangible, the possible? All I knew was that my head felt as if it was punctured with needles and my memories played havoc with my rational mind.

My guard turned to one side, and when I saw his jawline jutting forwards and the slightly hooked nose, I knew precisely who he was.

'Hadrian! Hadrian!' I repeated louder. 'Talk to me.'

He stepped to one side.

'I know it's you,' I said. 'Why?'

I paused, waiting.

'I thought we were friends. Did Maxine force you into this?'

But his shadow moved away from the doorway and his footsteps faded along the decking.

My throat ached, and each time I wrestled to free my hands and feet, my skin burned and my head throbbed harder.

'Hadrian? I need water and I must talk to Maxine…' My voice broke and the room turned in circles.

Chapter 26

No Escape

When I opened my eyes white spots darted through the gloom. Judging by the dryness of my tongue and throat I could have been here for days, but I knew it could only be early morning still. The dawn chorus was in full flow - a cacophony of crows drowning the tweets of smaller birds. Chinks of sunlight criss-crossed like lasers over the floorboards and walls. I straightened my back as much as I could, and craned my neck to look at the desktop now visible in daylight. Typed pages were stacked in two piles. They had to be my manuscript, and Maxine had left it in full view, well aware I had no chance of retrieving it.

My best and only hope was to free myself and get as far away from here as I could. Neither Maxine or Hadrian seemed in any rush to either talk to me or do with me whatever they had planned. I knew releasing me wouldn't be an option. Not unless I could persuade them that I'd leave and not go to the police. I'd studied enough real crime cases to understand how kidnap and hostage situations ended - if lucky they escaped or were rescued, otherwise it rarely ended well or with the victims alive to tell their tales.

But if I escaped, I'd go straight to the police. I'd done nothing wrong other than discover an unpublished manuscript of Maxine's that could potentially lead to the exposure of her husband's murderer. Maxine herself, I strongly suspected.

Maxine assumed I knew more - that I'd read the ending, and she couldn't risk me having this knowledge and leaving - not least because I was a lawyer. She might have hidden her manuscript in the attic, but what a risk to even write it and expose her story in typed format, as I strongly suspected she had. She must have written it for catharsis, to unburden her mind of her husband's death at her own murderous and false-hearted hands -

or had she cast her twin sister as his murderer? I could only speculate.

My novel might be based on a true crime but I'd given it a fictional ending. At least, I'd hypothesised and made calculated assumptions. But what of Maxine's?

Footsteps approached along the decking. A key turned in the lock before the door creaked open and Maxine walked in. Without even catching my eye she crossed to the far side of the room and opened the curtains so that I could see out and down the slope to the trees by the stream.

'Maxine, tell me what I've done to deserve this.'

She turned to me, then walked slowly back across the room. She sneered down at me and spat, 'Don't play the little miss innocent with me. You took the wrong lady for a fool.'

Even before I could consider how to reply, she brought her hand back and slapped me, making my head swing and crack the back of the chair. I registered the impact and pain before my vision turned white and I lost consciousness.

A buzzing sound filled my ears and when my eyes flickered open, dazzling sunlight beaming through the windows blinded me, making me squint and turn away from the glare. My cheek stung, and my head throbbed in waves that grew and subsided.

I turned back to the window. Squinting through sunlight, I saw a frost like mist drifted past the window, and when I breathed in, a pungent aroma filled my nostrils. I watched orange flames throb and spark amidst spiralling smoke that rose up from a mound of logs a few yards down the slope.

Maxine stood at the fire, her eyes directed at the summerhouse. I watched her retreat a few steps, then advance forwards again, before turning a circle as though performing a strange ritualistic dance.

She swept one arm forwards in a courtly gesture and bowed. Then she reached down and held something aloft which I immediately recognised as my blue and pink suitcase. She pulled an item of clothing from it and dropped it into the fire. The flames flared brighter and swirled up into the air, as Maxine continued pulling clothes and personal items from my case, dropping them one by one into the flames.

When she finished her ritual by throwing the case onto the fire, I knew exactly why she'd burnt my belongings and had wanted me to witness her doing so. She looked my way again and held up something small and black. In an exaggerated gesture, she placed it on her outstretched palm. I couldn't think what it could be, until she lifted it and raised it to her ear to make quite sure I knew. My phone. My only means of contacting someone - Marcus, Mum, the police.

When she dropped that into the fire, she tipped back her head and laughed. She had no intention of releasing me, but every intention of leaving me here to die, or finishing me off herself.

Maxine was wrong about one thing, though. I hadn't taken her for a fool and neither had I tried to take advantage of her. She'd volunteered her help - I'd asked her for nothing.

But I had been naive. Why had I assumed she was a good person because I admired her writing and stories? And of course, she was smart - damned smart.

What was I missing? There had to be more.

Had Maxine somehow made the connection between me as the daughter of the lawyer character in my manuscript. Was she taking revenge on me because of her fall out with Dad all those years ago?

Or her assumption I'd read more of her manuscript than I had, and was concerned I knew details that would incriminate her?

Whatever her motives, if I didn't escape this mess, I'd miss nothing - I'd be dead.

Panic rose in me like boiling water making me pant and sweat, until something like a jolt of electricity made me sit up and see that survival was down to me alone. I had to be clever - smarter than the witch at her pyre.

I twisted and turned my hands and feet and the bindings scraped like razors against my skin. It felt like wire dug into my skin, which they must have covered with tape for extra measure.

One thing seemed certain, it was too painfully secure to wriggle out of.

Maybe a quick manoeuvre could snap it?

My law professor had once played us a crime docu series and I recalled one episode about a couple in their country home when thieves had broken in at night, tied them up then ransacked their possessions. The woman had previously worked in the forces and undergone training to escape capture. In an interview afterwards she'd demonstrated how she'd released herself before untying her husband and calling the police from their bedroom phone. The thieves had been successfully interrupted, captured and convicted of their crimes.

I pressed my right foot up tight against the leg of the chair and snapped my foot swiftly to the side. The pain made me gasp and nothing gave way, but when I wriggled my ankle I thought the binding felt looser. I counted to three and using all the force I could muster, repeated the movement. I heard a click and knew a section of the binding had snapped. I glanced out of the window to see Maxine still prodding her fire with a long stick. I stamped my foot, wrestled with the binding and kicked. With each movement the binding loosened, until finally I felt the tape come free. I raised my leg and saw grey tape hanging from my trainers and I kicked it off. The skin on my ankle looked red raw and bruised but a sense of elation revived my energy.

I refused to be left here to die. I had too much to live for, not least Mum, and maybe even Marcus. I said I'd message him today, so when I didn't he might assume I wasn't interested, which couldn't be further from the truth.

Outside, flames flickered as embers sparked and rose up from the fire, but I couldn't see Maxine. I looked for shadows behind the door and windows, and listened out for sounds or movement.

Where was she? And Hadrian, too?

I had to assume one or both of them were nearby.

I used the same technique on my left foot and snapped it away from the chair leg. After four futile attempts I felt something give and the tape slackened.

My hands were so tightly bound I could barely move my shoulders, let alone my arms. Frustration and anger grew inside me as I struggled to free my hands.

'Damn you!' I screamed, feeling exasperated and exhausted.

When I turned to Maxine's desk something caught my eye. On top of the paper tray, I spotted a knife - a paper knife with a metal blade. If only I could get hold of it. With my ankles free I braced my feet on the floor and lifted the seat. I only shifted the chair a millimetre or so nearer to the desk, but it was something.

I tried again and again, and each time I moved the chair inch by agonising inch towards the table and that knife, hope spurred me on. My knees nudged the table leg and I began to twist my body weight to swivel the chair around until I judged my arms and hands to be in line with the paper tray and the knife. Breathing hard, I turned my head and glimpsed the knife almost within reach. But the only way I could get the knife into my hands would be to knock it out of the tray with my elbow and attempt to snatch it as it fell. It was a risk, and I'd only get one shot, but it was my best and only chance.

I curled my fingers into a cup shape ready to catch the knife. Then I pushed back until I felt the cold of the metal blade against my elbow. I leaned gently against the knife and felt it shift. With the smallest movement I pushed the blade again and felt it slip over the edge of the desk and brush my forearm. I fumbled and grasped with all fingers and the knife hinged between my forefinger and index finger. I paused, panting but elated. I couldn't risk dropping the knife, but would it be sharp enough to cut through the tape and binding?

Slowly, I rotated the knife in my fingers and angled the blade upwards against the tape around my wrists. I pressed hard and began to move the blade up and down. My wrists and fingers cramped from being forced into an unnatural position, but I kept on sliding and pressing the knife against the tape. When I heard a tear I knew my efforts were working and I pushed on, praying neither Maxine nor Hadrian would come through the door and catch me in the act. I felt the resistance of the binding beneath the tape and redoubled my efforts.

I wasn't convinced the knife could even cut into the binding and so I gripped the knife in my right palm, took a deep breath and wrenched my hands apart. Nothing gave and I groaned at the futility of my attempts. I snapped my wrists sharply again, and felt the knife slip from my fingers and clank against the floorboards.

'Shit!'

It was then I heard the key in the lock. I turned my head to see Maxine pushing the door open. She clocked that I'd moved, and rushed at me.

I tugged desperately against my bindings and tried to stand up, but nothing gave. Maxine stepped squarely before me and with both hands shoved me back into the seat.

'You're going nowhere, Missy!' She sneered in my face.

Her breath smelt rank from booze.

'But why? I've done nothing.'

My final hope was to reason with her. And judging by the fury in her features, and the bile in her tone, reason was a likely lost cause.

'You're a menace! Worse - a pestilent parasite. When I started reading your manuscript, your fanciful made up story, it didn't take me long to work out who you were.'

'I'm a fan of your books. I told you that from the start. You invited me here!'

'You're a spy, and what's worse, you fooled me. You tried the same with Hadrian, and when that failed you began playing with Marcus.'

'You're wrong. I wanted to be friends. That's all. And yours too.'

Lank hair stuck to her scalp, and she brought her face to mine so that the tip of her nose almost touched mine.

I thought about headbutting her, but she withdrew a few inches.

'You really believe that - oh, I only want to be friends?' She mimicked my words.

The whites of her eyes were shot through with fine blood-red lines. 'Hadrian wouldn't touch you, you filthy bitch.' Her words slurred. 'He has better taste. Which he gets from me, not from his abysmal father.'

A thought came to me. 'At your talk you spoke of your devastation at Winston's death.'

'You fool! Winston isn't Hadrian's father.'

Then who was?

'Hadrian isn't alone,' I said. 'Plenty of us have crap fathers, I should know...' my words trailed away and shrivelled on my tongue.

'Oh my dear, Jodie. It's too late to be coy with me.' There was a flicker of triumph in her eyes. 'I know Brett Anderson is your father.'

Her words punched me in the guts.

She reached down, cupped and squeezed my chin with her fingers. 'I know because you're the spitting image of him. Oh, and your appalling manuscript only reinforced your connection with him. No doubt Brett did do away with poor little Sheila. At least you got that part right. I came to realise I was better off without him.'

'You mean as your lawyer?' My thoughts went into overdrive.

She snorted and with a sly tone, confided. 'Oh, my *relationship* with your father was far more than lawyer and client.' She cackled and whispered, 'Don't tell your mother.'

I listened, not daring to interrupt.

'And we would have been more, too, until he ended it.'

And I realised that what she was about to reveal was something I should have worked out myself days ago.

Maxine's pupils contracted to pinpricks, and she continued speaking as though from a distance. 'Brett might have fathered Hadrian, but that was where his responsibility ended. I never forgave him for abandoning me, and our beautiful boy.'

Now I knew Hadrian and I were related, it seemed blatantly obvious. And if it was Hadrian locked in here with me as a child, then Maxine and Dad's relationship had lasted several years.

'Let me go.' I kept my voice level. 'I'll go and never return. You have my word. You can go back to how you were.'

Her gaze lowered and trembling all over, she hissed, 'And I'll never forgive any child of Brett's who purposely concealed her identity. You're a spy of the most despicable kind and no doubt in cahoots with that journalist.'

'Give me my manuscript and let me go. I never see Dad, and even if I did I wouldn't speak a word of this. I detest him more than you do.'

'Oh, I doubt that. And no need to worry about your book. I've burned it.' She nodded to where the fire smoked.

I glanced at the table top to the pile of typed papers I'd assumed were mine. No matter, I had my own printout and backups so if she'd burnt it, all the better.

'You know that was all it was fit for - the fire.'

'So why offer to edit it?'

'I pitied you - pathetic creature that you are.'

I knew she lied. Maxine took pity on no one. My being hostage was proof of that.

'I thought I may be able to improve it,' she continued. 'But alas, it's a lost cause. Your ex was right about that.'

'Fine. I appreciate your honesty.' I paused. 'Untie me.' I tried again. 'I'll disappear and you won't see or hear from me again.'

She shook her head. 'I've never trusted the word of a lawyer.'

'Ex-lawyer,' I replied needlessly.

She stepped back, and I could see she was unsure of her next move, until her eyes turned dark with intent and her lips curled into a snarl.

I knew she meant me harm.

I kicked out and wrestled against my bound hands. Maxine cast her eyes around the room until they fell upon something behind me. She gave a sly smile and stepped around me, her footsteps heavy upon the floorboards. I turned my head, and in my peripheral vision I saw her lift something up. She clutched the object in her hand and walked towards me. And in that instant I knew she meant to bludgeon me with it.

I was in deep trouble.

Her shadow loomed large and I heard her breaths at my back. With heart pounding and muscles primed, I snapped my hands apart and heard the bindings crack and break. Finally, with my limbs free I sprang to my feet, just as Maxine brought the object down. As the weight cracked my shoulder, I lunged forwards and spun around. The door was open, with only Maxine in my way. I raised my arms, dived forwards and pushed her hard. For the briefest moment she loomed over me, her features aflame with rage. She paddled her arms and feet as her body folded, and like a tree struck by lightning she crashed to the floor.

A howl broke from her and as the floorboards shuddered beneath the impact, I leapt over her and made for the open doorway. Nothing would stop me now. I darted across the decking and took the steps in one clean stride. Maxine screamed from behind and glancing up the garden I saw Hadrian already charging down the slope and weaving through the trees.

I'd never get past him so I ran around the side of the summerhouse and hurtled down the hill, past the burning logs and onwards to the trees at the bottom. Hadrian's feet pounded the ground behind me, and I sensed he closed the gap between us with every stride. I turned and saw he was only feet away with hands outstretched to grab me, but I darted right, widening the distance between us once more.

I heard him yell and with a glance over my shoulder I saw he'd fallen.

I screamed at him. 'Stay away!'

I had to make it to the trees.

'You can't outrun me,' Hadrian shouted.

His goading spurred me on and I slipped into the trees and ducked behind a wide trunk. Hadrian was close once more but I heard him stop, pause, then shuffle through dead leaves and undergrowth. I pressed myself against the bark, inching slowly round to remain hidden.

Closeby, twigs snapped and leaves rustled underfoot.

'Why hide? There's only a stream and it's too wide to jump.'

My options were to fight or run. I peered round and through the trees I saw a wall and arch. It had to be the bridge over the stream and the lane past the house that led to the main road.

But Hadrian was close - too close.

'Come on, Jodie. I know you're here.'

More rustling and footsteps nearing.

'Mum explained what you've been up to. Spying on her and me. Lying, snooping and stealing her work. Seducing Marcus after trying it on with me.'

Of course Maxine had worked her poisonous lies on him.

I made a snap decision and stepped out from behind the tree. 'We should talk.'

Hadrian stood only yards away, and the moment he clocked me he lunged at me, grabbed my shoulders and shoved me to the ground.

So talking wasn't an option, and as I fell I summoned all I'd ever learned about self-defence.

I landed hard and winded, but I kicked at his crotch.

I missed, propelled my foot again, and this time aimed true.

Hadrian growled as pain erupted, then he clutched his belly and doubled up.

But he was still standing, and as I scrambled up I felt his hands grasp my top and he hauled me back down to the ground. He stood over me, dropped down and straddled me, pinning my hips to the floor.

I bucked and twisted to dislodge him but he grabbed my wrists and held me fast. Quickly turning my head, I opened my mouth and sunk my teeth into the soft skin of his wrist, tearing at his flesh until blood spurted into my mouth.

'Ahhh!' He bellowed, yanked his hand away and slapped me. 'You bitch!'

My vision reeled. I spat blood and tried to sit up, but he grabbed my wrists again and yanked them to the side.

His face was inches from mine. 'You liked me well enough on the train - what changed your mind?' he snarled.

'My mistake. I thought we could be friends.'

His eyes blazed. 'You prefer my dumb cousin, Marcus.' Spittle bubbled on his lips. 'I watched you fucking at the lake.'

'So it was you? I thought it was…' I paused, unsure, but no, he deserved to know.

My hesitation registered in his eyes and he tightened his grip on my wrists. 'Who?'

I shook my head. 'Let me go and we'll talk.'

The creases on his brow deepened. 'What are you hiding?'

'Maxine's never told you then?'

'She's told me enough.'

'What exactly? What did I do wrong?'

'You're a snooper and spy. You're in cahoots with that journalist.'

'That's bullshit and you know it.'

His hair flopped forwards like a cap falling, and he shook it angrily aside. 'I guessed as much even without Mum. Far more than coincidence you turning up with your book.'

'You're wrong. Maxine's wrong.'

We locked eyes - almost interchangeable up close.

'No, Hadrian. If you really want the truth - the real truth your mum's failed to share with you, is that…I'm your sister.'

He leaned closer still and I saw a flicker of something - a flash of recognition pass across his features. 'That's fucking impossible!'

'She admitted it to me just now. And it makes perfect sense. You must've seen you look nothing like Winston?'

Hadrian shook his head but I watched his face pale and his eyes flickered with confusion. 'I've never doubted.'

'Really? You and I, we're too alike. I didn't know before today, but the clues were there, we just couldn't see them. Before Maxine's talk I admit I knew Dad had been Maxine's lawyer, thirty odd years ago, but that isn't why I came to her talk. I've always loved her books. Whatever her faults...' and I thought, far too many faults to mention, 'Your mum's a brilliant novelist.'

His hands loosened their grip on mine, and I continued.

'I never imagined Maxine and Dad had an affair, but I knew they'd fallen out and Dad wouldn't allow mention of her name or her books in our house. I'm sure my mum doesn't know about Dad's affair with your mum, and definitely not about you.'

'You said your dad had died?' His words caught in the back of his throat.

'Your father,' I said, slowly. 'Dad's alive. I say he's dead because I don't see him and it's easier that way. But Mum has his address. She's never stopped me seeing him, but I chose not to. You can though. He has to know about you - that you're his child.'

'No! You're lying to get away.'

'I swear it's the truth. Ask Maxine - she cannot deny it.' I paused and looked at him straight. 'Would you want to be responsible for hurting your own blood? Because that's what I am.'

With those words, he released my hands and reeled back onto his haunches. He glanced at his wrist and the blood that oozed from the bite, then passed one hand over his eyes - his pain and confusion evident.

He lifted his eyes to mine and I saw he struggled to digest my words.

I glanced at the bridge over the lane and my mind fought between talking or running.

I scrambled to my knees. 'Tell your mum I got away. I won't go to the police.'

He reached out and gripped my hand. 'I can't!'

'You'll go to prison - both of you. Do you understand? Do you want that for your future - Maxine's? Mum knows I'm here and if I don't call she'll drive over. And Marcus, too.'

Hadrian shook his head. 'Mum'll know I helped. She'll go mental.'

'Say you fell - hurt yourself.' I glanced at the blood on his wrist. 'Your mum fell in the summerhouse. I pushed her - you should go check.'

Hadrian's eyes remained unwavering. 'You'll give me my father's number - his address?'

I nodded. 'I'll explain we've met and you want to meet him.'

'Will he want to?'

I thought about the ending of my book and how the murder of Sheila, Dad's ex-girlfriend, might finally be solved. If necessary, I'd use that to bribe Dad to agree to meet and talk to Hadrian.

'I know he will,' I said with conviction.

'What if I have more questions?'

'We'll talk.' I placed my palm on his arm. 'We're brother and sister, and despite all this, I'm glad. I have a big brother, David - your age. He'd want to meet you. He's like you in some ways.'

Doubt formed in his features. 'This is too fucking weird.'

I rose slowly to my feet and the surrounding trees swayed and turned. I leaned against a trunk - regaining my balance. 'It's a shock and a lot to take in. But you will. As will I.'

Hadrian gestured towards the bridge. 'Go then, but if you're lying...'

'Your mum admitted it. And there's something else. I remember being here with you in your house and the summerhouse. Dad brought me here.'

Hadrian's forehead furrowed as he tried to recall. 'We've met before?'

'When we were little. You don't remember?'

Doubt crossed his eyes, followed by the faintest recognition. 'I'm not sure.'

I heard a shout and searched through the trees. 'I must leave or she'll catch us talking.'

He nodded. 'On the bridge, turn right. Stay low and hidden.'

'Thank you...brother.' I reached out, and with hesitation, he raised his arms too.

But our brief embrace felt forced, on both our parts.

Shouts echoed through the trees and I knew Maxine was on the hunt for me.

Hadrian pulled away. 'Go!'

Chapter 27

The Chase

At the stream, which flowed fast and deep, I headed down an overgrown path, making my way between the scrub and ducking beneath overhanging branches. Moments later I reached the bridge and scrambled up the bank, through loose stones, bramble bushes and nettles. I peered over the wall before finding a foothold and hauling myself up. I swung my legs over the top and dropped onto the verge.

The lane was empty. I just needed to make it to the main road, unseen by Maxine. Once there I'd flag down a car and beg for a ride into Hexham. My legs trembled with adrenaline as I ran, and when The Blue House came into view behind the wall, I crouched down, still running. The sun blazed hot on my back and up ahead the road shimmered with translucent light. My mouth felt parched and my head pulsed with pain and thunderous beats, but nothing would halt my escape from this mad woman. I should have taken heed of the warnings and left before Maxine totally lost her mind.

The boundary wall at the front of the house was lower, and approaching the gateway to the drive I crouched down and crept up to the gatepost. When I peered round I saw movement at the front of the house. The front door was open and the sound of raised voices travelled. I stood up, sprinted across the gap and onwards to where the lane sloped steeply downhill. In front of me the tarmac and stone walls grew fuzzy and blurred and my head started to swim. I was in danger of passing out and I stopped and leaned against the wall to steady my breaths. Sweat dripped down my face but I set off walking - willing myself to remain upright. My legs felt weaker with every step and I sucked in each breath in a desperate attempt to remain conscious. But despite my efforts white spots sprinkled my vision and every step felt like it could be my last.

The rumble of an engine approached from behind and I spun around. Maxine's Audi advanced at speed with her behind the wheel. I staggered onto the verge and scanned round for a stile or gate to escape through. But there was nothing. I reached for the top of the wall and in my peripheral vision I watched the Audi mount the verge.

Maxine's intention was dangerously clear and I fumbled for a foothold in the stones. The following moments became a blur. Hands grappled at my clothes and I lost my foothold and tumbled back onto the tarmac. As I scrambled to stand she kicked me and I fell to the ground again. I raised my eyes to hers which were filled with hatred and bitterness. Maxine bent down and punched me, then raised her leg and stamped her boot on my belly forcing the breath from me. I rolled away, coughing, sputtering and struggling to get up. But again she kicked me down.

'No better than your bastard of a father.'

Her accusation fuelled me with rage and I rose up again. I turned and screamed at her. 'I'm nothing like my father!'

She growled incomprehensible words, reached down for a rock and raised her arm.

She hurled it at my face. 'You don't want your book back then?'

I'd already anticipated her move and when I ducked sideways the rock skimmed my cheek.

I turned on her. 'I should have known you wrote from bitter experience.' And with youth on my side, I lunged at her, booted her in one knee then the other in quick succession.

As Maxine toppled backwards I raced to the car. She'd left the engine running and I jumped in, slammed it into reverse then steered around her body sprawled at the side of the road. With my foot to the floor I glanced through my wing mirror to see gravel and dust spinning in the air and Maxine rising to her hands and knees. Christ, if anyone had seen me they'd think I was beating up an old lady.

I'll never know how I made it to Evelyn's house - sheer desperation to find someone who would help and protect me from Maxine. I remembered banging on Evelyn's front door, but nothing beyond that - who answered the door, what I said to them or what they said in reply.

But even before I returned to consciousness I felt a warm hand in mine, and when I opened my eyes the blurry face that looked down on me, and slowly came into focus, was the one I'd wanted to see more than anyone else's.

Marcus' features were taut with concern. 'You're okay.' He stroked my hand.

A question or a statement? 'I'm not sure.'

'Your face and head are bruised, which is probably why you passed out. Mum's called the doctor.'

I coughed and my tongue stuck to the roof of my mouth. 'Could I have some water?' My lips felt numb and a whiteness filled the room.

'Of course.' He released my hand and hurried out.

He returned with a glass and I held it to my lips.

I gulped several mouthfuls, swallowed and sighed. 'Water has never tasted so incredible.'

I drained the rest of the glass.

'What happened - you've got blood around your mouth? You texted early this morning.'

I wiped my lips. 'What did it say?'

'Wait.' He reached for his mobile on the coffee table, and handed it to me.

"Stay away. I want nothing to do with you. EVER!"

I shook my head. 'You'll never believe what I've been through with your sociopathic aunt and cousin.' I took his hand. 'I didn't send that. I hope you know.'

'After last night, I was confused by it. I replied and tried to call you.'

'Maxine incinerated my phone. Watched her do it, along with my suitcase and belongings. That was after she and Hadrian tied me to a chair in the summerhouse and I had to fight Hadrian to make him listen.'

Marcus exhaled a long breath. 'Oh God!'

Evelyn came into the room followed by Philip.

She perched on the end of the sofa and scraped a hand through her hair. 'My sister and nephew did this?' Her breaths were jagged and her eyes welled with tears.

I nodded slowly.

Evelyn clasped a hand to her mouth. 'I'm so sorry. I should have insisted you stay here.'

The three of them sat round and listened as I described what had happened, from the moment I said goodbye to Marcus the previous night. I knew by their expressions and gasps that they were shocked, but possibly not as surprised as they might have been had they not already known Maxine.

Evelyn's features darkened and she stood up. 'I should call the police.'

'Please, no. Not yet.' I protested. 'There's something else you need to know.'

'What - more horrors?' said Philip.

'It's a biggie.' I drank more water. 'My father, who I'm estranged from because he was abusive... is also Hadrian's father. I didn't know but Maxine confessed, and I believe it's true. Hadrian was in the dark until I told him. It's how I persuaded him to release me. Hadrian is damaged, unsurprisingly with a mother like Maxine, but he has feelings.'

I looked at Evelyn whose complexion had paled and tears pooled in her eyes. Philip took her hand and held it protectively.

Marcus looked over at his mum. 'You knew this?'

She nodded and with lips trembling said to me, 'Your father is Brett Anderson?'

'Yes,' I replied. 'Sadly, we can't pick our fathers.'

Evelyn rubbed a finger into the corner of each eye. 'I've always suspected he was Hadrian's real father. I knew Brett became more than Maxine's lawyer. And I must admit when I developed those photographs of you, the possibility you were related to Brett crossed my mind. I pushed the thought aside as a ghost from the past.'

Marcus aimed an accusing glare at his mother. 'I can't believe you knew, and yet never said a word.'

We looked at Evelyn, expectant.

She gave a long sigh. 'How could I? It happened years ago - before you were born.'

'What difference do the years make? He's my cousin, your nephew, and our father is fundamental to who we are.'

Evelyn sighed, and turned to the window for some moments. 'Maxine fell in love with Brett. Well, as in love as she could be with a man.'

'But she was married to uncle Winston,' said Marcus.

'Of course, although I believe she was in love with Brett even before her marriage. Their affair was on and off, but ultimately Brett married.' Evelyn turned to me. 'Brett didn't want Maxine and he certainly didn't want his illegitimate child. Ultimately, he rejected Maxine in every way he could, and she was devastated.' Evelyn paused. 'And when he began to pursue me, her feelings of rejection turned to hatred.'

'You had a relationship with my father too?' I said, then glanced at Marcus.

'No! I detested him. Sorry, but it's the truth. I saw through his charming exterior, and I told him so, repeatedly.'

Thank God for that, I thought.

'So Maxine discovered Dad was pursuing you?'

'Yes, Maxine turned up here unexpectedly when your father had dropped by, yet again.'

'That must have damaged your relationship with Maxine?' I said.

'Well, it severed the few remaining strands. We'd grown apart, largely because Maxine has always been so resentful and bitter about everything.'

'It's hard to imagine you were brought up together. You and Maxine couldn't be more different,' said Philip. 'Thank goodness.'

'And yet, she's brilliant in her own way. An egocentric, self-centred bitch, but one cannot fault her storytelling,' said Evelyn.

'It's strange how some rising to the tops of their professions aren't the kindest of people. My father was another,' I said.

'Maxine has a sharp, dark and twisted mind, and after what you've been through, she's far more dangerous than even I imagined,' said Evelyn.

I nodded. 'I'd broken off the wrist ties when Maxine came in, but I believe Maxine would have finished me off herself.'

'Then we must inform the police,' insisted Evelyn.

'And this is why I haven't given up on finding out the truth about Winston's death,' said Philip. 'Jodie's horrific experience only confirms my suspicions.'

'There's more,' I said, and they all turned back to me. 'I feel really uncomfortable bringing this up, but given the revelations about Dad being Hadrian's father, and him also pursuing you, Evelyn, should we not also talk about Marcus' father?'

'My father?' Marcus shot at me.

I looked at Evelyn who turned to Philip.

Philip nodded. 'I think given today's revelations, it's only right that you speak openly.'

Evelyn shook her head, and a frown of uncertainty etched across her features.

Colour rose in Marcus's cheeks and he directed at Evelyn. 'So you do know my father?' He turned to me and when he spoke his words were barely audible. 'Am I the only one in the dark?'

'I couldn't say before. It wouldn't have been fair,' said Evelyn, softly.

'Fair on who? As if knowing my father is unimportant to me.' The words caught in his throat and I took his hand.

'It isn't that I didn't want to tell you,' said Evelyn. 'I've wrestled with my conscience. But I couldn't risk upsetting Maxine any more than she already was about it.'

I watched as a shadow of realisation passed across Marcus's face. 'You cannot mean Uncle Winston?' His jaw clenched and the muscles stood out in his cheeks. 'You damn well *should* have told me!'

A new expression came into Evelyn's eyes - her eyes shuttered and her lips pressed together with regret. 'So many times I almost did. But I believed you'd be more upset knowing, and with him being dead, too.'

'You're wrong! I'm upset that I've reached the age of thirty-three and only now know who my father was, when *you* knew all along.' His voice rose in anger. 'So sleeping with married men is your thing. Yeah?' With mouth taut he glared from Evelyn to Philip.

'No, it wasn't like that and never has been.' Evelyn spoke quickly, desperate to appease him. 'What happened with Winston, happened only once, even though we fell in love.'

Marcus scraped his hands through his hair. 'So why didn't he leave Maxine and become a father to me?'

'He was going to, but he died before we could make it happen,' said Evelyn, and overwhelmed, she let out a sob.

Philip wrapped an arm around her and she leaned against him.

Marcus turned to me. 'Quite the Miss Marple, aren't you?' He didn't disguise his bitterness.

With a deep sadness and regret in her eyes Evelyn turned to me too. 'Did Maxine tell you?'

'No,' I replied, and I tried to frame my words. 'The connection sparked in my mind that night in your studio. The unnamed sculpture you'd placed so precisely, so lovingly between the two of Marcus. At first glance I thought the three were of Marcus, but there was the beard, build and subtle differences, and later I realised it must be Winston after having seen his photograph at Maxine's. And the likeness is uncanny. As are all your sculptures.'

'And his likeness to his father, too,' said Evelyn, gazing fondly at Marcus.

'I must have been blind not to have seen it for myself,' said Marcus, realising his father had been closeby all along.

'But we often don't see what's become too familiar,' I said. 'I'm in a new place, I'm new to your family, so as an outsider it seems obvious - now that I know you all.'

'It would have been kinder if you'd talked to me yesterday,' said Marcus.

'I know, and I'm sorry. But I was confused and didn't know for certain. And it's why I've spoken to both of you, not with your mum behind your back. I'd have wanted to know too if it was my father.'

'I'm sure, given a little time, both Marcus and Evelyn will respect your directness,' said Philip.

I looked at Marcus and he nodded. 'Well, I am glad I know late rather than never, but Christ, it'll take some sinking in.'

Evelyn nodded. 'Please know I was only ever thinking about you.'

Philip stood up and looked out of the window. 'Is Maxine likely to come looking for you? You have her car, so she might report it stolen.'

'I only wanted to get away. I couldn't think beyond that,' I said.

'I could drive over and ask to see you?' suggested Marcus. 'See what Maxine discloses. That way she won't suspect you're here with us. She already knows she sent that text saying you want me to stay away.'

'Good idea. And she shouldn't be a danger to you if you keep quiet about Jodie being here,' said Evelyn. 'In the meantime I rang my doctor friend, Thomas. He's retired, but he's coming round to check you over.'

'What did you tell him?' I asked.

'I said you'd fallen and banged your head then driven here.'

'I'd like to avoid hospital if I can. They'll ask difficult questions.'

'Let's see what Thomas says first. You cannot take risks with head injuries or concussion.'

'Listen, Maxine is unhinged and dangerous,' Philip urged. 'Hadrian, too. We must call the police. Maxine must be arrested and locked up. Look what she's done to Jodie. She almost killed her.'

Evelyn took his hand. 'I know you want to protect us, but let's do this our way. We'll call the police if we need to.'

'What do *you* think Jodie?' Philip turned to me. 'Wouldn't you feel safer with Maxine arrested? After all, you were the one she so violently attacked.'

He looked at Evelyn and Marcus.

Marcus nodded. 'Yes, your call, Jodie.'

I thought for a moment. Truthfully, I agreed with Philip that Maxine was an unhinged sociopath and should be arrested. But given the revelations, and that this was Marcus and Evelyn's family, and Hadrian was my half-brother, I said, 'I would prefer that Evelyn decide.'

Evelyn exhaled. 'Thank you, Jodie. We'll see what the doctor says and if any of us are concerned for our safety, we inform the police. Agreed?'

As we nodded our agreement, I got the strongest sense that this was not the last I'd heard or seen of Maxine.

Chapter 28

Thrown off the Scent

'What did she say?' I asked, when Marcus returned from driving over to Maxine's.

He sat with me on the sofa which I'd barely moved from since I'd arrived earlier that day.

'She made up a cock and bull story about you leaving without explanation. She looked grey as a ghost but with a whopping great bruise on her cheek. I had to hold myself back from punching her other cheek.'

'Understandable. And I didn't hit her, only pushed her off me.'

'She made her story sound utterly convincing, and especially when she embellished it with nonsense about what a lazy, deceitful and ungrateful young woman you were. She advised me to give you a wide berth.'

'She didn't mention the imprisonment, trying to run me over, bludgeoning me, or that she wanted me dead?'

'Unsurprisingly, no,' he said, and grimaced.

'What about the Audi?'

'I've dealt with that. Philip followed me and I drove it to the train station in Hexham - left the keys inside. Hope that's all right with you. When she reports it missing - she probably already has, the police will find it and think you caught the train home. Or maybe someone else will steal it and she'll be carless for a while.'

'Good thinking. If the police think I stole the car, I'll explain that I was insured even if Maxine denies giving me permission.'

'I don't think she'll say you stole it. That could come back to bite her.'

'Yep. She's walking on dangerously thin ice.' I paused. 'And how are you feeling about your father? I know it's a shock.'

'Mostly, I'm gutted he died before I got to know him.' He took my hand. 'But I am glad I know, finally.'

'You're not too upset with your mum?'

He thought for a minute. 'Not sure. She didn't tell me for what she believed were good reasons, even though she was wrong to have withheld from me.'

'I wonder what you'd have thought seeing how Hadrian looks so different, and yet your mums are identical twins?'

He nodded. 'I'm glad I know that odd piece of the puzzle too. And I reckon Hadrian might be, too.'

'I hope he isn't disappointed when he meets Dad. Dad isn't a kind man. Quite the opposite.'

'At least Hadrian's dad's alive. I'd do anything to have a conversation with mine.'

'I know and I'm so sorry you can't.'

'Philip is even more hell bent on finding out the truth about Uncle Winston, I mean, Dad's death, but I don't know what more he can discover.'

I thought again about Maxine's manuscript hidden away in her attic. Did that reveal the truth about Winston's death? If Winston had been pushed off that cliff by Maxine or someone, that would be devastating news for Marcus.

'Doctor has given me the all clear,' I said, changing the subject. 'But I must rest for a few days.'

'I think I should stay to keep a close eye on you. Make sure you don't slip into unconsciousness.'

I leaned over and kissed him. 'I'd love that.'

Chapter 29

Three Months Later

Since escaping Maxine's clutches and moving back to Mum's I'd worked tirelessly editing my novel and submitting it to literary agents and publishers. At the same time I'd been applying and interviewing for roles in law firms. I'd been offered a couple of positions but the firms hadn't felt right. I knew I was employable and was holding out for a position that I really wanted and with an appropriate starting salary to match. Thankfully, Mum was happy to have me home and the freedom gave me time to travel over and spend time with Marcus.

'Do you look like your mum?' asked Marcus, sitting beside me in the passenger seat.

'Definitely. I'm a couple of inches taller - she's petite, but our colouring, hair and eyes are the same.'

'A dark haired senorita, then?'

'Yes, if you like. I look like Dad too, and like Hadrian, I guess, but I prefer to think I'm like Mum.'

'For obvious reasons,' he said.

Marcus turned down the hill into Bamburgh and we drove past the townhouses and the magnificent castle on the cliff came into view. The flags along the turrets fluttered in the breeze and clouds drifted merrily across the skyline.

'What a picturesque town. I can't believe I've never been before,' said Marcus, gazing out of the window.

'You haven't lived,' I said and laughed. 'It's much quieter than Hexham. Not a lot goes on here other than holidaymakers, walkers and visitors.'

'I can see how that could be dull for a young lawyer.'

'I still love it though, and staying with Mum is never dull,' I admitted.

'We're lucky to have great mums.'

'I hope you don't mind but I told her about you and your Uncle Winston. I didn't want any awkwardness when we talked about family. I had to tell her about Hadrian, too. That was a difficult conversation.'

'I'd rather people know about my real dad, so that's cool. How did your mum take the news about your dad and Maxine's affair, and Hadrian - their love child?'

I sighed. 'You know, Mum thinks Dad is such a shit that she wasn't overly shocked at his betrayal. She was upset, understandably. She said she'd like to meet Hadrian, but I'm not sure about that yet.'

'I feel sad that it didn't go so well when Hadrian met your dad.'

Marcus turned into my road, The Wynding, and pulled up outside, Ocean View, our home.

'I feel bad that I put them in touch,' I said.

'It's what you promised.'

'Yeah, and that freed me, so I don't regret it. Plus it was Hadrian's choice to meet Dad.'

Marcus looked out. 'What a beautiful house.'

'Only home I knew until University.'

I unlocked the front door and we carried our bags inside. 'Mum won't be back til five so we've got an hour or two. We can walk down to the beach.'

'I'd love that,' said Marcus. 'Breathe the ocean air.'

After showing Marcus my bedroom, or more precisely, how comfy my bed was, we walked down through the dunes and the miles of beach and ocean opened out in front of us.

A scent of sea salt swept up in the breeze, and I gasped. 'This is my favourite view in the entire world.'

Marcus gazed one way and then the other. 'Incredible! You were lucky to have this as your playground.'

'Yep, me and David spent hours down here. Complete freedom.'

Marcus took my hand and together we ran and leapt over the stream that flowed down to the sea.

He turned to me and took both my hands. 'Fancy going into the dunes and getting naked?'

'We've only just got dressed,' I said with a grin. 'Let's go further up - it'll be deserted.'

'Oh, you've done it before, have you?'

I laughed. 'Not that, no, but me and my friends did occasionally sunbathe nude, or topless.'

'Let's go then.' We ran, laughing, along the sand.

'Up here.' I pointed to a path that sloped between the dunes and tall grasses. 'I know the exact spot.'

I stopped and gazed around - not another soul within sight.

We walked a path that meandered between mounds of sand topped with grasses, to a hidden dip in the dunes.

Marcus stood and slowly turned a full circle. 'It's so quiet. I can't even hear the waves.'

Together, we looked up as a seagull flew silently over until it turned in an arc and dipped out of sight.

I looked at Marcus, and smiled. 'This is it. I swear no one else even knows about it. My friends and I named it the outer zone.'

'You mean like the Twilight Zone.'

'Exactly. We nicked the idea.'

'So making love here will take us to another dimension,' he said, with a twinkle in his eye.

I kissed him on the lips. 'That happens whenever and wherever we make love.'

We knelt on the sand facing each other and beneath the late afternoon sun we removed one another's clothes. As we kissed and touched it felt like I'd been waiting my entire life to make love with Marcus in this special, secret place from my youth.

When my phone rang, Marcus paused, kissed me and said, 'It might be your mum?'

'I doubt it's Mum.' I sat up. 'But I should answer it.'

'Could be a job offer,' said Marcus.

I reached for my mobile in my shorts pocket.

'Hello,' I said.

'Jodie Rivera?' asked a man.

'Yes, speaking.'

'I'm Simon Trimble from Albatross Publishing. You sent us your manuscript - The Truth.'

'Yes,' I said, expectantly, and widened my eyes at Marcus.

266

'I don't know if you're aware, but we're also Maxine Croyett's publisher?'

My heart began to pick up speed and I sensed his formal tone. 'Right. And yes, I knew that.'

As I waited for him to speak my imagination went into overdrive.

'We're currently preparing Maxine's latest novel for publication, with a publication date four weeks from tomorrow.'

'Okay, I enjoy her novels,' I said.

'Do you know Maxine Croyett personally?'

'I have met her before. Has she mentioned to you that I've written a book?' I asked.

'No, she informed me that you are close to her nephew and that you came to one of her talks and turned up at her house some months ago.' His tone had turned officious.

'Is there a problem?' I said.

'I'm afraid so. Having read your manuscript, it's obvious to see that you have stolen, almost word for word, Maxine's latest novel. This is a clear cut case of plagiarism and we are consulting with our lawyers to decide how to proceed.'

I let out a gasp, and my breath juddered. 'No, you don't understand,' I protested. 'It's Maxine who has stolen *my* novel. She volunteered to edit it for me and I acted as her housekeeper. But I had to leave because she became aggressive.'

'So, you were Maxine Croyett's housekeeper?'

'Only because she was editing my book for me. I'm a lawyer.'

'Which law firm do you work for?' he asked.

'I don't at present. I'm applying for positions.'

'Have you ever worked as a lawyer?'

'Yes, I worked for O'Mara-Reeves Associates in Newcastle until a few months ago.'

'But you left to become a housekeeper?'

'No, I left because…' I heard my voice rise and felt the words claw at my throat. 'I just left.'

'I see…' he said.

I tried to speak calmly, even though feelings of panic threatened to surface. 'Can I come and meet you? Maxine has stolen my manuscript. It's mine! I've spent two years writing it.'

I heard him sigh and I knew he didn't believe me.

Why would he believe an unknown and unpublished writer had written this novel, rather than Maxine, a multi best-selling author who had submitted it as her own work?

'We don't need to meet, but I'll be back in touch,' came his clipped reply.

'Maxine's lying. She's stolen it. She's completely mad.' I continued to protest, but the line went dead.

I looked at Marcus and raked my hands through my hair. 'Holy shit!'

He nodded as if it came as no surprise. 'Maxine's stolen your book? The book that implicates your dad, the man Maxine loved and was rejected by, as the murderer of his girlfriend all those years ago?'

'Yes, you got it in one. So Maxine will get her revenge - not only on Dad, but me, too.'

I leaned upon Marcus and clasped my forehead. 'I need to think what to do. I wish I'd never met her. And I never should have trusted her with my book. And now she's stolen it and will make a fucking fortune from it.'

My eyes stung and I pressed my fists into them to restrain my tears.

'Don't blame yourself. I'm angry with myself for not anticipating this and warning you to be cautious.' Marcus handed me my clothes. 'Come on.'

My hands shook as I dressed, and a raging fury rose within me, burning my insides and firing my blood. If only I'd thought rationally and gone straight to the police after Maxine had taken me hostage. She'd have been arrested, tried and imprisoned for what she did to me. Despite my promises to Hadrian, I'd been a fool to let such a serious incident go.

'I'll bloody kill her,' I fumed.

'If I don't get to her first,' added Marcus.

'I have to decide what to do, and fast,' I said.

Marcus and I sat opposite Mum at the dinner table, but the weekend I'd planned where Mum could get to know Marcus and enjoy our company had taken a dark turn even before they'd met. When we'd walked back from the beach and through the front door Mum saw I'd been crying and I spilled the news about Maxine stealing my novel as her own.

It wasn't often I saw Mum lose her rag, but she was all set to drive over there and have it out with Maxine, threaten to reveal her holding me hostage to the police and have her arrested.

'It's too late for that,' I insisted. 'We need a clever and radical approach.'

Mum opened a bottle of red wine and poured three large glasses. She lay a sheet of paper on the table, gave us each a pen and wrote in capital letters - *THE TRUTH.*

'Okay, brainstorm. Any idea, however impossible it might seem, write it down,' she said.

She raised her glass. 'May the best idea succeed and take Maxine Croyett down.'

We clinked glasses. I took a long drink, eager for a rush of alcohol fuelled inspiration, then set my glass down and picked up my pen.

An hour later we'd emptied the bottle of wine, were half way through the next and had almost filled the sheet of paper with our ideas, none of which inspired me with great confidence.

I turned to Marcus.

'I don't think writing letters, going round to reason with Maxine, or threatening lawsuits is going to work. There's no time for that.'

'What do you suggest then?' he asked.

'Do you think your mum would be prepared to help out?'

'I'm certain she would, but how?'

I stood up decisively, 'I'm going to give her a call.'

Marcus and Mum's eyes followed me as I went to the phone on the sideboard. 'What's her number?'

When I came off the phone, a plan of action was decided and I hoped to God that it would work.

We'd begin in the morning.

Chapter 30

Albatross Publishing

I stood together with Evelyn on the pavement of Clayton Street in Newcastle City Centre, outside Maxine's publisher - Albatross Publishing. Their office was set midway along a beautiful four-storey Georgian terrace. Architecturally, like so many of the terraces in Newcastle, it was grand, and looking up at it, a little imposing given the plan I was about to implement - if we could gain entry. Evelyn had made a special effort to look professional as opposed to arty, in a smart, burgundy Chanel skirt suit, and I wore my black dress suit with blue shirt, navy tie, tights and heeled court shoes.

I held my brown leather briefcase filled with what I hoped was convincing evidence.

I turned to Evelyn. 'Ready?'

'If you are?' she asked.

'I'm terrified, but prepared,' I replied.

I buzzed for reception on the intercom and a woman answered.

'Hello. Who are you here to see?'

'We're here to see Simon Trimble.'

'And your name?' she asked.

'Jodie Rivera and Evelyn Hall.'

There was a short silence. 'What time's your appointment?'

'This is an impromptu visit. Simon is Maxine Croyett's editor and we are here on her behalf.'

'You're not in his diary.'

Evelyn stepped forwards to the intercom. 'I'm Maxine's twin sister and she sent me. She prefers not to come but has important details about her new novel she's asked me to hand over to Simon, in person.'

'Bear with me,' came the receptionist's curt reply.

The intercom silenced and I turned to Evelyn with adrenaline fluttering through me. We only needed to get through these doors and into his office, or we'd be in for a long wait.

The intercom clicked and the woman came back on. 'Mr Trimble is busy all day. 'Appointments only, I'm afraid. Please ask Maxine to ring him, in person.'

The intercom fell silent.

Evelyn turned to me. 'What now?'

I sighed. 'We wait, if you don't mind?'

A young man in a bright orange T-shirt walked up the steps to the door. He carried a large icebox and pressed the intercom. The receptionist answered.

'It's Paul's Buns with the lunch orders.'

The door buzzed and clicked.

He pushed the door open and I stepped forwards, held the door and we followed him in.

The young man turned to us.

'Oh, don't worry, we were waiting for the receptionist to open the door,' I said, with a broad smile.

He crossed to the lift and we followed and waited beside him until the lift arrived and the doors slid open. I was so relieved to be inside the building that I felt none of my usual fears of stepping inside the lift, and didn't even look around for the staircase. The young man pressed the button for the third floor. I had no idea which floor Simon Trimble worked on, but we had to start somewhere.

'Do you deliver to Simon Trimble?' I asked.

He lifted his clipboard and looked down a list of names. 'There is a Simon,' he replied. 'Salmon and cucumber in a wholemeal bap,' he added.

'Ooh, my favourite,' I said.

The lift pinged and the doors opened. The young man gestured politely for us to go first and we walked into a foyer. It was small but well lit and with smart, contemporary chairs and striped wallpaper. Classy black and white framed photographic portraits hung on the walls, which I presumed were of their most renowned and celebrated authors.

A pretty woman with shiny black hair looked up as we approached the main desk. She didn't speak, but smiled and waited for us to introduce ourselves.

'I'd like to speak with Simon Trimble, please,' I said.

She frowned - realising we were the women she'd turned away from the intercom. 'I assume you have an appointment?'

'We don't, but I must speak with him. I'm Jodie Rivera, a lawyer, and Simon has been reading my manuscript submission. He rang and spoke to me in person on Saturday. And this is Evelyn Hall, Maxine Croyett's twin sister.' I smiled at Evelyn. 'Please would you ask if we could have two minutes of his time?'

The girl raised her eyebrows. 'Mr Trimble lets me know if he has an appointment. Are you the woman I spoke to on the intercom?'

'Yes, but I know Simon will be grateful he spoke with me. I have *vital* information for him.'

She pressed her lips together, clearly unconvinced. 'Please take a seat,' she said, finally. 'But I'll call security if there's any trouble at all.'

'There will be no need. We're not here to cause problems,' I insisted. 'In fact, we're here to save Simon from a damaging lawsuit.'

Moments later a tall, middle-aged man came into the reception. He was elegantly dressed in a checked blue suit and bow tie.

He looked from Evelyn to me, then turned and spoke directly to the receptionist. 'Beth, are these the ladies downstairs who were asking for me?'

'I'm afraid so, Simon.' She pursed her lips again. 'They barged their way through with Paul's Buns.'

Simon glanced at his watch before turning to me. 'I have five minutes before my next meeting.'

He turned and we followed him to the end of a corridor and into a spacious and brightly lit office. His office was surprisingly neat for a publisher, I thought, with contemporary floor-to-ceiling bookshelves, filled with colourful book spines, all perfectly aligned. On the other walls were more black and white author portraits. Traffic sounds rumbled from the street below, and Simon walked to the window and pulled the sash down.

He sat behind his desk. 'Please close the door.'

He spoke with a light geordie accent, similar to my own. I'd never tried to tone mine down, but I think it happened naturally after working with lawyers and clients from all over the country.

I closed the door and he gestured for us to take the seats in front of his desk.

I sat down, placed my briefcase on my knees and clicked it open in readiness. Then with a smile, I looked across at him. 'Thank you for seeing us.'

He looked at me stony faced and I noticed how heavy hooded his pale lashed eyes were.

'Let me be blunt,' he said, and brushed a speck of something from the sleeve of his jacket. 'Your manuscript - The Truth, may have a different title but the plot is exactly the same and not a great deal different from Maxine Croyett's novel, other than the setting.'

Of course, I thought, Maxine wouldn't have rewritten the ending, despite suggesting to me that it should be rewritten, because my ending already incriminated Dad.

'I assume she set it at Hadrian's Wall?' I asked.

He watched me closely as I spoke and I felt suspicion and judgement in his gaze. 'You said you were Maxine's housekeeper?'

'No,' I said. 'I temporarily helped her out in her home whilst she volunteered to read and then edit my novel manuscript. It was purely a business exchange for her expertise and time. I am a trained lawyer with professional qualifications and a decade of law experience. I worked for O'Mara-Reeves Associates, as I explained when you rang me. Please ring John O'Mara, a senior partner. I'll give you his business card. John began reading my manuscript before I left his employment and he can assure you I spent well over a year writing and editing it - evenings, weekends, every spare moment.'

Simon smoothed his hand over his hair. 'This John fella, was your boyfriend I assume?'

'Yes, but no longer. He has no reason to mislead you, and neither do I.'

'I see.' Simon turned to Evelyn. 'You look familiar. Have we met before?'

'I'm Evelyn Hall, Maxine Croyett's twin.'

He nodded. 'Ahh! Of course, the strong resemblance. And you're the sculptor. I saw your exhibition with my wife at the Edinburgh Festival last summer.'

'That's right. And I'm here to support Jodie and her work - her novel. I assure you that Maxine did not write this novel, and if you publish it, then it will be fraud on a criminal scale.'

'And I will have no choice but to file a lawsuit should you choose to go ahead with publishing my novel under Maxine's name,' I added.

Simon's eyes narrowed. 'Is that so?'

But I recognised uncertainty in his features, and I pressed on.

'It's also important for you to know that my novel is based upon a real life crime story. I set it elsewhere and wrote an alternative ending to the conclusion the police and forensic examiner came to.'

'That is called artistic licence and allowable in fiction,' said Simon.

'Of course, I realise that,' I said. 'But for Maxine the crime is as personal to her as it is to me.' I paused.

'Okay,' he said slowly and sat up straight. 'Now I am intrigued.'

'I thought you might be,' I said.

I continued. 'The man arrested for the crime in my novel is based on my own father - Brett Anderson. He was the young woman's, Sheila Morgan's, lawyer boyfriend at the time of her drowning. I named her Sarah in my novel.'

'And why would you wish to implicate blame on your own father? Wouldn't that rather upset him?'

'My father and I have been estranged for years. I found out at my own cost what a violent and cruel man he is. So you see, I have no qualms about placing the guilt on him for this crime. More importantly, I believe what I have written to be the truth - although I have no evidential proof as he wasn't convicted and unlikely to ever confess to what really happened - should I have sought the opportunity to ask him.'

Simon cupped his chin and listened intently. 'And how is Maxine involved and why would she want to steal your novel when she is quite brilliant at writing her own?'

I took a deep breath. 'Because she hasn't published a book for five years - as you know. I believe she is struggling, creatively. But most importantly, after reading mine, even giving it a different setting away from where the crime was committed, she recognised it as the crime story involving my father, her ex-lawyer and ex-lover, and the father of her only child.'

'Good Lord! This all sounds too fantastic to be remotely possible.'

'I assure you it's the truth. And what is more, she was extremely upset and resentful when my father, Brett, rejected her, stayed married to my mother, and the icing on the cake, went in hot pursuit of her twin sister.' I turned to Evelyn.

Simon's mouth opened as he looked from me to Evelyn.

'That is the sort of man my father is, unfortunately.'

'Your surname is Rivera, not Anderson like your father's?'

I nodded. 'Yes, my mother and I changed our names to her maiden name when she threw my father out.'

Simon looked at Evelyn. 'This is all true? This man, Brett Anderson, who fathered Maxine's only child, pursued you?'

'Yes, but I saw him for the monster he was. A revolting excuse for a man, a serial philanderer, and so I had nothing to do with him.'

'And you are prepared to swear to all of this, even though Maxine is your sister? You have no loyalty to her?'

'I don't know how well you really know Maxine. She may be a brilliant writer, but she is not a warm or loving human. And in the short time I've known Jodie, I was shocked by Maxine's behaviour towards her and how low she has sunk by stealing Jodie's work. I have since read Jodie's novel and believe her writing style shines brightly, and is quite unlike my sister's, but is unique and superbly written.'

Simon glanced impatiently down at his watch. 'Indeed, I read the whole manuscript. I'm afraid I'd need to see concrete evidence to prove it is your novel and not Maxine's.'

I reached inside and pulled out John's business card and handed it across the desk. 'If you can't take my word as a professional lawyer, then please call another lawyer, John. He will verify that this manuscript and story is written by me and me alone. As I said, he witnessed me writing it.'

I reached inside for my notebooks and an early draft of my novel.

I placed them on the desk in front of me. 'As you will see in these, all of my character outlines, my considerable research notes on the real life crime, setting research, plot and chapter plans are all here. Lots of notes, too. You can also read my first printed draft which is rough but has my handwriting all over it. Physical and forensic evidence that will stand up in court, should it need to. My manuscript files are also dated and saved on my hard drive and discs. Maxine has nothing other than the printed manuscript and computer file I gave her - no previous revisions, of which I have several dating back eighteen months.'

I might be no technical whizz, but when it came to computer work, I'd learned to my cost the importance of being rigorous with document backups.

I fell silent and awaited Simon's response.

'Well, well, ladies! This has been a most interesting and enlightening meeting. I am left feeling disturbed, but nevertheless, glad that I met with you.' He stood up.

'And what do you plan to do?' I asked, feeling more hopeful by the second.

'With your agreement, I'd like you to entrust your notebooks and evidence with me. I shall be ringing this John fella too.' Simon sucked in a breath. 'And then I will be speaking to Maxine.'

I watched his features and body language. I considered myself a pretty astute judge of when someone was lying and he *appeared* to believe my story, or at least be worried enough to take it seriously. But I knew leaving my evidence here left me vulnerable.

'I should advise that I've taken the precaution of making photocopies of my evidence, and I've logged the details with a senior lawyer and former colleague.' I gestured to my draft manuscripts and notebooks. 'Can I trust you to keep all of this safe and locked up?'

He gave a thin smile. 'Of course. I do not underestimate the serious ramifications of this matter.'

'And I hope you will then be talking to me again?' I asked.

He reached out and shook first my hand, and then Evelyn's. 'Indeed. You can expect a call within a day or two,' he replied.

He showed us out to reception. 'It's been both a surprise and a revelation to meet you, Jodie Rivera.' He turned to Evelyn. 'And yourself, Ms Hall.'

Chapter 31

Six Months Later

After the meeting with Simon, things progressed rapidly. My aspirations to become a published author had become a reality. Simon Trimble reported that John had backed up my story, and had even admitted to enjoying what he read of my book, despite the main character, aka murderer, being named Johnny. Even more astounding after everything that had happened, was that I'd been signed up with the same publisher as international best-selling author, plagiarist and sociopath, Maxine Croyett. Of course, Albatross Publishing had little choice but to drop Maxine from their author portfolio, and the publicity surrounding this had sparked some high profile news stories.

One morning as Marcus and I were sitting in bed munching on jam on toast, Marcus' mobile phone rang from the bedside table.

He peered down. 'It's Philip.'

'I wonder what he wants,' I said, curious.

'Morning Philip. Everything okay?' Marcus said, and listened. 'Yeah, Jodie's here, hold on.' He turned to me. 'He wants to speak to you.'

'Oh.' I took the phone from him. 'Hi Philip.'

'Morning. I'd like to read you an article I've written for the Observer. They liked my brief for the background on Maxine and her attempt at book theft and plagiarism.'

'Who is your source?' I said, already knowing the answer.

'Well, obviously I know what happened to you, but I won't be citing you as my source. I wouldn't want to damage your career now it's taking off.'

'So, Evelyn's agreed?'

'Yep. She regrets not going directly to the police after Maxine held you hostage and attacked you so violently. We both agree that what Maxine is should be known publicly.'

'Good.' On that we agreed. 'Let's hear it then.'

Philip spoke and I listened. I turned the volume up and Marcus listened in too.

I savoured every sentence and detail of the controversial and damning article. Philip had spared none of the incriminating evidence, all of which was true. "Outright plagiarism and theft... assault and kidnap... affair with her lawyer... love child... reclusive... mysterious and unsolved death of her husband at the time of her affair.'

I devoured every word and had to admit to relishing each new detail that would add to Maxine's downfall. I felt Maxine was finally receiving just and due punishment for her attack on me and theft of my work.

'It's brilliant, Philip. Keep my name well out of it, but I agree with every detail. How's Evelyn feeling?'

'She feels desperately sad that her relationship with her sister has come to this, but she realises that without publicly telling the truth, she's condoning her sister's crimes.'

'Thank you, Philip. How I'd love to be a fly on the wall when Maxine reads this.'

'Better to be well away. Any fly on Maxine's wall is unlikely to survive for long.'

We hung up and Marcus put his arm around me.

'I'll call Mum later,' he said. 'I know she wanted to build bridges with Maxine, but it's too late. Maxine will never forgive Mum for her betrayal with my dad, Winston. And it seems Dad paid the ultimate price for Maxine's revenge.'

Maxine's professional reputation had plummeted and shattered beyond repair. She was guilty of committing the worst possible sin for any writer - plagiarism, and for a successful author, this discovery had resulted in a shameful and damning finale to her career. There was no way she could touch me or my career now.

I didn't ask Simon Trimble, but I presumed Maxine was aware that prior to publication, he'd signed me up with my book. I could only conclude that her grandiose delusions and over-inflated sense of worth had convinced her she'd get away with such a monumental theft. I assumed she was more dangerously unhinged than ever, and feeling vengeful, and I hoped to God I wouldn't bump into her at any book events or that she would try to stalk me or seek me out. Given she was virtually a recluse, I hoped that would minimise any opportunities for her to confront or attack me in person.

During the past year, and despite all the upset and drama, my life and career had changed almost beyond recognition. Marcus and I were moving in together. We both agreed that being out of the immediate area of Hexham and The Blue House was essential - no accidental encounters - so we signed up for a flat on the outskirts of Newcastle, and Marcus could still drive to work at the education centres along Hadrian's wall.

We settled in quickly; it felt so wonderfully right being with him that any regrets I'd had about going to Maxine's talk and staying with her began to fade into the recesses of my mind.

My book, simply titled, *The Truth*, was published at the end of January, and all manner of publicity events and articles had been scheduled. That someone else was doing all the organising for me felt like a huge privilege and I vowed I'd never take this feeling for granted.

Some things had left me feeling uneasy though. Hadrian had, according to Marcus, pursued getting to know Dad, and after an unsuccessful initial meeting, Dad had relented and allowed Hadrian into his life. I heard on the grapevine that they'd been spending time together and that Hadrian got on with Dad's second wife, too.

Whilst I didn't resent Hadrian knowing Dad, as I would never want to bridge the void between Dad and I, I was fearful that their newfound relationship might affect me or Mum in some way. What did Maxine think of her only son knowing Dad, the man who'd abandoned and rejected her all those years ago? Not that I felt in any way sorry for Maxine - she'd no doubt been treated by Dad in the only way she deserved, at least from what I'd experienced during that fateful and traumatic week I'd spent with her last summer.

During the editing of my book, Simon Trimble and I had sat down together and had a long discussion about the truth that my book explored and revealed. Was it indeed the truth that explained the real life drowning of Sheila Morgan? Or had it been a figment of my imagination or revenge to incriminate Dad?

Either way, it couldn't be proven, unless Dad came forward and confessed his involvement, which was an impossibility. People like my father didn't feel guilt, let alone confess to their crimes or mistakes. He still hadn't ever acknowledged or apologised for the way he'd treated me, David and Mum. No, the precise truth of Sheila's death would remain a mystery, Simon and I concluded.

In the preface, we stated that my novel was based on a real-life drowning and declared where and when it took place. We'd had to, really. If we hadn't, someone would have read the book, speculated and revealed the actual news story - not least Maxine.

Evelyn's lover and journalist, Philip, had also advised that we state the real story, and as a media professional and friend, I trusted his advice.

A month after publication I was both excited and terrified to be invited to talk on The Book Review. It was an hour long TV programme aired each week which invited a mixed panel of authors and celebrities to discuss three books, read them beforehand, and share their opinions on the programme. What was even more nerve-wracking was that one of the books to be discussed was my very own - *The Truth*. I had given several interviews for newspaper and magazine articles, but nothing for TV or even radio.

A fortnight before the show I travelled to Manchester to meet with the producer. I got the feeling she wanted to sound me out to see if I could answer questions coherently about my book, and if I had what it took to speak about literary matters generally on a national TV show without embarrassing either myself, the programme makers or their celebrity presenter and renowned Oxbridge academic, Robert Fulford.

'I love that red dress you're wearing,' she said as I got up to leave. 'And for sure the camera and audience will love you.'

'I hope so,' I replied.

'Your appearance on the show will do wonders for your book sales and lead to other publicity events.'

If I don't mess it up, I thought.

'I'm looking forward to it. I'm bringing along a couple of friends for moral support.'

She grimaced. 'Not Maxine Croyett though, I hope?'

'Simon's spoken about the controversy then?'

'Simon and I are old friends.' She paused. 'And obviously I read the papers.'

At least the programme would be pre-recorded, but in front of a live audience. I imagined the small auditorium would be full of book enthusiasts who were primed and ready with their questions, a few of which would be selected and asked during the programme. I'd invited Simon Trimble, Marcus, Mum and Evelyn. I'd also invited Evelyn's boyfriend, Philip, who had declined, for obvious reasons.

When Marcus opened up the TV Schedule magazine and showed me my name listed amongst the other authors and celebrities, my tummy did a massive flip.

'Oh my God! How am I going to control my nerves amongst that lot?'

'Remember you have to pretend scary people are naked and that way you won't feel intimidated.'

I gave a nervous laugh. 'That's the audience, I think.'

Marcus laughed too, 'Okay, imagine that I'm naked and watching you as you talk.'

'Seriously? And you think that's going to help me stay cool and calm?'

I dissolved into laughter, which then led to Marcus having to kiss me to quieten me, after which things quickly progressed to us making love on the sheepskin rug.

Afterwards we lay with limbs entwined on the floor and Marcus pulled two cushions off the sofa to rest our heads.

We lay facing one another - our noses almost touching. 'All this publishing stuff is making you even more sexy.'

'It's only because I'm happy, and that's more because of you than my book.'

'I wonder if after you become a TV celeb and poster pin up author, you'll want more than we have here.'

I stroked his cheek. 'First of all, you've made me happier than I've ever felt before, by a thousand miles, and secondly, are you sure that authors ever become pinups?' I giggled. 'I sincerely hope not.'

'No, but if you were on a poster I'd buy it.'

'Stop it, Marcus. I'm feeling humbled by the whole book thing so far. I think I have a serious case of impostor syndrome.'

'Well, when you're on that programme don't forget that you wrote that book, not my wicked aunt of the north.'

I kissed him on the lips. 'Thanks for the reminder, and if I mess up on camera, you can heckle from the back row.'

Chapter 32

The Book Review Programme

I sat beneath the spotlights, about to be questioned and with an audience only metres away. It felt weirdly akin to being in court, but the faces were friendlier and all chatted away as the crew finalised their equipment preparations and the make-up artists checked and tweaked our hair and faces. I'd worn the same red dress the producer had admired - well fitted with a neckline that wasn't too low, nor the skirt too short. I wore black Mary Jane heels, sheer tights and crossed my knees modestly, holding my book in my hands. I'd placed post-it notes in a couple of pages as I knew I was going to be asked to read an excerpt or two.

I took some calming breaths and tried not to feel overwhelmed by the fame and proximity of the other guests. I was seated beside the programme presenter, Robert Fulford, and to my right sat Stephanie Morgan, a scholarly looking British author of historical fiction, then next to her, Harley Mason, renowned book review editor for The Sunday Times. To the left of our presenter sat Helena Bonham Carter, even more beautiful in person, with reading glasses perched on her nose, coming next, Greta Rubinstein, Scandi noir novelist and famed advocate and activist for LGBTQ+ rights.

I looked up at the audience and Marcus gave me a wave from the middle of the back row where the steps led down between the audience seated on either side. Beside him sat Evelyn looking amazing in a purple trouser suit, with her hair beautifully styled in an updo, and next to her, my mum in a floral green dress bought especially for the occasion. Both mums were engrossed in conversation. Ever since we'd introduced them a month ago, they'd hit it off, and Mum had even travelled over and stayed at Evelyn's for a weekend. I imagined they had lots of history to talk about, and were anticipating becoming in-laws at some point in the future.

I hoped for that, too.

The ten rows or so of seats in the TV studio were full and a handful of people stood at the back to one side. The lights dimmed above the audience and white lights illuminated the stage. The opening credit music started and the audience hushed as we turned our faces to our presenter, Robert. He was a distinguished looking man, hair prematurely grey, but attractive with brown perceptive eyes and a voice that commanded both interest and attentiveness.

He invited each of us to introduce ourselves and what we do or have written.

I turned to the audience and smiled. 'I'm Jodie Rivera, I'm a lawyer by profession, and the author of *The Truth*, a novel set in Yorkshire and about the mysterious disappearance and drowning of a young female lawyer back in the fifties.'

The audience applauded as each of us introduced ourselves, and I began to relax and even glanced up towards Marcus. But he wasn't looking my way, rather he had turned his head to the people who stood behind the back row. My gaze followed his, but when Robert spoke my name my attention quickly returned to him.

'I wonder if you'd be able to read us an excerpt from your novel that might give our viewers an idea of what it's about.'

I opened my book to the first fluorescent post-it. 'I'd love to, thank you, Robert.'

I turned to the audience. 'This story is narrated by Sarah, the murder victim. Through naturalistic flashbacks and her deepest thoughts, the reader is given an insight into her life and her relationship with boyfriend, Johnny.'

I began to read. "Late in June we drove into the heart of the Yorkshire Dales and Johnny turned his car onto a dirt track at the base of Whernside. I gazed out of the car window in awe at the landscape that surrounded us. As I stepped out of the car, I heard the haunting call of a bird of prey and spotted a Red Kite that circled the air high above us..."

But as I continued to recite the passage from memory, I glanced up, and when I glimpsed the face of a man I hadn't seen in over a decade - my father, and the precise murderer who I portrayed in my novel, my insides erupted with panic. He hadn't

284

changed, and especially his eyes which lasered into mine. Beside him stood Hadrian - his young doppelganger. I hadn't anticipated or imagined that either of them would know about this programme, or if they did, would want to attend the recording of it.

Christ! How had Dad even known about the recording of the show, and how the fuck had he wheedled or sneaked his way in? Had Hadrian found out and told Dad? Maybe Maxine had a spy at Albatross Publishing, and told Hadrian because she wanted to cause trouble?

I managed to finish reciting the passage, forced a smile, and the audience applauded as if entirely satisfied with my reading.

'I felt myself right there on that hillside with Sarah and Johnny, thank you, Jodie,' said Robert.

I turned to him and tried to calm my heart which was catapulting into my mouth knowing who was watching and listening to my every word. But I refused to feel intimidated or repressed by the presence of my father and I decided I would speak freely as if he weren't here. He couldn't touch me here on the stage. I wondered if he'd spotted Mum and Evelyn or if either of them had spotted him with Hadrian only feet behind them.

Christ, the whole situation felt horrifyingly surreal.

Stay focused, I thought.

As we began to discuss one of the other novels we'd read in preparation, I tried not to allow my eyes to be drawn again to the back of the auditorium. My cheeks grew flushed beneath the lights and my hands felt clammy on the cover of my book. I realised I should contribute to the discussion, but my mind was struggling to come up with even one coherent sentence.

I blurted out. 'I can't say I was convinced by the main protagonist. I mean, who would willingly set off on a long journey through a forest without at least a bottle of water, or leaving a note to tell their family where they were going? It's almost as if they were wanting to die.'

The other members of the panel turned my way for what felt like long moments, surprised and unsure how to respond.

Until Helena Bonham Carter nodded and laughed. 'I completely agree, Jodie. He was a fool, and it's hard then to empathise with someone, an experienced explorer no less, who acts without a modicum of common sense.'

The audience erupted into laughter.

'I did enjoy the book though,' I continued. 'Extremely readable and I was keen to know if he'd survive or was rescued.'

'That is true,' agreed Helena. 'A real page turner and probably why it's already sold over a million copies in its first year.'

'And is a best-seller what you are after?' Robert asked me.

I thought for a moment. 'That isn't why I wrote it.'

Robert leaned forwards in his seat. 'And why exactly did you write it, given that you were already enjoying a successful career in Law?'

I kept my eyes fixed on his and I felt a shiver run over my skin. 'I wrote it because of my past - my childhood.'

'Your childhood? Does this story relate to your upbringing?'

I swallowed hard and my eyes smarted. And I didn't care who was listening - my mother, my father, Evelyn, or the entire bloody nation.

I lifted my chin. 'Yes, I wrote it because of my father.'

Robert nodded, his eyes intensely focused and sincere. 'Please, go on.'

I glanced up to where my father stood. 'My father was a lawyer, like I am, like I was, but that is where our likeness ends. Growing up in a house with him was hard. It was difficult, and ultimately, it was painful and traumatic. He treated me, my brother and my mother with contempt, with anger, with violence - never the love I craved from him, and needed. And it is for this reason that I chose to write about and exorcise these feelings that have festered and remained inside of me all these years, through a novel that is both fictional and real. Real because it is based upon a true crime, and real because my father was, I believe, the perpetrator - the murderer of the young female victim portrayed in my novel.'

There were murmurs amongst the audience.

I took a breath, unsure how to continue. 'So you see, the title of my novel, *The Truth*, is the truth of the crime as I see it. And I believe that although the crime itself remains unsolved from all those years ago, knowing who and what my father was and no doubt still is, I believe that he murdered Sheila Morgan - who was his girlfriend in real life.' I blinked through tears and through my blurred vision I saw movements where my father stood.

A tall woman appeared behind my father, and I glanced at the seats where Evelyn had been seated, thinking she'd got up, but no, Evelyn was still seated beside Mum. My eyes flicked sidewards again to the woman's face. The same face but with cropped grey hair - Maxine, her eyes fixed upon my father with a look of pure hatred I could clearly discern from here on stage. I stood up.

What happened next was beyond my control and my reach, and happened too rapidly for me to intervene.

Maxine held something in her hand and I watched as Hadrian, finally seeing his mother and realising her intention, moved to cut in. Maxine raised her arm and swung the knife at my father's back at the precise moment that Hadrian stepped between them.

I screamed out, 'Stop her!' to warn my father, but at the same time another scream echoed through the auditorium. A young man's agonised cry. Hadrian's back was turned to all of us, other than Maxine, and I watched as his head, shoulders and torso folded over and he collapsed. Everyone in the audience and on stage had turned in their seats to see what caused the disturbance.

I sprinted across the floor between two cameramen and hurtled up the auditorium steps. Hadrian lay in a heap on the floor, and beside him Maxine sank to her knees with the knife dripping blood in her hand. Instinctively I reached down and grabbed the knife from her and threw it down the stairs. Maxine looked up at my father, her head shaking in confusion, before falling upon Hadrian's body, screaming and howling.

My father looked at me with deep loathing, before he stepped over his son's body, pushed open the exit door and disappeared through it.

Chapter 33

One Year Later

My father and I would never be reconciled and the void between us only widened further. I couldn't stop picturing the horrific TV studio incident when Hadrian had attempted to protect his father, been stabbed by his own mother, and subsequently died and been revived on the operating table. By some miracle and the immense skill of his surgeons, Hadrian had survived and recovered, minus one kidney.

My book prompted the Sheila Morgan drowning to be reopened. The revelations in the studio that day meant the authorities had no choice but to reexamine the evidence, albeit forty plus years old. Furthermore, after Maxine's murderous outburst, the police had reopened the case of Winston's fall from the cliff at Housesteads Fort. The evidence against Maxine grew stronger by the day. On top of all this I'd reported the incident where I'd been knocked out, locked up and bound when staying at Maxine's. I knew this would add to the evidence against her.

Philip had already written and published the story with the added detail of Maxine turning up to the TV studio with the intention of doing harm to Brett or possibly me, but the far worse and unanticipated outcome of almost murdering her only beloved son. Maxine, and potentially my father, were in for a prison sentence, and as far as I was concerned both deserved a lifetime of punishment.

Marcus and I were happily settled in our first owned property - a first floor flat in an old Victorian town house. We'd even adopted a rescue dog to join us in our new home. She was a sweet natured miniature schnauzer named Tiger and she loved nothing more than to curl up beside me, whether I was relaxing with Marcus in the evenings or sitting at my desk writing.

One Saturday morning, Marcus came into our study, placed a cup of tea beside me on my desk and went to sit in the easy chair by the window.

I swivelled my chair round and sipped my tea. 'Are you excited about tonight?'

'Of course. It'll be fun catching up with all my mates.' He looked down at his wrist and tapped his watch face.

I sensed he had something on his mind.

'And getting hopelessly drunk, I expect,' I said.

'I'll have no choice given I'm the stag and they'll have high expectations of me.'

'Were any of them surprised we're tying the knot so soon.'

'Mmm.' He scrunched his nose. 'There have been one or two comments, but I reckon they're all pleased for me, maybe even envious.'

I lifted Tiger off my lap, popped her on the floor, and went to squeeze in beside Marcus.

'Funny how our family dynamics have changed and now our families are joining,' I said, snuggling up to him. 'I can't wait for you to meet David, too. Mum's thrilled he's coming to the wedding.'

'I still can't quite believe how much like Hadrian he looks,' said Marcus, glancing at David's photo on the bookshelf.

'Shared genes, but altogether different, personality wise.'

He wrinkled his nose. 'I wonder how they'll get on?'

'Hopefully they'll bond, rather like we all have since the incident.'

'I hope so,' Marcus said, thoughtful.

He glanced at his watch again. 'Hadrian will be here soon.'

'Generous of him to drive all the way over to pick you up.'

'I mentioned that me and Hadrian are going to walk a stretch of the wall today, before we go out tonight?'

I shook my head. 'No, which part?'

'Housesteads Fort.'

I straightened up, and a sense of unease rose inside me. 'Really? Where you both work every day?'

'Yeah. I don't mind though. I get the feeling Hadrian wanted us to go together to the spot where Dad died. Now that the inquest into his death has reopened.'

'Do you feel okay about that?'

He scrunched his nose again. 'It might feel uncomfortable, but I think so.'

I sensed his disquiet and taking his hand I leaned over and kissed him. 'Please don't stand close to that edge. I feel peculiar even thinking about you looking over that drop.'

'Don't worry. Hadrian and I are all good now. That's the one positive change to come out of this past year. Oh, and you of course, my beautiful, almost wife.'

In Marcus' eyes the terrible events from our recent past were history. They were effectively lost in time, meaning they could no longer darken our present or future. And I realised that ultimately we each weaved our unique, but oftentimes, fictional reality - the fusion of wishful thinking, experience and reality, which became the truth we chose to believe in and live by.

Marcus wanted to move on, and I didn't want to hold him back from doing so.

I sensed movement and a shadow in my peripheral vision, and when I turned to the window I saw a crow had landed on the windowsill. It looked enormous up close, and it stood completely still looking in at us with round, black eyes, its feathered wings gleaming like jet-stone in the sunlight.

'Where on earth did he come from?' I said, turning to Marcus.

He made a little hand gesture to the window. 'The tree on the street, I imagine.'

My heart juddered in my chest as I watched the crow, watching us. I rose and went to the window, and with my forehead to the glass, peered closer. How strange, I thought. The crow had the same distinctive white fingerprint mark on the top of its head and my memory returned to that early morning at The Blue House when the crow had flown in through my bedroom window.

The crow's head twitched my way and I swear it looked straight into my eyes. It felt oddly unnerving to meet its direct and unafraid gaze.

'Look. It's got a white mark on its head,' I said without turning around. 'Isn't that unusual?'

Marcus came closer to have a look. 'Sure it's not a magpie?'

The bird switched its focus to Marcus.

'Definitely a crow,' I said.

'Yep. Reminds me, Winston, had a Mallen streak.'

'Really?' I turned to him. 'Aren't they supposed to be hereditary?'

'Often, yeah.' Marcus continued watching the crow. 'If I had one I'd have guessed my father's identity long ago.'

'True,' I replied and took his hand. 'Maxine and Hadrian, too.'

With a curious smile I watched Marcus. 'Are you trying to out-stare it?'

'You bet I am!'

The doorbell rang downstairs and the crow startled, spread its wings and flew away into the tree across the road.

'Ha!' cried Marcus. 'Beat him.'

'A persistent little fellow though,' I remarked.

I peered down to the garden path below. Hadrian stood a few feet from the front door - I hadn't seen him approach. He must have sensed me watching because he raised his head and we made eye contact through the glass.

His dark eyes and gaze reminded me so much of my father's, and I felt a nervous flutter in my tummy.

I turned back to Marcus. 'I'm going to miss you madly, you know?'

'I'll miss you a whole lot more,' he replied, and gave me a final lingering kiss on the lips.

He turned away and walked to the door.

My heart lurched and an overwhelming sense of foreboding filled my mind. 'Wait!' I called.

Marcus stopped in the doorway and turned around.

I ran over, wanting to hold him close to me and insist that he send Hadrian away. I wanted to wake up tomorrow morning with him, sleepy and warm, hip to hip, his thigh against mine.

But instead I clasped his hand in mine. 'What I really meant to say was, we will both miss you.'

And feeling a flutter of a different kind, I placed his hand with mine upon the soft swell of my belly.

I watched Marcus and Hadrian head down the garden path and climb into Hadrian's jeep. And when Marcus closed the passenger door, wound down the window, and waved up at me, he appeared happy and at ease despite all that had passed within their family.

Even so, as I picked up our tea cups and carried them to the kitchen, I felt sick with unease and my thoughts were in turmoil.

I sat down at my desk with Tiger ensconced on my lap once more. As I stroked her ears, for my own comfort as much as hers, I read through the page I'd typed only that morning. Other than my editor, Simon Trimble, I'd been cautious about sharing any details of the book I'd been writing for the past six months, and with genuine reason. Like my first novel, my second book, titled, *A Tale of Two Writers*, was also based upon a real life crime story. But this time it was my own story, featuring a young ex-lawyer and aspiring novelist, who is mentored by a reclusive and sociopathic best-selling crime writer.

The End

Acknowledgements

A special thank you to all those who helped me during the writing of my fifth novel - my publishers, Gwen and David Morrison, A J Humpage for her critique, superb editing and advice, proofreading and amazing advice from Robin Avalyn, feedback and reading support from, Liz Best, Kate Trelawny, Kerry Newton, Shirley Jones and Katharine Wilkinson.

About the Author

Olivia Rytwinski was born in Worcestershire and now lives in North Yorkshire with her family. She has a degree in English Literature and a postgraduate degree in Marketing. Olivia is a full-time writer and previously worked in marketing and education. To date, she has written five contemporary thriller novels - *A Family by Design*, set in the Scottish Highlands, first published in 2017 and again in 2023, *I Never Knew You*, set in rural Wensleydale, published 2019, *Shadowlake*, set in The Lake District, published 2021, *The Actor*, set in Whitby - Yorkshire, published 2022, and *The Blue House*, set at Hadrian's Wall, Northumberland, published 2024.

Olivia's writing and stories stem from her fascination with the workings of the human mind and how adult relationships and family dynamics evolve over time and struggle amidst all the pressures that modern society brings - and on top of this how we are all under the influence of our inbuilt biological drivers that shape our behaviours. Olivia gives author talks and presentations about her writing and her novels to community groups throughout Yorkshire - sharing her journey to becoming a published author.